**THIS MAY BE THE MOST FRIGHTENING
BOOK
YOU WILL EVER READ.
IT IS ABOUT AN ALL-AMERICAN BOY
WHO KILLS FOR FUN.
AND IT'S BASED ON FACT.**

THE B

D1103075

THE BOY NEXT DOOR

Chris Loken

ⱕ

BERKLEY BOOKS, NEW YORK

Although this novel is based in part on an actual case, its characters are not intended to portray real people, and they should not be understood as doing so.

This Berkley book contains the complete
text of the original hardcover edition.
It has been completely reset in a typeface
designed for easy reading and was printed
from new film.

THE BOY NEXT DOOR

A Berkley Book/published by arrangement with
Dodd, Mead & Company

PRINTING HISTORY
Dodd, Mead edition published 1985
Berkley edition / February 1988

ISBN: 0-425-10626-8

A BERKLEY BOOK®TM 757,375
Berkley Books are published by The Berkley Publishing Group,
200 Madison Avenue, New York, NY 10016.
The name "BERKLEY" and the "B" logo
are trademarks belonging to Berkley Publishing Corporation.

PRINTED IN THE UNITED STATES OF AMERICA

10 9 8 7 6 5 4 3 2 1

"But you are a great sinner, that's true. And your worst sin is that you have destroyed and betrayed yourself for nothing. Isn't that fearful? Isn't it fearful that you are living in this filth which you loathe so, and at the same time you know yourself (you've only to open your eyes) that you are not helping anyone by it, not saving anyone from anything! Tell me," he went on almost in a frenzy, "how this shame and degradation can exist in you side by side with other, opposite, holy feelings?"

Feodor Dostoevski
CRIME AND PUNISHMENT

The
Investigation:
Part 1

1

"Linda . . . Linda Lou . . ."

Irene Craig sat up in bed, vaguely aware she had spoken aloud, but not knowing what she had said. The bedside light was on; she wondered why. Her eyes automatically sought her digital clock. Its glowing dial read 6:47 A.M.

Then it came to her with a scary rush, so she said the words again, this time calling out her eldest daughter's name with conscious urgency. "Linda Lou!"

There was no answer from the opposite bedroom, although Irene had purposely left her door open onto the hallway so she would be sure to hear Linda when she came in.

Mrs. Craig hurriedly threw off the coverlet she had pulled over herself when she lay down to wait for Linda's return and slid off the bed. Though she still had on her bathrobe and bedroom slippers, she suddenly felt chilled. Her entire body shook. She stumbled as she took the first step, but righted herself and ran the few steps across the hall to Linda's bedroom.

She stopped in the open doorway, clutching the door casing. Linda's bed was empty.

The soft satiny bedspread was neatly arranged, tucked in primly around the canopied four-poster bed. There was no indent where a body had lain along its length. The frilly, feminine pillows remained fluffed against the headboard. No head had rested against them in the night and left its little mark.

Mrs. Craig stiffened. She didn't realize how tightly she was clutching the door frame until she felt a fingernail break. Her mouth opened to scream.

3

"Behave yourself!" she hissed instead, shocking even herself by the almost animal unintelligibility of the sound. Hoarse, guttural, it was more like hot steam hissing forth from some fissure way down deep inside her than recognizable words.

Mrs. Craig tried to reason with herself, to fight back the eerie foreboding that had been growing within her, awake and sleeping, since she had returned from her New Year's Eve Bible class supper at 1:30 and not found Linda home. For goodness sakes, Irene, what is happening to you? Do you think you're the first mother whose daughter has failed to come home? Stayed out with her boyfriend overnight? Just because it's never happened before doesn't mean it can't sometime. There has to be a first time for everything. Everybody. Even Linda. Why panic?

Yes, indeed, why panic, she asked herself again in lieu of an answer, her eyes subliminally cataloging Linda's room to see if anything was out of order—nothing, it appeared, at least from where she still stood in the doorway, her fingers now relatively relaxed against the door frame . . . Why panic? All she knew for sure was that Linda wasn't in her bed, hadn't been all night. Which certainly wasn't to say that she couldn't be a thousand and one other places, safe and sound . . . Yet, she really couldn't think of any. The Browns? Naturally, they would be the first logical choice; after all, she was out with Bill.

Mrs. Craig took one or two halting steps toward the telephone. For some reason she was loath to call the Browns, just as she had been last night when she came home from the Byersdorfs' and found Linda not home.

The nameless fear filled her again, so intense she felt giddy. She had to fight the foolish impulse to throw herself on Linda's bed and sob. "What am I so frightened of?" she heard herself say aloud, kind of hoping that the bare words would scare away the answer. "If something . . . awful . . . had happened . . . I surely would have heard by now. The police . . ."

Mrs. Craig sank down on the edge of Linda's old-fashioned four-poster bed. Could it possibly be that her daughter was not quite as good a girl as she believed? Was not telling her quite everything? Of course, no mother ever expects it to happen with her daughter. But maybe even Linda could do something like most other girls nowadays. Get into a little mischief. Maybe even have a drink or two. Smoke one of those horrible cigarettes . . .

Mrs. Craig shook her head, flung the word out. "No!" Besides, Linda was out with Bill Brown. He was even more dead set against such things than Linda. Somebody else maybe—young lovers could forget to let parents know and spend the night together, maybe just falling asleep in each other's arms —but not Bill and Linda, they were too good, they'd more likely stay up all night discussing Scripture. Like they used to do half the night before she had to put a stop to it . . .

"The basement!"

Linda could be down in the family room. Maybe even both of them. Sure, they had come in late, real quiet, slipped in the back door and down into the basement to watch a late movie on the TV and fallen asleep in each other's arms like regular lovers and were still down there sleeping right now.

Sure, it was New Year's Eve!

Hope followed Mrs. Craig down the two flights of stairs from Linda's bedroom to the family room in the basement. It was so quiet in the house she could hear her slippered feet on the carpeted stairway. She could already see the two young lovers sleeping innocently in each other's arms when she cleared the last step and rounded the stairwell to view the television area.

It took at least a few seconds of standing there in the dark before she even realized she could see nothing. There was such an oppressive silence, such absolute dark, that it took the last vestige of her strength and will to lift her arm and finger the light switch.

Now she finally screamed. As the lights came on and illumined that empty couch in front of that cold barren television set, Mrs. Craig somehow knew that something awful had happened to her daughter.

She turned and stumblingly ran up the basement steps and into the living room. She couldn't remember the Browns' telephone number and had to look it up. Her fingers shook so she had to dial twice before she was able to complete the call. Somebody answered on the second ring. A voice said, "Yes?" The single word was so subdued Irene Craig wasn't sure who had spoken.

"Leona?"

"Yes." Stronger, more defined now, but the voice still didn't sound like Leona Brown's.

"Leona, this is Irene Craig. Sorry if I woke you but—"

"Oh, that's alright, I was up."

"Is Linda Lou there?" The question came blurting, followed by what seemed a lifetime silence.

"Well . . . no."

"Well . . . is Bill there?" Irene held her breath.

"Why, yes, of course he's here."

"Of . . . course?" Panic fought for control of Irene Craig's voice. "How do you know . . . so sure?"

"I was up when he came in."

"When?" Irene asked, not even knowing why.

"Ah . . . two. Yes, right around two."

"Alone?"

"Of course."

"I see. Of course. But . . . where then . . . is Linda Lou?"

"She's at home. Bill told me he dropped her off."

"No, Leona, she's not at home."

Their voices seemed almost casual, Leona Brown's somewhat stubbornly sure, Irene Craig's publicly polite, as her South Georgia breeding had taught her.

"I've gone through the entire house."

"Have you looked everywhere, Irene?"

"Well, yes . . . everywhere she would be."

"Have you looked in the bathtubs?"

"Bathtubs?"

"Under the beds?"

"Well, no."

"Well, then, go look."

"Leona . . . you know, she's nineteen years old. Why would she do that?"

"Well, she's got to be there because she's not over here."

"Do you think . . . I really ought to?"

"Yes." The voice affirmed her question almost fiercely. "You go look. Call me back."

Irene Craig hung the phone up and did as she was bid. She knew it was insane, but by this time horror so held her that it led her through the house again. She looked under the beds. She looked in the bathtub and went back to the phone and redialed.

"Leona, she's not here. She never came in. She's not in her bed. Her bed hasn't been slept in."

"Well, we'll come over, Irene," Leona Brown said softly.

The Browns lived only two blocks around the corner. Irene Craig heard their car tires crunching the frozen snow in her driveway, was waiting at the front door for them.

"What on earth happened!" she demanded of Bill Brown, grasping his upper arms and asking her questions directly into his face. "Did you let her out of the car someplace? Have a fight and she left you?"

"No," Bill Brown answered quietly, looking back directly into her eyes. "I brought her home at two minutes till two—"

"But Bill, she's not here!"

"I dropped her off, Mrs. Craig, just like I'm telling—"

"But she's just not here, Bill." Mrs. Craig persisted fiercely. "Are you sure you two didn't have a fight or something? You dropped her off someplace else?"

"No. Right here. Right out there," Bill corrected, gently pulling one arm loose from Mrs. Craig's clutching fingers and turning his body partially to point in the general direction of the front porch. "The last thing I saw, she was sitting on the porch in the snow waving good-bye to me."

"Bill! In the snow! It was freezing cold, way below zero!"

Bill nodded, a quizzical look of disapproval showing on his face too. "She took off her jacket, sat on it. Kind of wrapped the rest of it around her legs."

"Took off her jacket! Bill, how could you leave her like that . . . just sitting there!"

"You never wanted me to come in the house with her if it was after twelve, Mrs. Craig," Bill reminded her matter-of-factly.

Fred Brown, Bill's father, spoke through the deadly silence. "I always taught Bill to see a girl safe in the house before he took off, unless, of course, their parents wish otherwise."

"She's got to be here somewhere in the house," Leona Brown insisted, as she had on the telephone.

"Leona. I looked . . . called, screamed her name."

"Asleep. Sound asleep," Leona insisted stubbornly. "Sleeping so sound she didn't hear you calling." With that Leona wheeled and headed for the stairs, turning her head quickly from side to side as she strode calling, "Linda! Linda Lou!" as though fully expecting the girl to materialize from almost anywhere. Bill Brown just stood quietly alongside his father, his face blankly white. Irene suddenly brought her hands up to shield her ears and began to wail, "Who would hurt Linda? Who would hurt Linda? Who would hurt Linda? Who would—"

Fred Brown moved close, in an attempt to console her. "Irene, we don't know that anybody has. Maybe she just went to a girlfriend's house? Came in and warmed herself and decided it wasn't time to call it a night. New Year's Eve, you know. Went over to a girlfriend's house, some party she heard about—"

"No . . . no . . . not Linda."

"Kids are funny sometimes, Irene, you never quite know just exactly what they are going to do next, no matter how well you think you know them. Goodness knows, I have two of my own."

Leona returned from her inspection of the house. "She's not here," she stated quietly, in a strangely subdued voice reminiscent of the one with which she had answered the phone that morning. "I looked everywhere."

Mrs. Craig spun away from Fred Brown's consoling hand, stood staring out through the partially frosted living room window at the snow-covered front porch. "I'm going to call the police."

Fred Brown nodded. "Fine. I think you should."

2

Officer Hal Porath of the Little Falls Police Department—the LFPD—took Irene Craig's call at 7:30 A.M. and proceeded immediately to the Craig residence at 1402 Drake Street. Some of the things Mrs. Craig had said and the manner in which she had said them seemed to Officer Porath to indicate that there might be more to this situation than just another coed slipping out for an overnight shackup.

There were a number of people present when Officer Porath arrived at the Craig residence: the lady he had spoken with on the phone, the mother of the alleged missing girl, Mrs. Irene Craig; the boyfriend, Bill Brown; his father and mother, Mr. and Mrs. Fred Brown. Officer Porath already knew Fred Brown slightly, so they exchanged a perfunctory greeting as he walked in. "Hi, Fred."

"'Lo, Hal."

Mrs. Craig quickly fleshed out the facts she had given him over the phone. Her daughter was missing, last seen by her when Linda had left with Bill Brown to babysit with the Henderson child at 6:30 the evening before, had not returned home by the time Mrs. Craig had finally slipped off to sleep around 2:00 A.M. this morning, still had not been seen or heard from. Yet Bill Brown stated emphatically that he had brought Linda back home at two minutes before two. Mrs. Craig reiterated that she had waited up until at least two for Linda Lou, but had heard nothing before going to sleep, neither a car pulling in the driveway nor her daughter coming in the house, both of which she as emphatically insisted she would have heard, awake or asleep, had either happened.

9

Of course, Officer Porath had heard such emphatic statements enough times in his three years on the force to know that "absolutely positively" often became "gee, maybe not," but for some reason he tended to believe Mrs. Irene Craig. There was something about this lady that brooked no nonsense. When she said something, Porath found himself letting it slide into his investigative mind as fact. Not that he disbelieved the others. So far as he knew the entire Brown family were good, solid, churchgoing Little Fallsians. Bill Brown, the boyfriend, seemed to be honest and sincere, as puzzled as anyone by his fiancée's disappearance after he had dropped her off at her door at two minutes till two last night.

What about that though? Porath asked himself. A polite, sincere young man like Bill Brown not walking his girlfriend —hell, his fiancée—all the way into the house at two minutes till two in the morning, New Year's Eve, fifteen below zero outside!

"Let's go over this one thing again, folks—particularly you, Bill. You say you just pulled into the driveway, went around and opened the door for Linda, she got out, you walked around your car and got back in, watched her walk up to the front porch, saw her sit down on the porch in the snow. . .?"

"I . . . you forgot one thing, Officer," Bill said, kind of hanging his head sheepishly. "Or maybe I just forgot to mention it. We kissed good night first . . . just a little kiss . . . there by the car."

"OK, you kissed by the car. But what I'm trying to get at, you just sat in the car and watched her walk up to the porch by herself, sit down on the—"

"Excuse me, Officer," Bill interrupted diffidently. "She kind of just leaned. She never really got all the way down in the snow, just kind of leaned, one hip holding her weight."

"I thought you said she took off her jacket and wrapped it around her legs," Mrs. Craig interposed.

"She did that too," Bill agreed, "kind of tucked in around under her . . . seat."

"Bill," Porath pursued, "didn't that seem mighty weird to you?"

"No," Bill answered guilelessly.

"I mean, it was cold, man. Somewhere near fifteen below zero cold. Didn't you think Linda might get frostbitten or something? At least, catch her death of cold?" Mrs. Craig let out a little wrenching sob. Porath mentally cursed himself for his tactless choice of words. "I should think you would have stopped the car, got out, said something like, 'Linda, you ought not to sit out here like this. You ought to go right in.'"

Bill shook his head slightly, a barely perceptible motion, said in his soft, low voice, "No, sir, she looked ... perfectly comfortable to me. Just sat there on the edge of the step like she was going right up ... gave me her little smile ... waved good-bye."

Fred Brown stepped into the general silence that followed his son's strangely chilling reply. "Hal, this all goes back to Irene here telling Bill that she didn't want him coming in if it was late, after midnight. Of course, I can understand that, I know what it's like to try to get a good night's sleep after working all day if you have children coming in and going back out all hours of the night. I'm not saying I'm blaming her one bit for not wanting Bill to see Linda all the way inside at two o'clock in the morning no matter what the weather was like outside—"

Mrs. Craig suddenly turned away, brought her hands up over her ears, her body jerking with partially suppressed sobs. Porath stepped up to her, placed one hand lightly on her bowed back. "Mrs. Craig, if you would be so kind, could you show me where your daughter's room is? I'd like to see if there might be a note or something. Who knows, there might just be a perfectly normal explanation to all this."

Mrs. Craig's back shuddered beneath his hand two or three more times, but she managed to nod her head and led him toward the stairway leading to the second floor. Porath observed that Mrs. Craig walked partially stooped, as though she could not quite shoulder the frightful burden the new year had rung down upon her.

Officer Porath found nothing in the girl's bedroom to assuage his own growing fear that something untoward had befallen Linda Lou Craig. In fact, he found considerable circumstantial evidence to augment that suspicion. Apparently, everything Linda owned, with the exception of what she was wearing when she left with Bill Brown at 6:30 the evening before, was still in her room, including 125 dollars in cash in her top bureau drawer, the exact amount of a check her mother had cashed for her the day before; hardly the procedure of a runaway.

Porath didn't think she was a runaway—or an airhead floating thoughtlessly off for a New Year's late night on the town. He tended to take Linda at her mother's word, substantiated by her boyfriend, the whole Brown family: a very stable young lady. "The last thing she would do was run away from home in the middle of the night." They had all more or less agreed to that, one way or another.

Her room tended to bear this consensus out. Artifacts of a religious nature were scattered throughout the room. A well-worn Bible lay opened on her bedside table, with numerous marked passages. Her framed confirmation diploma from St. John's Lutheran Church hung on one wall, a benevolent Christ spread his arms over the headboard of her little-girlish, canopied bed. Literature from a Bible study group, clasped praying hands on another wall—it went on and on.

But . . . then again, young people do some strange things. Particularly in a college town like Little Falls. Christ knows, Porath had seen students from the very best homes, kids brought up in the lap of luxury, go out and steal cars when they had one of their own sitting in front of their dorm. Booze, dope, even prostitution—it didn't make any difference what kind of a background a kid came from, they could get into most anything. And did. Ninety percent of the investigations he had participated in had involved University of Wisconsin at Little Falls students, and probably half of them had something to do with sex, one way or another.

No, Officer Hal Porath—only twenty-four years old and three years out of UW-LF himself—reminded himself, don't go jumping to any hasty conclusions when you have students and possibly sex involved. That's the first commandment of the LFPD bible.

"Linda have any other boyfriends?" he asked Mrs. Craig softly.

"Not now, since Bill. Before . . . there was one, Jack Dun from high school. Yes, we had some trouble with him once."

"Trouble?" Porath asked, the inflection in Mrs. Craig's voice turning him toward her. "How so?"

"He became very upset when Linda broke off with him. Broke into our house one time."

"When was this?"

"Just about this same time last year. When Linda Lou was home from Augustana for the Christmas break—she went to Augustana her freshman year, transferred home to UW this past fall."

"Do you think he could be somehow involved with . . . this?"

Mrs. Craig's gaze traveled by Porath to Linda's high school graduation picture atop her bureau. "I suppose . . . anything's possible."

The Brown family had a suggestion for Porath when he and Mrs. Craig returned downstairs. Possibly Linda Lou had forgotten her house key and was unable to let herself in.

It was a possibility, so they all searched the house. But when they did not find the key, Mrs. Craig pointed out that even if Linda had left it home or mislaid it, had she been brought home at two minutes till two, Linda would have seen her car in the garage and, knowing her mother was already home rung the doorbell. "Surely, I would have heard the doorbell," Mrs. Craig averred adamantly.

"Remember, though, Mrs. Craig," Bill demurred politely, "you don't hear so well in one ear."

"I certainly would have heard the doorbell. It's only when a sound is made close to that ear that I can't hear it."

Porath straightened. He had been looking under the living room couch for the key. "Is that a fact, Mrs. Craig? Your hearing is impaired in one ear?"

Mrs. Craig nodded. "But it doesn't affect my hearing things from a distance."

"How much, would you say, your hearing is impaired in that one ear?"

"Totally. But—"

"So if your good ear was turned away from the sound . . . pressed down on a pillow . . . then, would it be fair to say, that you wouldn't be as likely to hear that sound?"

"No, I don't think so. Not when it's from my bedroom down to the front door. I always hear the doorbell no matter where I am in the house, which side I am sleeping on."

When you're sleeping on that good ear? Nah, I don't buy that one, Mrs. Craig, Porath thought. Up till now, I've bought almost every word you've said, but that one I can't put in the bank. In fact, that might just put a little different light on things altogether. "Could I use your phone, Mrs. Craig?"

"Certainly."

"I'm going to call the station and see if there is anyone available to help me conduct a search of the outside area."

Officer Don Meyer came over immediately. Porath met him outside as he was getting out of his patrol car, and together they conducted a search of the immediate area, knocking on the doors to either side of the Craig residence, but the occupants had not heard or seen anything unusual in the course of the night. They cursorily examined Linda's blue 1966 Chevrolet station wagon parked on the left-hand side of the drive leading to the garage. Snow had drifted against the northwest side of the wheels; no tire tracks led to or from its present location. Upon later questioning, Mrs. Craig confirmed that, as far as she knew, Linda Lou had not used her car since they had returned on the twenty-eighth of December from a Christmas holiday trip to visit relatives in Minnesota. Nothing significant in the way of foot tracks or other markings could be determined by examining the drive or the surrounding yard, though there were indications that a number of people had at some time walked in the area. Due to the blustery winds that had prevailed most of the night and were still blowing, any track or marking was either partially or totally obliterated. The ground was frozen rock hard; ice crystals winked off the tundraesque areas where the wind had swept the earth clean of snow. Drifts in wavering columns marched across the yard, flanked trees and fence posts, closed ranks against the house and attached garage. There had been only about three inches of new snow in the past few days, just a few flakes in the last twenty-four hours, and very few of them had remained where they had fallen.

At this juncture, Fred and Bill Brown joined the two young officers in their search, stood with them contemplating the drifted-over footprints. "Looks to me like any number of people have been milling around out here, Hal," Fred Brown observed.

Porath shrugged. "Yeah, sometime." Bill Brown stood forlornly staring down at the ephemeral footprints. "Bill, what do you think happened to her?" Porath asked suddenly, on impulse.

Bill finally looked up, his eyes a thousand miles from nowhere. "Somebody must have come along . . . been hiding . . . and taken her off."

Fred Brown nodded abruptly. "Yes." Then he wheeled and strode back toward the Craig residence, Bill following his father.

Meyer and Porath watched them go. "You go along with that, Hal?" Meyer asked.

Porath continued watching father and son until both had disappeared through the front door. Suddenly he shivered, his body jerking involuntarily. "Helluva night to just go wandering off somewhere."

"That what you figure she did?" Meyer pursued.

Porath reflected, but not for long. "Not really." Then he turned and headed for the house himself, utilizing Bill Brown's footsteps for easier walking through the drift that had built up near the front door.

Again inside, he addressed Mrs. Craig. "I'm going to put out an MP—missing person—on your daughter, Mrs. Craig. Ordinarily, we wait twenty-four hours, but I think in this case we'll just go ahead and do it now."

It took some effort, but Mrs. Craig's eyes were able to meet his. "Thank you," they said.

Returning to the police station, Officers Porath and Meyer were joined on the case by Officers Ed O'Brien and Fred Walters. Checking over the various stories told by the Brown family and Mrs. Craig, they were able to verify that Bill and Linda had arrived at the George Henderson residence to baby-sit with little Tami Henderson at approximately 6:30, leaving there just before 9:00 P.M. The times were verified by George Henderson. Then, according to all the Browns, the young couple had returned to the Brown residence to finish watching a movie on television they had begun viewing while babysitting, going down into the Brown family room in the basement to do so. At approximately 11:30 P.M., according to all the Browns, Bill and Linda had left to pick up Bill's sister, Elizabeth, who was attending a New Year's Eve function at Unitarian Church. There had apparently been some kind of mixup there, though, as they had somehow missed the sister and she had gotten a ride home with a friend. Bill and Linda had then spent the remaining time between roughly midnight and his stated return to the Craig residence riding around and looking at Christmas decorations on houses. Of course, other than

Bill's say-so, the officers had no way of knowing this to be the case. Yet, all agreed, this was not in itself an unusual pastime for people during the holiday season—particularly young lovers. Such festive tours were usually relieved with a little dillying and dallying at the various "lover's lanes" scattered around the campus and throughout the Big Falls area. The Greater Big Falls area is not what one would refer to as solid city, a sprawling metropolitan area, but is rather a series of contiguous cities and townships with the University of Wisconsin at Little Falls, the Hi-Tech research center, and Chevrolet dominating the landscape and lives of the citizenry. Numerous parks, golf courses, Lake Waupaca, Star Lake, the Little Wolf River, "two-track" roads, and so forth afford parking spots galore for young lovers, not to mention the actual rural country within fifteen to twenty minutes' drive in almost any direction. The young officers were unanimous in their opinion that Bill and Linda had probably done as much stopping as starting. "He probably didn't want to get into that in front of the folks," Officer Meyer observed.

"Yeah, we'll go into that when we call him in for further questioning," Porath agreed absentmindedly. He was involved in finishing the MP report on Linda Lou Craig. Bill Brown had been able to furnish a more complete account of what Linda had been wearing last evening than her mother. Obviously very observant, he had remembered almost every article of her apparel in detail, while Mrs. Craig could remember only the blue fake-fur-trimmed ski jacket and red/orange plaid slacks. So, according to his account, Linda was also wearing brown Earth Shoes, a gray crewneck sweater over a blue pullover, and blue mittens. She carried a "thick, bulgy," tan, strapped purse. Her eyeglasses were of the large, round, dark horn-rimmed variety.

Porath filled in the vital statistics: Linda Lou Craig, 1402 Drake, Little Falls; White Female; nineteen years old, 5'5" 120 lbs.; blond/blue; brown-rim oval glasses. Missing 1-1-77.

Porath inserted the pretty young girl's picture into the reserved space. She looks a little bit like Sandy, he said to himself, the thought of his wife allowing him to catch an ever deeper glimpse into Mrs. Craig's grief.

"Meyer, take this MP and Xerox up a few. Walters, you call public transportation, check all buses, trains, flights having left between . . . ah, let's say, nine o'clock last night till now—"

"Why, nine? We got eyeball on her till 11:30 last night, Hal."

"Family eyeball, man, family. Don't you know by now you don't ever take the word of family in these kinds of deals."

The rest laughed. "Hell, Hal, I know you're buckin' for detective, but you don't have to start talkin' like Badger already," Meyer kidded.

Porath blushed. Maybe he had gotten a little carried away. After all, he was the youngest cop in the room.

"Hey," O'Brien piped up, "maybe we ought to call Badger in on this, somebody from Detective Bureau."

Porath wasn't that crestfallen. "What for?" he shot back. "We got this in hand. It's only a MP."

"That's not the way you're actin'."

"Aw, what the hell, let him have a holiday off for a change," Porath said. "Christ knows, the old bear can use one." Besides, he continued to himself, it'll give me a chance for a change.

Aloud, he continued marshaling his troops for a day. "Eddie, you and Don hit the all night restaurants within a mile or so radius of her house, the Big Boy next to the University Inn, Friendly's, you know the ones. I'll stick here at the desk, check out this Jack Dun, call Bill Brown in for questioning. Let's say we meet back here at 1300 hours. I'll try to set him up for then."

"You can't have much confidence in us finding her if you're already calling him in before we leave to look," Meyer pointed out.

3

They didn't find her either. Reporting back to the station as agreed, they found Bill Brown already there with Porath. Detailing Walters to continue searching, Porath huddled briefly with Meyer and O'Brien off to one side before ushering Bill into the interrogation room, the other two officers following. Porath seated Bill at the largish rectangular conference table, took the chair directly across from him, Meyer and O'Brien flanking Porath to either side.

Porath positioned the tape recorder between himself and Bill Brown, watching him as he did. Bill seemed totally relaxed, completely at ease. Now freshly groomed, his youthful appearance struck Porath even more forcefully than it had earlier that morning. My God, this guy doesn't look a day over sixteen—slender, dark blond hair sliding down his forehead in a boyish bang, baby-blue eyes, that scrubbed squeaky clean look on his almost pretty face, clothes spick-and-span, the whole works just stepped in off the back of a Wheaties box.

"How old are you, Bill?"

"Just turned twenty-one, the 27th of December."

Porath reached out and flipped on the tape recorder. "OK, Bill, do you know Linda Lou Craig?"

"Yes, I do."

"How long have you known Linda?"

"Well, I've known her ever since she was in high school a little bit and going down to church and that."

"How long have you been going out with Linda?"

"Well, ever since then. Ever since I've really got to know her."

"OK. Do you have any plans on getting married?"

"Yeah, we do. We haven't set any date or anything, as we have finances and school to get straight, and we want to make sure that we both are grown up in these two areas before we do set a date."

"OK, Bill, let's go back to last evening, that would be the thirty-first of December of 1976. Could you briefly tell me what time you picked up Linda and what followed after that?"

"I picked her up about quarter after six as she was supposed to be babysitting at 6:30."

"OK, what time did you get there at the Hendersons' residence?"

"Oh, well probably about 6:30. I didn't look at my watch. We just walked in and talked to them for a few seconds while they put their coats on. After a short while we put Tami in her crib and turned the TV on shortly after seven, and the movie came on at eight and we watched the movie, and then later the Hendersons came back."

O'Brien interrupted, "OK. When you say later, what time was that when they came in?"

"Well, I don't know exactly when they came in, but by the time we got back to my house I think it was about quarter after nine."

"Were your mother and father there at that time?"

"Yes, they were."

"What did you do at your house, if anything?"

"Well, we finished watching the movie and had pizza and 7-Up, and after the movie we talked a little bit, and then we went over to Unitarian Church because my sister was going to be there. We looked there, and she wasn't there. Then we left and drove around a little bit to look at Christmas lights on houses."

"How long was that drive approximately?"

"Well, probably a good hour."

"OK. What car did you have then?"

"My car, it's a 'seventy-four Chevy."

"OK. Approximately what time did you drop Linda off at the front door there?"

"A couple minutes to two."

The exactness of the time intrigued O'Brien. "How do you know it was a couple minutes to two?"

"I always check my watch when I drop her off. I've had

her home late before, and her mother, you know, wants her to be in early and insists on having it, and I know on certain holidays like she really doesn't get fussy too much."

Porath took over the questioning again. "OK, you said you let Linda out. Did you walk her up to the door, or did you stay in your car?"

"I, umm, you know, opened the door—"

"Car door?"

"Yeah, and opened her door, and I kissed her good-bye there, and then she walked up and I got into my car and waved, you know, and backed out, and she sat just on the edge of the step like she was going up in a couple of seconds, just on the edge, just on the very tip edge not even really being seated almost, just the edge . . ." Bill seemed caught in the groove of that memory. It played over for him every time he got to that part of his story. It looked to Porath like Bill was seeing her sitting there again right now, so he gave him a fair chance, just waited till he resumed. ". . . anyways, she smiled . . . and I drove on home."

"So the last you remember her, she was sitting on the step waving good-bye to you?"

"Yeah."

"When you picked Linda up last night, did you notice anything different about her?"

"Well, she, her face seemed kind of glum. For half an hour she seemed kind of moody where she wouldn't say much and you have to carry a conversation, but after a half an hour she just didn't seem moody at all and was fine the rest of the evening."

"Did she mention any problems that she had with friends here or her mother or any other of her associates?"

"No, no."

"How about her father? I understand he is living in Iowa? Did she make a statement that she might like to go see him over the break or that her sister was there?"

"Well, she's really concerned about her sister Pat, because her sister doesn't want to go to college and sometimes her sister and her will get into arguments and vicious arguments. The reason she told me this and everything was because they felt that Pat was really kind of a mixed-up kid, not really but kind of, and she wanted me to pray with her and to pray on my own, and her mother and her said they were going to set up a time too when they could also pray for Pat."

"OK, getting back to last night," Porath continued, hesitating briefly—he was vaguely uncomfortable about Bill's long-winded nonanswer but he didn't know why—"you said you had pizza and 7-Up. Did you have any alcohol of any type to drink, or did Linda have anything last night at all that you are aware of?"

"No, no way at all. We abstain, and we just don't like to drink at all."

"OK, was Linda under . . . was she using drugs or prescription medicine for any reason?"

"Once in a while she might take a pill, I see her, but she says that's just a, ah, girl problem . . . something like that." Apparently, Bill wasn't too comfortable talking about "girl problems," Porath noted. But, then again, neither was he.

"OK. Do you have any idea yourself where she might be?"

"No, I don't. I really don't." Bill answered quickly, but sincerely.

Neither did Investigating Officer Porath. Nor could he think of anything else to ask Bill Brown. But he had done his job, got the alleged facts. Handled Bill nice and easy, buddy-buddy, kept his kids gloves on, softened him up for Meyer and O'Brien, just like they had agreed beforehand. Now it was up to them to pounce on the fatted rabbit, just like Badger would, had he been there. Turning toward Meyer, Porath cocked his near eye. "OK. Do you have anything, Officer Meyer?"

Meyer did. "Did you have an argument with her last night?"

"No, I didn't," Bill answered easily, showing no emotion whatsoever. Porath watched him throughout the rest of the questioning, never taking his eyes off the smooth boyish face.

"Did you hit her?" Meyer was asking.

"No, I've never hit her."

"Did you drive to a park in another area and mess her up and leave her out there?"

Bill's eyes suddenly flicked; his negative response was barely audible.

"Uh-uh."

"Did she get mad at you and get out of the car?"

"No, she—"

Meyer bored right through Bill's answer. "Did she leave you last night?"

"No, she's never stomped away or anything."

Meyer tried the old trick bounce-back question. "Have you ever hit her before?"

Bill fielded it right off the wall. "Never touched her. I've always believed in talking."

O'Brien relieved Meyer. "Isn't it a little unusual not to walk a girl right in to the door?"

"Well, I've never walked her right in to the door," Bill answered, deadpan. "Sometimes I walk her up to the door."

"Do you ever wait until she gets in to the door before you leave?"

"Not in the winter."

That one got O'Brien. A puzzled frown slowly spread over his big Irish map of a face as he dumbly repeated, "Not in the winter."

Is this guy for real? Porath asked himself. Is he jerking O'Brien off . . . or what? "Do you know whether she had a key for the door last night, or did she forget it? Did she mention that to you?"

"She didn't mention anything about her key, not having it or not, but if she thought she didn't have it she would have flagged me down or else called me because they also gave me a key."

Well, he must be in pretty good with the mother if he's got a key, Porath thought.

O'Brien came back with a little more of his homespun logic. "Bill, do you have any idea what the temperature was last night?"

"No, I don't."

"Would you say it was below freezing?"

"Yeah, I guess," Bill allowed. "But when I'm with Linda sometimes I don't think about temperatures and that like."

Bill suddenly began telling of another cold night with Linda, how warm she made him feel. Again Porath felt Bill was right back there with Linda. Maybe he's in some kind of shock? Is this his way of reacting to the trauma of his fiancée's disappearance?

He listened even more closely to what Bill was saying. "We went walking, you know. We put a blanket around ourselves when I come back from Oyster Island . . . we were just walking around the street . . . just talking about the summer and how much we missed each other."

He doesn't want to come back to the reality of now, Porath guessed. He wants to continue walking around under that blanket with Linda.

Meyer moved into the short silence that ensued. "Does Linda have any other boyfriends?"

"She's not seeing any other men right now or anything, and if she ever did she said she'd tell me about it because that would be the proper thing to do."

"Has she dated anybody since she started dating you?"

At first Bill didn't seem to even quite comprehend Porath's question, but when he did he seemed offended. "Since she . . . no, no sir, uh-uh."

"Do you know of Jack Dun?"

"I know what he looks like, and I talked to him a little bit at a party, her graduation party high school, but that's the last time I've seen him. Linda has seen him at U.W. walking around a little bit," Bill added, almost as an afterthought.

"Have they talked to each other recently?"

"No. She said she didn't talk to him or wanted to and kind of veered away 'cause she's kind of scared of him."

Hmm, thought Porath, noting that statement both in his head and on the yellow legal pad before him.

"When is the last time that you know that Linda talked to Jack Dun?"

"Just shortly before he broke into their house one night last year, I don't know the date. It was in the winter, winter vacation. About the same time as now, last year."

A silence crept across the squad room. The four young men, all relatively the same age, sat there in the lengthening silence, just kind of numbly looking at each other. Porath reached out, forefinger extended over the "stop" button of the tape recorder. "This interview is now concluded at 2:23 P.M. on 1-1-77."

The three officers remained seated silently for some moments after Bill Brown exited, no one of them apparently quite ready to voice an opinion.

"Well, what do you guys think?" Porath finally ventured.

"Seems straight to me," O'Brien responded, slowly. Yet his open honest face crinkled with perplexity. "Square."

"Yeah, about the straightest arrow I've come across in a long time," Meyer agreed, "square as Donnie Osmond. Still . . ."

"Still, what?" Porath pursued.

"Still . . . I don't know," Meyer said, spreading his hands palm up. "There's something goofy about that sonofabitch. He's too good to be true. Don't smoke dope, drink, screw, who knows what he does!"

"He didn't say nothin' about screwing, Don," the logical O'Brien pointed out. "'Course, we didn't ask him, neither."

"No way," Meyer mimicked, his imitation considerably more prissily effeminate than Bill Brown's actual voice. "No way at all. We abstain!"

They all laughed, breaking the tension that had seemed to linger in the room even after Bill Brown left. Porath chalked it up to a kind of growing uncertainty, a fear that he and the other young uniformed officers, essentially patrolmen, might be getting in over their heads on this case. Might better call in Badger and his detectives . . .

Banishing the thought, he put both hands on the table, cleared his throat, firmed up his voice. "OK, guys, where do we start on this MP?"

Their silence answered him. "We got any kind of a file on Brown, Hal?" Meyer finally asked.

"Nah, you kiddin'? Clean as a new whistle. Not even a traffic."

"What about this Jack Dun?"

"A few little scrapes. Speeding, DWI—the biggest, the B and E last year on the Craig residence."

"What was that all about?"

"Drinking mostly. Dun had been to a New Year's party and got all snockered up, came looking for his old girlfriend, Linda. She wouldn't let him in, so he broke the door down."

"Nice guy."

"Beaut."

"Does have a kind of freaky ring to it though," Meyer mused, back on the break-and-enter. "Jilted boyfriend comes back one holiday season to kick his ex's door down. What's to keep him from coming back this year for the whole bundle?"

"Yeah, finds her sitting all nice and easy on the front stoop two o'clock in the morning," O'Brien chimed in. "New Year's Eve, he's blind as a bat, lays in wait for her to come home, hides behind the garage, watches, waits for little Billy here to pull away, runs out, and snatches her—"

"Fifteen below zero?" Porath asked quietly. "Wind chill factor something like forty below? I don't think anybody would lie in wait very long."

"Car could have been parked out on street," Meyer observed. "Could have been sitting in there warm as toast, the heater on, slumped down, watching the driveway. Got lucky when Linda didn't go in right away."

"Possible," Porath admitted.

"Plus a thousand other possibilities," Meyer continued. "She ain't quite the angel everybody says she is. She purposely didn't go in because she didn't want her mother to hear her come home, had made a little rendezvous with the captain of the football team. Ran off to Timbuktu, joined one of those goofy religious cults—"

"OK. They're all possible. At this stage, anything is." He came to his feet. "She's been missing for anywhere from twelve to sixteen hours already, depending on who you want to believe. Meyer, you do a complete background and whereabouts on Dun. Eddie, you stay here, check out law enforcement, state, county, city, say, fifty-mile radius; hospitals—"

"Morgues?"

"Definitely. I'm going back out to talk to Mrs. Craig a little more. Have her put a call through to her ex-husband down in Iowa. While I'm out there, I'll check the neighbors close about, maybe, a strange car parked along the street last night. Any questions?"

Nobody had any, so they broke to go their several ways. As Porath was going through the station, he spotted Officer Charles Dinato signing in at the main desk. A little older, more experienced, maybe even a little wiser, Chuck Dinato would be just the guy to pull in on this case. "Hey, Chuck, wanna take a little ride?"

Dinato turned. "Sure, why not? What you got?"

Porath waved a Xerox of the MP at him. "MP. Coed living at home over on Drake disappears in the middle of last night."

Dinato grinned. "Ah, yes, good ole New Year's Eve."

"I got a hunch there's a little more to this one."

4

Mrs. Craig was in a state of near collapse by the time Officers Porath and Dinato returned to her home at approximately 3:00 P.M. Friends, a Mr. and Mrs. Blank, had come over to offer whatever help they could, and the three of them, at Mrs. Craig's insistence, had gone out and searched the surrounding yards themselves. When the two officers entered her home, Mrs. Craig was slumped on a kitchen chair, still in her outdoor gear, her face red and swollen from the bitter wind-driven cold, and crying. At the sight of Porath she started to rise, but Mrs. Blank restrained her, saying, "Please, Irene, you must try to catch your breath—"

"Officer," Mrs. Craig cried, breaking away from her friend's arms, "it's so cold out there!"

Porath caught her by her upper arms and purposely squeezed down hard, hoping the abrupt action would shock her out of this spiraling panic. "Mrs. Craig, we'll find her. I have men searching in every direction. We're checking the trains, planes, buses, girlfriends, old boyfriends, door to door—"

"I had to go out and look myself."

"I know you did, ma'am," Porath soothed her. "But you must leave that sort of thing to us. You're much more important telling us things, Mrs. Craig, supplying us with facts that might help to find your daughter."

"Like . . . what?" she finally asked in nearly a normal tone of voice, her fear-ovaled eyes pleading with him.

"Like what you already have. And more." Porath consciously slowed his speech pattern even more, striving for a normal conversational tone. "Linda's hopes, dreams, fears, habits—the slightest little thing. Has she had any problems that you know of lately?"

"No," Mrs. Craig said, shaking her head, her eyes still in the land of terror but starting to come back home. "No."

"Her health's been good?"

"Yes."

"Both physically and mentally?"

"Mentally . . . ?"

"Has she had any psychological problems? Has she ever been to see a psychiatrist?"

"Why . . . no. Of course not!"

"OK, Mrs. Craig, does Linda always let you know if there was any change in plans? If she was going to be late for any reason?"

"Yes, surely, something like this . . ." Her face began to pucker.

Officer Dinato stepped in quickly. "Ma'am, Officer Porath here tells me your other daughter—I'm afraid I don't know her name—"

"Patricia—Pat."

"Pat is down visiting her father, your ex-husband, in Iowa."

"Yes."

"Don't you think we better call—"

"I . . . already have." She turned her eyes back to Hal Porath, seeming to seek out his more familiar face to render this personal information. "Right after you left this morning. I knew she wouldn't be there. There was really no way she could be, yet I still held some kind of a crazy hope." There was a long silence, broken only by Mrs. Craig sucking in short sob-trembling breaths. "Of course, she wasn't there. How could she be? But still I hoped. Pat answered. I said, Pat . . . Pat . . . That's all I could say. She recognized my voice and said, 'Happy New Year, Mother!'"

The last four words came out in a spiraling, blood-curdling scream, riveting even the superficially hardened police officers where they stood. Mrs. Craig threw back her head and screamed again—a primordial lament, a mother seeing her firstborn child pulled from her arms and smashed bleeding to the ground before her very eyes.

"Somebody has hurt Linda . . . somebody has hurt Linda," she wailed over and over, "somebody has hurt Linda."

She somehow knows her daughter is dead! The thought seared through young Hal Porath's mind.

He knew it was brutal, but he knew just as surely that now was the time to ask this particular question: "Could Linda have made some arrangement to run off with another man?"

He could just as well have slapped her. Her head snapped backwards as though dodging an actual blow. Her face hardened into a sneering vicious cast. "Linda is a good girl! She does not make rendezvous in the middle of the night with strange men. She is not promiscuous! She is still a virgin!"

"I'm sure she is, Mrs. Craig. But you know I have to ask those kinds of questions, whether I want to or not."

Mrs. Craig's face softened. She started to reach her hand out to him in a forgiving gesture. "Surely. Yes, surely, I understand."

Officer Dinato spoke up. "Mrs. Craig, might I search Linda's room more thoroughly? Officer Porath here told me that the two of you had only made a casual check earlier this morning."

"Of course."

"It's right up there at the head of the stairs, Chuck, the first one on the left," Porath directed, pleased to hear the Blanks offer to accompany Dinato.

Alone with Mrs. Craig, Porath got right to the point. "Mrs. Craig, how do you and Bill Brown get along?"

She hesitated just long enough to let Porath know she was giving the question more consideration than it should normally require. "OK, I guess."

"That's not exactly a ringing endorsement of a future son-in-law."

"They were in the process of breaking up."

"They *were?*"

"Yes. Linda Lou tried to give him his ring back the night we returned from Minnesota, but he asked her to keep it. Just as a gift, was the way he put it. 'Let's just continue to see each other as friends,' he told her, 'see what happens with time.'"

Porath could feel his investigating-officer hackles rising. "Obviously, Linda must have told you these things?"

"Certainly. As I think I said before, she told me everything. We had no secrets from each other. That's how I know something awful must have happened to Linda for her not to be here. She was very protective of me, particularly since my divorce."

"Could your husband have come up here . . . and—"

"Jon?" Mrs. Craig exclaimed incredulously.

"I'm sorry, I mean . . . you implied, the divorce must not have been easy. Was there a battle between you and your ex-husband over custody of Linda?"

"No. Absolutely not. Jon and I . . . well, we may have had our difficulties, but we are civilized." Mrs. Craig hesitated, then continued. "Jon used to be a Peace Corps volunteer, you know. A number of places, Hindustan . . . when Linda Lou was little."

Another silence started to gather sorrow, so Porath pushed gently on. "Why do you think . . . ah . . . she wanted to give Bill his ring back?"

Her answer took Porath somewhat aback. "He wasn't enough of a man for Linda. 'He's just a little boy, Mother,' she told me. 'He's never had another girlfriend. I don't want to hurt him, but I don't want to live with him either.' She was very kind, you know, always picking up some stray dog, things like that. That's why we have these two half-breed mutts; Linda brought them home." Hal Porath followed her eyes to the two dogs crouched beside her chair. One of them, a terrier cross of some sort, seemed to know she was talking about him because he suddenly let out a series of low, drawn-out groans, as though he was having a bad daydream. "It's alright, Meatball," Mrs. Craig said automatically, reaching down to stroke the dog's head. "Meatball is her favorite. He's been acting strangely all day. He knows something is . . . wrong."

"Is this too painful for you, ma'am?"

"No, it's worse when you're not here."

"Thank you." They caught each other's eyes for a split second. It was one of the nicest compliments Hal Porath had ever received as a policeman. "Now, then, we were talking about why Linda was breaking off with Bill. You said, if I remember correctly, 'He wasn't enough of a man for Linda.' Is that your characterization of Bill Brown or your daughter's?"

"I would have to say both of ours. She was also fearful of his, ah . . . future possibilities."

"Such as?"

"He's not a good student. Linda likes to study, and he doesn't. All he seems to want to do is hang around her and talk religion. I mean, Linda is religious, but he's almost a fanatic! He never takes her anywhere but to some kind of religious function. That's one of the things that kept me from calling his house to see if they were there when I came home last night and found she wasn't. I sat by the phone debating, my hand even reaching out sometimes. 'Should I call the Browns or not? No,' I said, 'maybe they found some friends someplace for a change, went out for something to eat or something—'"

"So they had few friends?"

"Linda did. Still does, of course." Mrs. Craig hastened to correct the slipped tense. "Still does. A lot of friends."

"Certainly, I'm sure she does, but they, together, didn't seem to have many friends?"

"None. No, sir, not one that I can think of. They never went anywhere in a group like kids normally do, parties, dancing, out to eat. All they did was sit around talking in low voices, go to Church functions, Bible studies. Of course, there's nothing wrong with that in itself—I'm religious myself—but kids should go out and have more fun, not just sit around like old fogies talking about sin and salvation. They should be talking about life. Living."

"Certainly. Yes, I agree."

"That was another reason Linda wanted to break it off before she got in too deep. She felt Bill was monopolizing too much of her time, keeping her from her friends, the rest of her life, other activities . . ." Mrs. Craig's words dwindled off, but this time her reticence didn't seem to stem from emotion or lack of something further to say.

"Yes? You were saying?" Porath prompted quickly.

Mrs. Craig began shaking her head no, then suddenly stopped the motion resolutely. "Yes, I am going to say it. Maybe I shouldn't, but she did tell me so I am."

"Yes?" Porath prompted again quickly.

"She didn't like the whole Brown . . . atmosphere. They seemed so . . . kind of, in a way, petty, to her. Oh, she didn't necessarily mean personally, she would go to great lengths not to demean them. They make a good living, probably have more money to do with than we do. I'm sure Fred has a good income, and Leona is a certified teacher if she wanted to go back to work or they needed her additional income. The kids seem to have every material thing they need and more. Apparently, the grandparents have money, too. They bought Bill his car—it was a brand spanking new Chevrolet back when he graduated from high school. Linda told me Elizabeth was to get a thousand dollars from the grandparents when she graduates in the spring . . . or is it next year? Let's see, Elizabeth must be seventeen now, she's either a junior or senior—"

"Mrs. Craig," Porath started to say, trying to head her off, work her back to more pertinent facts than when Elizabeth Brown might graduate.

". . . I'm certainly in no position to do that for my girls, much as I would like to."

"Ma'am—"

"They have any number of sailboats around the place, recreational equipment. They're always forever off somewhere together, camping, cross-country skiing, whatever it is they do . . ."

Again, Mrs. Craig's words dwindled off, but this time Porath felt it was for another reason. Obviously, she was starting to realize the same inescapable conclusion that had formed in his mind.

He said it for both of them. "Sounds like a perfectly healthy atmosphere to me, Mrs. Craig." He went on, knowing he was prodding a little. "I mean, what healthier atmosphere could a young girl marry into than a family like the Browns? Doing so many nice, clean family activities together? Camping, sailing, skiing—I mean, like they say, the family that—"

"—Plays together, stays together," Mrs. Craig finished for him, even managing a little bit of a wry grin. "Though, of course, it used to be 'pray.' Then again, they do that too, in spades." She fell silent. This time Porath merely waited. He was starting to get the funny feeling she was trying to tell him something important, if either of them could ever figure out what it was. "Yes, who am I to cast the first stone? Heaven knows, our own family hasn't been all it could either, not even able to stay together, but . . . but, somehow, there was still that . . . atmosphere in the Brown home that Linda didn't like.

"They're real clannish. Kind of . . . ingrown, it seems. Like everything only seems to have meaning for the family. Noth-

ing outside really means anything. I don't know, but whatever
it is, Linda was uncomfortable there. 'Mother, I get strange
vibes,' I remember her saying once. 'Though everybody
seems so squeaky clean, there's still these weird vibes in the
air.' Like Fred seems so jolly, but in a way too, he's real strict
underneath. Dominates Leona something awful—she has to
serve him breakfast in bed every morning! Elizabeth too—not
breakfast in bed—I mean, the way he treats her . . . it's like
the men over there are worth a whole lot more than the girls.
Linda didn't like that. She said, 'Mother, if we were to get
married, maybe Bill would end up treating me like that too.'"

"Treating? You mean, physically?"

"Oh, no, I'm sure Fred doesn't beat Leona or Elizabeth,
anything like that. It's more mental, emotional—which can
sometimes be a whole lot tougher to take in the long run than
regular old-fashioned beatings. At least then a woman can
look down at her bruises, see them, say, 'My goodness, what
am I doing here!' And get the heck out. These other bruises
. . . sometimes it takes an awful long time for them to swell up
big enough for a woman to really see them."

"Yes, I don't doubt that, Mrs. Craig. But, to stay a little
closer to home, Bill Brown sure doesn't seem like the type to
me that would dominate a woman, in any way."

"Oh, I'm not suggesting that he would do . . . anything
physical. No more than Fred would." Mrs. Craig was obviously picking her words very carefully now, her fists
clenched with strain.

"But . . . I feel he has the capability . . . to be very
domineering . . . emotionally . . . given half a chance."

"But, so far, at least, so far as you yourself know"—Porath
was being just as careful—"neither you nor your daughter
Linda have ever been subjected to any . . . let's say, abuse . . .
of any variety, from Bill Brown?"

Mrs. Craig sat silent, frozen perfectly still. But finally, in a
deathly still voice, she said, "No. Not so far . . . as I know."

Another long silence—there was nothing further for Porath
to ask, so he just waited.

"Strangely enough, that was one thing Linda liked least
about Bill, his lack of emotion. He never seemed to get angry
at her, no matter what she did."

* * *

Dinato's search of Linda's room produced little more than Porath's of Mrs. Craig's head did. There was a small green address book though, containing numerous names and phone numbers, also a desk calendar, with the words "617 Kenmore. Sat. Bring Cookies, 7:00 P.M."

Today was Saturday.

Dinato called the station and had dispatch run a cross-reference on the address, found it to be the Martin Greenburger residence with a telephone number of 828-6109. Calling the number, Dinato found that, yes, Linda was invited to Jackie Greenburger's for a party to begin at seven o'clock this evening. But, of course, she wasn't there yet.

This slim lead having been worked down to nothing, the two officers thanked Mrs. Craig for her continuing cooperation, assured her they would continue to work on Linda's disappearance "day and night, with all available personnel," and took their leave.

"Get anything of value?" Dinato asked Porath as they walked up the drive to their marked patrol car.

Porath shrugged. "Not really." Yet, somehow, he kind of felt he had, if only he knew what. Seemed like there had been something fairly important somewhere in what Mrs. Craig had been telling him. Something that would give him a handle on this case. *Damn, I wish I'd paid a little closer attention in some of my psych courses*, he thought.

They got back in the car, Dinato behind the wheel. "Where to, back to the station?"

Porath started to say "Sure," but when he opened his mouth the words that came were, "Say, what say we take a quick drive past the Browns'? It's only a couple blocks around the corner on Fauntleroy. See if his car is in the driveway."

"What do you want to see if his car is there for?"

"Damn, I . . . you know something, Dino, I'd sure like to take a look inside that car. That's the last place she was, you know, that we know for sure, inside that car."

Dinato frowned. "Boy, we're supposed to have a search warrant for something like that."

"Not if the guy consents. Why shouldn't he, if he's clean? I'll come up with something to make it sound plausible . . . the key! Yeah, Linda's house key, we looked for it this morning. Perfect, it was the Browns who brought it up in the first place. They should have no objection to us continuing to search for it."

5

The two officers walked up to the front door of the Brown residence and rang the doorbell. Fred Brown opened the door. "Hello, Hal, what can I do for you?" Porath introduced Officer Dinato, explaining that Dinato would be in charge of the Linda Lou Craig case during the next shift and that they were still searching for Linda's house key.

"We were wondering, Fred, if we could take a quick look through Bill's car, to see if it might possibly have fallen out of one of her pockets, maybe slipped down between the seats or something?"

Fred frowned. "Doesn't seem like there'd be much chance of that."

"I know, but there doesn't seem to be much chance of anything in this case—we've run up against nothing but nothing. It seems like she's just vanished into thin air."

Fred nodded. "Well, I see no reason why you shouldn't look through the car. Bill couldn't give you anything to go on when you had him down to the station?"

"Not really. It was just a chance to get on record his recollections of last night. See if there might have been some little thing he overlooked when we all met together at the Craigs' this morning."

"He tells me you taped the visit you had with him?"

Porath shrugged casually. "We always do. Just a matter of procedure."

Fred nodded—skeptically, Porath thought—and abruptly switched to Linda. "She's a pretty hardheaded, headstrong little gal. Bill tell you that?"

"Yeah, more or less."

"Used to having her own way. Of course, Irene has her hands full, trying to raise two teenage girls without a man in the house, not that she hasn't done a terrific job of it. Linda is a fine girl, we're going to be proud to have her as a daughter-in-law, but Bill was just telling Leona and me now a few things at least I wasn't aware of. How terrifically moody Linda's been lately. How she might sit for hours on end when they're together not saying a word, then all of a sudden want to jump out of the car and walk alone for a while, praying to herself—"

"Bill indicated to you that she did that last night, Fred?"

"Well, now I don't know if he said exactly last night, but enough times of late. This thing of not wanting Bill to see her all the way into the house, not even remain in the driveway till she's safely all the way inside—why, that seems to have become a big thing with her of late. Insisting on standing and watching him drive away before she would go in the house. He'd have to get out of the car and go back and say, 'Well, you should go in the house,' and she wouldn't."

"Fred, apparently Bill didn't do that last night. According to his testimony to us—"

"And so, finally, he'd say, well, this is the normal way she wants to do it. She wants to see me drive away and wave to me and then go in the house, and so that's what happened."

"Yes, it appears it did—"

"In fact, I hear now—Elizabeth tells me—that sometimes Linda went for a walk around the block even in these subzero temperatures and prayed while she walked and then came back to the house."

Officer Porath looked at Fred Brown levelly. "Fred, do you have any reason to believe that Linda did that last night?"

"Well, no, not really, but if a person does something once, there's a good reason to believe she might do it again."

"Fred, right now, the main thing we're concerned about is finding her before she freezes to death. If she is still out there somewhere."

"Certainly. Of course, so am I, Bill, Leona, we all are. That's why I'm telling you all this. I just thought maybe by filling you in on a few things about Linda you might not have heard so far, some of her little quirks her mother might not want to bring up, it might give you a better idea where to look—you know, Bill is very polite, loyal, gallant, I've taught him to be. He won't tell you a lot of things like this—"

"Like what, Fred?" Porath asked him point-blank.

"Hal, Linda just doesn't have her head screwed on quite as tight as Irene would like to believe. She's a pretty disturbed little gal. Things aren't all that hunky-dory between her and Irene at home. Bill tells me back there right now Linda's been badgering him to go out and find an apartment with her so she can move out of her mother's house. Bill's talked her out of moving out dozens of times. He knows it's not the right thing for two religious young kids like—"

"Fred, I'd appreciate it . . . Could you please call Bill out here, check with him if it would be alright for us to look through his car for Linda's house key? If we could find that and knew she couldn't get in the house, that might put a different light on things."

"Certainly. I've been meaning to do it all along. Bill, come on out here a second, Hal and—what's your name again?"

"Officer Chuck Dinato."

"—Chuck here want to look through your car for Linda's house key."

Bill Brown entered from the hallway leading to the bedrooms of the Brown ranch-style home. The two officers were standing in the living room just inside the front door, facing Fred Brown. To their right lay the combination dining room and kitchen. Bill's mother, Leona, followed closely behind her son, one hand on his shoulder, almost as though she was subconsciously trying to steer him. Bill appeared much as he had through what by now was becoming a long day: quiet, subdued, a vaguely perplexed look in his deep-set baby-blue eyes, neatly trimmed hair parted on the left and combed down and across his forehead. He was dressed in well-pressed, light-blue slacks and a royal-blue pullover sweater/vest over a white dress shirt, the unbuttoned collar worn outside and folded back over the neck of the sweater—almost exactly as his father was dressed, Porath realized now, looking from one to the other. He was also struck by how much they looked alike, wore their hair; take away twenty or so years and pounds, they could easily pass for brothers. There was something distinctly old-fashioned about Bill Brown. It was a number of things other than just his haircut and clothing. He was a smooth-faced, untroubled kid from the fifties, no later than the early sixties, some throwback to "Happy Days," a "Gee whiz" kid steered out by his mother because the cops were here to find out if he knew anything about who threw the overalls in Mrs. Murphy's chowder.

His mother didn't have him by the ear, but she looked worried. Distinctly agitated, her watery blue eyes darted nervously from her son to the two officers, back to her husband, and started all over again. She appeared somewhat older than her dapper husband; Porath wondered if she was. Whatever, the years hadn't treated her as kindly, appeared to have scarred her more, wrought their worry lines more deeply into her broad Holbein face, rounded her shoulders, bowed her strong body slightly. Maybe it's from all those years of carrying breakfast trays, Porath thought.

"Bill, we'd like to give your car a quick looksee for Linda's house key."

"Sure, go ahead."

The two officers turned and let themselves back out the door, leaving the Brown family standing as they were. "Talkative mother, ain't he?" Dinato observed out of the corner of his mouth as they walked along the front side of the rectangular house. "Sure wanted to make sure we knew how kinky Linda's been lately."

"If it's true, I don't blame him. The kind of disturbed girl he described could be most anywhere, have done most anything to herself."

"Suicide?"

Porath shrugged. "Some kind. Cults . . . run off to join some kind of slower suicide. Maybe Bill even helped her."

Dinato nodded. "There's something screwy here."

"My sentiments exactly. Notice how hard his mother is taking Linda's disappearance?"

"Sure did. 'Course, that's only natural, kindhearted woman, something scary like this. Doesn't have to mean she thinks her kid's got anything to do with it."

"No, not necessarily. But I think she does."

Dinato nodded. "So does Mrs. Craig."

"You catch on fast, don't you?"

"My ole lady didn't whelp any idiots."

Bill's car was parked in the side drive, just a few feet around the northwest corner of the house, to the rear of the residence. The two doors of the chocolate-brown 1974

Chevrolet Impala were unlocked, so Porath opened the passenger side door and Dinato the driver's side, and together they searched the front seat area, under and between the seats. Dinato was the first to find something, several light-colored hairs on the surface of the tan vinyl seat covers, also a blue thread. Just about that time Bill arrived and leaned over Dinato's shoulder, apparently attempting to see what he was doing. "Could these be from Linda's head?" Dinato asked Bill, indicating the several light-colored hairs he held between his thumb and forefinger. Bill allowed as how they might well be, they were about the right shade and length. The blue thread he felt was the wrong color blue and would not match her ski jacket.

"Hey, what's this?"

The tenor of his partner's voice caused Porath to straighten. Dinato was crouched low over the front seat, his eyes not four inches off the level of the seat. "What is it, Chuck?"

"This here," Dinato answered, drawing back so his partner could see, pointing to a minute discoloration in the fabric just to the right of center and approximately six inches from the front edge of the seat. Porath crouched low over the spot. The stain was reddish brown in color.

"What is this, Bill?" Porath asked him. Dinato made room so Bill Brown could squeeze beside him and peer down at the stain too.

"Beats me," Bill answered casually. "Looks like ketchup or something."

"More like blood to me," Dinato stated unequivocally.

"Me too," Porath agreed, pulling back so he could get a better focus on Bill's face. Bewilderment slightly purpled the normally China-blue eyes. He doesn't know any more about this than we do, Porath found himself thinking.

"Blood?" Bill asked incredulously, the awesome word inflected with a curiously childish intonation. It was as if he could not only not believe its existence, but was even a little afraid to say the word out loud.

"Yeah," Porath repeated flatly, "blood."

"How'd that get there?" Bill asked, in much the same manner he had said the word "blood." Porath had the feeling he was asking himself as much as he was them.

"That's kind of what we'd like to know," Dinato said, turning to thrust the question right in Bill Brown's face. Bill just stared back at Dinato, without moving, their faces only about twelve inches apart. Finally Bill just shook his head slowly from side to side in complete bewonderment.

Bill's father came around the corner of the house just then and, seeing his son and Officer Dinato apparently squared off face to face, asked rather stridently, "What's going on here?"

"We found something that looks like blood here on the front seat, Fred," Porath said bluntly.

"Blood!" Fred Brown threw a quick glance at his son, then pushed by him to peer where Porath was pointing. "Where, I don't see anything?"

"Right there." Bill's father started to poke at the stain with his forefinger.

"Don't touch it!" Dinato commanded sharply.

"You mean that little spot?" Fred asked, the words colored with indignation. "My goodness, that could be most anything."

"We don't think so," Dinato disagreed, "and I've been around long enough to know blood when I see it."

Fred Brown ignored Dinato's observation, turned to his son. "You know what that is, Bill?"

"No, I sure don't, Dad."

"Think hard now, son. Could you have been doing something here in your car, stopped in a drive-in or something, spilled something—"

"Sure. Lotsa times."

"This looks mighty recent to me, Mr. Brown," Dinato observed. "Been there any length of time it would have been worn into the seat by bodies rubbing over it—see how it still shows a distinct outline around the edges? After even a few days a blood spot tends to blur around the edges, become rounded off."

Porath didn't know if Dinato knew what he was talking about or not, but it seemed to be working with Fred Brown.

"Bill," Fred asked, "you cut your finger or anything here in your car recently, anything like that?"

Bill started to shake his head negatively, then reversed direction and nodded emphatically. "Yeah, come to think of it, I did have a nosebleed here in my car a few weeks ago. That might be where it came from."

"You actually remember some dropping on the seat here, Bill?" Porath asked.

"No, not really. Actually I thought I caught it all in my hanky. I try to be real careful about getting anything on my clothes or car, but some could have leaked through without my noticing it."

"Probably did," his father agreed.

"Bill, you say it was a few weeks ago?" Dinato asked.

"Yeah, something like that."

"I don't think it would show up as distinct around the edges—" Dinato began, when Fred Brown interrupted.

"Why, Bill, seems to me, I remember you saying something about this nosebleed before. Don't seem to me like it was no 'few' weeks ago, more like last week if I recollect correctly, wasn't it?"

"Yeah, I guess it was, Dad, just the beginning of last week. Monday, I think it was, I was going to one of my psychology classes, Abnormal Behavior Problems, I believe it was."

"School's been out for Christmas break since a week Friday," Dinato was quick to point out.

"Well, I must have been going somewhere else then," Bill countered meekly, "because I do believe it was just this past Monday."

"You say you're a psych major, Bill?" Porath asked.

"Yeah, third year."

"Me, too—was. Of course, I graduated three years ago, class of 'seventy-three."

"I graduate spring of 'seventy-eight. Say, is it hard to get a job on the LFPD? I'd like to get in a few years of on-site training before I settle into what I really want to do, maybe work for the Public Defender's Office, something like that, where you get more of a chance to help people who really need it."

"I didn't have much trouble—course, I put in my application while I was still in school, was already working part-time on the force as a trainee. Now I've already got my application in to test for the FBI—"

"Ah, you boys can get together for a frat party some other time," Officer Dinato scowled. He had been no closer to a psych major than riding alongside Porath in the patrol car. "Bill, you mind if I take a little sample of this blood—I mean, this stain here—so I can get it typed?"

"Help yourself." Bill shrugged.

Porath, properly rebuked by Dinato, fell to assiduously

searching the car, while Dinato was lifting a very small sample off the edge of the stain with a pair of tweezers procured from his evidence kit. He did find some interesting little items in Bill Brown's car—several marks on the right inside door panel, salty white in color; they appeared to be foot marks. Several longish blond hairs were located in both the front and rear seat along with what appeared to be one blond pubic hair located on the right rear of the back seat.

"Take a look at this little gem, Chuck," Porath whispered when he found it. Dinato straightened up from lifting his sample of what he, at least, was already absolutely certain was blood and leaned over the front seat. "C-hair, eh?"

"Yeah, blond," Porath confirmed. The two young officers remained locked in this posture, staring into each other's eyes. "You know what I'm thinkin', buddy?" Dinato finally asked.

"Yeah," Porath nodded, "about time to call in the big boys."

Dinato strolled casually by the waiting Browns to the patrol car, got in and shut the door behind him. He radioed the LFPD desk, advised Kozelowsky, the duty detective, what they had, asked for permission to impound, so a complete search could be made by the Crime Lab. Kozelowsky didn't feel he could authorize seizure on what they had, suggested they call the Helvetia County prosecutor's office. This had to be done by telephone, so Dinato retrieved Porath from Bill's car, told the anxiously observing Browns that they had to swing around to Dinato's house—he only lived on the next block—to pick up some evidence envelopes. They didn't want to spook the Browns unduly. If they couldn't impound, they would need their continuing cooperation.

On the way over to Dinato's house to make the phone call, Porath suddenly thought of something. "Say, Dino, what's all this about fresher bloodstains being more distinct around the edges? I didn't know you could age blood that easily after it's completely dried?"

Dinato, driving, turned his head toward Porath and winked. "Boy, that's common knowledge where I come from."

"It is?"

"I mean, you psych majors don't know it all. There's a lot of little things us street guys just know from common sense—"

"Why, you big baloney head! You made that up, didn't you?"

Dinato let out one of his patented laughing roars. Porath joined him, giving Dinato a huge punch to the shoulder. It was the first time he'd been halfway happy this new year.

As Porath's 6:00 A.M. to 2:00 P.M. shift had long since officially expired, Officer Dinato now technically became the investigating officer, so he made the call to the Helvetia County prosecutor's office. A Mr. Walter Self advised Investigating Officer Dinato that he did not believe they could legally impound the Bill Brown vehicle at this time but that the two officers could obtain evidence from the vehicle with the permission of the owner of the vehicle. Armed with this nebulous blessing from on high, Dinato and Porath returned to the Brown residence and asked Bill Brown if he had any objection to their taking a few small items from his car. Again, Bill Brown had no objection, following them back out to his car. At this time, Porath took a bigger sample of the possible dried blood from the seat of the vehicle; he also removed one hair that appeared to be pubic from the right rear of the back seat and the several longer blond hairs and the blue thread sample from the front seat.

While Dinato was obtaining the items from the inside, Porath examined the exterior of the vehicle. He noticed several lateral scratch marks along the passenger side, extending practically the entire length of the car, but most clearly etched along the front fender area. These lateral scratches were just in the salt stains on the car, not in the paint itself. It appeared as though the marks were caused by branches from a tree or a stiff plant. Porath asked Bill Brown if he knew where he might have gotten these fresh marks on the side of the car. Bill indicated that he hadn't gone anywhere where he could have received them, had no idea how they could have gotten there. What interested Porath the most was that the entire car was covered with a great deal of white salt, while the scratch marks contained just a small amount of spray. Due to the condition of the roads on New Year's Eve, the vehicle would not have had to travel very far to get the small amount of spray over the fresher scratch marks. One could draw the conclusion that the lateral scratch marks had been placed upon the car very near the end of last night's driving, particularly as

Bill Brown had already stated, and again reiterated, his car had been "sitting parked right here" since he returned home at a few minutes after 2:00 A.M.

Dinato, having finished obtaining the items inside the car, now also began examining the exterior. While Porath and Bill were discussing the possible origin of the fresh scratch marks, he noticed sand and frozen mud in the right rear wheel well of the vehicle, the same side as the scratches. There was no sand and frozen mud in the wheel wells on the left side of the vehicle. Dinato took a sample of this frozen sand/mud mixture from the wheel well and placed it in another evidence envelope. Throughout the two officers' examination, Bill had stood stoically watching them, answering their occasional questions as casually as they asked them.

"You mind showing us where you drove to last night, Bill?" Porath now asked, in the same casual manner.

"You mean, all last night?"

"No, just from the time you left the Hendersons' till you got back here, parked your car a little after two."

"Well, first we did just come here, you know, like I told you, to watch the movie."

That was another stupid little thing that had been bugging Porath. Dropping his voice so Dinato wouldn't hear his totally irrelevant sophomoric question, he asked it. "Incidentally, what was the movie, Bill?"

"It's a Mad Mad Mad Mad World."

Dinato stuck his head up around the corner of the car, a big grin on his face. "You can say that again."

Porath returned to Bill's itinerary a bit more officiously. "OK, now then, Bill, you stated that you left here at approximately 11:30 to pick up your sister Elizabeth at Unitarian Church?"

"That's right. We both looked for her, but she wasn't there, so we just drove off and looked at the Christmas decorations—"

"Where?"

"Well, now," Bill said, thinking, ". . . I don't think I know the actual names of all the roads we went on, but I guess I could take you back over the general route."

"Why don't you just do that, Bill, before it gets too dark out?" It was fast approaching dusk, an icy gray gloom had begun to settle over the modest middle-class ranch-style homes of the relatively recent development. Porath could smell wood smoke being driven to ground by the lowering cold of another subzero night. He shivered, thought of Sandy, wished he was home sitting in front of his own wood stove, their Christmas present to each other and the Arabs.

"OK," Bill was saying. "You want to take my car or yours?"

Dinato had finished his wheel-well work and joined them in time to hear Bill's question. "No thanks, Bill," he said dryly. "If you don't mind terribly, I think we'll go in the patrol car. Just let your car rest on its laurels."

As they came around the corner of the house and started down the drive to where the patrol car was parked on Fauntleroy, Fred Brown stepped out on the open front stoop and called. "What's going on now? Where you taking him?"

"Oh, Fred," Dinato said apologetically, turning back and throwing up one hand to acknowledge he knew he should have informed him but it had completely slipped his mind. "Bill has volunteered to take a little ride with us. Show us around where him and Linda drove last night."

"What for?" Leona Brown now crowded out on the narrow stoop porch behind her husband, extreme concern clearly marking her mobile features.

"Oh, just to see where the kids went on their little ride last night, looking at the decorations. Maybe, by just retracing the drive, something Bill might spot will trigger him to remember something Linda might have said or done, give us a little clue to work on . . ." Dinato spread both his hands wide, palms up. "The way it is now, we haven't got a darn thing to go on."

Fred Brown stood staring down the driveway at them. "You sure you want to do this, son?"

"Why not, Dad?"

The father had no answer for his son's query. Finally he nodded his head brusquely, turned, and ushered his wife back into the house.

Bill guided the officers from his residence directly through the Beechwood Hills area of Little Falls to Unitarian Church on Applelane. There, as he had stated earlier, he had looked around for his sister, Elizabeth, but did not find her. Then, proceeding out on Radies Road in Harrison Township, Bill stated that he had pulled in several drives and parked for no more than five minutes each time, just long enough for them to get a closer look at a particularly fetching Christmas display. Some he claimed to remember distinctly, others he was not as certain about. In any event, it mattered little, as the officers had only his word to go on, and the clean snow-cleared drives could give no indication of whether his car had stopped there or not, were it important in the first place.

Continuing off Radies Road in a roundabout way back to Linda's house, Bill said they had turned in at the water treatment plant on the Beechwood extension just east of Keller Lake Road, a fairly extensive complex of land, buildings, and concrete treatment reservoirs dissected by numerous one and two-track trails. Here they had parked a bit longer, Bill admitted somewhat sheepishly, getting in some fairly heavy discussion about their future marital plans leavened by a little light petting. From there they had proceeded to the Craig residence on Drake, where Bill had, by previous testimony and emphatic reiteration, dropped Linda off at two minutes till two.

Dinato didn't turn in at the brightly lit Craig residence, just drove on by, glancing down at the odometer as he did so: 15.2 miles. "Bill, doesn't seem like it would take no two and a half hours to travel the route you just showed us, only fifteen point two miles."

"Gee, was that all it was?" Bill asked guilelessly.

Dinato nodded, trying to drive and observe Bill's face at the same time. Porath was leaning forward from the back seat, his forearms resting on the back of the front seat attempting to do the same. They both could see Bill's face clearly as they cruised slowly through a well-lit intersection of Drake and Fauntleroy. "Unless, of course, you two lovebirds perched a good deal longer at one of those spots than you're telling us?"

Bill ducked his head slightly, appearing to blush, but it could have just been a reflection off the blinking red caution light.

"Say, there by the water treatment plant?" Dinato suggested. "That's a dandy little lover's lane. Before I got married, I used that trail myself for a little dallying and dillying, not to mention diddling."

Bill straightened somewhat rigidly, squaring his shoulders, pointing his chin prudishly, his voice sounding almost prissy. "Linda and I do not engage in premarital sex. We promised each other that right from the beginning, exchanged that vow again when we got engaged."

"Who said you did?" Dinato asked innocently. "A guy can spend all night parked without getting laid. I've done it more times than I like to tell myself, though not by choice—"

Porath stepped in with a little Psych 101 smoothness. "Bill, all we were suggesting is that conceivably you two got so deeply involved in your marriage planning that you sat there talking a good deal longer than you thought you had; it's a natural thing to do."

"Yes . . . yes . . . I suppose we could have," Bill admitted, seemingly completely mollified.

The patrol car was approaching the Miller driveway. "Bill," Porath asked suddenly, as though he had just now remembered, "which one of those spots where you parked you think you could have scratched up your car?"

Bill turned his head slowly till he was looking directly back at Porath, but he didn't answer until Dinato had turned in and stopped the patrol car in the Brown driveway. Porath reached up and snapped on the overhead dome light.

"You know something, Hal," Bill finally said unblinkingly, as though it had just dawned on him too, "it might have been back there at the water treatment plant. There were some trees there, and that trail is pretty narrow."

"Could have been," Porath agreed casually. "Did you, by chance, go down that trail a little further than you showed us?"

"No, I don't think so. Seems to me we parked just about where I showed you."

"Bill . . ." Porath left the name hanging, as though he was going to pursue the same subject further, and suddenly asked instead, "Did you know Linda was planning on going to a party at the Greenburgers' without you this evening?"

"Greenburgers'?" Bill finally asked, his brow crinkling in what appeared to Porath to be total incomprehension.

"Yeah, Jackie Greenburger's house," Porath said quickly, feeling a quick glow of pride at remembering the girl's first name too, "scheduled to start . . ." Porath made a fairly elaborate show of working back his tunic cuff and looking at his wristwatch. "Just about now, seven o'clock. You mean to say Linda never even said anything to you about it?"

"Why . . . no. She never even said a word."

"That's odd—of course, you know Jackie too?"

"No, I can't say I do."

"Then it does appear she was going to go without you, doesn't it, Bill? I mean, you just weren't invited, were you?"

Bill appeared to Porath more bewildered than at any previous time this day. "Doesn't . . . look that way."

"Was that typical of your relationship with Linda, Bill? That she would just go around accepting invitations to New Year parties without inviting you, her fiancé, along? Not consulting you, not even letting you know about it?"

"Why, no. We went everywhere together. Never kept a thing from each other. I don't think there was a thing of any importance we haven't shared with each other over these past months, particularly since we got engaged—"

"Unless there had been a change in your relationship, Bill."

"Change? What . . . what do you mean?"

"You were no longer engaged."

"No longer . . . engaged? Why, no, just last night we were talking about our marriage plans, how long we should wait, how we could get the finances together. Finances can be one of the biggest problems if they aren't worked out properly, we—"

"Bill, maybe *you* thought you were still engaged . . . but she didn't?"

"She . . . Linda . . . certainly we were still engaged!"

"Didn't she try to give you your ring back just a couple of days ago? Wednesday, the twenty-seventh?"

"No. That was my birthday!" Bill exclaimed, seemingly aghast at even the thought. "She tried hard to get back from Minnesota to be at my house for the little party we had planned, but her mother kept dawdling along purposely, so they didn't make it—"

"Purposely?"

"Well, I don't mean purposely against me, just wanted to stay to visit her friends down there longer. Linda finally got back the next day, called me the minute she got home, apologizing all over the place—"

"Bill, what I'm saying is this: Maybe, though you didn't realize it, Linda, in her own mind, had kind of broken off the engagement. That's why she could accept the invitation for this party at the Greenburgers' tonight, without inviting you too. Without even so much as telling you."

A heavy breath-holding silence pervaded the patrol car. Hal Porath thought he heard the dashboard clock thumping, but then he realized it was his heart. Not a car moved past on Fauntleroy, no movement occurred within his vision. Another deadly cold night was stealing upon them, the car windows had already begun to glaze over in the short while since Dinato had pulled in the Brown driveway and cut the motor. Porath suddenly had the weird image that the three of them were somehow trapped within an icebound casket and were slowly freezing solid. That the only thing that could save them was—

"We . . . are still . . . engaged. Anybody who says different . . . doesn't know what she's talking about."

"She?"

Bill ignored Porath's thrust, continued flatly, stubbornly, little-boy stubborn, Porath thought, "The only people who know what's between Linda and me is me and Linda. And that's where it's going to stay . . . unless she decides to come forward and tell you differently. Now, I think it's about time you two get back out there and try to find her and leave me alone."

Whereupon, Bill Ray Brown got out of the patrol car and shut the door behind himself firmly.

The two officers sat as they were for some seconds and then turned to look at each other, letting out their collective breaths as they did so. "Guess he told you, eh?" Dinato said, his face crinkling in a wry smile.

"Yeah, guess he did," Porath had to admit, reaching up and snapping off the dome light. "But somebody's lying here."

"Might be Linda. Telling her mother one thing and Bill another."

"Could be. They both seem to believe what they're telling us."

Dinato reached down and turned the ignition key; the engine jumped to life. "Where to, Govnuh? Back to the station? Your shift's long over, and those pricks don't know what overtime means."

Porath barely heard what Dinato said. If he could just catch somebody in a provable lie, then maybe the whole thing might start to unravel. "Back to the water treatment plant."

Dinato twisted in his seat, trying to see his partner's face in the uncertain light. "You see something back there?"

"No. But it checks. That could be where he scratched up his car. According to him, it's the last place he and Linda stopped; probably only would have gotten about that much new salt spray in the scratches coming that relatively short distance."

"Yeah, that would check out distance-wise," Dinato agreed. "But I didn't see any bushes or anything he could have driven up against if he drove where he said he did."

"If he drove where he said he did."

Dinato nodded. "I see where you're coming from, buddy." He was just turning off Fauntleroy onto Keller Lake Road, snapped on the siren and flashers, stomped down on the accelerator and held it there till they got back out to the water treatment plant.

They could have saved the gas and rubber. There was nothing more to be found this time than last. Though they car-prowled every one- and two-track trail within the entire complex, they could find no place where outgrowing bushes or down-hanging tree limbs made contact with a moving vehicle as long as it remained on the roadway and there was no indication in the snow of a car having driven off the roadway. Backtracking, the two officers easily found again where Bill had indicated earlier he had parked the night before. His tire tracks—the only tire tracks—were clearly visible in the two to three inches of snow that lay undisturbed in the theoretically off-limits area.

Yes, it looked as though Bill Brown had parked his car exactly where he had showed them and had driven no place else within the water treatment complex. But, conversely, that being the case, he absolutely could not have scratched his car in the manner that he had where he had driven with Linda last night.

The question remained then: Where had Bill Brown scratched his car?

That night Porath had trouble sleeping, spent most of it clinging to his sleeping Sandy's back, thinking of Linda.

And Bill Brown.

There was this one thing that just wouldn't go to sleep. Something about him . . .

Waiting until it was nearly decent, 6:00 A.M., he got up and called Mrs. Craig. She answered midway through the first ring. He apologized quickly, hoping he hadn't frightened her with his call. She assured him she had been awake all night, was more than willing to talk to him.

"How did Bill seem to you when you first saw him yesterday morning," Porath asked her, coming right to the point, "when he first came to your house in response to your call about Linda being missing?"

"Why . . . well, I'm not sure I really looked at him so close right off the bat. I was so upset, almost half crazy, just asking all of them at once, but particularly Bill, I guess. He kept repeating how he had dropped Linda off at two minutes till two—"

"You're not answering my question. Would you say that he acted different than usual? The same?"

"Well, maybe a little . . . strange. Though, of course, it might just have been he was in as much shock as me. I suppose I was acting strange too."

"Forget that. Forget everything except just your feeling."

A heavy silence—Porath could almost feel her sucking in her breath.

"He almost acted like he really didn't care!" The words came boiling into his ear.

"Thank you." Porath mumbled some amenities, hung up. He finally had what he had been stalking all night. Mrs. Craig had corroborated an eerie feeling he had had a number of times while with Bill Brown in the course of yesterday. Either Bill was in some sort of deep traumatic shock and was just woodenly going through the motions, or he just simply didn't care—or, somehow, couldn't. There was something lacking within him. Like, as they used to say in the old days, he wasn't quite all there. Something had been left out of him. Feeling. Where was Bill's real, deep-down, warm-sad feeling?

That young Hal Porath didn't know. He couldn't answer that big question about Bill Brown, any more than he could about so many others of Bill's, and his, generation. For it hadn't only been with Bill Brown that Hal Porath had noticed this particular phenomenon, but with too many others of his friends, classmates, and colleagues. A lot of them didn't seem to "really care," as Mrs. Craig had so aptly put it. Wouldn't? Couldn't?

Porath shrugged, wondered what to do with his answer, now that he had it. An alleged lack of feeling didn't a murderer make. Or cause Bill Brown to have done something to cause the disappearance of one Linda Lou Craig . . . did it?

6

Dinato was up and calling into the station by 9:00 A.M. that Sunday morning of January 2, 1977. Advised by the desk that Porath was there and had called in Lieutenant Zarling to brief him on the MP Linda Lou Craig case, Dinato, though not slated for duty until two in the afternoon, decided to go down to the station and present what he had to Lieutenant Zarling also.

After hearing his two young officers, Lieutenant Zarling agreed that there did, indeed, appear to be "something strange" about the case. Acting on Officer Porath's request that a polygraph be run on one Bill Brown, Zarling, after briefing Chief of Detectives Badger by telephone, contacted Corporal Sam Atwell, resident polygraph expert, and asked him if he would be available to administer the test. Corporal Atwell, though it was his Sunday off and his wife was having the in-laws over for a big Sunday dinner, agreed to forgo the festivities and run the test at approximately 1:00 P.M. that afternoon. Porath then made contact with Bill Brown by telephone and asked him if he would submit to a polygraph examination. Bill indicated that he would and could be in the station at one. Lieutenant Zarling also authorized Dinato to contact the Wisconsin State Police Crime Lab to see if they could run a test on the suspected bloodstain on the front seat of Bill Brown's vehicle before the polygraph. Dinato contacted a Roland Nehring at the Crime Lab who agreed to attempt a make on the stain immediately. Dinato met Nehring at the Crime Lab at approximately 11:00 A.M. and turned over to him five evidence envelopes, three containing the hair and

53

thread samples and two containing the blood samples. After running a preliminary test, Nehring stated that the substance was blood but it would be several days before it could be determined if it was human blood and, if so, what type of human blood.

In the meantime, Porath had advised Dispatcher Hotaling to place a computer printout statewide for MP Linda Lou Craig. Officer Meyer's follow-up report on possible suspect Jack Dun, the ex-boyfriend, indicated that Dun had a corroborated alibi for the time in question and could, for all intents and purposes, be eliminated as a possible suspect in this case.

It now remained to be seen just how possible a suspect the polygraph machine made Bill Ray Brown out to be.

Quite possible, the polygraph machine seemed to be saying, quite possible, but not positively.

Corporal Atwell sat hunched over his desk, studying the read-out before him. Bill Brown sat calmly across the desk from him, in the single straight-backed interview chair. They were the only ones in the small, instrument-crammed office.

"Bill," Atwell said abruptly, "you flunked on four, whether or not you know what happened to her; on eight, if you lied about leaving her at home; and nine, if you had directly caused her to be missing. What do you make of that?"

Bill didn't even blink. "Beats me."

"OK. Let's go over this piece by piece then." Atwell leaned forward toward Bill, turned the printout so he could see. Bill hunched forward on his chair. "See here, on whether or not you know what happened to her, the way the needle jumped when I asked you?"

"Yeah."

"Yeah, what?"

"Yes, I see how the needle jumped."

"Why do you suppose it jumped like that?"

"Beats me."

Atwell felt like saying, "You bet it did," but he checked his tongue. "And here again on question eight: Did you deliberately lie about leaving her at home about 2:00 A.M. on January 1, 1977?"

"I'm sorry . . . I really don't know."

Corporal Atwell found himself staring across his desk into the wide-open, unblinking blue eyes, thinking, Damned if I don't almost believe that he believes what he's saying. But, then, he had Bill's polygraph printout, and he also almost believed what it was saying. "What about question nine then? See here, the needle jumped again when I asked you that one: Did you directly cause Linda Lou Craig to be missing from her home?"

"I dropped her off," Bill explained again patiently, without the slightest indication of prevarication, or doubt, "just the way I keep telling you, everybody else. She was just sitting there in the snow, more like kind of leaning, just one hip against the step looking at me, waving me good-bye."

Atwell had heard this story enough times already, from both Porath and Dinato when they briefed him, from Bill himself when they had gone over his version before the polygraph examination. That was another thing—in total honesty, Atwell wasn't completely satisfied with the results of the polygraph reading. Though the machine had definitely indicated untruthfulness in the areas he had questioned Bill about, the reaction had not been as clear-cut as he would like it to be; it was almost as if the polygraph machine wasn't completely sure itself. Atwell had never seen anything quite like it; the machine appeared to be reflecting the subject's uncertainty. Almost like it was saying the subject doesn't know whether he was telling the truth or not!

"Bill, do you drink by chance?"

"You mean, whiskey, things like that?"

"Yeah, demon rum. Were you drinking New Year's Eve?"

"7-Up. We had 7-Up with our pizza."

The kid was starting to get on his nerves, too cute for his own good. "Forget the 7-Up, I'm asking you about the hard stuff—"

"Corporal, I've never had a taste of hard liquor in my life. We don't believe in it; my family, Linda, we all abstain—"

"How about drugs?"

"Sir, I wouldn't let something like that in my body at the point of a gun."

"I don't blame you," Atwell agreed dryly. "The only thing here is, Bill, I'm trying to give you a hand, if you can call it that. You see, if you were under the influence of alcohol or certain drugs and you did do something to Linda to cause her to be missing, then it, ah, would be easier to explain. Like, ah, you did it, but you were so far gone, you didn't know what you were doing, can't quite remember now—"

"But I didn't, Corporal. You see, that's just my point, the one I've been trying to make with all you people. I just didn't do anything to cause Linda to be missing."

"But the machine—"

"No matter what it says, I dropped her off."

Atwell didn't like to be interrupted. "Bill, the Crime Lab found blood in your car. Human blood."

Some of the smug surety slid off Bill's face, but there was more perplexity in his eyes than fear. "Honest?"

"Cross my heart. How do you suppose that got there, son?"

"From the nosebleed I had Monday, I guess. I thought I had caught it all in my hanky, but I guess some must have leaked through on the seat—"

"On the door panel too? It leaked through your hanky way over there on the passenger-side door panel?"

Atwell thought he detected some confusion in the baby-blue's now. "I don't know anything about no blood on the door panel," Bill said slowly.

Neither did Atwell. He had just thrown it in to read Bill's reaction. The Crime Lab hadn't been able to tell in its quick preliminary test that morning what the stains were on the passenger side door panel. "Bill, what did you and Linda fight about New Year's Eve?"

"We didn't fight about anything."

Atwell shuffled through some papers he had on his desk, picked up one at random, made like he was reading it. "Says here that you got into a 'pretty heavy discussion' New Year's Eve—"

"When did I say that?"

"To Porath—says here that you two got into a 'pretty heavy discussion' New Year's Eve about Linda Lou wanting to break off the engagement, give you your ring back—"

"No way. I never said anything like that."

"Oh, oh, excuse me, Bill, I'm terribly sorry. I have the wrong paper. This isn't your deposition at all. It's a Mrs. Irene Craig, apparently Linda's mother—"

Bill sat up straight, his face showing more emotion than it had at any time during the interview. "Her mother said that? Mrs. Craig said Linda was trying to break off our engagement? Give my ring back?"

"That's what it says here."

"No way! That's just simply not true, Corporal sir. If Mrs. Craig said that she must be . . ."

"Lying? A mother would lie about something like that at a time like this?"

"Well, no, I surely wouldn't like to think so. She's always claimed to be real religious too, but she just . . . had to be mistaken."

Atwell started to reach for the telephone. "Should I call her up and ask her?"

Bill called his bluff. "Go ahead. But I'm sure if that's what she mistakenly believes, she will just say the same thing over again anyway. I mean, Mrs. Craig thinks she knows Linda Lou so well, but she doesn't really. Linda hated it at home; she was always after me to help her find an apartment so she could move out of the house. Even wanted me to move in with her, but I knew better than that, told her so right there New Year's Eve even, that wouldn't be right. We had taken vows together not to have a sexual relationship until after we were married, and I know that would be next to impossible to do if we lived in the same apartment—"

"So you weren't involved sexually?"

"That's what I'm trying to tell you—

"You didn't do . . . *anything?*" Atwell cocked his left eye, wrinkled up his face with a large dose of male disdain, leaned the whole concoction across the desk closer to Bill. He dropped his eyes, squirmed in the hard straight-backed inter- view chair, blushed to the roots of his carefully groomed hair. "Well, we . . . did do some fairly heavy petting."

"Such as?"

"Kissing and hugging."

"No more than that?"

"What do you mean?" Bill asked innocently.

Corporal Atwell asked himself the same question every other officer had. Is this guy for real? "You stayed on top of her clothing?"

The boyish-looking young man seemed to grow even younger right there across the desk from Atwell, ran through his entire repertoire of adolescent sexual nose-picking, still didn't look up. There was something about the way Bill combed his hair that annoyed Atwell. Parted high and sweep- ing down and forward across his forehead, a thick lock coyly tumbling toward his left eye. Maybe it was just because he had so little left himself, Atwell rationalized.

"Bill, you haven't answered me."

"We . . . touched each other . . . a little."

"Under your clothing?"

"Outside . . . outside."

Atwell let that go; he felt sorry for the poor devil. "Bill, why did Linda want to get her own apartment?"

"She was tired of fighting with her sister, constantly being reminded about her parents' divorce—"

"What do you mean by that?"

"Well, Linda felt that, by living with her mother, just seeing her all the time, constantly reminded her about the fact that her parents were divorced, that if she lived away from home she would start to forget about it."

"Was she upset about it, I mean, New Year's Eve?"

Bill shrugged. "No more than usual."

"So, you would characterize it as, more or less, a routine discussion you'd had many times before?"

"Yeah, I guess so." Bill suddenly sat bolt upright. "Say, sir, on that blood on the seat of my car."

"Yes?"

"I just thought of something. That could be from my sister."

"How so?"

"She rides in the car with me all the time, sits in just that seat." Bill ducked his head again, seemingly somewhat embarrassed. Atwell knew what he was driving at, but made him say it.

"So?"

"Maybe she . . . was on her period."

Atwell let the silence lengthen, waited for Bill to look up. "It's possible," he finally said, letting a goodly glob of skepticism color the words. "I suppose anything's possible." Atwell again waited, just sat there staring at Bill. Bill just sat there staring back. Doesn't this kid ever even blink? Atwell asked himself, noting his annoyance, then asked himself another question. What is there about this kid that annoys me—other than the fact he might be one of the most skillful liars I've ever met?

In lieu of an answer he tapped the polygraph readout with

his forefinger again. "Bill, I think there's enough here to proceed further with you."

Bill nodded as though he expected there would be.

"You go on out there and wait in the waiting room by the main desk. I'm going to go over this readout with the investigating officers." Bill merely stared back at him blankly, so Atwell got to his feet and moved toward his office door, Bill getting up from his chair and following along. Reaching the door, Atwell pulled it open. Louder than necessary, considering Porath and Dinato were lounging against the wall just a few feet down the hall, he said, "C'mon in, men. I think we got a little something here we ought to take a close look at before we decide what to do with him."

Fred Brown, who with his wife Leona had been standing down the hall to the left of Atwell's office, now strode forcefully forward. "What are you talking about?"

Atwell made like he didn't know who Fred was, tilted his head forward and peered over his glasses. "Who are you?"

"The boy's father. What's going on here? You've had him down here for three hours already."

"He may be here a whole lot longer. He flunked a substantial part of the polygraph exam." Ushering in Porath and Dinato, Atwell shut the door in Fred Brown's face.

"What you get, Corporal?" Porath asked, the moment the door was shut.

"Yeah, you find the little bastard out?" Dinato asked tensely.

Atwell shrugged. "Mebbee yes, mebbee no. Call Badger. I think it's time to drop the heavy hand on young Lochinvar."

7

Detective Sergeant Floyd Herman Badger was out rabbit hunting near his boyhood home in the Sand Lake area when he got
beeped. Forty-five years old, he had been with the LFPD seventeen years, fourteen of them in criminal investigation, five
as boss of the Detective Bureau. By the time he arrived at the
station, near 6:00 P.M., Bill Brown had been undergoing interrogation, including the polygraph, for five hours, broken only
by an occasional recess while Corporal Atwell conferred with
Porath and Dinato and took the supper break he was on now.
The only additional information of note Atwell had gained
from Bill during the period they awaited Sergeant Badger was
in relation to the "discussion" Bill and Linda had New Year's
Eve. Bill now indicated that it might have been "a little more
of a discussion" than he had stated earlier and that Linda had
become so upset at one point that she had "wanted to get out
and pray."

Atwell felt about ready to pray himself when Badger
walked in. "What you got, Sambo?" he growled. Flinging his
old greasy gabardine backpouch hunting jacket behind the fil-
ing cabinet, Badger crossed into the bathroom without waiting
for an answer. He had been keeping a pretty good running
track of what was going on in his lively little detective warren
over the holiday weekend, tapping into the desk by telephone
or car radio three or four times a day, so there wasn't a whole
lot about the Linda Lou Craig disappearance for him to hear.
The girl had disappeared. They suspected the boyfriend. But
they didn't quite know why. Or how. Or, even, quite when.

Atwell listened to his boss relieve himself—he wasn't one

60

to bother shutting the door—waited until the toilet bowl quit yowling, then called in, "You want to talk to the two investigating officers too?"

"Yeah, you all come over to my office."

They all did. Atwell slouched in the suspect's chair. Officers Dinato and Porath stood more or less at attention in front of Badger's desk until he waved an impatient hand, setting them down in the two remaining chairs as quickly as if he had leaned over and whacked them in the chest. Damn, he's a craggy mother, Dinato thought. That face looks like it was left over from Mount Rushmore.

Badger listened to what they had to say, leaned back in his frayed vinyl swivel-back chair, scratched down under the neck of his red thermal underwear, noting how ferociously it will scratch when a man first comes in out of the cold. "You know something? If it was me handling this case, I'd call the whole shooting match in. Get them all together in the same room, have me a little eyeball to eyeball. See if we can't straighten out these stories a little. Was the girl trying to break off the engagement or wasn't she? Mother says she was; the boyfriend says no. That one could make a whole helluva lot of difference. The time span differential New Year's Eve— where were the two kids for those two and a half hours between 11:30 when they leave the Brown house and get back to supposedly drop Linda off at this 'two minutes till two,' if the route you guys," indicating Porath and Dinato, "drove only took a little over an hour? That is, if we can believe any of the times. The Crime Lab says there's some kind of blood in the seat of his car, maybe some more on the door panel, something else Porath here says looks like foot smudges from feet walked in salt slush. That could be explained easy enough by a couple of kids humping in the front seat, but all you guys keep telling me we're dealing with a couple of angels here. Yet you're finding short hair, long hair—tell you what, fellas, if it was me, I'd just throw out anything anybody has told you so far and just start over again from scratch, and I don't mean this underwear. Actually, coming in on this a little late like I am may be a plus for me, kind of give us a fresh start, we'll just get them all down here if they'll come—"

"The boyfriend, Brown's folks are here already, been here all afternoon," Atwell pointed out.

"Good. Get Mrs. Craig down here, too, throw them all in

the same room. What about those scratches along the side of the kid's car that he says comes from those phantom trees out at the water treatment plant? Crack down on him on that. If they couldn't have been made any place where he took you on the ride, where didn't he take you . . . for a ride, fellas, for a ride. Maybe this smart little cookie took you guys for a ride. Find out where he didn't take you!" Both Porath and Dinato nodded simultaneously. "If there's a body in this case, and the boyfriend did her in, that's most likely where it is. But we can't just conclude we've got a homicide on our hands. We got to keep all our eyes and ears open. Maybe the kid is telling the truth, somebody else snatched her, she's a weirdo, ran away. Anytime there's this much religion lurking around, anything can happen. Maybe she ran off to join a convent, Holy Rollers, became a Moonie, Hare Krishna. Who the hell knows, there's so many weirdos out there now, any one of them could have swallowed her up. If we don't crack this one tonight, tomorrow we start checking the farout religious groups, the communes, those wild-eyed mothers on campus, The Path, The Road, Highway to Heaven, whatever they call themselves."

A big callused hand, moving deceptively fast, suddenly leaped out and snapped up the polygraph printout off his desk. "But look at this thing! That mutha machine ain't none too sure neither, it kind of thinks the boyfriend did it—at least, did something. Pound away on what it seems to be saying. That Bill Brown maybe yes/maybe no knows what happened to her. That he lied about leaving her at home. That he directly caused her to be missing. Though the machine's none too damn sure on any of these, don't you be unsure. You keep pounding away like you know for damn sure he did something. But don't always think only of homicide. Yes, sure, he could know what happened to her, just like the machine seems to be saying, but so could she. He helps her run away to the convent but has taken a vow with her not to tell. Yes, sure, he lied about leaving her at home, because he drove her to the disco in Milwaukee where she started working New Year's Eve as a topless dancer. Yes, sure, he directly caused her to be missing, because she wants to be missing. I'm telling you, you can't overlook any possibility no matter how farout when these university kids are involved. Christ knows I've found that out these past seventeen years."

Badger paused for breath, but just. "So see if you can get them all down here, both families, try to take some of the kinks out of these stories, see if we can crack this thing tonight, break through the ice. If we don't we could be in for a long skate. If there is a body involved, cold as it is now, all this wild country around, practically nobody's stirring out there these days but a few half-wit rabbit hunters, we might not find it till spring."

Mrs. Craig came right down. Badger courteously invited everyone into his office, along with Corporal Atwell, Officers Dinato and Porath, who brought in extra chairs from the squad room and arranged them around the perimeter of the, by now, cramped room. Badger stood behind his desk, signaled for Atwell to seat the boyfriend directly across his desk in front of him. When everyone was seated, Badger started to sit himself but, on impulse, remained standing, his bones telling him that he might do better if he stood above all the others, particularly this Bill Brown. Seeing him for the first time now, Badger was struck—as all the other cops involved had been—with Bill's straightforward clean-cut good looks. Damned if he don't even look like a choirboy was the way he characterized Bill Brown to himself.

"Folks, I'm Detective Sergeant Floyd Badger, commander of the Detective Bureau of the Little Falls Police Department. I hope I haven't inconvenienced you by asking you all to come down here, but, obviously, considering the gravity of the circumstances, I thought it best for all of us to visit together as quickly as possible to see what else we might possibly do to find Linda Lou." They all nodded. "Now we have done all we could think of toward finding Linda, but so far," he said, looking directly at Bill Brown, who stared unblinkingly back, "we haven't been able to find her. In the course of our investigation, we have come up with a few minor inconsistencies in the stories told by you people—and some not so minor. Corporal Atwell has given Bill here a polygraph examination this afternoon, the results of which I hold in my hand. It also points out some minor inconsistencies in Bill's story—and some not so minor." Fred Brown sat sullenly; Leona Brown nervously worked the fingertips of her right hand into the cupped palm of her left. "Now I know this could be difficult for all of you, possibly even very unpleasant, but we feel that anything we might do to find Linda would far outweigh whatever inconvenience this might place upon you people. We also realize we have had Bill here at the station for some six or seven hours already, but I am sure he would gladly give six or seven more hours if it would help to locate his fiancée."

Badger stressed the last word, flicking his eyes from Bill to Mrs. Craig. Mrs. Craig's eyes flashed, her face clenched rock hard. Bill merely nodded, his impassive face revealing nothing. "I want to make one thing perfectly clear: We are not here to blame anyone, throw any stones. We are here to visit together to try to find Linda Lou Craig. So, if any of you has anything whatsoever to tell us, particularly something that has not been told before, that might help us to find Linda Lou Craig, now is the time to tell it."

Detective Sergeant Badger waited. They all did. The supercharged silence was broken by the dispatch radio squawking down at the main desk. It was a floor and three doors away, but it sounded like it was right there in the room with them. Still, no one in the room even moved.

Badger purposely brought his right hand up and stroked his two-day-old rabbit-hunting grizzle—any experienced rabbit hunter knows better than to shave in this kind of sub-zero weather. It made him realize he was still wearing his hunting clothing, having come right from the woods to the station. He found himself thinking of the peaceful quiet of the snow-covered swamp he had tramped that afternoon, the smell of cut cedar clearing his head, wistfully comparing that spritely cedar scent to the sickly stench of frightened people and dusty unsolved cases.

"Alright then, let's get to it!" He heard himself almost snap, "The inconsistencies. Bill here tells us that he and Linda are still engaged. That nothing was ever said to him by Linda about her returning his ring." Watching Bill nod as he said it, Badger swiveled his eyes to the grim-faced Mrs. Craig. "What do you have to say to that, ma'am?"

She could barely answer. So many emotions crowded her voice box there was barely room left for the words. "He . . . Linda told me . . . she had tried to give his ring back Wednesday night but that he told her keep it anyway as a gift . . . 'Let's just be friends.'"

Badger looked past Bill at Mrs. Craig, trying to get both their faces in his vision at the same time and somehow hear the true voice of the missing girl. Though Mrs. Craig's face was easy enough to read, he gained nothing from Bill Brown's. He's a stone-face alright, he told himself, just like the boys been telling me. "So, you're saying, ma'am, in fact, that Linda was still wearing Bill's ring on New Year's Eve?"

"I really don't know if she was physically wearing it or not," Mrs. Craig retorted, indignation carving a passage for the words, "but she was no longer emotionally engaged."

"Try to think, ma'am, was she still wearing it or not? It could make quite a difference."

"I really don't . . . can't remember."

"Have you noticed it around the house, since she's been missing?"

"No, but then I can't say I've really looked!"

Badger turned to Porath and Dinato. "Did either of you come across it when you looked through her room?"

Porath and Dinato looked at each other, shook their heads. Porath spoke for both of them. "Sergeant, I can't say we have as yet conducted a total search of her room—"

"We will tomorrow." Badger turned to Bill. "What do you say, Bill? Was Linda still wearing her . . . your . . . ring, New Year's Eve?"

"Of course," Bill answered simply, "we were still engaged."

Chalk one up for you, Billy-boy, Badger said to himself. Until we find out otherwise, if that ring's still on her finger, you're still engaged.

Mrs. Brown broke silence by adding, "I saw it there too New Year's Eve. When they came over to watch the movie, I distinctly remember seeing it on her finger when she reached for a slice of pizza."

"You're sure, Mrs. Brown?" Badger asked.

Leona Brown nodded emphatically. "I remember admiring it. It was such a lovely ring."

Badger wasn't sure, but he thought he heard Mrs. Craig sniff. Whether she did or not, he could almost feel the battle lines being drawn through the room. Of course, this would be perfectly natural. A man didn't have to be an old-line detective to know that whenever, wherever, there are children and their respective parents involved, particularly as prospective in-laws, it's Nelly bar the door. "Mrs. Brown, you say Linda and Bill left your home at 11:30 to go over to Unitarian Church to pick up your daughter?"

"Well, that was if Elizabeth was there."

Badger glanced over at the two young investigating officers. Porath particularly looked a bit puzzled.

"Let me get this straight, ma'am. From what I've been led to believe, it was just a matter of them going over to Unitarian Church to pick the daughter up, but they somehow missed her. Are you now saying that you weren't sure Elizabeth was going to be there even before they left to pick her up?"

"Yes, I just told them they were supposed to go over to Unitarian Church to see if Elizabeth was at the church services at that time."

Porath raised his eyebrows quizzically. "I see," said Badger, "and what were they supposed to do if they found your daughter there?"

"Why, bring her home, of course."

"Did they?"

"No." Mrs. Brown shrugged. "Elizabeth wasn't there."

"Where was she?"

Mrs. Brown's eyes widened. She spread her hands slowly, palms up. "You know, there's been so much going on, I've never even thought to ask her."

No need, Badger thought, I'll ask her myself. "Certainly, I understand," he said aloud, then asked casually, "When did you next see Linda and Bill then?"

"I . . . why, of course, I never did see Linda again, but Bill came home a few minutes after two."

"How can you be so sure of the time?"

"Well, I was waiting up. I glanced at the clock when he came in."

"I see. How . . . ah . . . how did Bill seem to you when he came back?"

Mrs. Brown shrugged. "Same as always."

"I mean, did he seem happy, depressed, excited—"

"Happy. Very happy."

"What did he do when he first came home?"

Mrs. Brown shrugged again. It seemed to Badger as much a nervous habit, a quick inturning of her already slightly slumped shoulders, as a ploy to gain time to think. "Just walked in . . . was in real good spirits, seemed to be very happy."

"How could you tell?"

The nervous little shrug. "Well, just by looking at him. Then by the way he talked."

"Oh, so you talked awhile?"

"Yes."

"About what?"

Again, "Oh, he said they just drove around and looked at the Christmas tree lights."

"Then what?"

"Then he dropped her off. Kissed her good-bye and left her sitting on the front steps of her house."

"All that?"

"What do you mean?"

"You must be very close with your son." Badger smiled. "I never remember coming home after two in the morning and telling Ma all about kissing my girl good night."

"Neither did I," Leona retorted unsmilingly, "but times have changed, and I am very close with my son."

Badger nodded slowly. "I'm sure you are . . . and times have changed. Now, as to Linda sitting down in the snow, didn't you think—"

"Yes, as a matter of fact, I did. I jokingly said to Bill, isn't that a little odd, or why did you do that, something like that, and he said, 'Oh, we always do that; it's not uncommon for Linda just to go up and sit on the steps before going in—'"

"Leona!" Mrs. Craig suddenly blurted. "That's not true, and you know it!"

Leona Brown turned slowly toward Mrs. Craig. "No, I don't, Irene. I don't know that's not true at all."

"In the middle of the winter! Fifteen below zero! You're making my daughter out to sound like some kind of nut."

Fred Brown spoke up for the first time. "Irene, she's only telling what Bill told her. Verified, I might add, on other occasions, by our daughter."

"Then she's lying too."

"Perhaps," Mr. Brown said, "but I doubt it. We didn't raise our children to be liars."

"Well, neither did I," Mrs. Craig snapped. "Granted, Linda may have done that at some other time, maybe last summer when it was warm, but not last night. Besides, I would have heard the car drive in—"

"Irene, you know you don't hear so good—"

"Forget my hearing!" Mrs. Craig almost screamed. "I would have heard Bill's car drive in. I heard cars crunching by out on Drake while I laid awake. I always hear Bill's car drive in, even when the snow is not frozen. I would have heard Bill's car drive in New Year's Eve. He never brought Linda home! He never brought Linda home! He never—"

Badger came around his desk and took her by the arm and led her across the room and out his office door, closing it behind them. "Mrs. Craig, you've had enough. Done enough. I'm going to ask you to go home now. I'll have one of my men drive you—"

"I can drive."

"I know you can, but I'd like you to let him drive you. Conceivably you will think of something more to tell him on the way."

"I can stay, I'm tough enough, if it'll help to try to find Linda."

"Mrs. Craig, I think you can help more now by leaving. There's a few things I think I can use on Bill to better effect without your being here."

"So you think . . ."

"I'm not sure just exactly what I think. But let me tell you, I've just begun, and I don't mean to stop till I find your daughter."

"Thank you. You've all been . . . most helpful."

"We try," Badger said grimly, "we do our best."

"I know you do."

Badger opened the door again and called, "Dinato, come here. Give Mrs. Craig a ride home." Then added, purposely, "She'll undoubtedly have a few more things to tell you, so take your pad and pencil along."

"Right, Sergeant."

Badger said good-bye to Mrs. Craig, reentered his office, strode grimly back behind his desk, faced his shrunken audience with a stern set face. "Alright, now we're going to get down to real business. Some real serious business. I didn't want Mrs. Craig to hear any of this, purposely got her out of the room because, frankly, it's just too much to ask a mother who's lost her daughter to hear."

Watching the Browns' faces closely, particularly Bill's, Badger observed a widening of the eyes, a rigidity of body as they leaned forward tensely, a holding of breath. The mother appeared most apprehensive, Bill least. "No, we didn't find her body. All I meant was what I said. She has lost a daughter, hopefully, temporarily. But the Crime Lab has definitely found blood on the front seat of Bill's car. Now I know Bill has told us he had a nose-bleed in his car a few days ago—"

"It could be from Elizabeth too, you know. She sits there all the time," Mrs. Brown interrupted, somewhat defiantly.

"Certainly, it could," Badger agreed amiably. "It could be almost anyone's, maybe even mine, but I don't think so." He leaned forward for emphasis. "Linda Lou Craig was the last one we know of who sat in that seat, and she hasn't been seen since."

"Sergeant," Fred Brown said flatly, "that stain means nothing until you type it, and you know it, so let's cut out the theatrics. Now that Irene Craig has gone, I've got a few things to say myself. Certainly, we are all greatly concerned about Linda—she was becoming like another daughter to us—but I've now got to try to protect my own. Just how long do you think you can keep Bill down here?"

"That depends, Mr. Brown, that depends."

"Now we've been more than cooperative all along, haven't stinted ourselves one minute since Linda came up missing, been out searching around and asking questions ourselves, have hardly slept a wink since Irene's phone call yesterday morning, let your people come in and search through Bill's car without a warrant, take him for rides, tape record interrogation, let him come down here and spend darn near all day with you today, give him polygraphs—"

"Ah, yes, Mr. Brown, I was just coming to that."

"I know you people, if you had really found out anything, if he was lying about anything, you'd come down on him with both feet. We wouldn't be all sitting here in a circle chat—"

"Corporal," Badger said, by way of interruption, "would you come up here please?"

"Sure, Sergeant," Atwell said, coming forward.

"Here, you're the unbiased polygraph expert. You tell Mr. Brown what the polygraph had to say about Billy's truthfulness."

That did it. The scared people and dusty file silence was there again. It seemed to take forever for Corporal Atwell to pick up the polygraph printout and look it over. Fred Brown had been stopped talking literally in the middle of a word, and his mouth still hung slightly ajar. Leona Brown's eyes grew progressively rounder, became somewhat bulbous, a nervous tic pulled at the left side of her cheek. Badger couldn't help but feel sorry for her, but if her son had done something to the girl, he had no time for such niceties as sympathy.

Atwell cleared his throat, but that was all. Badger was beginning to think Atwell had decided to add to the war of nerves, and whether or not he knew what happened to Linda. He lied about leaving her at home. And he lied about if he had directly caused her to be missing."

An even louder silence followed the scholarly Atwell's words. The Brown parents' eyes slowly left Atwell—it seemed to Badger to take them a lifetime—and slowly, oh so slowly, their heads turned simultaneously sideways to look at their son seated between them. Their son continued to impassively stare straight ahead. At first, Badger thought he was staring at him, but when he tried to catch Bill's eyes in his own and couldn't, he realized the clear blue eyes were looking somewhere over his left shoulder and beyond.

"What do you say to that, son?" the father was asking, gently.

"I haven't the slightest idea what they're talking about, Dad."

"Bill," the mother asked beseechingly, yet her words were overlaid with such surety that they came out as much a statement of fact as question, "everything happened just the way you told us, didn't it?"

"Certainly, Mother."

Badger felt sick to his stomach. He wasn't sure whether it was because he hadn't eaten since breakfast, or from having to eat the permissive potpourri the Brown family was serving him now. What the shit, did they think the little pot-licker was just going to jump up and say, "I did it, Dad, Mother, now make it all better"?

The father tried to, swiveled his eyes to lock with Badger. "You know full well, polygraphs been wrong before, Sergeant."

"Not nearly as many times as they've been right."

The father dropped his eyes briefly, then brought them back up again, but some of the arrogance had slipped away. "Do you mind if we talk to Bill alone for a few minutes, Sergeant?"

Badger thought about that one a few seconds. Maybe now was the time to jump over all of them with both feet, try to break into the kid, play the parents off against the son if it was humanly possible, try . . . suddenly, he was bone tired. Tramped all day through rough and tumble boggy cedar swamp, all he had in mind was a few four-legged bunnies, maybe even a snowshoe, called back to this . . . Badger looked at the clean-cut, boyish face, the fearful parents hovering beside him, thought of his own twelve-year-old son, Dave. This kid didn't look much older, still staring somewhere up there over Badger's left shoulder, dealing with something or somebody beyond his ken—

It hit him then. Yes, Badger told himself slowly, I believe . . . I do believe the little pot-licker's praying.

A slow sad feeling settled over Badger. The gray-faced companion that had been strolling over so often of late, they would soon have to sit down for a real visit not just a quick cup of coffee.

"Sure, go ahead. Try to talk to him. If he did do something to her and he tells us now, I'll try to do the best I can to save him, at least, a piece of him. If he did and doesn't tell us now, I'll get him sooner or later . . . all of him."

Badger turned and walked from the room, Atwell and Porath following. When they were out in the hall and closed the door on the Browns, Atwell reached out and patted Badger on the shoulder. "Good show, Sarg."

Badger merely grunted.

"I think we're getting close, Sergeant," the youthful Porath said, boyish enthusiasm coloring his words. He wanted to pat Badger on the other shoulder, but he didn't quite dare. "You going to keep after him, sweat him all night?"

Badger had a sudden impulse to reach out and give Porath a quick little bearhug, but, of course, stifled it. He said instead, "Boy, this ain't one of those half-wit television shows where Dinato comes popping back in after the next to the last commercial with the big clue that breaks the case."

"Did you see the change on them when Corporal Atwell hit them with the polygraph?"

"I didn't see no change on the kid." Badger grunted. "Tell you the truth, I got a feeling in my weary bones that we wouldn't break that kid if we sweated him for months. There's something about him . . ." Badger stopped himself, shrugged. "Then again, maybe there's nothing in him to break."

After about fifteen minutes Fred Brown came out in the hall, walked up to the trio of waiting lawmen. "Tell you anything we should know?" Badger asked him.

The father shook his head. "He has nothing to tell. Other than what he already has."

Badger nodded. "Alright, take him home. We'll catch up with you again tomorrow." He turned abruptly and walked down the hall toward the main desk, Atwell and Porath trailing along beside him. As they passed the desk, Badger suddenly stopped, turned to Porath. "What status you carrying Billy-boy under?"

Porath shrugged. "Subject, boyfriend, whatever—"

"Change it to suspect," Badger growled.

8

The next morning Badger had Chief of Police Dick Mackey convene an all departmental briefing concerning the missing Linda Lou Craig. Present were Chief Mackey, Badger, Detective Sergeant Poulous, Sergeant Sievert, Atwell, Detectives Jensen and Kozelowsky, Officers Dinato and Porath. After all involved had contributed their findings and educated guesses, Chief Mackey ordered a general search to begin that day, January 3rd, including ground to air by the Big Falls Police Department helicopter unit. At the conclusion of the general departmental briefing, Badger called an assignment briefing for his department in his office.

Porath was detailed to take Poulous out to the Brown residence and obtain the clothing Bill was wearing on New Year's Eve, then seize his vehicle for the Wisconsin State Crime Lab. After some consultation with his parents, presumably as to exactly what he had been wearing New Year's Eve, Bill went into his bedroom and shortly returned with various articles of clothing in a brown shopping bag. Poulous then had Bill's car towed to the Little Falls City Garage, where it was processed by Crime Lab chemist Rollie Nehring in conjunction with Dinato. Nehring removed many suspected hairs from the front seat and several from the back seat. He also took more of the blood sample off the front seat and a substance off the right passenger side door panel, which he felt might also be blood. Measuring the two scratches in the salt and dirt on the right side of the vehicle, he found them to be one and a quarter inches apart and twenty-seven inches off the ground.

Meanwhile, Badger and Jensen went out to the Craig residence and met with Mrs. Craig, Linda's younger sister Pat, and their father, Jonathan Craig, the latter two having just arrived from Iowa. Neither had any idea whatsoever as to where Linda might be. Pat suggested Badger call her cousin, Shirley Hogan, nineteen years old, of Ivanhoe, Minnesota, with whom the Craigs had been visiting during Christmas vacation. Shirley and Linda, the same age and close friends, were known to exchange confidences. Badger made the call, questioned Shirley closely as to what she might know about Linda's relationship with Bill Brown. "Thank you, miss, you've been very helpful," he finally said, replacing the phone in its cradle and turning to the waiting group. Mr. Jon Craig stood with his arm around his youngest daughter, Pat, her soft, rounded cheeks streaked from crying. Her mother stood to the other side of Pat, her right hand instinctively reaching out to touch her on occasion, patting her forearm, stroking along her back now. "What did Shirley say?" Mrs. Craig asked.

"Linda had confided in her. Said she wasn't sure about Bill. Wasn't sure about marrying him. Stated that . . ." Badger wasn't just exactly sure how he should say the next, then decided the same way Shirley had said it was the only way. "Bill Brown wasn't aggressive enough for her. Didn't know when to kiss and when not to."

"Aggressive?" repeated Mrs. Craig, singling out the word Badger suspected she would.

"Yes, that was Shirley's word," he said matter-of-factly, "but she implied that it had originally come from Linda."

"What do you suppose Linda meant by that, Sergeant?" Jon Craig asked.

"It would seem to me, linked as it was by the cousin in the same sentence with 'not knowing when to kiss or not,' that it could be very likely have a sexual connotation."

"Are you implying that Linda was the aggressor in their . . . relationship?" Mrs. Craig asked rather stridently.

"No, not just that way," Badger said slowly, casting for the right words himself, "that cut and dried. As you have indicated all along, Mrs. Craig, your belief is that there was no sexual relationship as such, and maybe that is one of the things that we have to take under consideration, that there wasn't and, unconsciously or otherwise, Linda wished there was."

"That's putting it rather . . . bluntly, Sergeant," Jon Craig finally said.

Badger spread his hands. "Folks, we have to face facts—if they are in fact facts—as facts. It can only mislead us if we don't."

"There can be any number of constructions placed on the word 'aggressive,' Sergeant," Mrs. Craig pursued. "Quite possibly Linda meant in relation to life goals. As I'm sure I've already told you, Linda was becoming quite concerned about Bill's apparent apathy toward work, study, seriously considering what he was going to do for a future—all this mumbo jumbo of his about getting into something where he could 'help people,' become some kind of missionary, whatever."

Jon Craig said nothing, but his face assumed a cast that Badger could only characterize as annoyed, impatient. It seemed to be saying, "Let's not bring up this old song and dance at a time like this," and Badger couldn't help but agree. "You may have a point here, Mrs. Craig, but I don't think we should overlook the possible sexual connotation either. After all, we are dealing with a girl of nineteen and a boy of twenty-one—"

"Don't let their ages fool you, Sergeant," Mrs. Craig interposed. "In many ways Linda is much older than Bill Brown, the perennial sophomore."

That's just about what I was trying to say, Badger thought. One of the "many ways" may be sexual; he merely nodded.

"Yes," Pat Craig agreed, speaking up for the first time. "That's one of the things Linda doesn't like about Bill. He seems so young, even looks like a baby."

"Did she say that, Pat?" Badger asked.

"Well, maybe not just that way, but I know that's what she meant."

"What else did she say about Bill, Pat?" Badger asked her gently. She was a pretty little thing, big round violet eyes, darker complexion and hair than her mother or sister. Yes, she looked more like her father, larger boned, softer features— both probably softer all the way through.

"Well . . . he isn't very . . . romantic, you know."

"No, I'm afraid I don't know." Badger smiled. "I'd like you to tell me."

"Well, he never really wanted to do anything very much."

"You mean in a romantic way?"

"Oh, no." Pat blushed brightly. "I mean, maybe not that either, but Linda likes to have more fun, I guess, like normal kids."

"Normal?"

"Well, yes, just doing things like most kids like to do."

"Would you say Bill Brown was not exactly normal?" Badger pursued.

"Oh, I guess he was normal enough alright—I mean, he isn't a retard or anything like that, but he just seemed so young. Always wanted to have his own way, almost like a baby. Keep Linda all to himself, away from her other friends, trail her around like a puppy dog. That Linda didn't like."

Badger nodded. What Pat had said tended to solidify his thinking: Brown's another one of the instant gratification kids the country is crawling with these days. The kind that get mightily pissed by rejection. Born and bred to believe that they are something really special, they don't take kindly to growing up to find out they're not. They used to just drop out, take it out on themselves. Now they're really getting pissed, taking it out on others. "Pat, is Linda the type . . . would Linda break off an engagement with Bill, verbally—they talk about it and agree to no longer be engaged—yet still continue to wear the ring?"

Pat blushed slightly but held Badger's penetrating gaze, nodded slowly. "That's possible. Linda likes pretty things—"

"Pat!" Mrs. Craig broke in sharply. "The only reason she would continue wearing that little ring was so as to not hurt Bill's feelings any more than she felt she already had."

"I'm sure you're right, Mother," Pat said sullenly.

"He begged Linda to. 'That way we can still be friends.'"

Badger turned quickly to Mrs. Craig. "Ma'am, was that the word Linda used, 'begged'?"

"Well, I . . . now that I said it, it seems . . ."

"Think hard now, it could be important."

Mrs. Craig shrugged, almost angrily. "Well, no, I can't honestly say . . . seems now the word she used was 'asked,' but I definitely feel she implied it was a very strong 'ask.' So pathetic she didn't feel she could turn his request down, obviously."

"Folks, what I'm trying to get at here is this: If Linda did in fact attempt to break off her engagement with Bill, or actually did, short of physically giving him his ring back, just how did it affect him? Just how upset did he become over it? Now, Mrs. Craig, you tell me that Linda had told Bill she was breaking off the engagement on Wednesday night, the twenty-ninth. Yet Bill and Linda went out again on Thursday night, the thirtieth, to a party at Bill's grandparents' home, then again on New Year's Eve. What bothers me is, if a guy is really going to get ... ah ... that angry over something like this, my experience tells me that the time they usually ah, overreact, is right then! Not some two, three days later. So, I've got to ask you again. If Linda did verbally break off her engagement with Bill, just how upset would he become over it?"

There was a protracted general silence, broken only by the scratching of Jensen's note-taking pen. Finally, Pat Craig spoke up. "Bill Brown never seemed to me like the kind to get very upset over much of anything."

"Yes, I have to agree with you there, Pat," Mrs. Craig said. "I can't honestly say I've ever seen him get angry over anything."

"He was the one always trying to make peace between me and Linda," Pat admitted. She hesitated, then continued. "It almost seemed like Linda sometimes tried to make him mad and couldn't."

Jon Craig had said very little throughout, just stood patiently looking from ex-wife to daughter as they answered Badger's questions. Badger had the feeling that this may have been his usual role in this family, listening more or less patiently while his women did most of the talking. But now Mr. Craig suddenly reached back and found something to say. "Of course, I don't know Bill as well as the rest of the family, but maybe what Pat just said—about it almost seeming like Linda sometimes tried to make Bill mad but couldn't—maybe that's part of what Linda meant when she said he wasn't aggressive enough for her. Subconsciously—even though Linda might not have been sure herself what all she meant."

Badger was looking at him now, really seeing him for the first time. "That's very perceptive, Mr. Craig. You might just be right there."

"Maybe." Mr. Craig nodded, a certain sadness settling back over his harried features, the realization swimming in his watery blue eyes. Badger had the feeling Mr. Jonathan Craig was somehow blaming himself now for whatever had happened to his eldest daughter.

An awkward silence followed.

"OK. I think that will be about all for now," Badger found himself saying. "If any of you think of anything further, don't hesitate to call me anytime, anyplace. Though Detective Jensen here will be assigned this case on a daily working basis, all the rest of us will be involved too. I'll be going over everything he and the rest of my men bring in, trying to put it all together. As I already told you, we had the police helicopter searching today. Starting tomorrow, we will organize searches as well. Suffice to say, we will keep on looking for Linda with every means at our disposal till we find her."

9

But they couldn't look for Linda the next day, at least, physically. The means Badger had at his disposal were as nothing matched against what old Mother Nature mustered January fourth. A snowstorm the likes of which is only remembered struck the greater Big Falls area just before daybreak and howled on through that day and well into the night, bone-chilling winds driving snow into drifts four feet deep in places. To attempt a ground search would have been fool-hardy, so the duty detectives stayed put, forced by the blizzard to restrict activity on the MP Linda Lou Craig case — tying clerical loose ends and checking out slim leads by telephone. Badger spoke for all of them when he looked out his office window, the snapshots of Linda Lou Craig lying before him on his desk. "Baby, if you're out there now, we'll play hell trying to find you."

A few people found them though. Mr. and Mrs. Craig fought their way through the blizzard together to huddle with Corporal Atwell over a few things that had come to them as they spent a mutually sleepless night. The one that intrigued Atwell the most was Mr. Craig's traveler's check test, as a means of ascertaining whether or not Bill and Linda were still engaged. It seemed that Jon Craig had sent two traveler's checks to Linda shortly before Christmas, one in the amount of twenty dollars to be given to Bill as a birthday present, "If she was going to continue her relationship with Bill Brown." Therefore, if Linda had not given the traveler's check to Bill, it meant that she, at least in her mind, had terminated the engagement and very likely had informed Bill of her decision, as she had stated to her mother.

It made sense to Atwell. "How come you sent the check to Linda with that proviso?" he asked Jon Craig.

"Frankly, I was surprised they got engaged in the first place," the father answered. "I kind of looked at it as just one of those 'kid' engagements, more for the novelty than anything else. And I had heard something to the effect that she was unhappy with the relationship—obviously, at least enough to have worded my letter that way."

"Just how did you word it?"

"To the best of my recollection, I told her that if she was going to continue her relationship with Bill Brown to give him that twenty-dollar traveler's check for his birthday present. And if she was not going to continue her relationship and was going to break it off, to keep that check for herself, as well as the other one I sent."

"Just how was this check made out, Mr. Craig?"

"It was completely made out except for filling in Bill's name."

Atwell nodded. "OK, you bring us in the data on the checks, both of them, and we'll check it out." For various reasons—if Linda was still alive and hadn't cashed the checks as yet, when she did they would tell where and when.

"There's another thing too," Jon Craig continued. "I had also told Linda that, if she wanted to, she could invite Bill to come with her to Chicago next weekend—the weekend of the eighth—to meet Pat and me when I brought her back from Iowa, just to spend the weekend, shopping, maybe taking in a show, whatever. Well, now, of course . . . but what I'm getting at here now is, if Linda hadn't gone ahead and mentioned anything about this to Bill, invited him, then wouldn't that be a pretty sure sign she was planning, or already had, broken off with him?"

Atwell nodded. "Yeah, I'd say so. We'll check that out too."

He didn't have to wait long. Bill and Fred Brown were next in his office, just minutes after the Craigs. Atwell had called them in to propose another polygraph examination of Bill, to see if they couldn't clear up a few of the "obvious inconsistencies between what Bill here is saying happened and the machine says didn't," as he put it to the two Brown men.

"You see, the whole reason of these examinations is to find out the truth of the matter. Not to persecute or prosecute Bill or anyone else. It's merely a helpful device to try to find out what actually happened. If Bill is not involved in any way, we are as anxious to eliminate him as a suspect as you are to have him eliminated. Atwell was addressing this line of reasoning primarily to the father, feeling it very likely would be him making the ultimate decision. "So we can get on to digging up other suspects, if something actually has happened to Linda at the hands of another."

Fred nodded. "I think that's an excellent idea. If I were you, I'd be looking right now."

"Don't worry, we are," Atwell assured them both. "And if Bill is as innocent of any wrongdoing in this matter as you both say, he's got nothing to lose by agreeing to another polygraph, everything to gain."

Fred Brown turned to his son, who had been standing listening quietly. "What do you say, son?"

"It's alright with me, Dad," Bill answered easily. "I want to do anything I can to help."

Fred nodded slowly, still looking at his son. "He'll be here."

"Good. Tomorrow at 1:30. Now then, you can have your car back, Bill, we're through with it—"

Bill smiled at that news, the open-faced, boyish smile lighting the sparkle in his clear blue eyes. "Terrific, that'll make it a whole lot easier to do some of the things I have to do."

Atwell didn't ask what they might be, though a wry thought or two crossed his mind. He merely nodded. "You can pick it up at the city garage." Turning back to Fred, he added, "One more thing, we need Bill's blood type—as a matter of fact, both your children, to see if we can determine just whose blood that is in Bill's car. Again, if it would turn out to be one of the family's, obviously it would help to eliminate Bill."

"Certainly. We'll have them for you as soon as I can get them from our doctor."

"Good. I guess that's all—oh, Bill, the Craigs were just here. Did Linda give you a twenty-dollar traveler's check from her father for your birthday present?"

"Check? Birthday present? Why, no, I never even heard anything about any check," Bill answered, with obvious sincerity, then added, obviously annoyed, "Of course, she never did make it back in time for my birthday party."

"No big deal," Atwell said casually. "Was there ever any talk about you joining Linda to go to Chicago this coming weekend to meet Pat and her father when he brought her back from Iowa?"

"No," Bill answered, but more slowly this time, his face starting to wonder a little about something. "But . . . seems to me, she did mention something about maybe me and her going somewhere to meet her dad and Pat some time—"

"But not specifically Chicago? This upcoming weekend—the eighth?"

"No. Nothing that . . . definite."

Something different was starting to show on the father's face. Now he said it. "You think maybe she just didn't get around to telling Bill about it, Corporal? Decided to just go ahead to Chicago by herself, not telling anybody about anything?"

Atwell shrugged as casually as he had asked the questions. "Anything's possible."

"You checking this out?" Fred Brown pursued, rather aggressively, Atwell thought. "Have you people contacted the Chicago police?"

Atwell looked at Fred Brown levelly. "Chicago's a big town, Mr. Brown. Lot of people there."

Despite the still drifting snow, Badger called a progress and assignment meeting at his office for 8:00 A.M. the next morning, January 5, 1977. It took some digging out first, but all hands showed up.

"OK. Where do we stand on Linda Lou Craig?" he asked the assembled detectives, by way of getting the snowball rolling. While he waited for the obvious answer, he glanced out his office window at the sparkling clean blanket of snow, which had temporarily tidied up Little Falls—along with the entire Midwest—hiding from sight the scars of the old year. Funny, he thought, today seems like the first day of the new year to me.

Sergeant Poulous brought him back to January 5, 1977. "The same as yesterday."

Badger turned toward Jensen. "Cliff, hit the campus, go around to all her classes. Here's a copy of her curriculum for this semester. Show her picture to the profs, students. Who knows, maybe she'll show up for class."

I'll bet, their faces said.

Jensen nodded. Badger turned to Corporal Atwell, cleaning his nails with a deadly looking switchblade. "Sambo, you cop that off some Milwaukee pimp?"

"Naw, got it from my kid for Christmas."

They all laughed. "You stay here, run another poly on Brown."

The phone rang. Badger picked it up. "Detective Sergeant Badger. Yeah, sure, John, tomorrow's paper. Something like 'No Clues to Missing Girl.' Sure, you can quote me: 'At this time we have nothing to indicate a homicide.' Yeah, try to keep it in front of the public. Say, can't we do better than the second section? This could still be a matter of life and death. OK. See what you can do. Try to get a spread on the front page, say in a couple of days at least. What's that, I don't sound very optimistic about finding her alive? Well, no, as a matter of fact I don't, but for Chrissakes don't put that in the paper!"

Slamming down the phone, he turned back to his waiting men. "OK. Everybody got their long johns on? Foul weather gear along?"

The detectives collectively groaned. "You can't be serious, Floyd?" Poulous asked. "There must be four feet of snow out there if there's an inch."

Badger grinned. "Keeps your circulation up, arteries from hardening. Everybody's who's not doing something else I've told you, meet me at the intersection of Radies Road and Van Buren."

Part of Corporal Atwell's decision to reexamine Bill Brown had been based on the fact that Bill had submitted to the first polygraph the very next day after Linda had disappeared. A lingering shock factor may possibly have had some bearing on Bill's responses. Also, after that first polygraph, during the course of the extensive interview he had had with Bill, Bill had ultimately stated that Linda was very upset over various matters New Year's Eve, a state of mind on Linda's part he had previously denied.

Yet, Atwell decided to ask Bill virtually the same questions he had asked him on the first polygraph. Of the five relevant questions, the only change was in the wording of numbers four and five. Four—"Did you directly cause Linda Craig's disappearance?"—now became "Did you directly cause Linda Craig to be missing from her home?" And number five—"On that night did you physically harm Linda Craig?"—now became "Did you plan with Linda to have her missing from her home?"

To these questions, as he did to the other three that were relevant, Bill answered no.

Yet, again, Atwell felt that the emotional responses Bill Brown exhibited when asked these five relevant questions were sufficient to indicate deception on the issue in question. To check his opinion, Atwell now took both polygraph charts to the Wisconsin State Police barracks and showed them to Sergeant John Julien, a WSP polygraph examiner for the district, and Lieutenant Ron Wunderly. Both of these experts concurred.

Jensen, returning to the station, contacted Inspector Kelly, New York City, a member of the inspection department of American Express traveler's checks. Inspector Kelly agreed to open an inquiry file on the check in question to see if it had been cashed; and, if so, where, and by whom.

Badger was still out leading the ground search for what the searchers were by now openly referring to as "the body." Fighting through drifts up to their chests, Badger and his men were only able to cover a small area off Radies Road, a fairly secluded pocket of jack pine and hazelnut bushes conducive to the dumping of a body. Unable to see anything because of the snow depth, they were forced to rely on "foot-feel," walking shoulder to shoulder, forcing one foot ahead of the other, hoping or not to make foot contact with what they were searching for. "Damn, I hope I don't step on her!" the young Porath said out of the side of his mouth to the grizzled Sergeant Poulous. "What you out here for then?" Poulous grunted back.

Badger, though he could think of a thousand other reasons —all of them rabbits—why he'd rather be out here, didn't mind the snow or bitter cold. A good ole country boy from the Sand Lake area north of Big Falls, when he had his druthers, would surely rather be out in the bush than buried under his usual blizzard of paperwork. Battling nature, he was at least one on one. He could see where he was going, look back over his shoulder and see where he had been. That sure's hell wasn't true with detective work.

All they found was frostbite.

10

They didn't find much else during the next few days either. Searches, both ground and air, continued in an ever-widening radius, constantly hampered by the bitter cold and subsequent snowfalls adding to the depth registered by the blizzard of January 4. Yet the LFPD persevered the best they could, with what they had to work with. Jensen continued his dogged daily rounds, telephoning friends and acquaintances gleaned from Linda's green address book, interviewing those he felt at all promising in person.

"She meets people and gives them the benefit of the doubt immediately," said Nancy Ladd, one of Linda's closest high school chums. "When somebody turns out to be weird, she doesn't learn very fast. I guess what I'm saying is that Linda wants to find the good in people." Then, on a more somber note, Nancy added, "You look too hard for the good, you overlook reality sometimes."

"Caring, sincere—a person who would like to see the world a better place," was the way another one of Linda's close friends described her. "She treasures people. She's the kind of person who always keeps pictures of her close friends with her."

As the days dwindled away along with the leads, Officers Porath and Dinato were sent back to patrolling, forced to trade the heady pursuit of what was by now accepted within the department as murder for the mundanity of traffic violations and college drunks. Work on the MP Linda Lou Craig file fell almost exclusively to Badger and Jensen now, with Atwell filling in as needed, particularly when something turned up that might have some bearing on the two polygraphs he had given Bill Brown. On January 7, he sat in on an interview with Dr. Russell, pastor of St. John's Lutheran, who had talked to Bill Brown on two separate occasions and had also talked to Mr. and Mrs. Craig and Mr. and Mrs. Brown, all members of his church. Dr. Russell could see nothing in the behavior of Bill that was extremely out of the ordinary or that would lead him to disagree with the version of what had happened New Year's Eve, as related by Bill to him. Yet, later that same day, Jon Craig told Atwell that Dr. Russell had told him that he was not convinced Bill was telling the complete truth in reference to Linda's disappearance. Apparently, Dr. Russell and the polygraph machine had considerable in common.

But, life being what it is, in Little Falls as everywhere, with each passing day other people got in other trouble and the rest of Badger's small detective bureau had all they could do to keep up with these other cases. Even Badger and Jensen couldn't commit themselves or their time exclusively to MP Linda Lou Craig. Particularly Badger, who still had the supervisory responsibility his title carried. The paper blizzard raged across his desk daily. Yet he did what he could, whenever he could. There just wasn't all that much to work with. Other than their uncategorized suspicions of Bill Brown, what did he have? The girl was missing, period. And unless he found her or her body, as he saw it, there was no way they could move on Bill Brown on what they had. So the only thing they could do was to continue to search for the girl, dead or alive, and try to find some further information with which to more deeply implicate Bill Brown.

Working on the latter, he telephoned Crissy Hogan, cousin to Linda and sister to Shirley Hogan, to whom Linda had confided her doubts about marrying Bill Brown. Crissy was in the army and he telephone-tracked her down in Greely, Colorado. Yes, Lieutenant Crissy Hogan told Badger, she had talked to Linda about Bill when they were both visiting in Minnesota over Christmas. Linda had told her that she was scared to go through with the marriage, that she was so much smarter than Bill and she thought that he was a weak individual and if they married she would have to wear the pants in the family.

But the two girls had also talked of other things, with other

implications—such as joining the Peace Corps together, for
one thing. But after the older Crissy had advised Linda that
she would have to have graduated from college to be able to
join the Peace Corps and she have finished her stint in the
army, the subject had fallen from grace. Yet it did indicate, to
Badger's mind, a sort of vague or otherwise restlessness in
Linda Lou Craig. Some kind of yearning to be off somewhere
else, doing something else. Maybe change her life completely?

But he still didn't think she would leave for this new life at
two o'clock in the morning New Year's Eve . . . or would she?
Sometimes people did use the advent of a new year for just
such a purpose. Walk away from the old, start anew with the
new. A young impressionable girl goes out New Year's Eve
with the thought in her mind of cutting all old ties to the old
year, the old life—particularly an unwanted boyfriend,
fiancé, a strangling engagement. Whether she was planning or
running away to a new life or not? Yes, looked at this way,
there was something about the whole set of circumstances that
told Badger that, if Linda was really set on breaking off her
engagement with Bill, she would not have let the new year
ring in without giving him his ring back. Most likely, she did
it some time after they left the Brown home at 11:30, if that is
when they did leave. Therefore, even if Leona Brown saw the
ring still on Linda's finger when she reached for a slice of
pizza at ten, it wasn't there when the clock struck midnight.
And it very likely left that finger sometime between 11:30 and
midnight. That half hour that was beginning to intrigue him
more and more.

The tempo picked up measurably on the tenth of January.
The official results of the extensive chemical tests run by
Nehring at the Crime Lab on the bloodstains in Bill Brown's
car were made available to the LFPD. The blood was human.
Nehring was further able to demonstrate the presence of the
blood group factor of Type B, but there was such a minute
amount of blood present that he was only able to perform one
test, one time. There are four international blood groups, A,
B, O, and AB. Blood group A contains only the blood factor
A; blood group B contains only the blood factor B; blood
group O contains neither of these blood factors; but group AB
contains both the blood factors A and B. Therefore, a person

with blood group A or O could not have deposited those bloodstains in Bill Brown's car. Bill Brown and his sister were blood group A. Only a person with blood group B or AB could have deposited these bloodstains. Linda Lou Craig had blood group AB—as do millions of other people, any one of whom could theoretically have bled the blood Nehring removed from Bill Brown's vehicle.

But Badger didn't think so. His bones told him it was Linda Lou's blood. The question remained, however, how had it gotten there on the front seat and the passenger side door panel of Bill Brown's car? Though Mr. Nehring stated by telephone that there were tests which can assist in determining whether the blood could possibly be menstrual blood, they would require substantially more samples than he had had to work with.

"Let me ask you this then, Rollie," Badger pursued. "Our measurements show the stain to be located seventeen inches from the right side of the front seat—the passenger's edge or the passenger's door side—and eight to nine inches from the front of the seat."

"Yes, that checks with my measurement. The stain was essentially on the top of the seat cushion on the right side."

"Could a woman in a menstrual cycle have deposited that stain in that location, Rollie?" Badger asked. "Just so far as the location goes?"

The scientist paused. "Well, I certainly have no idea of the number of places a woman could sit on the right side of that vehicle, but no, if you want just my opinion, I don't think the seat stain is located directly under the seat of a person. It's a little more to the left; maybe towards the left leg area and up farther than the vagina would be in a normal seated position."

That also jibed with Badger's thinking. "OK, Rollie, now as to the hair; would you say them short hairs were definitely pubic?"

"Absolutely."

"Dinato tells me you were pulling out quite a batch of them?"

"Yes, there were quite a number."

"Could you be a little more specific, Rollie?"

Nehring chuckled. "Well, I didn't sit here and count them, but I have a whole package full."

Badger whistled. "Another unscientific question, if you

will, Rollie. Would you say that, in order for there to get that
many pubic hairs in a car, there'd have to be a little hanky-
panky going on?"

"No, not if the occupants rode around bare naked all the
time."

"Well, assuming they did keep their clothes on most days."

"It's been my studied observation, Sergeant, that under
normal circumstances pubic hairs do not work out through the
clothing. We at the Crime Lab feel they usually are shed
through some form of friction, one might say, while the shed-
ders are unclothed."

Badger laughed. "You find them mostly in the front seat or
where?"

"About evenly distributed, front and back."

"Rollie, could you tell me whether they are male or female?"

"I think so, but I'm not sure it would stand up in court.
Better yet, pluck a few from your suspect and your victim,
and I guarantee I'll match them."

"Wish we could, Rollie. But you know our problem as
well as I do. We find the victim, and I don't think I'd need
you."

That evening Mrs. Craig decided that she and her ex-husband should take matters into their own hands and confront
the Browns' if they had to walk through their living room
wall. She just couldn't get it out of her head that the key to
Linda's disappearance somehow lay with Bill Brown. If it
turned out that Bill wasn't involved in Linda's disappearance
and she turned up later safe and sound, she would crawl to
them begging their forgiveness on hands and knees. If he was
in some way involved, then anything she might do to his family, short of murdering him, would not be enough anyway.

But they didn't have to storm through the brick wall of the
Browns' living room. They merely rang the doorbell, and Fred
Brown came to the front door and courteously invited them in.
Nor did the Craigs really confront the Browns. They merely
sat down in the living room and talked, though their conversation was very strained, and little or nothing of seeming consequence was said, all participants holding rigidly to their by
now oft-declared positions. Yet it seemed to the Craigs that a
certain change had come over the Browns. An awful finality

seemed to color their words about Linda. Leona Brown continuously talked of Linda in the past tense. When Mrs. Craig asked Bill what he had been doing the past week about finding Linda, his answer seemed to her to indicate hopelessness. There was also a not very subtle accusatory ring to Leona Brown's voice, as though she felt the Craigs had somehow brought Linda's disappearance down upon themselves. She mentioned several times to Irene Craig that she should not have "that red light" on at the front of her home.

"Leona! What are you trying to say!"

"You just shouldn't have that red light on in front of your home, Irene—"

"Leona, it isn't even red—though what that should mean I'm sure I don't know—it's yellow!"

"Well, it certainly looks red to me—"

"It's yellow! But what either color would have to do with Linda's disappearance is beyond me!"

The men appeared rather uncomfortable, but said nothing. Even the normally talkative Fred Brown said little. Finally, Irene Craig could stand the desultory conversation and strained silences no longer. She suddenly turned to Bill. "Bill, you keep saying you and Linda just drove around town for over two hours looking at Christmas decorations. Why don't you drive us around now and show us where you went."

"Why? What would be gained by that?"

"Well, you know, just driving the same area may jog your memory or something. Anything is better than sitting here doing nothing!"

Bill cast about for a little help, looking first toward his mother, then his father, but at the moment none was forthcoming, so he shouldered the proposition himself. "Well certainly, I can understand that feeling, Mrs. Craig. Sometimes I feel much the same way myself, but I don't really see how it could accomplish anything. You know, I've already driven the police around where we were and that didn't help."

"But, Bill, you drove the police around during the daytime."

"Evening, it was almost night."

"But it wasn't night. Maybe all the decorations weren't on, you didn't see all the same things."

"Irene," Leona Brown interposed, "I'm sure lots of people

have taken down their Christmas decorations by now, it's the tenth of January."

"I don't care! Bill, if you'll take us around now, at night, maybe you'll see something and something will remind you of something, anything." Even while she was almost manically insisting, Mrs. Craig knew why: If you just sit here and talk about her, it seems like she's dead. But if you get back out there and keep looking for her it means you think she's still alive.

"I don't know, Irene," Fred Brown said finally, "I'm afraid I have to agree with Bill. What actually could be gained by it? Besides, look at Bill, he's exhausted. Out on his feet. So am I. We've been out every waking moment looking for Linda ourselves."

"Where?" Mrs. Craig asked flatly.

"Well, of course I've had to go to work and Bill's in school—not that he's doing more than going through the motions—but I thought it better for him, all of us, to try to keep up some semblance of normality. Still all this past weekend Bill and I have been out checking with the trains, planes, buses. I've been on my CB practically day and night talking to truckers on the highways. Yesterday Bill and I went to every church service in the area hoping to see her walk in to one of them."

It took all the willpower Irene Craig had left to keep from bringing her hands up over her ears and screaming. Appealing to her ex-husband, she said, "Jon, please . . ."

"Fred," Jon said quietly, "why not? Maybe we've got nothing to gain, but what have we got to lose? I agree with Irene. I just can't sit idly by either. I've got to keep moving, looking, so, why not?"

Fred Brown looked from one Craig to the other, finally nodded his head slowly, swiveling to look at his son, seated slumped in an easy chair by the end of the piano. "Alright, but I'll drive." To Bill directly, he added, "You come along and tell me where to turn."

The four of them, Bill and Fred Brown, Irene and Jon Craig drove for over two hours all over town, it seemed to Irene Craig. Bill sat in the front seat next to his father; Jon and Irene sat in the back seat. Even to see the houses was difficult. Many homes were almost obscured by the huge banks of snow plowed to either side of the streets. Here and there a lonely leftover Christmas decoration straggled a melancholy greeting out at them. They hadn't gone a block before Irene started to feel the utter futility of their action. The other occupants of the car must have felt much the same way for very little was said throughout the drive. Just about the only break in the oppressive silence was Bill's terse directions to his father to turn here and there. Finally, at some late point in the drive, Fred pulled into a 7-Eleven store to get something, and Jon Craig volunteered to accompany him "just to stretch my legs."

Irene Craig and Bill were alone in the car. The only light spilled sporadically from the blinking neon storefront sign onto their facing windshield, each blink painting a pale eerie mask over Bill Brown's face. Irene sat huddled in the dark of the back seat. It seemed to her that she was waiting for something, her eyes searching the right side of Bill's face. He appeared to be studying something somewhere out his passenger side window. I've never seen that face before, thought Irene. No matter how many times I've seen it, I've never seen that face before.

Even she didn't know for sure what her thoughts meant, or why she was so devilishly fascinated by watching the neon light blink on and off the right side of Bill's face. It was like some hideous horror show on late night television, one she wanted to turn off so she could just go to sleep, but somehow couldn't. His dead white face repelled her yet fascinated her. The light blinked on, then, one-two, button your shoe—she found herself counting, saying this foolish rhyme—it went off again. Three-four, close the door, back on.

"Bill, where's Linda?" she heard a voice say.

Five-six, pick up sticks. Off. Seven-eight, shut the gate.

"I'm sure I don't know, Mrs. Craig."

11

They lowered the boom on Bill Brown the next day, the eleventh of January. Calling him in for a 9:00 A.M. meeting—again he came of his own free will, blithely signed the recognition of rights form—ostensibly to go over the polygraph charts that were obtained in the reexamination, they sat him down in Atwell's electronic lair of an office and hit him with every watt they had.

Atwell started it off. "Bill, let's go back to New Year's Eve. You stated to me a number of times before that you left your house at 11:30 to go to Unitarian Church to pick up your sister, Elizabeth—"

"That's right. My mother asked me to."

"But when you got there, your sister wasn't there, is that correct?"

"Well, actually, we were never sure she was going to be. I was just supposed to go see if she was there."

"Why didn't you go back home and let your mother know she wasn't there? I live over on Applelane. It's only a ten- or twelve-minute ride from Unitarian Church to your home."

Bill shrugged. "I don't know. Just didn't think it was important enough, I guess. My mother didn't say we had to do that."

"Tell me what you did again to find out if she was there?"

"Well, I stopped in the parking lot—"

"Were there a lot of cars there?"

Bill hesitated, a puzzled look sliding over his face. "You know, I don't seem to remember. It seems like there were, but, then again, I can't honestly remember seeing them."

"Were there or weren't there?"

"Yeah, seems like there was, there must have been, but I can't say I took any particular notice of them. Maybe it was because my windows were so frosted over—"

"But you did stop in the parking lot and park your car?"

"Yeah."

"Then what did you do?"

"Went in the church and looked for Elizabeth."

"Linda waited in the car?"

"No, she went with me."

Atwell glanced over at Badger. He was seated to the corner of Atwell's desk so he could look past the side of Atwell's face and stare directly into Bill's. "Forget it, Sambo," Badger grunted, "get inside."

"OK, Bill, what did you see when you got there?"

"What . . . what do you mean?" Atwell had the feeling that Bill understood his question perfectly but was stalling for time. Badger had the same reaction, but said nothing.

"Describe for me what was going on inside the church at the time you entered it?" Atwell rephrased, making sure there was no area for doubt or equivocation this time.

Bill hesitated. "Well . . . when we entered the church, the congregation was, ah, singing."

"Standing or sitting?"

"Ah, standing."

Atwell nodded. "I see. So it must have been like some kind of regular New Year's Eve service or something, right?"

"Yeah, well, I guess so."

"You don't seem very sure."

"I don't usually go to church New Year's Eve, so it's hard for me to say whether this was a regular—"

Atwell cut him off. "Now where was the congregation standing and singing?"

"Well, in . . . in the church there."

"Where the congregation would normally hold services?"

"Yes, in the main worship area . . ." Bill shrugged, apparently unable to be more explicit. "The church."

"The minister was standing up there in the pulpit leading them along in the song?"

Bill shrugged again, then shook his head somewhat evasively. "I suppose so. Or maybe he was standing there in front of the altar, kind of facing the choir, leading them. I can't say that I remember that part too clear, where the minister was standing and all. I was more involved in looking around for Elizabeth."

"Did you two go in and sit down, then look around for her?"

"Oh, no, we wouldn't just walk in and intrude on a service in progress like that!" Bill exclaimed, seemingly somewhat aghast at Atwell's lack of ecclesiastical cool. "We just kind of quietly went in and stood there by the door looking around."

"The door—this would be to the rear of the church?"

"Well, yes, I guess you could say that, the rear from inside, but it would be the front from outside."

"The main entrance?" Badger broke in to ask. "Would you call that the main entrance?"

"Yes." Bill nodded.

"Did you have to go up any stairs or steps to get in the main entrance to where these people were standing and singing in the main entrance area?" Badger pursued.

"Gee, I don't remember that for sure, Sergeant, I've only been to that church once before, and it was night. I was mainly only thinking about finding my sister."

"I see." Badger nodded. "How far would you say this main worship area was from the entrance where you stood?"

"Oh, gosh, I don't know, maybe . . . twenty-five feet."

"So you could clearly see from where you stood whether or not your sister was among these people standing and singing?"

"Yes. She wasn't."

"Did anybody see you?"

"I doubt it. They were all more or less standing facing away from us."

"The minister? Didn't you just say he was standing facing your way, leading the rest?"

"No, I don't think I quite said that, maybe more like he was standing facing the choir, kind of sideways."

"Oh, now you remember just exactly how the minister was standing?"

"No, Sergeant," Bill explained doggedly, "I just said seems like he wasn't really facing us either."

"What time do you suppose this was?"

"Well, we left home at 11:30. Like the corporal here says, it probably only takes about ten or fifteen minutes to drive from my house to Unitarian Church. We went right in to look for her . . . oh, I'd say, somewhere near 11:45, ten of twelve."

There's something fishy here, Badger told himself, something ain't kosher. He just couldn't see Bill and Linda in the church before midnight. For one thing, that would conflict with his theory of her breaking off the engagement before the old year ended. But then, that was just some half-cocked theory he had dreamt up, not a shred of evidence to base it on. Yet . . . He made a mental note to himself to contact the minister of Unitarian Church and find out just what time it was when he was leading the congregation in song. "What song were they singing?" he asked Bill suddenly.

"What? Song?" Bill appeared more confused by this simple question than any other Atwell or Badger had asked, but it may have been just the way Badger so suddenly asked it, after holding silent for some time.

"Yeah, song. 'Old Lang Syne,' maybe?"

Bill shook his head slowly, answered in all seriousness, "No, I don't think so, Sergeant. Something more religious, but I just didn't pay much attention—"

Atwell cut him off. "Bill, you're aware, of course, that we only have your word that you went to Unitarian Church to look for your sister at all—"

"I can't help that. Look, I've got Elizabeth checking with people she knows at Unitarian Church to find out who all was there that night, see if anybody saw me and Linda come in looking for her. As soon as we find out somebody that did I'll let you know."

"Do that," Atwell remarked dryly. "Bill, you told us that Linda had requested that you let her get out and pray at some point when you were driving around New Year's Eve. Where was that?"

"Ah, right near University Apartments. Yeah, just shortly before I dropped her off."

"What time would you say that was?"

"Well . . . I guess I can't say very close on the time, but it wasn't all that long before I dropped her off."

"Why was she so upset with you, Bill?"

Bill shook his head slowly, seemingly more hurt than disgusted. "Corporal, I wish you would quit this tiresome game of trying to trick me with such childish questions. I told all of you thirty times it had nothing to do with me at all, it was her parents she was upset with, not wanting to be like her parents and end up being divorced, the troubles she was having with her sister, Pat—"

"Maybe that's why she wanted to break off your engagement, Bill," Atwell asked softly, "she was afraid you two would end up getting divorced too?"

"Please, Corporal, I've already asked you to quit trying to trick me. This is much too serious a problem—"

"I'm being very serious, Bill. I'm saying that the reason Linda wanted to break off the engagement may have had very little to do with you at all, it was her fear of marriage itself—"

"Corporal, I have that fear myself. Particularly with Linda. As a matter of fact, because of the track record of her family, it was one of the things we discussed most—"

"New Year's Eve?" Badger asked softly.

Bill flicked his eyes at Badger, but answered to Atwell. "No, I don't think that was said exactly New Year's Eve. It was one of our common understandings—"

"But at some point, you two did discuss the possibility that your engagement could conceivably be . . . not end up in marriage?" Badger asked carefully.

"Of course, an engaged couple must always consider that possibility. That's why people get engaged rather than leaping directly into marriage. But we only discussed the possibility in hypothetical terms. Linda said that the only way she would ever break our engagement was if God directed her to a different mission or to someone else with whom she could work better doing God's work."

"You . . . you think that may have happened, Bill?" Atwell asked softly.

"No. For she never said anything to me about giving back my ring."

"Bill, did it surprise you any that Linda didn't give you the check her father sent her to give you for your birthday?"

"Yes, if he did send the check."

"He did, Bill. We found the letter that Mr. Craig had enclosed with the checks, spelling out what Linda should do with them. She was supposed to give you the one for twenty dollars, Bill, if—and I quote Jon Craig—'you intend to continue your relationship with Bill.'"

A hurt look had settled over Bill's face. Badger thought of his twelve-year-old son when he struck out in Little League.

"Yes," Bill finally said, "then I am . . . disappointed."

"Bill, we have information from any number of very reliable people that Linda was thinking seriously about breaking off her relationship with you." Atwell, who had spoken softly, kindly, throughout, now waited patiently.

Bill finally looked up, resolution shining in his eyes. "I'm going to tell you something right now, Corporal, both of you. If anybody was going to break off that engagement, it would more likely have been me. Particularly now, since she got interested in the Mormon religion. That's one of her big problems, always running from one religion to another, trying to find all the answers outside of herself and her own religion."

"You think that's what she's doing now?" Badger asked quickly.

"Who knows. Last year it was The Path, last month it's the Mormons, who knows who it is now."

"Our information says it was you that was involved in The Path."

"Sure, I took her . . . because she wanted to go. But I only went three times. It didn't take me long to figure out they didn't have the answer, but it was her who was always having private little talks with that Reverend guru, whatever his name is—"

"You're not trying to say now that it was you who broke off the engagement with her."

Bill turned to face Badger full face. "Sergeant, let me make this perfectly clear, once and for all. There was no talk by either of us about breaking our engagement. All I want to do now is get her back. See if we can't get this whole mess straightened back out and then look to our future again."

"Certainly." Atwell nodded, glancing at his notes again. "I can understand that, Bill, but what I can't understand is why, if you had nothing whatsoever to do with in some way causing Linda to be missing, how come the polygraph keeps saying you do?"

Bill drew a deep breath, let it out slowly, shaking his head slowly all the while. "All I can say is this . . . and I've thought a lot about this too, even tried to do some research on the subject in the library, talked to my psychology professor . . . it must be because of some makeup in my character, some paranoid reaction or something . . . it's just that questions of an accusatory nature bother me."

"That is your answer?"

"I'm afraid that's the only one I have. I've always been that way. Whenever somebody accuses me of something, whether I've done it or not, I get all hot and sticky all over."

"Bill, you tell me then. Where do we go from here?"

"What do you mean?"

"With finding Linda? With you? No matter where we look, what little we find keeps somehow invariably coming back to you. What do you suggest we do?"

"Well, my father wants to go to Chicago and look there. There's talk of bringing in psychics, though I personally think that's foolish. I've talked with Jon Craig about the possibility of my folks and him going in together to hire a private investigator."

"What for?"

"Well, to look for Linda, of course, but mainly to actually investigate the circumstances surrounding her disappearance, after I dropped her off, to substantiate my belief that she was abducted from her doorstep—"

"Bill, we consider that a low percentage possibility."

"I know you do. That's exactly why I want to hire a private investigator."

"I see. What else? What else are you planning on doing?"

"Praying. A great deal of praying, Corporal." Bill turned his clear blue eyes toward Badger, who was hunched morosely over the corner of Atwell's desk, big jaw parked in even bigger palm. The grizzled man and the smoothfaced boy eyed each other warily. "I suggest we all do," Bill finally said softly.

"Best you do most of it," Badger said. "The blood in your car is Linda's."

A moment of stunned silence ensued, the staring match continued: Badger and Bill Brown at each other, Atwell at Badger. Possibly, Atwell was even more taken aback than Bill, for, with the exception of a slow widening of the pupils of Bill's eyes, Badger could detect no visual signs of turmoil within Bill Brown. Somehow, this lack of emotional response to damn near anything thrown at him had come to bother Badger more than anything. Badger had the feeling he could announce to Bill Brown that the Russians had just dropped a hydrogen bomb on Washington and he might answer, "Really? How many megatons?"

Now all Bill finally said was, "How can you be sure?"

"The Crime Lab, Buster, the Crime Lab. They have a way of finding out things for us, you know, that's their job. How'd it get there?"

"Beats me."

"Don't give me that 'beats me' shit! There's Linda Lou Craig's blood on that seat, and I want to know how it got there!"

Bill shook his head slowly from side to side, his big baby-blue eyes never leaving Badger's. "I honestly don't know, sir. I don't even know if you're telling me the truth."

Atwell took a chance and broke in on Badger. "Bill, I have the Crime Lab report right before me here. It states categorically that it cannot be your blood or your sister's."

"So?" Bill asked, simply.

"You and the rest of your family have blood group A. The Crime Lab found blood group B, which is Linda's." Hurrying along, hoping Bill hadn't covered blood groups in any of his college classes yet or, if he had, hadn't done his homework, Atwell added, "Now, we ask you, if this is Linda's blood that the Crime Lab found in your car, both on the front seat and the passenger door panel, right below the door handle, how could it have gotten there?"

It appeared that Bill's lips were forming the words "Beats me," but he glanced at Badger and swallowed instead, his eyes flicking back to hold on Atwell's. Good, Badger thought, it's working. He's more comfortable with Atwell; he'll tell him more rather than have to talk to me.

"Gosh, that's hard to answer," he began. "She rode in my car so much, it could have gotten there so many different ways, I suppose—"

"Name one," Badger snapped, pleased to see Bill didn't turn to look at him but kept his eyes on Atwell.

"Well, maybe she had a nosebleed."

"You remember one?" Badger growled.

"Well, no . . . but that doesn't mean something couldn't have happened sometime when I wasn't in the car."

"Quit stalling! Dammit, Bill, I want to know how Linda's blood got there all over your car, and I want to know now!"

Bill cringed, but Badger had the feeling it was more from his rough talk than what he had asked. If rough talk would shake this choirboy's story, rough talk was what he'd get. Still looking at Atwell, Bill finally said, "I suppose she could be, ah, on her period too sometime, over all the months she sat there—"

"The blood is fresh, Bill. The Crime Lab said the blood is fresh," Badger snapped, "no more than a day or two old!"

"She could have had her period that night."

"Did she have her period that night, Bill?" Atwell asked softly, kindly. "New Year's Eve?"

"How would I know, sir?"

"Because you fucked her!" Badger sneered.

That brought Bill's head snapping around toward Badger, opened his mouth naturally. "I did not!"

"Well . . ." Badger sneered back. "I'm glad to see our little angel knows what the word means, at least."

"I know what the word means, Sergeant," Bill said righteously. "But that doesn't mean I would stoop to use it, much less do it."

Badger leaned in across the corner of Atwell's desk until his nose was almost touching Bill Brown's, brought his right hand up from where he had been concealing it alongside his leg, stuck what he held between thumb and forefinger directly under Bill's nose: "Then tell me, choirboy, how did all these get in your car?"

Bill literally had to pull his head back a few inches to even see what Badger held clenched between his fingertips. "What is it? I can't see."

"C-hairs."

"C-hairs?"

"Yes, c-hairs, you little shit, cunt hairs!"

Bill's eyes opened wide, very wide, his mouth dropping simultaneously. It almost appeared his lips were about to repeat Badger's school-yard vernacular, but when he spoke, it was in Websterese. "Pubic . . . hairs . . . ? They were in my car?"

"Yessir, yessir, three bags full," Badger chanted, leaning in close again, "one from my master, one from his dame, one from the little boy who lives on Fauntleroy Lane."

Bill, appearing as much bewildered by the strange antics and verbal gymnastics as he was astounded by what Badger kept poking under his nose, once again turned to the more reserved Atwell for explanation. "Corporal, what does this all mean?"

"Just exactly what he's telling you, I'm afraid, Bill. The Crime Lab also found a great quantity of pubic hair in both the back and front seats of your car." Atwell again picked up the piece of paper off his desk, appeared to be reading. "To quote Mr. Nehring of the Crime Lab, his exact words are 'Though I didn't count the pubic hairs found in the Bill Brown vehicle, I have a whole bag full.'"

Bill appeared aghast. "Pubic hairs. In my car?"

"Bags of them," Badger said again, cackling maniacally. "Sticking out everywhere. Crawling up through the fabric. Nestled in corners, coating the walls—why, that car was virtually held together by c-hairs. When ole Rollie Nehring picked them all out with his little tweezer, the shell just collapsed all over the city garage . . ." Badger couldn't continue and commenced cackling like a full-blown madman this time, slapping the top of Atwell's desk with his big hands till the papers danced, some of them sliding off onto the floor. Suddenly, stopping laughing as quickly as he had begun, Badger stuck his flushed face back close to Bill's, startling him even more, pop eyes staring owlishly into a rapidly aging face. "How'd they get there, Billy? These little beggars. If you don't ever carry on in that car like the rest of us sinners, how in good gracious did they all get there?"

"I . . . gosh, sir, Sergeant, for the life of me, I . . . could they work out through your clothes?"

Badger slammed his fist down at Atwell's desk again. "See! I knew it! I told you he'd ask that, Sambo. Hot diggity damn, I knew it—" Suddenly stopping his wild peroration, Badger stuck his nose to Bill's again. "Got you this time, baby, I'm way ahead of you this time. Sambo, read what the good scientist said when I asked him that."

Atwell did as he was told, picking up the piece of paper and intoning, "Question: Rollie, short of sexual intercourse, how could this large amount, this great number, this whole bag of pubic hair find their way into Bill Brown's car? Answer: Well, of course, if the occupants rode around naked all the time. Question: Seriously, Rollie, could there be any other way—I mean, is it possible for pubic hairs to work out through clothing? Answer: Of course not. Question: So, then the only way you would say this extensive amount could be found in a vehicle would be through extensive—"

"Foreplay," Badger suddenly boomed. "Foreplay. I believe

Little Lord Fauntleroy here, Corporal. I don't think our Little
Lord would go all the way, force himself upon some unsus-
pecting little damsel like Linda, but I bet they could have
some fast furious foreplay, Corporal. Some real fast furious
foreplay can burn off just as many c-hairs as plain old screwing, ain't that right, Lordy-boy?"

Bill didn't answer. He sat rigid, his face impassive again
now but still drained death-white. He wouldn't even look in
Badger's direction, no matter what provocation. The kindly
Atwell stepped into the breach once more. "Bill, now tell us,
it's the only logical explanation anyway, nothing to be
ashamed of. Christ knows, everyone in the world does it at
one time or another."

"Corporal, I don't want to be like everybody else in the
world. That's just it, I've worked all my life not to be."

"I know, Bill, I know how you feel. I always tried to do the
right thing myself, but we all slip once in a while, it's as
natural as eating. See, we're not saying you had sexual relations with Linda. Even Badger here is willing to admit that he
believes you, doesn't think you had sexual relations with
Linda. All we're asking you is, if maybe you didn't have a
little foreplay with Linda now and then."

"Yes."

"Yes? Did you say, yes, Bill? Speak up, I—we can barely
hear you."

"Yes."

"Yes, you had sexual foreplay sometimes?"

"Yes."

"Did you engage in sexual foreplay New Year's Eve, Bill?"
Bill nodded his head mutely.

"Say it, Bill, you have to say it."

"Yes."

"You engaged in sexual foreplay New Year's Eve?"

"Yes."

"Where?"

"When . . . when we parked."

"Where? Which time?"

"In the . . . church parking lot."

"So you didn't go in right away? To look for your sister?"

"No, we . . . snuggled."

"Snuggled?"

"Yes, snuggled. That's what we call it."

"What did you do, Bill? When you 'snuggled'?"

"I . . . felt of her."

"Where?"

"All over."

"Under her clothing?"

"Yes."

"Did you remove any of her clothing?"

"No."

Atwell could just see the needle of the polygraph in his head jump. "Are you sure, Bill?"

"Well . . . I didn't exactly remove them, but we . . . pulled down her panties."

"We?"

"Linda helped me."

"Just her panties?"

"Well, her pants too, first."

"How far?"

"Down to her knees."

"Then what did you do?"

"I . . . felt her some more."

"Felt her?"

"Felt her . . . up."

"Did you finger . . . did you insert your finger into her vagina, Bill?"

"Yes."

"Many times?"

"Yes."

"In and out?"

"Yes." Bill suddenly looked up, directly into Atwell's eyes, some form of remembrance flooding his direct childlike gaze. "I think she was on her period."

Badger sat bolt upright in his chair, spoke as softly as Atwell now, "Bill, are you saying for sure that Linda was having her period?"

Bill didn't look at Badger, still gazed at Atwell. "No, I'm not saying it for sure, but I kind of think she was on her period."

"Did you encounter any Kotex? Any sanitary napkin of any kind?"

Bill thought. "No."

"Well, doesn't she wear them when she has her period?"

"I suppose so. But . . . but I think she just goes ahead and takes them off beforehand . . . when she thinks we're going to snuggle."

"You've done this before then, is that it, Billy-boy?" Badger concluded dryly.

Bill merely nodded, still not looking at Badger.

"So what is it that you're now saying, Bill?"

"What do you mean?"

"Why did you just happen to bring up the possibility that Linda was on her menstrual cycle?"

"Oh, I just thought that might explain the bloodstain in my car."

"Bloodstains, Bill—stains. What about the one on the passenger door panel? Did you finger her so hard she squirted way over there too?" Badger asked brutally, suddenly changing tactics again.

Bill grimaced noticeably, but answered quietly, "When we snuggle, we're all over the front seat. Then too, it could have been on my hands. Then when I went to open the door for her . . . I mean, I could have leaned over her and opened the door for her when we went to get out of the car to go look for my sister, I could have got some on the door."

"Just like that, huh, Bill?" Badger asked softly.

"It could have been."

"Polite little mother, ain't you, Billy-boy? Always jump right up and open the door for your girl—'course, then, you drive away leaving her sitting in the snow."

Bill ignored this thrust, still appeared to be conjecturing to himself on the bloodstain beneath the door handle. "Of course, she could have got some on one of her own hands too, brushed it against the side of the door."

"Bill, how would she possibly have gotten blood on her own hands if it was you that was . . ." Atwell trailed off, left the question dangling. Bill chose not to answer, though Atwell was sure he understood the implication. Disgusted, Atwell let it slide, asked instead, "Bill, did you ever, at any time in the course of the night, ever observe blood on your own hands?"

"No."

Badger picked this up. "How about when you got back home for the cozy little get-together with your mother after 2:00 A.M. Did you just go ahead and chow down on the baloney sandwich your ma says she fixed you with your bloody fingers?"

"Sergeant, I always wash my hands before I eat. It's a normal practice in my house for my mother to wait up for me and fix me a munchie when I get home. I'm sure I just walked in like always and went immediately to the bathroom and washed my hands, then joined my mother for the lunch meat sandwich."

"Baloney!"

"It was lunch meat."

"You lying bastard! Your ma says you walked in the door and dropped your coat on the couch like you always do and then just came in the kitchen and ate your baloney sandwich! Or are you saying your mother is lying?"

"I'm sure mom just forgot to mention me washing my hands first. I always wash my hands first."

"No, you always do just exactly what is necessary after the fact to lie your way out of whatever bind you get your psalm-singing little ass in, don't you, Billy-boy? Just like you're lying now about the blood, conveniently remembering she was on her period today after you been swearing on all your Bibles all along that you never even touched her, but all of a sudden today you're fingerin' all over the front seat of your car, New Year's Eve, nights on end . . ." Badger suddenly let out an animalistic growl, reached and flicked the pubic hairs he still clenched between his fingertips into Bill's startled face. "I'm gonna get you, Billy-boy. I'm gonna catch your dirty-white ass. This is one little bind you can't run to your ma with, get your folks to bail you out. This baloney sandwich you gonna eat all by yourself." Drained, his frustration temporarily exhausted, Badger pushed back his chair, wheeled away from the desk, was across Atwell's small office in two lionish strides, and stood looking out the window at this latest of snowfalls painting fresh clean strokes over Little Falls, wishing to Christ He could snow a little in people's dirty filthy minds. "Get him outta here," he muttered.

But Bill Brown didn't go. He just sat there looking from Badger's turned back to Atwell. Finally he reached in his inside jacket pocket and took out a slip of folded paper, carefully unfolded it, smoothed it out, and cleared his throat. "I have a few questions myself I'd like to ask—particularly you, Sergeant Badger. What are you doing in the shiny blue car that all the media are saying was seen in the vicinity of 1402

Drake the night of December 30, 1976 and/or the early morning hours of January 1, 1977?"

Badger turned slowly, stood staring at Atwell, while Atwell stared back, both too flabbergasted to answer. Bill, in turn, sat there staring at the both of them, his wide-open eyes dead serious, calmly awaiting their answer. Atwell was the first to reconnect his tongue to wits. "Ah, Bill, we've heard about this alleged 'shiny blue car' this newsboy who delivered the *Times Union* claims to have seen."

"According to what we've been able to ascertain—" Bill began, somewhat pedagogishly.

"We've?" Badger growled.

"Dad and I," Bill continued smoothly. "This newsboy, Ismael Kohani, has stated that he delivered the *Times Union* to the Craig residence on January 1, 1977 between approximately 1:30 and 1:45 hours A.M. That he delivered the paper on the front porch, that the front porch light was on and also possibly the garage light, that a shiny blue car was parked directly in front of the garage near the front porch. He stated that the shiny blue car was medium size, not big and not a small compact, two-door, and the color was blue. Ismael further stated that he did see three or four couples leaving the Brant residence two doors down the street from the Craig residence, and these couples did walk down to Harlequin to get into their cars."

"Bill, did you . . . ah . . . interview the, ah . . . what's his name?" Atwell finally got it out, coherent speech still being rather hard to come by.

"Ismael Kohani. I'm afraid I can't divulge my sources at this time."

Badger growled deep in his throat.

"I see. Bill," Atwell said patiently, "we figure the blue car this guy saw is Linda's."

Bill dismissed that out of hand. "No way. Hers is blue and that's as far as it goes. A station wagon, certainly not shiny, it's been sitting there collecting dirt for months."

"You should know, Bill," Atwell interrupted, starting to make a comeback. "It's amazing how two different people can see things six different ways when it comes to an investigation."

Bill dismissed this also. "What about all those people he saw walking?"

Atwell chuckled. "Oddly enough, they were cops. Some of ours. Attending a party at the Brants."

"Another thing," Bill continued, unobtrusively consulting his list, "a big thing. What about the girl that has come up missing from the Roller Derby out east of town?"

"We're investigating that."

"I see. But you've found nothing."

"Not so far."

"I see. The kidnapping in Big Falls?"

"Out of our jurisdiction."

"What about my clothes, the ones that were confiscated by Sergeant Poulous. When will they be returned to me?"

"As soon as the Crime Lab releases them back to us. That is, unless they find something that requires us to retain them for evidence."

"You won't, Sergeant," Bill said suddenly, turning directly to Badger for the first time since he produced his checklist. "Frankly, we're concerned about your manpower."

"Are you?" Badger asked sweetly.

"Yes. We're just not sure you have the manpower to handle a case of this complexity. Simply too unsophisticated and ill-equipped to cope with a case of this type. We feel—"

"Ah, Bill," Badger asked, showing remarkable forbearance, "who's we now, still you and your daddy?"

"Yes, and some of my people from the university. I've brought your handling of the case up with some of my professors."

"So what's the consensus," Badger asked casually—a little too casually, Atwell thought—"between 'your people' at the university and 1546 Fauntleroy? What kind of grades can us unsophisticated, ill-equipped slobs expect this quarter?"

"Now, Sergeant, you seem to tend to take things person-ally, which can be a mistake in itself. I've always believed in trying to talk things out rather than allowing myself the luxury of losing my temper. So I want to assure you now that what I've said and am about to say is nothing against you person-ally. I'm sure you and your men are doing the very best you can with what you've got to work with, but we just think that you just simply don't have enough to work with."

Badger nodded amiably. "You're right there. I sure could use a few more men."

Bill, apparently emboldened by the unpredictable Badger's

seemingly sincere acceptance of his and his department's obvious shortcomings, decided to lay it right on the line. "It's just not the quantity, Sergeant. I'm afraid a lot of people think it's the quality too. I mean, I hate to say this, but just how are you using the men you have? Of course, I understand you all are mostly used to dealing just with drunk college students, but I must say, that almost every time I come in this station I see most of your men. So, one must ask the question, are you really getting out there trying to find Linda? Or are you all just sitting around inside your offices trying to conduct your investigation from here?"

Atwell feared for Bill Brown's life—right then and there, on the spot, his blood and guts all over his reasonably tidy office. Badger turned casually from the window where he had been standing and started slowly back across the office toward Bill, still seated as he had been all along, directly across the desk from Atwell. Atwell could already see the headline in tomorrow's *Times Union:* MURDER SUSPECT MURDERED IN ATWELL'S OFFICE, followed by, "Det. Sgt. goes berserk, breaks suspect in two with bare hands."

Badger was there now, right in front of Brown. Atwell could see the familiar time bomb ticking away just over Badger's left eye. His big hands hung dangerously close to Bill's head, swinging slightly, loose and at the ready. Atwell thought of the night he and Badger had been having a few beers out at a roadhouse outside of town a few years back—quite a few, that was when beer cans were made of real metal. Badger had taken an empty in each hand, the long way, and crushed them flat between fingertips and the palm of his hands.

But Badger surprised him this time. Not by what he said, but the way he said it. Quiet. Hardly above a whisper. It sent chills up Atwell's spine.

"Pray, Bill. Pray hard. Because if you hurt that little girl, I'm going to send you to hell."

Bill seemed to nod, but said nothing. Just got up and left, taking his list with him. Badger stood transfixed for what seemed to Atwell the longest while, appeared to be staring at a spot on his office door. Atwell finally, without even realizing he was doing it until he had, leaned forward to see if there was anything there. His movement seemed to free up Badger; he turned to Atwell, said in almost his normal growling voice, "If that mealymouth little bastard don't take the cake."

"He's something else," Atwell agreed.

Badger grinned ruefully, wiped his mouth with the back of his hand. "You know something, Sambo? This little bastard comes in here, I use the c-hairs to browbeat him into the sexual involvement, maybe force him into admitting a little lie to cover the big one—he turns it into the perfect alibi on the bloodstains in his car."

Neither said anything for a while. There wasn't a whole lot to say after that. There was just one thing though, kind of off the subject, at least the serious one, but Atwell just had to ask it. "The c-hairs, Floyd, I thought they were still over to the Crime Lab."

Badger grinned, sheepishly. "Pulled 'em out of my ear."

12

Later on that morning Badger had Jensen take Mr. and Mrs. Craig for a reenactment of the trip around Little Falls and Big Falls that Bill, his father driving, had shown them the previous night. Jon Craig, again proving the old adage that those who say little remember much, was able to guide Jensen around this latest New Year's Eve Christmas decoration sight-seeing route within, he felt sure, a block, give or take. Instead of just getting out of the Brown car to "stretch his legs," as he had said then, he had actually gone into the 7-Eleven store to purchase a map of the Greater Big Falls area, and as soon as he returned home sat down and inked in the route they had just traveled while it was fresh in his mind.

Jensen, in turn, taped the route as they drove it, paying special note to the direction of travel and the streets that were used. When he had completed the trip, he dropped the Craigs off at Mrs. Craig's residence and returned to the station to draw up a scale map detailing the trip. It covered 34.4 miles and required approximately one hour and fifty-three minutes to drive. This compared to the much shorter drive Bill Brown had shown Officers Porath and Dinato on the late afternoon of January 1, which was exclusively in the Little Falls area, comprised only about 15.2 miles and required approximately an hour to traverse.

Therefore, now, ten days later, Bill Brown had theoretically at least accounted for the time span differential that had bothered investigating officers so from the beginning. The missing time between the young couple's leaving the Brown residence at approximately 11:30 P.M. and Bill returning there at approximately 2:05 A.M. had shrunk to just over a half hour; all things being roughly equal, thirty-seven minutes. Allotting the young couple those thirty-seven minutes at Unitarian Church—or wherever—for "snuggle" time and the quick look-see into the church for the sister, Elizabeth, it all came out just about perfect.

"Too perfect," Badger grunted, when they went over Jensen's figures in his office later. "If any of those times mean anything to start with."

Just another little thing about this case that was turning out "too perfect."

"Well, all we got to do now," Badger concluded, "is to find out why Billy-boy gave us the two different routes."

Meanwhile, Atwell was assigned to look further afield in an attempt to find something that might indicate that Bill Brown wasn't quite the "choirboy" he pretended to be. More specifically, as Badger put it to Atwell, "See if you can't find something in his past behavior that might indicate him capable of murder," and/or, under the right circumstances, if sufficiently provoked, likely to murder. They knew now that he would lie about relatively small things, and the polygraph machine insisted that he would just as easily lie about the big ones. But it's a big jump from lying to murder, whether a polygraph needle or a man. And the lies they had actually caught him in so far could be construed as much an attempt to protect and preserve Linda's religio-sexual reputation as self-serving—unless, of course, the real lie here was that they actually had *not* engaged in strenuous sexual foreplay, New Year's Eve or at any other time, with Linda conveniently "on her period" to cover the bloodstains.

The bloodstains were small. Tiny. Minute. So minute that there wasn't even enough there to run a second test to complete the blood group factoring. Nowhere near enough to determine if it was menstrual blood or not. In the course of a homicide using external force—some kind of weapon—normally much blood is spilled, and quantitative amounts can be recovered by sophisticated technicians, no matter how careful the killer is at the time of the crime or afterward, particularly if the homicide occurs in a car. If a victim is murdered by some internal means, say poison, naturally there is less blood, though severe convulsions, internal hemorrhages, and the like can produce some bleeding from the various orifices of the body, along with other secretions, as easily detected and categorized by the skilled Crime Lab technician.

So, if the blood was Linda's and not menstrual and Bill had killed her, how?

Strangulation, Badger thought. It can produce flecks of blood from the nose and throat from the capillaries rupturing while the pressure is being applied and seepage from these crushed capillaries afterward. Also, in the thrashing about that ordinarily takes place in the course of a throttling, the victim fighting for his or her life, heads can be slammed against relatively sharp objects, particularly within a car—rearview mirrors, door handles—hard enough to break the skin, cause superficial bleeding. She could have torn off a fingernail fighting to save herself, a drop got on the seat, her hand flung out and grazed the passenger side door panel. She cuts the top of her head on the mirror during the melee. Later as she lies dead in the front seat beside him as he transports her body to wherever, her head rests against the door panel. Bill had said they "would be all over the front seat when we snuggle." Experience had shown Badger that a murderer and his victim would be all over the front seat of a car during a killing too.

Yes, it fit. Strangulation was the handiest means available during a passion killing—a tried and true method. And that's what Badger was 99.9 percent sure now had happened. She rejected him New Year's Eve, once and for all. Bill snapped, strangled her before he knew what was happening even, somehow kept his cool, drove somewhere and disposed of the body. He had two and a half hours to do that in, even accepting the supposed times given by Bill and his family, four and a half to five if they don't return to the Brown residence to finish watching the movie, go somewhere directly from babysitting with the Henderson child. Linda could be damn near anywhere. Under the snow.

Yes, it all fit—in theory. But that's all Badger had really at this point, a theory. So they had to keep looking somewhere out there in the real world till they found the pieces of the puzzle that fit the theory, at least so Badger concluded.

His men concurred—Atwell and Jensen, closest to the case, particularly. Stung by Bill's high-handed putdown of their department and themselves, they sallied forth this eleventh day of January with renewed vigor, redoubled determination, obsessed with the idea of getting Bill Brown.

As Jensen remarked after Atwell told him what Bill had said about them, "Can you believe the gall! Here we think he's maybe the murderer, and he comes in and as much as tells us we're not doing a good enough job catching him."

"Maybe he's right," Atwell ventured.

Atwell contacted Armand Luthke of Luthke Security on Oyster Island and requested him to begin an investigation on the island in an attempt to obtain any information in reference to Bill Brown's behavior patterns while working on the island the past summer, paying special attention to any problems Bill may have had. Badger's thinking here was that a guy like Bill might tend to act differently while away from home, and, as they had found nothing so far in his home area to indicate a tendency toward aberrant behavior or a propensity to solve a problem should it arise by resorting to violent action, maybe they would find some indication of this on Oyster Island.

Other than at the Delway Hotel where he had worked, it appeared to Armand Luthke that Bill Brown had made no impression whatsoever, was virtually the proverbial invisible man. Checking churches, judge, police, other hotels, the owner of the local coffee shop where the young people on the island hung out, Armand could locate not one soul that had known Bill Brown the summer of 1976 or had anything to do with him. He had made the right impression where it counted though, his boss. Speaking by telephone with Dave Graybill and his wife, owners of the Delway Hotel on Oyster Island, Atwell was told by them that they remembered Bill Brown very well, that he was a pretty good worker, that they had no real problems with his work, only a couple of minor disagreements in the course of a long busy summer, which would be entirely normal with any one of their young seasonal workers. Bill seemed to be quite religious and real clean-cut and quiet and did nothing abnormal during the summer that would lead them to believe that he was anything but a good, clean-cut kid. Mr. Graybill even went so far as to say that he "certainly would have let Bill go out with my daughter." The Graybills further went on to state that, though Bill didn't appear to have made any real close friends on the island, he did run around some with a group of young people from Symco State College, who were also quite religious, as opposed to another group of kids from UW-LF, who were good kids too but tended to have drinking parties and were more of the hell-raising type. Bill, they assured Atwell again, had nothing whatsoever to do with these hellions.

There was one kind of peculiar thing, though, Armand Luthke reported, almost as an afterthought. He had found this rather strange looking doll stuck back under the latticed porch of the cottage Bill had lived in. Of course, it could be any-one's. Bill had shared the cottage with others and literally hundreds of student employees had lived there over the years —who knew how long the doll had been there, though it did look fairly fresh. It was a homemade wooden doll, hand-carved, dressed with matronly clothing, no hands or legs, just a torso and head; but the really distinctive thing about the doll were the eyes, jet black, with tiny blood-red crosses superim-posed on the pupils.

"Looks like some kind of a voodoo doll to me," Atwell grunted. "Something you might wanna sit around sticking pins in."

13

Ken Knutson, junior partner of the prestigious Big Falls law firm of Wolcott, Barry, Anderson, Washburn and Knutson, located on the tenth floor of the Farmers State Bank Building, came into the case secondhand. Senior partner George Wolcott, a member of St. John's Lutheran Church, along with the Craigs and Browns, had been approached by Fred Brown and asked if he would represent his son, Bill Brown, primarily to act as a buffer between Bill and the world at large. Fred, as related by Wolcott to Knutson, was of the opinion that Bill was being treated unfairly, not only by the police but, as the days went by, the media as well. Wolcott told Fred Brown that his firm rarely handled cases of a criminal nature, being primarily a business oriented law firm. But when Fred Brown pointed out that this, in fact, was not a criminal case—his son being innocent of any wrongdoing whatsoever—but rather one of invasion of privacy and harassment, not to mention possible slander and libel, George Wolcott consented to take the case, more as a congregational favor than anything else. That is, if one of his partners, Ken Knutson, who did handle what criminal work they accepted, would take on the assignment.

Ken Knutson looked out over his medium mahogany desk at the distinguished, silver-haired lawyer. "Do I have much choice, George?" He grinned.

"Certainly, Kenneth. I told Mr. Brown of this contingency."

"Sure, I'll take it," Knutson agreed, leaning back in his

leather-upholstered swivel chair and spreading his hands wide.
"Why not?"

Why not indeed, he thought after George Wolcott left his
office. He was already intrigued by the situation, involved to
the extent of having followed the case through the media since
hearing a newscast mentioning the disappearance of Linda
Lou Craig New Year's Day. Since then the disappearance had
become a relatively hot item locally, something in the papers
about it regularly, on the newscasts daily. Not only was Knutson aware of the missing girl, he was aware of Bill Brown
as suspect. Furthermore, Ken Knutson already had a long-
distance, lawyerly position on the case before George Wolcott
ever happened into his office. He agreed with Fred Brown; he
thought this Bill Brown did need a buffer between himself and
the media. Of course, at this stage, he knew next to nothing
about Bill Brown's dealings with the police, but he could
make an educated guess about this facet too, and had. As to
the media, Knutson felt they had been unfair in some of their
reporting of the case, the loaded questions asked Bill Brown
and his family, the continuing presentation of Bill Brown as an
unbooked suspect of some unspecified crime. As a matter of
fact, lawyer Ken Knutson was already of the legal opinion,
based on what he had seen, heard, and read, that, unless this
kid Brown was actually charged with some type of wrongdoing in the disappearance of Linda Lou Craig, and damned
soon, he ought to limit further contact with the police and all
contact with the media.

Furthermore, he was intrigued by Bill Brown himself. This
clean-cut, soft-spoken, boyish-looking psychology major's
picture, as a member of UW-LF's famous marching band,
kept marching across the nightly television newscast. The picture was invariably followed by a heavy-handed recountal of
his having dropped his fiancée off on her snowbound doorstep
New Year's Eve, and she was never seen or heard of again.
The announcer's voice was as invariably dripping with skepticism. Yes, Knutson had wanted to meet this kid days before
George Wolcott dropped the case on his desk—to tell him,
"For Chrissake's, boy, you better get yourself a lawyer,
whether you did it or not, before you talk yourself right into
the can."

Yet, he was, as a good lawyer should be, open-minded

about the case itself. Maybe the girl had run away, joined one of those far-out religious cults like the media often theorized, when they weren't trying to journalistically indict Bill Brown. Maybe she was snatched off her icy perch, through some weird drunken New Year's Eve set of circumstances, like the boyfriend doggedly kept repeating. Ken Knutson, only thirty-four years old himself, graduate of UW-LF's bitter cross-state rival, the University of Wisconsin at Iola, knew very well what hijinks could go on in a college town on New Year's Eve, Homecoming, or just about any other night of the year when one or more students got together—seemingly innocent hijinks that could sometimes turn into tragedy. Then again, who knew, Knutson had to remind himself, maybe the sweet-faced boyfriend did do it, whatever "it" might be. Like the old saying goes, you can never tell a book by its cover.

Yes, Ken Knutson was open-minded about the case till he met Bill Brown. Then, as he remarked later, "I knew for damn sure the kid hadn't done anything criminal."

They hit it off right from the beginning. Not only was Knutson impressed with Bill, but with the entire Brown family. There was no doubt in Knutson's mind that the Browns were perfectly candid in all they were telling him, were heartsick over the disappearance of Bill's beloved fiancée, Linda Lou Craig, and were dedicated in their efforts to help find her. The Browns, at this initial meeting in Knutson's office, went into great detail on what they had been doing to find her; they were now even considering the hiring of a private investigator and consulting psychics in their desperation to locate Linda and prove to the world that Bill had nothing to do with her disappearance. Knutson had no feeling whatsoever that they were exaggerating in relation to their efforts or sincerity. Rather, he saw dedicated effort and righteous anger. They were almost pathetic in their desire to enlist him to their cause, eliciting his ideas, techniques, anything he might think of in reference to locating missing persons; no matter that he may have known less than they about such endeavors. Telling them that, he also advised them such activity would be better left for the police.

Speaking of police, the Browns were furious. Rightly so, it soon appeared, as they detailed the many injustices Bill had suffered at the hands of the LFPD, particularly chief of detec-

tives, Sergeant Badger, who apparently had gone slightly berserk while interviewing Bill the past Tuesday and more or less
thrown him out of his office. Ken Knutson knew Detective
Sergeant Badger professionally, having crossed swords lightly
with him over a couple of clients, and this surprised him
somewhat. Badger had always come across to Knutson as a
good cop, a little crude around the edges maybe, but honest,
just a guy trying to get a difficult job done. Of course, he had
never been a 135-pound murder suspect in Badger's office
either.

"Pardon my French, Mr. Knutson," Fred Brown continued,
"but this guy Badger is a real stinker! You just can't deal in a
civilized manner with him. Our objective has always been to
try to get to the truth of things. We've answered every question that the Police Department has asked us, we spent hours
down there, Bill sat down there at one sitting for seven and a
half hours, they run tons of people in, they gave him two
polygraph exams. We have to sign a waiver of our Constitu-
tional rights every time we set foot in the door of the police
station to as much as ask them what progress is being made in
finding Linda, or if we come up with another item of information that might be helpful in locating her—"

"Mr. Brown—"

"So Mr. Knutson, I says, if they have to have that to do
their job, OK, all right, but when Bill answers everything they
ask and then brings with him a little list trying to find out what
the current status is, if they had any more leads on finding
Linda, and Badger rants and raves like a prize loon, yells and
screams at him, we are not going to take that! Bill came right
home and called me. Even if he had signed away his Consti-
tutional rights, they are not going to yell and scream at him.
He was upset about that, let me tell you. I left work and went
down there and talked with a subordinate, and he sympathized
with me because he knows the man and what kind of a person
he is, and I said, 'Well, you know, it is time we should get an
attorney and here we are.'"

"Have you informed Sergeant Badger of this action?"

"I sent him a letter explaining our position—that he had
made it impossible to cooperate freely with him anymore because of his actions and that I did not want that to go on any
further or to impede the progress of finding Linda."

"You did the right thing, Mr. Brown." Knutson turned toward Bill, dressed quite elegantly in a rather formal-appearing, dark-blue suit with lighter blue tie and white shirt. He looked to Knutson more like a boy all dressed up for confirmation than a young man of twenty-one; I bet he doesn't even have to shave yet, Knutson thought, noting his smooth pale cheeks, skin creamy as a baby's. Bill had sat quietly between his parents throughout the meeting, respectfully allowing his father to do most of the talking. "Bill, where do you think Linda is?"

Bill Brown lifted his eyes to look directly into Knutson's while he spoke. Knutson was taken with his direct unblinking gaze, invariably the earmark of a man telling the truth. He has exceptional eyes, Ken Knutson noted to himself, as clear and blue as the lakes back home in Minnesota. "I . . . hate to say this, sir, but I'm afraid . . . somebody picked her up."

"Picked her up?"

"Forceably. Came along and saw her sitting there all alone on her front porch and just . . . forceably . . . took her away."

Knutson might have explored Bill's theory more fully with him, but his father interposed an expanded possibility that blew him right out of the water. "Mr. Knutson, if I may—"

"Surely."

"Now Bill here tends to lean over backwards to be fair—so do I, for that matter—but there's another little theory we have to kind of go along with that. I know Linda, we all do, Bill best of all, of course, and I say the only person that I think Linda would allow herself to go near under these circumstances, she just wouldn't pick up with a complete stranger without a struggle, it would have to be somebody official-looking!"

"Official looking?"

Fred Brown leaned closer over the front of Knutson's desk, his deep-set, dark-blue eyes glittering. "Or somebody that drives an official looking car, if you get what I mean."

"I think . . . I'm starting to," Knutson admitted, too astounded to say more.

"Now this official-looking person in this official-looking car slowly pulls up Drake seconds after Bill here pulls out of the Craig driveway, sees this beautiful young gal sitting all alone there on the front stoop of her mother's home, right directly under their garish porch light—which I have found out through my investigations was left on all night—thinks it's New Year's Eve, what the heck, can't help but conclude this beautiful young gal has to be drunk or drugged up or something just to be sitting here all by her lonesome in the snow, fifteen degrees below zero, two o'clock in the morning New Year's Eve, stops, rolls down his window, calls, 'Miss, are you all right?' or words to that effect. Linda looks over, the car is right out there on Drake, just three car lengths away at the end of her driveway, the street is well lit, there's a streetlight right there at the end of the driveway. Linda sees it is an official looking car, she says, 'Sure, I'm fine.' 'Come here, I want to talk to you anyway.' 'But, Officer, I tell you I'm fine, I always like to sit down to pray awhile before I go in.' But all the while she's talking, she's walking toward this official-looking car, by now she'd already be alongside, only a few seconds would have elapsed. 'Get in, I want to question you about' something or other. Linda, being a well brought up little lady, taught to respect, obey law and order, gets in— Whammo!" Fred Brown brought one ample fist crushing into the palm of his other hand. Knutson who had been unconsciously leaning forward throughout Fred's mesmerodic recital, almost as though his body was being drawn physically closer to the Brown family ranged in front of his desk, literally jerked backward when flesh met flesh. "It's all over and done within seconds. The car pulls away, nobody had seen it come or go. If they did, it's just another patrol car cruising New Year's Eve."

Knutson took a deep breath, wanted to lean back in his big, lawyerly, leather-upholstered swivel chair, but something within him bade him lean forward even closer toward the waiting Browns. "Mr. Brown, are you implying . . ."

Fred Brown held up both hands, palms out. Something curious struck Ken Knutson then, even then, while he was waiting with bated breath for Mr. Brown to dot the i's in "suspicion." His hands, Bill's hands—both man and boy had relatively large hands, somewhat out of proportion to the rest of their measurements. "Now I said, it's not maybe a Little Falls police car, but it could be an official-looking car of the same type and somebody with police type of appearance—"

"The paperboy saw men leaving the Brants' right down the street when he delivered the *Times Union* just about that time, Mr. Knutson," Bill's mother, Leona Brown, broke in. "And guess who they turned out to be."

Ken Knutson strained forward, staring from one Brown face into the next. "You're not saying—"

"Yes," Fred Brown blurted impatiently, "members of the Little Falls Police Department. We suspected they were. Brant is thick with the LFPD, but we didn't know for sure. But now we know for a fact, Bill got it right from the horse's mouth—Badger. Cleverly tricked him into telling him just who it was at the party just three doors away that went on all night New Year's Eve—his own men!"

"Detectives?"

"No, better yet—Uniform Division. So let's carry my theory one step further, a very logical step forward. One of them comes to the party while still on his shift, just stops by in the patrol car to run in and say 'Hi,' have a quick snort on the sly—"

This time it was Knutson interrupting Brown. "He wouldn't even have to be on duty, he could just be carrying his uniform in his own car, stick on his hat. Just roll down the window and stick out his arm and slap a police spot on the roof of his car. A lot of cops have their private cars equipped with almost as much para-police junk as patrol cars."

"Sure," Fred agreed emphatically, "you're with me now. All he has to do is *look* official. Linda is a young, gullible gal, her head full of who knows what all. Some guy she thinks is a cop or *is* a cop pulls up, calls to her, she'd just trot out to the end of her driveway without thinking twice." Fred Brown was straining so far forward toward Knutson that his body had almost left his chair, just the lip of his buttocks still made contact with the edge of the seat. More crouched over the balls of his feet than seated, he reminded Knutson of a knockout-hungry prizefighter straining off his stool just before the bell. A stocky middleweight in a vintage blue serge suit and tie much resembling his son's, both in color and cut.

"You agree with all this, Bill?" Knutson finally asked him.

The whole family nodded. "Yes," Bill answered quietly, "I believe it to be . . . a distinct possibility."

"Linda might, without thinking, walk out to the end of her driveway if somebody she thought was police hailed her?"

Bill thought that over, finally nodded gently. That impressed Knutson. This kid had a mind of his own, wasn't so well-trained that he would just go along with anything his folks believed. Better yet, even if it was something that might focus suspicion away from him.

"Now, I don't want to make Linda sound stupid or anything, but, sometimes she didn't use much common sense. Particularly when it came to . . . doing things." Bill hesitated again, finally stating quietly, "She always liked to be on the go. Always doing something. Never totally content just to sit and discuss something of value, more elevating subjects . . ."

Ken Knutson waited, thinking Bill was going to say more. When he didn't, seemingly sunk in thoughts of his lost love, Ken finally asked kindly, "Bill, are you implying that Linda might conceivably have gone off with someone of her own free will? Other than someone she might mistake for a police officer or some such official?"

Bill looked up. "Oh, no, she wouldn't just go off with another man, if that's what you mean, voluntarily . . . We are very much in love, engaged to be married. All I meant is that sometimes Linda doesn't exercise too much common sense, she is too good a person in some ways, too trusting."

"I see," Knutson said slowly, nodding his head sympathetically. It was obvious the young man was still in some state of shock, deeply distraught over the disappearance of his fiancée, still so close to her in heart and mind that he often spoke as though she were right there in the room with him, her presence shrouding each soft word of her.

Ken Knutson felt very sorry for the young man. There was something fragile within Bill Brown that wouldn't stand a lot of breaking—an old-world innocence, a trusting naiveté. Knutson could very easily visualize Bill Brown riding double with Don Quixote, desperately trying to joust his way through the much more complex windmills of the late seventies. He reminded Knutson of a rather delicate bird, a bluebird maybe, trailing a broken wing behind him, particularly when he had seen him on television trying to softly parry the savage thrusts of the media vultures. Those bastards aren't going to railroad this kid, he vowed to himself now in his office, not so long as I'm around.

"I'll take the case," he said aloud. "From now on, I advise you, Bill, all of you, the whole family, to refer all calls from the police, media, anybody and everybody, to me, effective immediately."

Tears spurted into Mrs. Brown's tired, frightened eyes, the

tears Knutson had felt trembling behind a sad mixture of inse-
cure stubborn defiance and some kind of societal inferiority
complex. Yes, he knew now where he had seen those eyes
before—in the head of a wounded doe he had struck with his
car, driving through the Nicolet forest.

"Thank you, sir," Mrs. Brown managed to say before she
ducked her head.

Fred Brown took the monogrammed handkerchief from the
breast pocket of his suit jacket and noisily blew his nose. Even
Knutson found himself busying some totally extraneous legal
documents from one side of his desk to the other. Bill, seemingly the most prepossessed of his family, stood up, stepped
forward the foot or so separating him from the front of Knutson's desk and leaned across it to offer his hand to Knutson.
While they clasped hands, Knutson found himself being
drawn once again into those deep, clear-blue Lake Michigan
eyes. They tugged at him, submerged him softly in their gentle undertow. "Thanks," was all Bill said.

"I haven't done anything yet," Knutson replied.

"You will. I know . . . you will."

14

It wasn't until the twenty-sixth of January that the LFPD finally got around to interviewing Reverend John Henry Johnson, pastor of Little Falls Unitarian Church. But, once there, it didn't take them long to realize they should have been more religious about their churchgoing.

"Why, nothing was going on in the church proper," Pastor Johnson answered, in response to Atwell's question as to what was going on in his church New Year's Eve. "If that's what you mean by the main worship area, it was locked and dark."

Jensen and Atwell looked at each other, momentarily at a loss for words. Atwell, finding his tongue first, asked, "Locked? What about the midnight services you conducted New Year's Eve?"

"There were no services New Year's Eve. Who told you that?"

Neither of the detectives wished to say that it was Bill Brown, so they chose to overlook the pastor's question, Atwell responding instead with another of his own. "Apparently we are laboring under some misunderstanding, sir. Ah, could you tell us if anything at all was . . . ah, if there was any kind of a function here at Unitarian Church?"

"Yes, we had a New Year's Eve social gathering down in Brotherhood Hall, culminating with a candlelight service."

"Down? Did you say, 'down'?"

"Yes, down in the basement. Brotherhood Hall is down in the basement, on the ground level."

"Sir, Pastor, so you're saying that whatever happened in your church New Year's Eve—this social gathering, I believe

126

you called it—happened in the basement, and nothing was going on upstairs in the main church?"

"That's correct," the patient pastor repeated, overlooking the fact that he had already told them three times. "The rest of the church was locked and in the dark."

"How would a person go about getting into this social gathering, Pastor?" Jensen interjected.

"Well, through the south doors of the Brotherhood Hall mainly, but maybe a few might have come through the parking lot doors on the northeast side. They were also unlocked."

"How many would have come in by the main entrance doors?"

"You mean the front doors?"

"Yes, those big double door at the top of the steps." The three men were standing talking in a glassed-in porch of the parsonage adjacent to the church, viewing the front of the church from where they stood.

"Why, nobody. They were locked. There was no reason for them to have been opened."

"There were no lights on in the church proper?"

"Not to my knowledge. There should not have been."

"So during that evening," Atwell pursued, wanting to make absolutely certain that they had this right, "New Year's Eve, there was no reason for any members of the congregation, or anyone else, to be in the main worship area, the church proper, standing and singing. Is that what you're saying?"

"Certainly not. That would not have happened."

Atwell paused, looked at Jensen. "Are you acquainted with Bill Brown?" Jensen asked.

"Only by remote acquaintance."

"Would you have recognized him had he come into this gathering at your church on New Year's Eve?"

"Not individually, but as a class of young person, I would have recognized him, for there were no young people of that age involved in what went on at that church that evening."

"Would it have been possible that evening for someone to have entered the Brotherhood Hall and observed what was going on down there in the basement, scan the crowd, and leave without your observing him?"

"I . . . yes, I suppose it could have been possible," the pastor had to admit, though he did it skeptically.

"When did the candlelight service you spoke of commence?"

"Oh, I would say 11:30 to 11:40, we broke up the socializing and went into the worship part of the situation. A few of the men and myself, my memory not serving me as to who the men were, took part in some informal singing without accompaniment. Other men led the service. We had a very short devotional by candlelight, there was prayer, and we had a service of communion."

"What time was the communion?"

"We attempt to have it as close to midnight as possible, so I would say, probably ten minutes of twelve."

"After communion, did anyone sing anymore?"

"No, the communion would have concluded at midnight with a single song and that would have been it."

"How long was the song?"

"Oh, one stanza. We were not using hymnals."

"What was the song, do you remember?"

"'We Are One In Spirit.'"

"Were you standing when you sang this song?"

"Hmmm, let me see. I don't think so. We had gathered our chairs in a semicircle, so I assume we sat."

Atwell took over again. "Do you know Elizabeth Brown, sister of Bill, Pastor Johnson?"

"Oh, yes, quite well."

"Did you see her that night?"

"No."

"What festivities, social or otherwise, were going on that night for the young people of your church?"

"Nothing. That is, at the church. There was a gathering at the home of UW-LF Assistant Football Coach Dale Simpson. Many of our teenagers were at that gathering."

"Is Elizabeth Brown a member of your church?"

"Not of record. However, as a matter of frequent attendance at our youth group and some attendance in our Sunday evening service. On one occasion, she asked to be baptized by immersion, which I was glad to do."

"You have regular Sunday evening services, Pastor?" Jensen broke in to ask.

"Oh, yes, they are one of our principal services."

"And they are held where, please?"

"In the church proper."

"This is like a normal . . . ah, you know what I mean, like regular Sunday morning services, say at the Lutheran Church?"

The pastor had a sense of humor. "Yes, just as normal as the Lutheran's, I should suspect, at least, as normal as I can make them."

"You give a sermon from the pulpit then, have a choir singing, that sort of thing?"

"Yes."

"Could Bill Brown have attended one of these regular Sunday evening services, Pastor?"

"Quite likely. Seems as though that is where I met him. I believe he did come once or twice with his sister, Elizabeth."

Atwell wanted to know more about the youth party at Assistant Coach Dale Simpson's home. "Pastor, how far is Mr. Simpson's home from the church?"

"Oh, I couldn't say exactly, short of two miles. Perhaps, one."

"But, surely, someone coming to pick up a person attending a party at Coach Simpson's house would not wait for that person in your church parking lot?"

The pastor chuckled. "Of course not."

"Again, sir, if someone were in your church standing either in the main worship area or looking onto the main worship area, would they also be able to look into the Brotherhood Hall where your social gathering took place New Year's Eve?"

"Absolutely not. It is physically impossible."

"One last thing: Does your main worship area look the same as your Brotherhood Hall?"

"Not at all."

"Could they be confused, one for the other?"

"There is no way that these two areas can be confused."

"Thank you, Pastor. As a matter of fact, I can't tell you how much we thank you," Atwell said, pressing the pastor's hand fervently.

The pastor's curiosity finally got the better of him. "I gather this young Brown fellow told you something quite different than I, might one be safe to say that?"

"Yes, one might be very safe to say that, Pastor," Jensen concurred. "One might even go so far as to say he lied through his teeth."

"Is that so," the pastor said, shaking his head sadly.

* * *

The two detectives were jubilant on their way back to the station. This might be what they needed all along to break Bill Brown! On this lie they had somebody to confront him with. The best possible somebody, the very reverend Pastor John Henry Johnson.

"By God, can't you just see Pastor Johnson on the stand, Cliff," Atwell chortled. "If somebody were to ask me what I thought God looked like, I'd describe Pastor Johnson."

"He's just what we've been needing to nail Brown to the cross," Jensen agreed. "Confront his folks too. If we can convince them that Bill is lying about going into Unitarian Church New Year's Eve to look for his sister, probably never even went near there at all, then maybe we can convince them that he's lying about a lot of things and get them to put the pressure on him to tell the truth."

Atwell's face sobered. "Yeah, if they even want the truth. Talking to those two, sometimes I get the feeling they don't want the truth, no matter what."

"Oh, I wouldn't go that far," Jensen said, glancing sideways at Atwell. Jensen was driving, so it was just a quick glance. "They seem like decent people to me. Sure, I can understand parents not wanting to believe that their only son is guilty of something like possible murder, but I don't think they would try to shield him if we could prove to them that, quite likely, he is involved to some degree."

"Hmm, I wouldn't be too sure about that. Ever hear of the Cape Cod Killer, Tony Costa?"

"No."

"Well, Tony's mother came across her little boy cutting one of his early victims into nice neat little bloody chunks in the family bathtub one afternoon—he liked to cut them up and bury them here and there. What do you suppose she did about it?"

Jensen shrugged, grimaced, almost like he didn't even want to consider it. "Telling it the way you are, probably nothing."

"You got it, buddy. Just went about her business for the next two or three years while Tony just kept on hacking away —local girls, small community, she had to know her boy Tony was responsible for all these subsequent disappearances too."

"She, the mother, she ever come forward?"

"Nope. Carried her grisly little secret to her grave."

"How'd anybody ever find out she had seen her son cutting up the one in the bathtub then?"

"Son Tony bragged about it after the cops finally caught him—after he'd killed and butchered eight or ten more."

Jensen drove at least another three blocks before he finally asked the question, stealing another quick glance at the older Atwell while he did so. "You . . . you don't think we're dealing with something like that here, do you?"

"Nah, I don't mean that exactly. Just passing along a little something about how far a mother might go to protect her kid—father too, I suppose, for that matter."

They were almost turning into the station before Jensen spoke again. "You notice that article in last Saturday's *Times Union* about the six area youngsters who disappeared over the last year and been found dead up around Sand Lake?"

"Yeah, the five girls and a boy."

"Yeah." Jensen parked the unmarked car, turned toward Atwell, his left forearm leaning on the steering wheel. "Now none of them was from right here in Little Falls, but sure close enough. You suppose Linda Lou Craig could be another one of these?"

Atwell continued staring straight ahead out the windshield. Finally he said, "Yeah, could be. If Bill Brown killed them too."

"You shittin' me?"

"No. Not that I mean Bill Brown got those other six too. You know as well as I do that we got nothing on that, but I'm saying I think he got Linda Lou Craig. So, I suppose, to use Pastor Johnson's words, one might be safe to say that, if he could get one, he could get more."

"What do you think, Sambo?" Jensen persisted, so caught up in this new wild theory that he forgot himself and addressed his immediate superior by Badger's pet nickname. "What do you really think about maybe Brown being involved in these other killings too? What's Badger say?"

"Well, he had me do a profile on all these other area cases as far back as a week or so ago . . ." Atwell hung out to his inferior tantalizingly, maybe just to remind him to address him properly.

"What'd you find?" Jensen asked hungrily. If he'd moved any closer he'd have been sitting in Atwell's lap.

"Nothing," Atwell had to admit. "I didn't come across anything that would indicate that we were missing anything of value in reference to this investigation."

When Atwell started talking like he wrote his police reports, Jensen knew it was time to back off, but he just had to know. "But what do you really think, you and Badger? Forget what you have to put down in the reports. What do you guys think, off the cuff?"

Atwell sat there stiffly, apparently chewing his answer over a little before he was ready to spit it out. "Me? I think it's a passion murder, just like Badger does. She wants to break off with him, so he snaps and does her in. A one-time deal."

"Yeah, me too," Jensen breathed, sort of relieved but at the same time sort of sorry too. "Now all we got to do is prove it."

15

Badger wasted no time moving on this first hard evidence of a
Bill Brown lie. Why in the world hadn't they thought to check
out Bill's version of what was going on inside Unitarian
Church sooner? Probably because Bill's description of the
events sounded so plausible, nobody in the department
doubted it. That was just it, Badger raged to himself, the little
bastard apparently spent half his time in churches, knew exactly what would be going on at any given holiday celebra-
tion—except this time he missed by one floor.

That explanation wasn't good enough though. Not for a
murder investigation. To overlook, for twenty-six days, direct
refutation by the best possible source of your prime murder
suspect's sworn testimony as to where he was and what he
saw there during the period the murder very likely took place
goes beyond rationalization, simply becomes poor police
work. Particularly when Bill Brown's evasive answers to
Badger and Atwell's questions on the eleventh should have
clearly suggested to them that he had not seen what he was
saying he had seen. Had not been there at all. And whether it
took the LFPD twenty-six days or twelve or seventeen or
whatever to find this out, verify this conclusion, is of small
meaning. It should have been done immediately. And Badger
knew it.

"Dammit," he raged, after his initial jubilation upon receiving Pastor Johnson's statement had worn off and he was
forced with translating its meaning into salvageable action.
"We should have had this knowledge two, three days after the
girl turned up missing. Ten minutes after we took Bill's state-

133

ment on what was going on at Unitarian Church, we should
have run right out and got Pastor Johnson's. Seems to me I
told somebody to go out and talk to him way back on the
fourth or fifth or thereabouts." Scanning the hastily assembled
detectives, Badger suddenly shot the finger at Kozelowsky,
sitting there quietly investigating his fingernails. "Kozelowsky! You, I told you to go see this minister sometime way
back then!"

"The other reverend, Sarge, you sent me out to see Reverend Russell, the preacher over to St. John's, about his counseling Linda about marrying Bill Brown."

"Oh," Badger said sulkily. He stood thinking a moment or
two, then wheeled on Jensen. "Cliff, then it must have been
you."

"That was the Reverend Hammer, Sarge, of Campus Action. You must remember him, you went with me. That was
just last week, Friday the fourteenth. It's all there in my work
report, dated—"

"Alright, alright," Badger said huffily, waving him off.
"You don't have to give me the time of day. Dammit all." He
smacked one big fist into the other. "There's just so many
reverends and pastors and half-assed preachers in this case, a
man can't keep track of them all. Sambo! Didn't I assign one
to you too?"

"Yeah, the Reverend Kennedy of Linda's church down in
Illinois, when she was going to school at Augustana—"

"See what I mean!" Badger roared, throwing his head back
and arms up in direct appeal. "They're coming out of the
woodwork. And if they aren't for real, you got the Browns
acting like preachers. I've had about all I want out of that
whole mealy-mouth crew, let me tell you. I'm going to get
that little lying, holier-than-thou Billy-boy Brown, if it's the
last thing I do—dammit all!" He said it again, pounding his
hairy fists into the airy Billy-boy before him. "If we could
have only hit him with this right off the bat when we had them
a little down. The whole family, that second day right after
your first poly, Sambo. That's as close as we ever come to
breaking him. The folks acting like they realized he was with-
holding something, now him and the whole family is hiding
behind Knutson's desk, we can't really get to him unless we
book him."

"Maybe we ought to?" Atwell finally ventured the suggestion into the ringing silence following Badger's outburst.

"Yeah, that's what I been thinking too," Jensen concurred.

Badger thought that over. "Boy, I would like to—I would surely love to. I got everybody from the mayor on down starting to snap away at my hamstrings. Don't think it was just by accident the paper run that article on them other MPs turned up dead in the last year. Them people out there trying to tell us something, boys, and I don't mean maybe—"

Atwell broke in on his boss, "But, Chief, they weren't even in our jurisdiction. They were over the line in Big Falls, out in Wyoming Township. Nobody can blame us for those status-open cases."

"Close enough!" Badger boomed. "Close enough so now that we got Linda Lou Craig, it's getting people to start thinking some pretty wild thoughts."

Atwell now asked Badger virtually the same question Jensen had asked him just a few minutes before. "But, Chief, you don't think Brown's got anything to do with those other six, do you?"

"Nah," Badger said almost disgustedly, "that's not the point. It's just that we're starting to look bad on this case. To a lot of people, this one looks open and shut. Lovers have argument, she tries to give him his ring back, he snaps and somehow kills her and dumps the body, all in two and half hours—just two and half hours, if we can believe the rest of the family. How much and how far can one person go and do in two and half hours? Let's say we believe this part of his story. She can't be that far away. OK, we know now that he never went near Unitarian Church that night. That gives him more time to do directly whatever he did and go that much further to dump the body, if he killed her. We should expand the radius of our search area by, say, at least a half hour, the distance a probably-scared, hard-driving kid could travel in a half hour. She still can't be that far away. We should be able to find her."

"But all that snow!" somebody exclaimed.

"Frig the snow. There was some snow on the ground New Year's Eve, too. He couldn't have gotten too far off any road with the body. Little guy like him, he couldn't have carried her too far. If his old lady gave us the right shoes that he was wearing that night . . ." Badger dwindled off. Suddenly shot a look at Sergeant Poulous. "Gus, what kind of shoes was he wearing that night?"

Poulous started opening his mouth, then suddenly shut it, did a little twist around his chair before getting it open again. "Gosh, Floyd, I don't believe I got any shoes along in the bundle his mother gave me."

"No shoes?"

"No, not that I recollect. When I got back to the station and catalogued them, all there was there was the pants, a shirt, socks, sweater, underwear . . ."

"Go on."

"That's all."

"That's all!" Badger almost shrieked. "No shoes. What about his outerwear, hat, gloves, coat?"

"There . . . ah, wasn't any in the bundle his mother gave me."

"My God! Man, it was fifteen below zero New Year's Eve. The little bastard had to be wearing two, three layers of clothes. Linda was. Look at the list we got on her. There was blood found in the car. Blood, particularly in small amounts like that, would more likely be found on his outerwear than in his shorts, yet nobody here thought to go after his outerwear the minute we found blood in his car?"

"Floyd," Poulous protested, "I got the clothes way back on the third, the same day I seized the car for the Crime Lab. How the hell do I know what they're going to find?"

"Uniform had already found blood, that's why we seized it," Badger acidly pointed out.

"Look, I don't have a search warrant. Uptown is afraid to issue one on what we had. I had to rely on Brown cooperation. What would you tell the mother when she and the boy go in his bedroom and come back out with a bundle? You're lying, these aren't the clothes the kid was wearing New Year's Eve?"

"You could say, shoes? He was wearing shoes, wasn't he, where are the shoes? He ain't Christ himself quite yet, he don't walk on snow fifteen below zero barefooted. In shirtsleeves. Hat? Gloves? Coat? You could ask for them."

"So could you have, Floyd," Sergeant Poulous replied stoutly, looking his slightly superior officer right square in the eye. "Every worksheet I file goes across your desk. Mine and everyone else's."

Badger couldn't deny that. That was one of the reasons he was so angry, probably the primary reason. He should have caught both his men's failure to interview Pastor Johnson sooner and the failure to requisition the set of outerwear that Bill Brown theoretically had worn New Year's Eve. Of course, the latter would probably have mattered little by then, some three days later. Any number of people could have washed or in some way disposed of whatever Bill Brown was wearing that night. For that matter, who knows but Bill and possibly Mrs. Brown or Mr. Brown or both what Bill was wearing? The bundle they gave Poulous could have been the clothes he wore the Fourth of July for all they knew. "Did anybody ever check back to see if anybody outside the family could remember what Bill was wearing New Year's Eve?"

"Give me a little credit, Floyd," Poulous answered acidly. "I checked with the only people known to have seen him, the couple they babysat for, the Hendersons, the couple that went to dinner with the Hendersons, Mrs. Craig. Nobody remembers what he was wearing. Though Mrs. Craig seems to think she remembers him wearing his father's old navy pea jacket, she's not even sure on that for that night, because Bill wore it most all the time."

Badger waved a hand at Poulous by way of apology. "Yeah, probably wouldn't have mattered anyway." He rubbed his hands together briskly, as a rabbit hunter too long carrying a cold shotgun might do to get the circulation going again. "OK. Let's quit crying over spilt milk and see what we can do with this new bottle we got. Atwell, call Mrs. Craig, ask her if she'd like to come down here. Yeah, go ahead, tell her what we got from Pastor Johnson, she deserves to know. Besides, that dame's got a good tough head, maybe she'll come up with something." Turning back to the rest of the detectives in his office, he said, "Jensen, you get on the horn to Knutson, tell him—I mean, ask him, we got to set up an interview with his client, Mr. Billy Ray Brown. Don't tell him what we got new on Billy-boy. Just say there are a few things in Bill's previous statements that we would like to clarify, you know, the usual." Jensen nodded, left for his office. Badger turned to Poulous, said mollifyingly, "Gus, sorry about the clothes. This case has just got me up a wall. I know that little bastard did it, but . . ." Badger spread his hands.

"Don't worry about it, Floyd. I should have pressed them

right then and there for the rest of the clothes, but they all seemed so damned decent about everything, cooperated so willingly about seizing the car and all."

Badger nodded in turn. "Yeah, yeah, that's how they struck me too at first. I should have caught it too when it went across my desk, like you said. Tell you what, let's spend a few more hours on this clothing thing, for what it's worth, see if we can't really find out, from an outside source, what Bill was wearing New Year's Eve. Try the Hendersons again, the other couple they went to dinner with, Mrs. Craig, really try to dig into them to remember what he was wearing."

"That's it, though, Floyd, if he went from the babysitting to his house to watch the rest of the movie like they claim, he could have changed his outerwear then."

"I know, but that's a remote chance we have to take. I think most people dressed for the night would stick with whatever they started out with unless they were changing for something special, more than going to pick up a sister. Check the dry cleaners in their area. Find out what the Browns have brought in since New Year's Eve, anything you can think of. If everything works out, I'd like to come down hard on this guy, hopefully book him. And I'd love to have a jacket with a few AB bloodstains or shoes with who knows what caught up in them wherever."

"OK, Floyd, I'll do my best," Poulous said wearily, trudging out.

Mrs. Craig wasn't surprised they had finally caught Bill Brown in a bald-faced lie, for she had believed he lied all along. Yet she still couldn't allow herself to think in terms of murder. Or any other set of circumstances that culminated in her daughter being dead.

Badger, realizing this, was forced to skate along on the thin slippery ice of mere fact with her too. Just as he couldn't book Bill Brown on what his bones told him, he couldn't very well tell her either. So he merely told her of this latest development, waited for her to voice the possible implication.

She didn't. Badger changed the subject. "Mrs. Craig, we have searched various houses in the Big Falls metropolitan area of late. Any that have anything whatsoever to do with the fringe religious cult groups that we've dug up—obviously, with no result. Other houses were searched in response to so-called tips that have been coming in since your ex-husband and the St. John's Lutheran Church posted the rewards. A press release concerning our activities will be put out—"

Mrs. Craig waved her hand wearily. "You don't have to tell me, Sergeant. I know you're doing your best."

"Obviously, it's not been good enough, ma'am. Therefore, and I feel you agree with me here, our best bet is to continue to concentrate primarily on Bill Brown."

"There's no doubt in my mind."

"Good. That's one of the reasons I asked you to come in. The fact that Bill lied about what was going on in Unitarian Church New Year's Eve means little in itself per se. It must be used in such a way as to lead to something bigger, more direct, something even more damaging to Bill Brown. Particularly now, since our hands are tied considerably by Bill's attorney, we can't slap him with it directly—"

"But if he's guilty," she said plaintively, spreading her hands palms up, "if he's really done something to Linda, can't you just arrest him?"

"No. Not unless we know for sure. Sure, I can physically arrest him, but can I hold him? No. Knutson would have him out in two minutes. We got to figure out some way to use what we got outside his attorney, some way where we might catch him up in some unguarded moment—"

"Sergeant," Mrs. Craig interrupted, "there might be something . . ."

"Yes?" Badger prompted.

"Dr. Russell. I have been talking to our minister, Dr. Russell. He told me that he had been seeing Bill. Maybe if he should start talking to Dr. Russell . . . and maybe I could go down there at the same time and just plain out and out confront him in front of our minister?"

Badger nodded. "Excellent. Yes, that's an excellent idea, Mrs. Craig. Possibly we could use some of his supposed religious beliefs to catch him a little off guard, get him to say something in front of your minister. Of course, I don't think we should say anything about this in advance to your minister. It might put him in a rather compromising position, seeing as how you're all members of the same church. The idea is, to see if this just couldn't all work out sort of, you might say, by itself."

Mrs. Craig nodded. "I'll see what happens."

"Good. In the meantime, on an official level, we'll keep trying to work through his attorney, set up an interview with Bill, try to use his lie about Unitarian Church to the best possible advantage. Incidentally, I don't think you should mention to Bill or anyone else what we have learned."

"Absolutely not."

Mrs. Craig turned to go. Badger felt obliged to say one more thing. "Mrs. Craig."

"Yes?"

"I must remind you of this. If Bill . . . has done something to Linda . . . do not confront him alone. He might come after you too."

Mrs. Craig held up her right hand doubled into a fist. "I hope he does, Sergeant." Her eyes glittered fiercely, fired again now by a desperate hatred. "I lie awake nights wishing he would come over and try something—anything that would let me know for sure."

Badger and Atwell just stood looking at this very proper Southern lady, carefully made-up and groomed, hair piled high in a bouffant style reminiscent of the fifties, striking this incongruous pose. Her entire being vibrated like a rubber band stretched far beyond its designed limits. No one spoke. There was nothing to say. The two men just continued standing respectfully till the lady suddenly turned and walked, stiletto high heels clicking, out Badger's office door.

"Whew," Atwell said, letting out his breath, "in a fair fight, my money's on her."

Badger thought on that a moment, then shrugged. "If Bill's our boy, it wouldn't be a fair fight."

16

After numerous letters and phone* calls back and forth between, first, Attorney Knutson and the Brown family and,
then, Knutson and the LFPD setting up the ground rules, the
partial interview of Bill Brown by the LFPD was conducted at
6:30 P.M. on February 7, 1977, in Knutson's office. It was
considered a partial interview by the LFPD, due to the fact
that written questions had to be submitted by Detectives Atwell and Jensen. They were then answered by Bill Brown with
the advice and consent of his attorney. The officers were not
present in the room where Knutson and his client conferred
over the answers, so it was only assumed that the answers
were written in Bill Brown's hand, though a later comparison
with other Bill Brown hand-writing tended to verify that as-
sumption. After having the questions answered in this manner,
the officers had a short opportunity of approximately two
minutes to talk to Bill Brown in Knutson's presence about the
questions and answers, but only in strict regard to his already
written answers.

At 8:00 the next morning Badger met with Atwell and Jensen to go over the partial interview of Bill Brown. The two
detectives explained to Badger the procedure that was used.

"So what did you ask him, Cliff?" Badger asked Jensen.

Jensen told him, adding that, when he had asked Bill, "By
the main worship area, do you mean the sanctuary such as
your own St. John's Lutheran Church?" Bill had answered,
"Yes." "Then I asked him what floor it was on, and he stated,

'The main floor.' So then I asked him if he had to go down any steps to get to the area, and he stated, 'No.'"

"Good." Badger nodded again. "Good work, boys. We got Billy-boy on that one."

17

The phone rang at the Craig residence. Mrs. Craig snatched it up. It was the call she had been waiting for. "Irene," Reverend Russell said, his carefully modulated voice betraying nothing, "Bill Brown has expressed a desire to speak with you. Will you come?"

"I'll be right down."

She ran out to her car and drove the short distance to the St. John's Lutheran Church in record time. Reverend Russell and Bill were seated in his office talking when she walked in. Both men rose as she entered, Reverend Russell coming to meet her with outstretched arms, taking both her hands in his. She was aware of her hands shaking. Apparently the minister was too, as he warmly gripped her hands tighter as he spoke.

"I'm glad you could come, Irene. Bill was just saying, he's looking forward to speaking with you, see if he can't close some of the distance that has, apparently, grown between you two since Linda's disappearance."

Bill stepped closer as the minister spoke. Now she turned her head so she could look at him. He held her eyes with no apparent effort, but neither spoke.

"Go ahead, just talk to each other," Reverend Russell urged, dropping Irene Craig's hands and stepping out from between the mother and her daughter's fiancé, so they faced each other with only a few feet of empty space intervening. "You can say anything you want to each other."

"Bill," Mrs. Craig heard herself say, "do you really love Linda?"

"Yes," Bill answered softly.

"Then why don't you do more to help?"

"I'm doing everything within my power, Mrs. Craig."

"But why won't you talk to the police? If you say you love her, you must talk to the police, try to help them find her in every way you can, Bill. That's all that matters now, Bill, is finding her."

"Mrs. Craig, they don't really want to talk to me. Just scream and harass me, keep making out like I'm somehow to blame for Linda not being here."

"Are you, Bill?"

"No. No way. That's what I keep trying to tell them, but they just won't listen, just keep screaming and yelling at me, swearing. That Sergeant Badger, he's not even civilized."

"He's just trying to do his job, Bill, find Linda—"

"No! All he wants to do is harass me. They don't even want me to come by the station to try to tell them things about maybe something I could help. All they want to make me do is sign away my rights so they can harass me some more, so I quit going, trying to help. I don't have to be yelled and screamed at, listen to the kind of talk that come out of Sergeant Badger's mouth."

"Bill, don't you see, that doesn't matter. It makes no difference what kind of man you think Sergeant Badger might be, how he talks to you. Bill, you're still here, Linda's been missing for over a month now, thirty-eight days to be exact, every one of them torn from my heart. Every morning when I wake up, I scream for Linda just like I did that first morning. So I try not to even go to sleep so I don't have to wake up, Bill, but that doesn't matter either because I'm still here, you're still here, but Linda isn't!"

"Mrs. Craig . . . I . . ." Bill took a halting step toward her, his mouth working over the words he was trying to say. "I know how you feel, honest I do, I keep trying to see her everywhere too, just like you, just like she was, but I can't see her either, even though I keep looking, just walking to my classes, driving down the road, every once in a while I see a girl that I think is Linda for a few seconds and then she fades away again, it's not her."

A sudden quick silence. Mrs. Craig sucked in a hot dry breath, shook her head sadly. "No, Bill, it's not her. That's why we must continue to try to talk, try to help each other find her. Help the police. Bill, talk to me . . . talk to me . . ."

"I am talking to you, Mrs. Craig."

She moved in a step closer to him. He held his ground. Now they were only a few feet apart. "Really talk to me, Bill. Tell me everything. Anything. Whatever pops in your mind. Like our minister said, Bill, we can say anything to each other. For our Lord's sake, Bill, tell me, where is Linda?"

"I . . . I don't know."

"Bill, we are in God's temple. This is our church. We both belong here. All our families do, Bill." She stepped in another step closer. "Can you say here in our church, God's temple, Christ's home, that you don't know where Linda is?"

Bill held her gaze, his clear blue eyes never wavering. "Yes. No, I don't know where Linda is. I dropped her off just like I keep telling you, everybody. Just pulled in there and walked around and opened the door and she got out and I kissed her good night and she kind of sat down in the snow, more like leaning than sitting, waved good-bye to me, a little smile on her face—"

"Bill! I can't stand it! Don't tell me that again! I didn't hear her come in. You couldn't have dropped her off that night like you say."

"I did. I don't care what you say about that. You don't hear so good anyway, you know that yourself. I dropped her off."

"Bill, I would have heard you. You never brought her home—"

"I dropped her off! And that's final."

This silence was mutual. They had reached some kind of a plateau, mesa in the mountains. Mrs. Craig glanced up, looking for new hand holds. "Alright, Bill, this is getting us nowhere." She tried to smile. "Isn't it something how something like this can make people start to not believe anybody . . . anything. Doubt makes a person start acting differently than they have anytime else in their life, say things, think things. It's getting so I'm not even sure anymore what I know or believe myself. Bill, we both love Linda very much, don't we?"

"Yes."

"We mustn't be at each other's throats. We believe in Christ, God the Father, the Holy Spirit. We are not heathen here to tear each other apart, are we?"

"No. All I've ever wanted to do with my life, Mrs. Craig, is help other people. That's why I was talking to Jon when he was here about maybe someday becoming a missionary when I get out of school."

"Bill, then we must act like Christians now. We must bare our souls. If there is anything evil within us, we must let it come out. Now is not a time to worry about petty things like hurt feelings, being yelled at by the police, even cursed. Now is the time to turn the other cheek, forget about everything but finding Linda. Cooperate with each other and the police—"

"I have been cooperating, Mrs. Craig. Just last night I spent the whole evening answering questions from the police—"

"In writing, Bill. Through your attorney. I've asked you this before, and I'm going to ask you again, Bill, keep asking you, for I don't understand your answer. If you have nothing to hide, why do you need an attorney?"

"It . . . I didn't really want one, Mrs. Craig, it's my father . . . he wanted me to have one."

"Bill, you're an adult now, Bill, twenty-one years old. You can't just continue to hide behind your father. At some point you have to take the responsibility yourself for your conduct."

"I have to obey my father, Mrs. Craig. That's what the Bible says. That's what I've been taught all my life, honor thy father and thy mother, and all should be well here on earth."

Suddenly, Reverend Russell spoke. He had been so quiet, ranged against the far wall, and they had been so caught up in each other and what they were saying, they had literally forgotten his presence in the room. His deep voice rolled like the voice of God. "Bill, you would be honoring your father if you speak the truth. The Father of us all. But if ye know the truth and speak it not, you shall dishonor Him and your father and mother here on earth. Your whole family, generation unto generation. But mostly you, yourself."

There ensued a silence so fraught with fear that Mrs. Craig felt herself trembling. God fear, she felt His presence in the room. Speak now, Bill, speak, roared through her head, carrying her that last step closer to Bill. Speak! Before God damns your mortal soul.

But Bill Ray Brown said nothing. She was so close now she could look deep into his eyes. Blue, they are, another part of her mind whispered through the immortal roaring, blue as my lost baby's.

Her hands leapt out and pinned Bill Brown's arms against his sides in a strangle grip. "Did you kill Linda?"

She could feel his arms swell beneath her grip, his arms turn rock hard. She had never felt mortal flesh feel this way. It scared her as much as the immortal God's presence had moments before.

But Bill Brown's gaze never wavered. The baby-blue eyes never blinked. He just continued staring deep into her eyes.

He answered, simply, calmly, "No."

It was Mrs. Craig who dropped her eyes and turned and fled.

18

FILE: 6–C–77 MP Linda Lou Craig
STATUS: OPEN.

The Investigation: Part 2

19

It was a beautiful, clear, crisp fall day, perfect for pheasant hunting. Nights had been freezing, the temperature dropping into the twenties. This cold snap, coupled with the generally dry summer and fall, had firmed up the low spots and would allow hunting closer in around the lakes than would be normally the case, so Luke Stovall and Sean Flanagan decided to take a day off from Chevrolet and hunt the swamp surrounding Hatch Lake. Too many times in the past they had flushed a pheasant in the thick underbrush adjacent to Hatch, only to have the wily ringneck sneak off into the natural sanctuary provided by the swampgrass bogs surrounding the muck base lake, an area virtually unwalkable except when frozen solid in the dead of winter.

They took Earl's pickup truck. Parked at the north entrance to Hatch Lake on a small access road, intending to skirt the lake to the west and hunt a fifty-square-acre plot to the south of the lake, an area not quite so overgrown with underbrush and containing an open field where pheasants ventured during the day to feed on weed seeds and whatever else suited their craw. After parking the truck, the two men walked south along Division Road, entering the woods at a little cut where, obviously, lovers had parked—beer cans and slightly used rubbers nestled in the tangled marsh grass choking the shallow ditch; here, as along much of Division Road in this area, the swamp extended right up to the roadway. Picking their way carefully through the whippy saplings, sticking to the higher ground as much as possible, jumping over bogs when they had to, they came to a large elm tree growing right in the middle

of a slightly elevated patch of ground, just like a little island in
the swamp.

They were only about a hundred feet in off Division Road.
It was just a little past noon. Sean was walking off to Luke's
right, carrying his sixteen-gauge pump shotgun at ready, scanning the leaf-littered ground for the squatting pheasant—the
bird played dead sometimes till the hunter almost stepped on
it—his finger on the safety. The only thing is, he thought,
how's a man gonna even get his gun up to shoot, thick as this
friggin' brush is—

Sean stopped, freezing himself. He had almost stepped on
something else . . . clothes? Yes, it looked like clothes, sticking up here and there through the fallen leaves. Sean leaned
over and brushed some of the gaily Jack-Frost-painted leaves
off the item of clothing nearest him. It was a coat, he could
see that now. A coat that once must have been blue, with some
kind of fur around the collar, but it was so faded now. Leaning
his shotgun against the huge elm tree and brushing away the
leaves with both hands, Sean soon had the whole set of clothing clearly visible. He sucked in a quick breath, held it. They
laid there just like somebody was still inside them! The coat to
the top, the slacks below the coat, legs spread at the bottom,
shoes at the end of the slack legs, each shoe on the proper
foot. Sean slowly extended his normally fearless hand and
lifted off the coat. A bra fell to one side—

"Luke!"

"Yeah," Luke yelled right back, obviously picking up the
urgency in his partner's voice. "What's up?"

"Come over here—on the double!"

Luke came crashing through the thick underbrush, pulled
up short when he saw what Sean was kneeling before. "My
God!"

"Yeah," Sean agreed, "looks just like somebody was in it."

"Bet your ass!"

The two hunters crouched in place, transfixed by the eerie
sight before them: an entire set of female clothing, laid out
faceup, were the wearer still inside them, feet pointing west,
the head end to the east. The coat was the only piece of apparel that was not being "worn." It had been carefully drawn
over the upper part of the body configuration, as though to
keep the upper torso warm, in its proper place but lying face
down, with the left sleeve tucked inside itself. The sweaters,

one inside the other, were under the coat, their bottom touching the waistband of the slacks. At the end of both slack legs were the corresponding shoes. To the north of where the coat had been, at the end of one coat arm, lay the scarf, bra, and mittens, the bra having "fell out" when Sean lifted the coat. The bra was unclasped, not broken or torn in any way. A small sapling grew up through the scarf. At a level of where the head should be and approximately two feet east, at the end of where the other coat arm had been, was the purse. Just like she was still carrying it in her hand.

"Luke," Sean asked slowly, "do you think there was a body in there once?"

"Yeah," Luke breathed, "looks like it just up and crawled out."

Sean looked some more, than slowly began to shake his head. "There'd be bones."

"Maybe the animals got them—the meat and the bones?"

Sean was still shaking his head. "Naw, they'd'a tore the clothes all up gettin' to 'em. 'Pears to me somebody just brought them clothes out here and laid them out real nice 'n' purty like that."

"Must'a been some time ago—look how that sapling's grown up through the scarf."

"Yeah, this spring at least, maybe way last winter when the swamp was all froze solid through here." As he talked, Sean began to pick the clothing up, looking through it for some kind of clue or other, tossing each examined item in a pile. As he began to lift the slacks, one leg kind of stuck in the dirt. "What's this here now?" he asked, as much to himself as Luke, pulling the intact slack leg free and holding what was left up close to his eyes. Inside the intact slack leg was pantyhose; in the proper location in the crotch was a pair of white cotton panties.

Sean almost angrily flung them in the general direction of the pile. "Let's get out of here. This looks like some kind of warpo-weirdo deal to me."

"Maybe we ought to check the purse, Sean?" the younger Luke said, walking around the pile of clothing to where the purse lay. Picking it up, Luke Stovall opened the large bulky purse, probably once an off-brown, maybe tan, but now darkened by exposure to the rains and subsequent drying sun, soft flexible leather hardening toward brittleness, the corners of the flap turning up. Luke had trouble with the latch. "Jeez, lookit all this stuff, even a Bible." He picked out a wallet, remarkably well preserved within the purse, flipped it open. "Here's a ID card—kinda blurry, but I can still make it out— Linda Lou Craig."

Sean shrugged impatiently, shook his head in quick jerking motion. This whole thing was getting on his nerves. Here he had just come out in the woods to get away from the never-ending assembly line stretching down through the years till the final punchout, they have to come across something like this.

And Luke was still talking. "S'pose we ought to go back out and call the troopers or something?"

Sean forced his civilized mind to consider this, but a much older one answered. "Nah. We'll do it on the way out. There's that little party store in Ghent; we can call from there. I mean, this is costing us. We took a day off to get some pheasant huntin', I mean to get me some!"

Luke Stovall agreed. "Yeah, them clothes been layin' here this long, a few more hours won't make no difference."

Putting the purse in Sean's hunting pouch, the two hunters continued stalking their self-appointed prey. Yet both men had difficulty concentrating on outsmarting the clever bird, a worthy adversary under the best of conditions. In the course of the afternoon both hunters missed shots they normally would have made. Neither could get his mind off the weird way the clothes just lay there, like some girl had just laid down and evaporated into the thin, cold, autumnal air.

Luke Stovall's mind was on the Bible he had found in the purse. She musta been a good girl though, or she wouldn't't'a come carrying her Bible along . . . 'course, she could'a just come right out here from church. But . . . just wiggled out of her clothes, just up and left them there!

Sean Mathew Flanagan kept seeing the clothes, the eerie way they were laid out when first he stumbled over them, just so, like she was on her back, her legs spread. He shuddered again, a quick flash of disgust burned his already weather-rosed cheeks, squeezed his good Irish Catholic heart, his thoughts leavened by centuries of both: A wee lass laid out for fornication. Perhaps some filthy bastard comes crawling in the night to fornicate them clothes.

Stopping, taking the pressuring purse out of his hunting pouch, Sean looked through the faded identification cards again. "Linda Lou Craig" he read slowly aloud, his lips moving with the words, "1402 Drake St., Little Falls, Wisconsin. Luke!" he suddenly yelled.

"Yow" came back his partner's startled cry.

"Luke," Sean continued in a relatively normal tone when Luke hove into view, "seems to me I've heard that Linda Lou Craig name someplace before."

"You know," Luke panted—he had come through the waist-high sawgrass on the double, cutting across the open field they had been sweeping at the sound end of Hatch Lake, halfway fearing Sean had stumbled over something even worse—"me too. I been saying that name over and over in my mind, Linda Lou Craig, Linda Lou Craig—"

"Let's get outta here," Sean said suddenly, jamming the purse back down in his hunting pouch atop the one pheasant he had managed to wingshoot, its blood flecking the overlap cover of the omnipresent purse. "This damn thing's startin' to weigh a ton."

Burning rubber till they got to Ghent, Luke and Sean went into Bartalotta's Party Store where Luke made a call to the Wisconsin State Police from the pay phone. The store owner, Al Bartalotta, overhearing Luke's end of the conversation and realizing its implication, called the Ghent Township Police Department from his personal phone behind the counter and told Officer Orin Lee what the two hunters had found. Officer Lee was at the store within minutes and commandeered the purse. Ascertaining that it appeared indeed to be the purse of Linda Lou Craig, the girl missing from Little Falls since January 1, he contacted Ghent Township dispatch and requested that they contact Little Falls police to inform them of the find and suggest that they meet him, Officer Lee, and the two hunters at Ghent Township Hall.

Ironically, Sergeant—now Lieutenant—Badger and the two factory workers from Chevrolet had been hunting only about two miles apart as the crow flies this beautiful Indian Summer day. Now, late afternoon, Badger was hiking across a freshly picked cornfield, watching his Irish setter, Shamus, work the cornpicker-battered stalks in a tail-wagging figure 8 about thirty yards in front of him. His shotgun was at chest-ready, but he was reveling as much in the pure, crisp autumn air and fresh clean dirt beneath his Wolverine hunting boots as the prospect of downing a pheasant. The pale bronze of the sun-bleached stalks gleamed against the encircling vermilion and yellow of the sugar maple forest that ringed the cornfield, all washed eye-dazzling bright by the sun setting out of a high azure-blue October sky.

October 20, 1977, 4:30 in the afternoon—the tiny radio receiver hooked on his belt beeped, and Badger reached down and switched it on. "Lieutenant." The tense voice of Officer Dinato came loud and clear. "Some pheasant hunters found Linda Lou Craig's clothes out in the swamp the other side of Ghent."

"How do they know they're Linda's?" Badger answered, bringing the two-way up to his mouth and pressing the transmit button, his mind automatically jerking back from paradisiacal meandering to the exactness of his other real life.

"They found her purse too—ID, everything."

"Everything?"

Dinato knew what Badger meant. "Everything but the body." Then Dinato said what Badger was already thinking. "But maybe her body is close by."

Badger could feel his skin start to crawl, the old familiar goose prickles work up along the back of his neck, the way they always did when he felt that he was about to move in for the kill. "Don't do a damn thing till I get there. Who knows about it so far?"

"Just the Ghent Township PD. State Police—"

"Hell! Dinato, where you at?"

"In my patrol car, heading toward you."

"Get on your horn. Call back to Ghent, the WSP. Tell them under no circumstances to put out anything to anybody till I get there. Nobody. I don't care if the governor calls. Tell them to keep them hunters right there till I get there, don't let them talk to anybody. Call Chief Mackey and request a surveillance on Bill Brown. I'm on my way."

"Lieutenant," Dinato said quickly, "they're at the Ghent Township Hall, near Sand Lake. Do you know how to get there?"

"Shit, I should, I grew up out there."

Switching off Dinato, Badger whistled for Shamus, who stood looking disgustedly back at his master—darn it all, the dog's soft brown eyes seemed to say, can't you ever leave that stupid thing to home?—and started on a dead run across the cornfield to where his car was parked on the rutted farm road. Damn, if that don't take all, he said over and over to himself as he ran crashing through the shredded waist-high stalks, if that don't take all. Finding her right up here where I grew up.

By the time Badger got to Ghent Township Hall, it was almost full. Chief Dick Mackey had raced up from Little Falls to take personal charge of his contingent, and Chief John Van Buren had come in from his home to command Ghent Township in what could very well be the first major break in the baffling disappearance of Linda Lou Craig ten months and twenty days ago, not to mention the six other homicides still open in his files. Jammed in with the steadily growing police ranks were the two hunters, Flanagan and Stovall. Chief Mackey deferred to his chief of detectives in the questioning of the two hunters. After gaining what information they had, particularly as to the peculiarly arranged clothing, it was agreed by all officers assembled that the Wisconsin State Police should be called in too. Their extensive manpower and statewide resources would very likely be needed for what was starting to take shape as a master plan. Calling WSP dispatch, Station Number 11, Badger advised them of what had been found near Hatch Lake. They in turn advised Badger that they would send Detective Sergeant Dave Baldwin of their Detective Bureau immediately.

An aura of barely concealed excitement and anticipation fairly crackled through the crowded room. Though no one said as much, the gut feeling was that they could very well be close to finally cracking through, on Linda Lou Craig, at least. The Ghent Township contingent was further hopeful, now that the Little Falls girl's belongings had also been found in the general area where the other bodies had been found the previous year, that this new discovery might end up shedding some light on those six victims, too.

Parceling out their available manpower, it was decided that one of the hunters, Luke Stovall, should guide Chief Mackey and Dinato to the site, there to secure the find and stand by for the arrival of the rest. Lieutenant Forseth was to return to LFPD and make sure that no word of the find leaked from that source, no matter who inquired, and handle communications there. Lieutenant Badger was to go to the corner of Division and State Roads to rendezvous with the en route Baldwin, taking the other hunter, Sean Flanagan, along to guide them into the site after Baldwin arrived. Chief Van Buren would remain at his Ghent Township police station with dispatch, to monitor communications at his end. After Detective Sergeant Baldwin arrived, they proceeded to the clothing site where the others waited. Once there, the two hunters carefully explained how the clothing had been laid out when first Sean stumbled upon it. "They weren't like this when I run up on them, let me tell you," Sean said, indicating the pile with a hooked thumb. "I didn't know no better. I just picked them up to see what all was there, then threw them in a pile like you see now."

"Is it your opinion," Badger asked, "that somebody could have just thrown the clothes down and they landed the way you found them?"

Both hunters were already shaking their heads negatively before Badger finished his question. "No way," Sean answered, speaking for both. "Them clothes were laid out neat, like I been telling you. Not in a hundred years could somebody just throw them down and they would land that way. Not just like a person just up and crawled out of them."

Badger turned to Dinato. "Can you draw, Dinato?"

"Draw, sir?"

"Yeah, like stick men?"

"Oh, draw—about that good."

"Good. Stick tight with these hunters, have them lay the clothes back out as close as they can remember, draw a diagram of what they show you. But first take a few pictures of what we have now, then some after they rearrange them, plus your diagram."

"Yes, sir."

Chief Mackey, Lieutenant Badger and WSP Detective Sergeant Baldwin huddled. "They're Linda's clothes alright," Badger said grimly, "match exactly with what we got listed."

"You say you got a suspect in this case, Lieutenant?" Baldwin asked.

"Yeah, the boyfriend."

"He some kind of a weirdo?" Baldwin asked bluntly.

Badger thought on that, finally shook his head wonderingly. "I didn't think so. At least, not till a few minutes ago."

"Where do we go from here, Floyd?" Chief Mackey asked, glancing at the sky, day-end gloom already starting to settle here in the shadow of the giant elm tree. "Seems to me it's getting a little late to start a search for the remains this evening."

Badger thought a moment on that too, watching as the clothing pile fast became an eerie outline of a young girl under the rearranging hands of the two hunters. The lowering light seemed to slide down into the garments, fill them up, give them the illusion of weight and substance, flesh them out. Badger shut his eyes and opened them quick. For a moment he had almost thought she was lying there in the gaily colored leaves, so soothing to him just a short hour or so before. It seemed like forever ago now—he thought, I'll never see Jack Frost leaves again without seeing those clothes lying in them. Blinking his eyes quickly again, the faded orange and red plaid of the slacks seemed to meld right into the Indian Summer leaves, become part of the whole. "Let's stake out her clothes tonight," he said slowly. "Sit up in this big tree here, just like we're bow-huntin' deer, see if a buck comes sniffin' around."

Chief Mackey and Detective Sergeant Baldwin threw him a quick look, almost like they thought he might be kidding. Deciding he wasn't, they agreed. "Good idea, Floyd," Chief Mackey said, "but with the surveillance on Brown, who we going to use for men?"

"Brown, that the suspect?" Baldwin asked.

"Yeah," Badger grunted, "but we're a little short of manpower to do both."

"You got it," Baldwin said quickly. "I'll put some of my men on him. Just tell me where and how many."

"Thanks," Badger said, getting what he had hoped for. "But first we got to bait the trap a little."

"I got an idea," Baldwin put in, warming to Badger's idea. "What say we put out a phony press release? Don't mention the clothes at all. Just say we found the purse of your girl somewhere away from here, say near a residential street in Ghent for instance, so we don't scare off this suspect of yours or whoever might be coming out here to jive on them clothes."

"You think that's why they were laid out this way?" Chief Mackey asked the sophisticated-sounding Baldwin, now compounding his image by taking a corncob pipe out of his tweed jacket and lighting up.

"If the guy's a looney. Whatever, somebody laid them out

that way for some reason, the very least to make believe that she isn't really dead, just lying there taking a little snooze, waiting for him to come rescue her or some weirdo thing like that."

Badger liked Baldwin's thinking, about a lot of things. "I say the phony press release is a good idea. We name a specific street, maybe the Ghent boys can even watch the location too. The guy might think if the purse got moved, the clothes might have too. But I think the first place he'll come running is to see if the clothes are still here, safe. He's gotta care about them, the careful way he laid them out, spread the coat over the top part to keep her . . . ah, I mean, the clothes, protected."

Turning to Chief Mackey, Badger regressed momentarily to New Year's Eve. "You know, Chief, how I always kept harping about how I never could quite figure how one guy could kill her and dispose of her body so well we've never been able to find it in almost eleven months with half the world looking, all in two and a half hours? Add this," he continued, sweeping a shotgun callused mitt at the clothing now completely laid back out under the big elm, the tricky half-light of October dusk slightly propping the upper torso against the base of the tree. "The middle of the night, fifteen below zero, the wind pounding icicles up your ass, he leaves home at 11:30 according to the folks, kills her, drives out here in the middle of nowhere, parks, takes her clothes off, carries them in here through blowing snow and brush thick as hair on a dog, lays the clothes out nice and pretty like the boys got them now, all in pitch dark! Then, unless we find the body right close by, he runs back to the car, drives somewhere else, does God knows what with the body, drives back home, walks in, says 'Hi Mom, how about a baloney sandwich,' all in two and a half hours."

Chief Mackey and Sergeant Baldwin couldn't help but chuckle at the fiery Badger outburst. "Maybe your guy's twins," Baldwin ventured, "Superman III."

"Superman, my ass," Badger growled. "I say he had more than two and a half hours—or some help! If he didn't bring these clothes out here New Year's Eve, when did he? We got to his car the very next day. He was either at the Craigs or someplace my men could lay their hands on him all the next day, from 7:00 A.M. on. We don't think his car was moved. So what did he do with the clothes? Take them in the house? Say,

look Ma, here's the clothes Linda was wearing tonight. I just
thought I'd bring them home with me."

"Floyd," Chief Mackey said soothingly, laying a restrain-
ing hand on Badger's red hunting-jacketed arm, "there's no
point in going over that now. The main thing now is to move
on what we got."

"Yes," Baldwin agreed, as much to get Badger back on the
current track as anything. "If it don't fit, maybe you got the
wrong shoe. It happens sometimes; I ought to know."

"I got the right guy alright," Badger growled. "It's just
that, with him, it's always like trying to pound square pegs in
round holes." Spitting his Skoal into the leaves off to one
side, he got back on track. "OK, it's 5:35. We put out the
phony news release tonight. If we hurry and call it in right
now, we can break it as a bulletin on the six o'clock TV news.
It'll be on the radio all night, television again at eleven, early
morning papers. Your guys sit on Bill Brown, me and my
boys will be up the tree, the Ghent boys on the residential
street where we say the purse was found."

"Floyd, somebody must notify Mrs. Craig before we release the story," Chief Mackey reminded.

"You betcha," Badger agreed. "You handle that, if you
will, Chief. Call dispatch right now, have Atwell and Jensen
do it. They've been working real close with her all along,
particularly Jensen. Have them go out to her house and break
it to her in person, tell her what we've found—just purse and
clothes, Chief, but not how the clothes were laid out, that's a
bit much right off the bat." Badger had up a head of steam
now and was on a roll. "Maybe I'll see what she's got to say
on that later. But, for Chrissakes, Chief, tell them to tell her
not to tell nobody nothing. Not even her other daughter."

Chief Mackey nodded, walked out to Division Road, got
on his police radio back to Little Falls.

"OK," Baldwin asked, "what are the logistics? When do
we get started? How many men do you want from me?"

"Soon as we break the news release, be set up when we do,
however many men you think. Dinato," Badger called, turning to the hovering Dinato, "you stay here. Don't take your
eyes off those clothes. We'll send Atwell out later to spell
you."

"You really want me up that tree, Lieutenant?" Dinato
asked, eyeing the huge elm, twenty or so feet to the first

branch. "How do I get down to arrest him if he does show up?"

"You don't arrest a buck, Chuck, you shoot him right between the shoulder blades."

Dinato kind of knew Badger was kidding; then again, he wasn't too sure. "If he does show up, you want us to use force . . . to take him?"

Badger nodded grimly. "Take him. However you have to. But first make sure it's him. Shine a light in his face. Have your five-cell with you. Put the light in his face, your gun in your other hand. If you have to do it, don't hesitate. Remember, whoever shows up out here is a murderer."

Dinato shivered in spite of himself. This night was going to be a long way from patrolling University Avenue. Chief Mackey had returned in time to hear the last. "You that sure on Brown, Floyd?"

"Unless I spent seventeen years in this racket for nothing, Chief."

"But we never figured Brown before for a . . . ah, 'weirdo,'" Chief Mackey persisted, first using Baldwin's word then switching to one thought in some circles to be more scientifically correct. "Not a psycho. You always told me you thought this was just a passion murder, though a little cleverer than most."

Badger backtracked a hair, but just a short one. "Who knows what to think of Brown. But I still think it's him. Maybe not a total warpo. I kind of go along with what Baldwin here said, some guy who doesn't want to believe his girl's really dead, so he fixes up her clothes to make like she's still alive. A little easier on the conscience, if the bastard's got one." Half turning to Dinato again, he continued, "But, however, whoever, laid them clothes out like that, you better believe he murdered the person who was in them."

Baldwin nodded. "Just from what he's told me so far, I got to go along with Badger on that. The news release we're putting out, the only guy showing up here will be the guy who placed the clothes here. And if you even think a guy's murdered once, you want to make damn sure you don't give him the opportunity again."

"Certainly, I go along with that," Chief Mackey said rather testily. "I've been in this business probably longer than you two put together. I just want to make damn sure if we catch anybody in this trap, and we treat him like a murderer, he is that. Remember, we haven't found a body yet. So, let's get on with it."

Properly cautioned, Badger turned again to Patrolman Dinato, all ears throughout this privileged colloquy between the grizzled murder-and-mayhem veterans. "OK, just watch your step. One of you stick real close to the clothes, up the tree, behind it, over there in the brush, I don't care where, so long as you can almost reach out and touch him if he shows. The other guy, Atwell, when he gets here, tell him I said to stay out by the road. The killer will undoubtedly come by car, probably park it out there on that little lover's cut where all the beer cans and condoms are. Tell Atwell to sneak over and slap a boot on one of the wheels, whatever, disable the car, the minute the guy starts back in the brush toward you."

"What shall we do with our cars, Lieutenant?" Dinato asked. It was already starting to get more than a little chilly, the sun sliding out of sight to the west. The stupid shiver twitched along his spine again.

"You won't have one," Badger answered brusquely. "We're taking yours. We'll send food, coffee, extra clothes, blankets, out with Sambo. Tell him to park his car out of sight on the Hatch Lake access road."

"Hello, what's this," Baldwin suddenly said softly. He had turned away while Badger was detailing Dinato, was bending over the clothing, had lifted the coat to take a closer look at the "upper torso," was peering at the outermost sweater. The sun, setting as it was, had slid low enough under the elm's canopy to cut through the brush tops and cast a ray directly on the "body."

"What do you see?" Badger asked, turning and taking the step to range alongside Baldwin.

"Looks like a stain. See this, now when the sun hits this sweater . . . this purple area?"

Badger bent over further. "Yeah. By God, I do."

Baldwin lifted the sweater—sweaters, actually, there were two, one blue turtleneck, the other a gray crewneck, one inside the other. Baldwin held the sweaters up directly into the dust-mottled ray of sunlight; now it fell full force upon the front of the sweater. There was no doubt about it, a fairly large section of the sweater, roughly over the heart area if the sweater was being worn, was discolored by a jagged-edged purple stain.

"You think it's blood?" Badger asked.

"Hard to say. There are no holes or other rents or markings that might indicate shooting or stabbing." Baldwin straightened, still holding the sweater. "You know what I suggest. It's too risky leaving these clothes out here, too much evidence. I think we ought to take them now."

"I'll go along with that," Badger agreed, hesitating only momentarily. "If he comes close enough to see if they're here or not, we should take him anyway."

They got no argument from Chief Mackey; naturally cautious, he had been thinking that all along. Baldwin picked up the clothing and placed them in a black plastic bag, noting each article on a clipboard as he did. Moving quickly now, Badger got on his radio and called Little Falls dispatch and gave them his various instructions to pass on to those concerned. After securing the clothing, Baldwin did likewise, detailing four men of his Intelligence Squad to pick up an immediate surveillance on one Bill Ray Brown at his residence at 1546 Fauntleroy Lane and continue it until further notice. Acquainting Chief Van Buren of Ghent Township with their plan, it was agreed that the news release should state that the positively identified purse of Linda Lou Craig had been located by his department on a residential street, Hope, in Ghent. It was further to be released to the media that the purse had been at that location for what appeared to be an extended period of time. This done, and ascertaining by radio that Atwell and Jensen had completed the personal contact with Mrs. Irene Craig and had gained her compliance to the plan, the phony news release was issued through Lieutenant Forseth at LFPD to all media. Just in time to break as a bulletin near the end of the 6:00 to 6:30 news.

Leaving Dinato to his lonely vigil, the rest went about their own business. For Badger and Baldwin, it was a quick sandwich and a bottle of beer at a country roadhouse called The Crossroads Tavern. "OK," Baldwin said through a mouthful of roast beef, "we keep the surveillance on both places till 9:00 tomorrow morning, then we go in with the tracking dogs from our canine division. If they don't find her, we call in the Citizen's Community Radio Watch search team and do a shoulder to shoulder search of the whole Hatch Lake area, concentrating primarily on the east side of the lake where we found the clothes. If that doesn't work out, we call in our underwater people and crawl right through that lake."

"Sounds good," Badger agreed readily. The longer he spent with Baldwin, the better he liked the man. Of course, it was one thing to make the kind of snap decision Baldwin made with the power and resources of the WSP behind you, another when all you had was the LFPD.

"Another thing," Baldwin continued, chewing away, "I've been thinking about the way her clothes were laid out, that purple stain on the sweater. We got a guy, Detective Sergeant Ralph Ravey in Sex. MO, kind of our resident shrink on weirdos and their actions. I got him on the radio on the way over here from the site, told him what we found, how the clothes were laid out and all . . ." Baldwin paused, laid down his sandwich. "It's his opinion that the body will probably be found within a half mile of the clothing. That, possibly, what should have been the head of the body in the clothing will point to the location of the actual body." Baldwin spoke carefully now, picking his words. Gone was the breezy casualness he had displayed before; now he was allowing the well-educated, highly trained detective to show through. "Ravey further commented that, in cases like this, it is unusual for the killer to lay the clothing and the body out in the exact same position. And that any damage caused to the clothing may be an indication of how the victim was actually killed."

Badger was listening as carefully as Baldwin was talking. "The purple stain?"

"Yes. I'll get the clothes to the Crime Lab as soon as possible. We'll find out what it is. But Ravey says it doesn't matter what it is, short of it actually being blood—and I didn't find any rents or holes in the sweater, remember?"

"Yeah."

"Ravey says, and I concur, that a fake bloodstain on a victim's clothing is not unusual either and may be placed there by the perpetrator to indicate the manner in which the victim was killed—in this case, either stabbing or shooting in the chest area, causing bleeding."

Badger took the last sip out of his beer bottle, sat the empty down on the bar. "You trying to tell me something, Dave?"

"Yes, for what it's worth. I think you're dealing with a weirdo here. Some psychosexual nut. So if your current suspect, this Brown kid, doesn't fill the bill, maybe you ought to start looking elsewhere."

Badger sat there digesting this, along with the last bite of his hot pepper and sauerkraut sandwich, the whole mess starting to swell sour in his stomach. Finally he nodded his head slowly. "Maybe you're right. Maybe—but I doubt it."

Baldwin grinned, got up to go. "See you in the morning."

"Hopefully before . . . if he steps in our trap."

Baldwin nodded, but he didn't look too hopeful. Lingering, he seemed to want to say something more, then said it. "How weird is this Brown?"

Badger had to say this. "Seems straight as an arrow."

Baldwin nodded thoughtfully. "Good. Those are the ones you want to watch the closest."

Badger swiveled his bar stool a few degrees more, looked Baldwin straight in the eye. "I am. Very close. For almost eleven months."

"I'm sure you are," Baldwin said lightly, then grinned quickly. "See you in the morning. Hopefully before."

"Right."

Badger dawdled a minute over a cigarette, ordered a cup of black coffee, wanted to be alone, let his mind slide back into the woods—not the woods he just came from, but the pretty Jack Frost forest that surrounded the cornfield he had been hunting when the call came.

It didn't work. What was Baldwin really trying to say? That maybe this case might be too big for the LFPD? Him?

"No way," he muttered half aloud, unconsciously using one of Bill Brown's favorite expressions, very likely one that he had equally unconsciously picked up from Bill during their various encounters in the flesh or on paper over the past eleven months. "No way." Billy Brown was his baby. He knew it in his bones. Nobody was going to get this one away from him. Or convince him that Brown hadn't killed Linda.

His brow crinkling, Badger had to examine these thoughts again. Who had said anything about trying to take this case or Brown away from him?

Badger dropped the smoldering butt in the acid black coffee, sniffed: Who'd want either of them?

Dinato lay belly flat in a small leaf-filled depression a few feet to the left of the base of the huge elm, facing the clothing site about ten feet away. Atwell had covered him with wool police-issue blankets and layered leaves over all. What had shortly before been a slight depression, probably the rotted out stump of the elm's mother, was now just another six-foot-plus-long hump among many comprising the generally uneven terrain. Lying flat on his belly, his gloved hands extended before him, a five-cell flashlight in one, his .38 Police special in the other, he was totally covered, the blankets and leaves carefully arranged in a cowl around his head. He, in effect, peered out through a little leafy archway; he could see and not be seen. There was no way an intruder could know he was there, unless he came up from behind or to either side and inadvertently stepped on him. Not that he would move if somebody did, Dinato vowed to himself. He would just steel his muscles and let the bastard think he was a log.

Not that it was very likely that anybody would walk up on him from any angle other than the one his vision commanded —what little he could see. It was dark by now, and there would be very little light here in the deep woods till the moon rose higher and could penetrate the leafy canopy. He had chosen this vantage point so he could look past the clothing site toward Division Road, the only plausible entry for any human. To the east was Hatch Lake, to the south boggy swamp, to the west acres and acres of swamp and doghair-thick brushy woods. And guarding the other end of this theoretical field of vision was Corporal—now Sergeant—Atwell, sitting huddled in blankets behind a log fallen across the ditch close by the lover's cut so he could "see" up Division Road for approximately 300 yards, until the road curved. The plan was that, if a car pulled up and parked and its occupant entered the woods, Atwell was to slip out of his nest, secure the car, then wait. If Dinato was unable to subdue, the person would undoubtedly run back out the way he came, back to his car, and Atwell would be waiting.

It didn't take long before Dinato realized that he would have to rely on hearing an approach. The night of October 20 began black as the inside of Hitler's heart, as Badger liked to say. Dinato lay there, straining every molecule of ear he owned. Surely he would be able to hear the approach of a car up Division Road; it was only 100 feet or so away. Possibly he would even see the car lights through the brush; that is, unless the killer came in with his lights off, just idling along. The

way Dinato was covered, he probably wouldn't be able to hear
a car just idling along. He would have to rely on hearing him
walking through the brush, when he got closer, his feet moving through the dry leaves—

What was that? It sounded like somebody coming through
the brush! But not from the way he was supposed to, from
Division Road. These sounds were coming from off to the
left, out of the woods.

Dinato lay there, trying not to breathe loud, straining his
ears till it felt like his head was about to pop, finally realizing
it was because he was holding his breath. He let it out and felt
better. Could hear better too, now that the buzzing inside his
head had stopped. There it was again!

Now it stopped. The sound stopped. No longer coming
through the brush, carefully bending saplings, occasionally
popping over a dry one—but now it started again. Now he
could hear the leaves actually rustling underfoot, he was that
close. The rustling-leaves sound seemed all around him.
Everywhere. Then he realized Brown was so close it just
seemed like the sound was all around him. The sound of the
stiff, dry, crackling, rustling leaves was so close it was rever-
berating within the leafy cowl that surrounded his head. A
hand was reaching down inside the leafy cowl—

Dinato froze. The modishly long razorcut hair on the back
of his head literally rose. It seemed like he could literally feel
it rise up and wave around frantically. Then the electric current shot from the back of his head down his neck up his arms.
He had trouble holding them still. He wanted desperately to
lift them and wave them around, anything. It took every ounce
of willpower he had to hold them stock still. The grip on his
flashlight and revolver becoming agonizing, his fingers were
aching.

The fingers touched his revolver hand. God help him, they
were brushing along his arm—"Yeaouuuu!"

He couldn't help it. The long, low, strangulated scream
tore through his gritted teeth; his squeezing fingers inadvertently pressured the flashlight on. It shone harmlessly into the
leaves his arms were buried in. There the little bastard sat,
grinning at him.

A mouse.

"What the hell am I doing here?" Dinato asked the light-
frozen mouse. "I'm a street kid!"

*　*　*

Along toward morning, dawn just cracking, Atwell had an even bigger scare, for his was human.

His eyes burning from the long night of staring up at the shadowy ribbon of moonlit asphalt, his muscles aching with cold and fatigue, he must have dozed off for a moment. Actually, it didn't even seem like he did, but he felt he must have, or how else could another have come up behind him close enough to grab him by the shoulders from behind?

Atwell damn near fainted. Had this other not held him with a grip that prevented it, he would have whirled and shot him. That is, if he wasn't too paralyzed to move.

"Don't move," the voice hissed in his ear. "It's me, Badger."

"My God," Atwell finally whispered back. "You scared the shit out of me."

"Sorry. But I didn't want to make any noise if something was on," the voice said in his ear.

Atwell, still not completely recovered but more pissed than scared by now, twisted half around to whisper into Badger's face looming over him in that phony first light of dawn, "What the shit, you some kind of Indian! How the hell can you prowl around out here in the dark, a man can't even hear you."

Atwell thought he saw Badger grin, that tight little half-grin of his, just one corner of his mouth jerking sideways. "Maybe I am half Indian. I was born in a cabin just up the road a piece."

The three Little Falls officers, two city boys and one good ole country boy, kept watch together until Baldwin and the tracking-dog contingent arrived at 9:00 A.M., but no other human, normal or otherwise, showed up.

The four-man WSP surveillance unit tailing Bill Brown and staking out his home could report nothing of value. Bill spent the evening at a movie with his new girlfriend, Sarah Fortunato. Then, returning to his parents' home, he parked his car, entered, and remained within those premises overnight.

20

Hatch Lake is a "no bottom" muck base lake approximately eighty acres in size, the water about three to five feet deep, extending then into muck God only knows how deep, one of many similar lakes comprising what is generally known as the Sand Lake area. Linda Lou Craig's purse and clothing were found forty yards to the east of Division Road and a quarter of a mile south of the Hatch Lake access road. Division Road runs north and south; Hatch Lake runs to the east off Division Road. There are houses along the south end of the lake and on the extreme northernmost end; on Division Road there are houses 200 yards north of the "lover's cut" leading into the clothing site, about the same distance south.

As promised, Detective Sergeant Baldwin and Trooper Hester from the Canine Division showed up at 9:00 A.M. with a tracking dog, Longtooth. First inspecting the "lover's cut" area, Longtooth took them directly into the clothing site. Obviously, he was merely following the many feet that had tramped in and out since the clothing was discovered, already beating down a clearly defined trail. From there, after sniffing the clothing site thoroughly—Trooper Hester said it was probably just habit; the dog certainly couldn't pick scent off clothing unworn for quite probably eleven months—Longtooth plunged into the woods. For four hours he worked himself and his followers, handler Hester, Baldwin, Badger, and Atwell, into jelly-kneed submission with no apparent results.

"You best call it a day, Sambo," Badger told Atwell when they finally got back out to Division Road again about 12:30. "You haven't slept since night before last."

170

"I'll stick it out," Atwell replied. "I want to be here if we find her."

At approximately 1:00 P.M., Baldwin called in the Community Radio Watch, the group of sixty to seventy local CB operators who had banded together to form a voluntary search team. They showed up some forty-eight individuals strong. Not expecting them all to individually find their way into remote Division Road, Tucker had arranged to meet them in the parking lot of Gohl's Grocery Store on US 49, where he briefed them as to the situation and his needs. After the briefing, the group was directed to the clothing site where Gene Moe of Civil Defense, also donating his time and expertise, set up a communication truck command post at Lover's Cut, as the debris-strewn cutout on Division Road automatically became designated.

They searched till dark. Badger, Baldwin, and Atwell joined ranks with the forty-eight CB volunteers and shoulder to shoulder, when they weren't on their hands and knees, the fifty-one men and women fought their way through the treacherous muck and slime encrusted swamp that surrounded Hatch Lake, not giving up until they had made the complete circuit of the lake and reassembled at command post Lover's Cut.

They were back on the search again early the next morning. The volunteer CB personnel were forty-five strong this day, three too sick and sore to "go it again." But their numbers were replaced by every man the LFPD could safely spare, five who had volunteered to "help find Linda." Her discovery had become a virtual mission with many of the Little Falls officers, most of whom, by now, had come to know Mrs. Craig personally through their part in the investigation or her innumerable trips to the station in her own unrelenting search. They had come to know her and respect her dogged efforts, to know her and pity her, as they watched her grow thin and wan as winter melted into spring into summer into fall, the grief lines in her face clearly etched. Many thought if they didn't find Linda soon, Mrs. Craig would collapse.

Conversely, as their care and admiration for Mrs. Craig grew, so did their hatred of Bill Brown. Guilty or not— though most thought he was—Bill Brown became the focus for many of their daily frustrations, whether related to the Linda Lou Craig disappearance or not. To see him tooling around town with his new girlfriend in his chocolate brown

Chevrolet Impala scot-free, strolling around campus to and from his classes, seated piously between his parents every Sunday morning in church, drove Badger and many of the LFPD up the wall. Whether Bill Brown realized it or not, he was under more than occasional surveillance the rest of that spring and, when he returned from a summer's employment as a youth minister at St. Paul's Lutheran Church up at Ogdensburg, again that fall. Sometimes the surveillance was official, when things were slow and Badger could spare a man or two or a little something came up that even halfway seemed to warrant it, but more often than not it was just one of the patrol cars picking him up as he pulled through an intersection and surreptitiously shadowing him for an hour or two, inobtrusively parking a few houses up or down from his parents' home on Fauntleroy to see just where and when he came and went. Other times it was just "running into him" at the supermarket or Old Dam Shopping Mall, checking to see what he was buying these days, tailing him back home or over to campus. They "just knew the little bastard had done 'it'!"

But this day, October 22, 1977, their loathing of Bill Brown was only a subconscious goad to Badger and the rest of the searchers. Their overwhelming motivation was simply to find Linda Lou Craig. Lining up on a north-south axis along Division Road, the assembled fifty-two officers and citizens made another shoulder-to-shoulder search of the woods, continuing to approximately seventy-five yards east of the clothing site. This producing negative results, they reassembled and made an east-west search of the wooded area across Division Road from Lover's Cut. This also availed nothing.

By now it was fast approaching dusk. Over fifty people and a tracking dog had searched for two solid days over and through some of the toughest terrain in Central Wisconsin and found nothing.

Sergeant Fernando Lopez, coordinator of the WSP Diving Squad, and Lieutenant Julien Mork of Helicopter Search and Rescue overflew the Hatch Lake area, paying particular attention to the far western shore of the lake. Hovering low, Sergeant Lopez slipped into his diving gear and dropped into the water, secured by a lifeline to the helicopter. Upon examining the bottom of the shallows of the lake, Lopez advised that the

only way to adequately search the lake would be in hipboots
with rakes.

This being impracticable if not impossible, Badger and
Baldwin then met with Jack Jones, supervisor of the Sand
Lake Department of Wild Life Research, who furnished them
with a motorboat behind which Lopez and five of his divers
fanned out on towropes and were slowly dragged around and
around the lake, feeling through the murky muck bottom for a
body with their hands and feet. Close in around the edges of
the lake even this was impossible as the water was so shallow
and the muck so thick that if a towline snapped a diver might
likely be lost. With his equipment added to his weight, he
might not be able to surface. But, brave as underwater divers
have to be, they kept at it, working in as close to the shoreline
as physically possible, until the muck was so treacherous that
it was even becoming dangerous getting the divers in and out
of the lake.

All for naught.

They decided to try to call the National Guard in. The
eastern side of Hatch Lake was just too large an area for the
volunteer group and law enforcement personnel at either
Badger's or Baldwin's disposal. Later that afternoon, Badger
had Big Falls Police Helicopter Unit 1 fly over that area to
photograph it prior to the proposed National Guard search.
These aerial photographs would then be enlarged in hopes of
their being shown to the National Guard to formulate a proper
search pattern for the area.

The clothing of Linda Lou Craig, minus the shoes, was
taken to the WSP Crime Lab by Baldwin and presented to
Rollie Nehring. Nehring lifted the two sweaters from the black
plastic bag Baldwin had placed them in on that evening when
they were first found, holding them up by the shoulders so
they hung full length. They were still one inside the other, the
blue turtleneck outermost, the gray crewneck inside, the arms
inside the body of both, just as they had been when Badger
and Baldwin had first viewed them in the pile under the huge
elm tree in the fading evening light. Now chemist Nehring
held them up to an extraordinarily bright laboratory light.
They both noticed the fact simultaneously. "They're inside
out," Baldwin exclaimed.

"Right you are," Nehring concurred, "here's the way the

sweaters would have been worn." As he spoke, Nehring reached his hands up inside the innermost sweater, including the arms, and, keeping them together, carefully turned them right side out. Now the gray crewneck sweater was on the outside, the blue turtleneck within.

A large reddish-purple stain, looking very much like old blood, covered virtually the entire front of the gray crewneck sweater. Turning the sweaters around, Nehring noted a smaller stain on the back side of the gray sweater. Moving to his lab table, Nehring ran a series of tests on the stain. Finally, shaking his head, he turned back to the waiting Baldwin. "Well, it isn't blood. I can't say with any certainty whatsoever on the basis of the tests I have just conducted what they are, but on the basis of these preliminary analyses we can exclude blood."

"Any idea at all, Rollie?"

"No."

"Would you venture a guess?"

"Put that way I might." The scientist smiled. "How about unsweetened grape juice?"

21

The last big search to find the remains of Linda Lou Craig in the general vicinity of the clothing site was undertaken by approximately 200 members of the Wisconsin National Guard Military Police squadron on the second and third of November, 1977. Not only did they search the large wooded tract to the east of Hatch Lake, they also re-searched the area between Hatch Lake and Division Road, to the north and south.

It was no easier this time. The woods were just as thick, the swamps no less wet and murky. The underbrush to the east of the lake was so thick it was impossible for the soldiers to walk upright and adequately see ground level so they went on hands and knees, as the CRW volunteers had before them. After two solid days of this, covering all plausible areas adjacent to the site and finding nothing, they, too, came to the conclusion that there was nothing to be found.

Sundown of the second day, the third of November. Eleven months and three days after Linda's disappearance. Badger stood off to the side of Division Road, in Lover's Cut, watching the convoy of drab green World War II army trucks pull out. The rack bodies were filled with mud-bespattered National Guardsmen hunched together in chilled, bone-weary fatigue, some standing, leaning against the rack sides, but most slumped on the floor of the truck bed in exhaustion. One of the noncoms, whom Badger had come to know by name in the course of the two days, waved at Badger as he passed. "Tough luck, Lieutenant. Sorry we couldn't find her for you."

175

"Thanks, Dobbe." Badger waved back. "You did the best you could."

The trucks pulled slowly past, one after the other, until all were gone. Now Badger stood there, in Lover's Cut, alone. Just a hundred feet away, over on elm tree island, was where Linda's belongings were found by the hunters thirteen days before . . . had it only been thirteen days before? Now here he stood alone again, apparently no closer to finding Linda than he had been before—or to getting Brown.

This is where the little bastard parked his car, he thought.

It was getting dark. He should be getting on. Going home to his wife and two children. He had missed supper again, it was long past time. He hadn't been spending much time with them since Linda, not nearly as much time as he should. They were all starting to gripe—

He turned and walked across the hundred feet, out toward the elm tree island. It was easy walking now, the underbrush trampled flat by the many feet of these long thirteen days. Getting colder with each passing day, the nightly frost probing deeper and staying longer each morning, even the foot-pounded mud was starting to stiffen toward its long winter quiescence.

She'll freeze solid again too, he thought.

Reaching the elm tree island, he stood and looked around. There was nothing there to see. Even the once gaily colored Jack Frost leaves had been shredded by the many probing fingers, ground to drab brown pulp underneath thousands of milling feet. The huge elm stood barren, bereft, denuded, giant arms sticking naked up into the stark, November-cold evening sky. Badger shivered. Indian Summer was over. A Mounds Almond Joy candy bar wrapper lay touching the base of the shrunken elm.

Badger moved to stand right where the clothes had been laid out. The soles of his feet tingled. He could feel her down there under him somewhere scratching away at the bottom of his feet. Trying to dig her way out of her premature grave with her bare fingernails. She had been buried alive.

He quick-stepped away, went back to lean against the trunk of the elm again, absentmindedly leaned over and picked up the Almond Joy wrapper. It didn't seem right to just leave it there.

It wasn't until he felt the tears sliding down his cheeks that he knew for sure he was crying. Lifting his hand to brush away the tears, he missed his face and let his hand keep going up in some kind of wave. "I did the best I could," he whispered to her brokenly, "honest I did."

The
Capture:
Part 3

22

Helmer Wrolstad was proud of his cornfield. Why shouldn't he be. Here it was only the twenty-seventh of June, and it was already knee-high. Chuckling to himself, he reached down and gently pinched a deep-green, nitrogen-rich leaf between horny thumb and forefinger, much as a father would tweak his young son's ear, said it right out loud for every budding ear to hear. "Yessir, folks always say, knee-high by the Fourth of July, here it's only the twenty-seventh of June!"

Best he get cracking on those stones though, Helmer reminded himself, while he could still get astraddle the rows.

Wiping his brow with the back of his corded hand, Helmer bent to his chore, picking the cobblestones he had cultivated up the day before, working away till he had the bucket of his old TO-35 Massey Ferguson tractor heaping full. "By golly," he told Massey, "there ain't never no end to this goldarn rock pickin'!"

Philosophizing on this and that, Helmer carefully steered Massey out of the corn rows and down the lane that led to a causeway out back behind the sugar house.

"Hello, what's that?"

By golly, that was some powerful smell. Must be some animal up and died, went to spoil. Seemed like it was coming from somewhere over there where he was going to build the new silo.

Keeping going down the lane, Helmer luckily drove out of the smell and thought no more about it. Just commenced to carry the cobblestone out back behind the sugar house and dumped them in the pile he was working up there in case he ever wanted to use them to patch the foundation or something.

The clock in his belly told him it was lunchtime, so Helmer started back up the lane. Again, as he hove into view of the silo site, he smelled the powerful bad odor. This time, pointing the direction he now was, heading back up toward the farm buildings, he paid a little more attention off to his right, to the north of the lane, where he had left some silo slabs and cement blocks and such laying. Seemed like some of them had been moved around a hair. Yah, a few kind of piled in a ring of sorts, built up like maybe a little altar or something. "Ain't no animal I know done that," Helmer muttered tightlipped, trying his darndest not to even breathe, the smell was so foul.

It got worse. The closer the tractor rolled—almost by itself, it now seemed—the worse the smell got, so Helmer found his hand jumping up to grab his nose. "Jeesus H. Keerist . . . !" he said, feet flying to hit the clutch and brakes, stopping the tractor no more than two, three feet from the weird-looking cone of cement block and silo slab, topped off by a tuft of dried weeds.

Weren't no doubt that's where the smell was coming from. There was something under there to see too—bluebelly flys aworking their way in and out the cracks between the slab, something oozing out low around the base of block, there was cinch bugs and maggots crawling slow in that goo, crawling slow like they had their bellies full.

Helmer sighed wearily, got down off the machine. Holding his nose with one hand, shading his eyes against the brilliant June sun with the other, he circled the pile like some kind of age-old animal himself, circled, peered, squinted, trying to work up the gumption to reach in and lift away the layer of dead weeds that covered whatever stuck up out of the pile of cement block and silo slab, the dead weeds looking for all the world like a big bouquet of flowers covering the top of a casket—

There! Helmer's hand shot in and knocked away the spray of dead weeds. A human skull stared up at Helmer Wrolstad. Eye sockets crawling with maggots, just like they were full of rising tears.

Helvetia County Sheriff's Detectives John Jankans and Tom Fallon were dispatched to answer farmer Helmer Wrolstad's frantic phone call and proceeded full siren to Helmer's farm on Old 49, a semirural side road just southeast of where I-97 crosses US-135. The farmer hadn't been exaggerating any on the phone. If anything, he had understated the "stinking mess." It was the grizzliest sight either of the veteran detectives had ever laid eyes on. There, alongside a picturesque rural lane running through a magnificent stand of sugar maple trees, crouched this conical pile of building block topped by a vermin-stripped death's-head. Forcing themselves to move closer, they were able to verify what their senses had already told them. There was a partially decomposed body under that skull.

"You touch anything, Helmer?" Detective Jankans asked quietly. It seemed oppressively hot and still here under the spreading sugar maples.

"No sirree, just knocked them dead weeds off the head with one fast swipe." The swatch of dead weeds was still lying there at the base of the conical pile.

"OK," Jankans said, nodding his head and backing slowly, yet never taking his eyes from the empty sockets staring so sadly back at him. "OK," he repeated, giving his head a quick shake to chase the devils away, "let's get outta here. Rope it off, secure it, call the Crime Lab." Returning to their car, Jankans radioed Detective Captain Henry Hague. "Captain, you better come out here. It's something else. And call the Crime Lab, prosecutors, the coroner, everybody..."

They all came. Heading the charge, Lieutenant Badger and Officer Chuck Dinato of LFPD arrived just ten minutes after the investigating officers, having picked up the original dispatch on their scanner. Detective Captain Hague and Detective Blackburn of Helvetia County Sheriff's Department were there by 2:00 P.M. Chief Assistant Prosecutor Jim Barry, Assistant Prosecutor Roy Egner, Assistant Prosectuor Pete Wright, from the Helvetia County Prosecutor's Office, were there by 2:44. At 2:45 Gaylord Lewison, John Guillen, and Lowell Sether from the WSP Crime Lab arrived on the scene and were briefed by Hague and Jankans. At 3:00 Detective Grant and Simonis arrived to augment the Helvetia County unit. Hague assigned Simonis as medical examiner representative, and he further agreed with all present that the crypt should be left undisturbed until the coroner/pathologist arrived. In the interim, Simonis took seven photographs with the medical examiner's Polaroid camera. At 3:06 Detective Sergeant Denny Erickson and Officer Art Lee from UW-LF University Police arrived on the scene. They were presently investigating a missing person, Danielle Forshey, from the campus and remained for victim identification, if possible. At 3:10 Dr. Jerry Salan from Riverside Hospital arrived, even the veteran coroner/pathologist appeared shaken by the macabre scene.

Now all was ready to dismantle the crypt or cairn or whatever the building block conically arranged around the body was meant to represent, if indeed it was there for any purpose other than to conceal the body. Forced to brave the overpowering stench, the members of the WSP Crime Lab team began slowly, carefully removing the block away from the body. Coroner Salan hovered over the crouched technicians, awaiting his grisly task. The various law enforcement officials encircled them, moving in as close as their various senses would allow.

It appeared to be a white female. What was left of her. Kind of kneeling, her legs doubled back beneath her, like she was praying for her life. Only thing was she had no hands left to pray with. They had been neatly severed at the wrists and lay to either side of her kneeling remains.

Her upper body was bereft of clothing and considerable flesh. The lower torso was partially covered with what appeared to be denim culottes. It was noted that the body was facing the east.

Dr. Salan estimated the body to have been there less than two weeks, and more than four days. He stated that his estimation would be seven to eight days.

Captain Hague now conferred with Lieutenant Badger of the LFPD and Detective Sergeant Erickson of University Police, in regard to their investigations of missing persons.

"What do you think, Floyd?"

Badger moved in even closer, leaned down over the sad remains, could feel the maggots working up his own neck. Slowly backing, he shook his head. "I . . . I don't think so, Harry. Looks to me like this one's . . . this one's a little too big boned to be Linda."

Hague turned toward Erickson. "What do you say, Denny?"

Erickson didn't hesitate, nodded immediately. "It could be . . . Danielle."

The three veteran officers just stood there momentarily, then suddenly Captain Hague wheeled and almost barked. "Alright, men, let's wrap it up."

The waiting CARE ambulance moved in closer. The two attendants, Ubby Wieman and Donnie Olson, under the close supervision of Lowell Sether of the Crime Lab, picked up the body and placed it in the ambulance. The CARE ambulance left the scene at 5:25, followed by Detective Simonis, who, upon arrival at Riverside Hospital, sealed the body in Vault Number One of the morgue.

It was 6:10 before all the lingering law enforcement and Crime Lab personnel finished their work and Detective Jankans was able to secure and clear the scene. The dismantled cement block and silo slab just looked like that again now, scattered cement block and silo slab. Even the ghastly smell had evaporated into the soft clean June air here under the spreading sugar maple trees. That's what trees are for, I guess, Jankans thought as he wearily checked the scene one final time. They take in all such stuff through their leaves and give it back to us fresh once more.

He turned and walked down the little grassy lane toward his unmarked police car. Seemed like something else was different now too, he thought. Yes, the birds were singing. Seems like they weren't when we came in.

23

Detective Sergeant Denny Erickson got two calls first thing the next morning. One was from Captain Hague of Helvetia County requesting the name and address of Danielle Forshey's dentist in Marion, Wisconsin. Hague also advised Erickson that word from the morgue was that the victim was wearing a pair of panties, a girdle with a flower design, and a pair of denim culottes. "Call up her folks, will you, Denny. Ask them if she could have been wearing this type of clothing?"

Just as he was reaching out to punch into another line to make the sad, fright-filled call—the kind a cop hates worse than poison—the phone buzzed under his outstretched hands. This one was from the Varsity Inn, informing him that a student employee, Cindy Fall, hadn't shown up for work and that a co-worker's call to her roommate in Irish Hall had garnered the information that the coed had not returned home from a class the night before either.

Jotting down the particulars—roommate Rosella Wagner, 720 Irish Hall, etc.—Erickson pushed back from his desk and just sat there leaning his hands against the front edge of his desk, still staring at the phone. "What the hell's goin' on here anyway!"

Could this be another one?

Sucking a quick breath, mind full of the godawful sight that might be their daughter, Erickson made the call to Danielle Forshey's invalid mother and heartsick father. Yes, the clothing could very well be Danielle's.

Last Sunday had been Father's Day.

* * *

At just about exactly the same time, 8:59 A.M., WSP Detective Simonis was back down at Riverside Hospital morgue. Checking the tape on Vault Number One, he found it to be sealed just the way he had left it the night before. Sliding out the body, he turned it over to morgue attendant Ray Brekke, who was to prepare the body for Dr. Salan's autopsy scheduled for 10:10.

Erickson was at Irish Hall interviewing Rosella Wagner. Something was a little peculiar here too, if this Cindy Fall was actually missing. Most, if not all, her belongings were still here in her room, including her purse. That's weird, Erickson noted. None of these girls ever go anywhere without their purse.

"So what makes you think Cindy has disappeared?" Erickson asked Rosella.

The slightly built girl looked away, fidgeted, possibly even trembled slightly, Erickson couldn't tell for sure. "Well," she finally said, "I heard on the news last night about some other girl's body being found. Cindy and I have even been talking about that other coed who disappeared a couple of weeks ago. She said she was going to start being more careful."

"What do you mean?" probed Erickson, "'start'?"

Rosella was almost turning herself inside out. "Cindy . . . Cindy is pretty impulsive, I guess. You might even say, spacey. She'd sometimes just pick up . . . people."

"Men?"

"Yeah, men, boys, whatever."

"And not always come home at night?"

The girl nodded timidly, not quite accepting the detective's probing eyes. "How often would you say Cindy doesn't always come home at night, Rosella?"

Rosella looked up, blinked. "I haven't seen her since Sunday."

"Sunday!" Erickson exploded, starting to swear but catching himself in time to modify down to, "Good God, girl, today is Wednesday."

"Yeah, I know, but they said down at the Varsity Inn she's been in to work every day but today."

"So?"

"So . . . you see, it's not so different what maybe Cindy's

been doing nights, it's the days. She usually always makes it to work, comes back here sometime during the day, to change clothes, get her books, take her pills. Sir, she didn't even take her pills this time, they're right there by her bed."

"What pills, birth control?"

"No," Rosella said as though shocked, bringing her right hand up to her mouth in a childish gesture, "her epileptic pills."

"Epilep—she's got epilepsy?"

"Yes, petit mal. Though she only had seizures once in a great while, she really hates them, so she was very faithful about taking her pills."

"She could have slipped a few in her pocket, couldn't she?"

Rosella was shaking her head. "She always carried her pills in her purse when she was going to be gone. And here's her purse and everything."

"Alright, we'll keep our eyes open. I'll check back with you tomorrow morning, if she hasn't come back by then. Of course, if she does or you run onto her or anything, you give us a call."

"Sure, but I just don't feel like Cindy just—"

"Rosella, where do you think she's been these last few nights?"

"I mean, she usually shows up at least once a day—"

"Rosella, I'm not asking you about her days," Erickson cut in rather brusquely. "I'm interested in her nights."

"Well, she has quite a few boyfriends. Besides them she just kind of . . . runs into."

Erickson sighed, flipped open his pad. "Names?"

"Well, the one I'd talk to first would be Gary Rierson. He lives on Main, 1860, she went with him the most."

"You think she spent the last few nights with him?"

"No, not especially. Lots of times she just pads wherever she finds herself, a girlfriend's, dorm lounges, wherever . . ."

Erickson just shook his head, headed for the door.

Prosecutor Salan was in the process of performing an autopsy on the unknown body, Ray Brekke assisting. Simonis left the morgue and drove to Marion, Wisconsin, to obtain the dental records of Danielle Forshey from her dentist, Dr. Langan, and to check the body's clothing with the suspected victim's parents.

Meanwhile, Erickson had tracked down Cindy Fall's alleged boyfriend, Gary Rierson, and was talking to him. "OK, Gary, so Cindy is, so to speak, impulsive."

"Yes," the slight, almost tiny, Rierson agreed readily. "She liked to, ah, experiment. Almost seemed like sometimes she liked to take chances."

"Like what?"

"Well, just picking people up. Every time something happens to a girl on campus I worry it's Cindy. She's . . . careless. I told her once already, 'If you keep this up, you're going to get yourself murdered.'"

Erickson looked at the fiery-eyed little student closely. He was mostly hair and eyeballs, but anybody can kill. Yeah, he reminded himself, sometimes it's the little guys who will kill a lot faster than the big boys; they got more to prove. "Do you mention murder because of . . . ah, recent local happenings or for some other, ah, more personal reason?"

"You know why I mention it, Sergeant," Rierson answered sarcastically. "There's been a lot of weird things happening around here lately. It's all over the news that a body was found yesterday. Everybody's betting it's either Forshey or Craig."

Erickson just nodded noncommittally. "Were you jealous of her, Gary?"

"Nah! Ours was never any great romance, no big thing. More mutual convenience than anything. You couldn't get that close to Cindy, if you wanted to. She's . . . disturbed, frustrated, all the time going around trying to seek out new people to help put her life in order."

"Were you one of those, Gary?"

He thought on that, finally nodded his curly mop of hair almost stubbornly. "Maybe."

"You seem to . . . know her very well."

"Why not? I'm no dummy. I've got my own problems, so I can relate to another's. Sure, Cindy got around, but it wasn't just some nympho thing. She was looking for answers, help. She made friends easily, lost them just as easily. Talked to just about anyone on the street. But she's afraid to get too close to people, and I'm sure some could get . . . offended."

"You get offended, Gary?"

"Not that offended, Sarge, not that offended. Save your brain power for them that need it. I got better things to do with my life than get that hung up on some spacey chick."

Erickson just grinned.

"I'll tell you one thing though, Sarge," Rierson continued. "If you want my opinion, Cindy almost had some kind of weird desire to be raped. The way she talked about sex . . . well, it was more like trying to tame a wild beast. And she wasn't afraid to let you know—anybody who'd listen practically—how she felt about it either. But she's not strong; I'm only five-three, and I could put her down like nothing. So, naturally I'm afraid something might have happened to her. Aren't you?"

Erickson just nodded again, asked softly, "How about you, Gary? When did you see her last?"

"Last night."

Erickson sat up straighter. "Last night? What time?"

"Right after her class."

"What time was that?"

Rierson shrugged casually. "A little after ten, I suppose. Her class let out at ten."

"Where was she—what class, where?"

"Outside the library—actually, between the campus library and the administration building."

"Go on. Was she alone?"

"No, she was talking to a young man beside her."

"What'd he look like?"

"I couldn't see very well; it's kind of dark in there. Besides, when I walked up, he kind of . . . slunk away."

"Slunk away?"

"Yeah, kind of slid back into the bushes there by the library."

Erickson leaned in even closer. "Gary, didn't you think that strange?"

"Yes . . . no . . . not really. I figured he might have known . . . or thought I was her boyfriend or something."

"Did you come on pretty strong to her?"

"Strong? What do you mean?"

"Loud. Say, 'hey, what's goin' on here, what you doing with this guy!' Let him know right off the bat that you were the boyfriend?"

Gary shook his floppy curls sadly. "No, nothing like that.

As a matter of fact, I came up on them quietly. Watched them for a while, kind of wondering if I should walk over and talk to her. We . . . we'd just had this argument a few days ago . . . about her habit of picking guys up—"

"Was she picking the guy up?"

"I think so. They were walking, real slow like. She talking, the guy listening. Every once in a while she would hesitate, look up at him, like she was looking to him for an answer, but he never said much, didn't seem to even want to look at her."

"Did you hear his voice at all?"

"Just barely. He said something once, not very loud, soft, almost careful like, seems like."

"Could you see him, Gary? What did he look like?"

"Tall. Yeah, tall, she looked up at him."

"How tall is Cindy?"

"Five five."

"He wouldn't have to be that tall—what'a'ya say, how tall?"

"I dunno, there isn't much light in there between the buildings, six foot maybe, maybe not quite—"

"Could he have just looked taller to you, Gary?" Erickson persisted, on a hunch, "because you're so . . . rather short. Considering you were trying to decide whether or not you dared step out there and try to claim your girl, could he have just looked that tall to you, Gary?"

Gary Rierson stared evenly at Erickson, a new look in his eyes now. "That's not bad, Erickson. In fact, that's pretty good, that's exactly what I was trying to decide."

Erickson didn't have time for compliments. "Could he, Gary, in reality, have been shorter?"

"Yes . . . yes, I think so. Probably not all that much taller than Cindy, maybe five nine or ten, somewhere in there."

"White, black—"

"White."

"Color hair?"

"Gee, I couldn't . . . I remember his clothes! Yeah, I thought they kind of looked like an odd couple, her in her usual jeans and backpack, long blond hair hanging way down over her backpack like it always does. She always went around looking like your stereotypical hippy, particularly alongside this dude in color coordinated shirt and pressed slacks. Yeah, I remember thinking then, he looked like some factory worker all dressed up for Sunday."

"Age?" Erickson was scribbling away like crazy.

"I'd say . . . twenties. Yeah, early twenties, no more."

Erickson looked up, pencil poised. "Gary, you could see these things but you can't describe his features better? What did he look like? Hair? Face—"

"Cut . . . fairly short. Seems like it was on the light side. Combed fairly slick."

"Shirt? Long sleeved or short?"

"Short. But seems like it was buttoned right up to the neck or something. He wasn't wearing a tie but he looked like he should. And something was glistening on his neck, maybe a cross?"

"But no jacket?"

"No jacket."

"But you never got a good look at his face?"

"No. Seemed like he always somehow kept it turned away from me, and when I finally stepped in to try to talk to her, he seemed to slink away."

"What did you say to her?"

Gary dropped his eyes. "Not much. It was brief . . . strained."

"What did you say, Gary?"

Gary let out a deep breath. "I asked her if she wanted to come with me or not. She . . . she just shook her head no. I asked her if she was picking the guy up. 'None of your business,' she said. Then I kind of got distracted. There was some arguing off to the side, my ears kind of went to listen to that rather than what she was saying . . . maybe . . . I think it was because I didn't want to hear what she was saying and rather listen to the other voices."

"Was this other guy involved in the argument?"

"No, it was just two other students arguing over some math problem, some stupid thing like that—"

"Where was this other guy now?"

Gary's head came slowly up, his eyes leaving that painful shadowy corridor between the library and the administration building momentarily. "You know . . . seems like . . . he'd even got further away."

"Physically?"

"Yes. Just while Cindy and I said those few words, me

dazing off to listen to the math argument, my eyes kind of drifted past Cindy to size him up . . . try to figure out what kind of a shot I had . . . seems like he'd gotten way over by the bushes somehow. Without me even noticing him go, just melted back into the bushes."

"Strange," Erickson said finally.

"Yeah, I thought so too." Gary tried to throw off a jaunty little laugh, but it came out more like a dying croak. "I mean, who am I to be afraid of."

"That's not what I was thinking, Gary—"

"Go ahead, I'm used to it," Gary interrupted defiantly.

Erickson just shook his head this time, ignored the little gamecock's final flurry, came in from his blind side. "Gary, knowing what you do about Cindy, do you think she ended up with this . . . shy factory worker?"

"Awww, damn . . ." He started to growl, then dwindled into a sudden sigh that seemed to suck a little more of his slight frame in with it. "Yeahhh. Yeah, shit yes."

"Just a shackup?"

"No, not just that. There's more to her than that. It's just that most people don't know how to see it, how to look at her—"

"Gary," Erickson interrupted gently, "I mean last night, with this guy?"

Gary started to nod his head, then stopped abruptly. "No, I . . . I can't answer that. There's no way I can know for sure what she does with him or any of those other guys. All I know for sure . . . is what she does with me." Gary stood looking down at his scruffy sneakers, even shuffled them once or twice. "You know, Sarge, there's one thing I didn't tell you."

"Yeah, what's that?"

Gary still didn't look up. "Well, after I last saw her there with this guy by the library . . . I goes home . . . about one or two in the morning I wake up. I was just laying there on my bed. I open my eyes. There she was, standing in my room." Gary took a second before he went on. "Then she disappeared. I don't know if I just blinked my eyes or not, but it seemed she was there longer than that, maybe twenty seconds, but now she was gone again." Gary raised his eyes, looked up at Detective Sergeant Erickson. A tear slid down a freckled cheek and spattered atop a scruffy sneaker. Erickson watched it all the way; it didn't have all that far to fall. "You know how ghosts are pictured as being transparent, Sergeant?"

Erickson nodded.

"Well, I couldn't see through her. I wasn't scared. I knew it was all in my head. But she wasn't wearing the same clothes. She didn't have her backpack on. She was wearing one of them flouncy party dresses little girls wear when they go to church or something . . . almost white it was . . . like her hair when she kept it nice and clean."

Erickson just nodded again.

"I couldn't see through her," Gary repeated.

Erickson felt like he had to say something. "Maybe . . . maybe none of us can, Gary."

Positive identification of the subject by comparison of dentition and postmortem x-rays with the dental records provided by Dr. Langan and Dr. Ward was made the twenty-ninth of June, 1978. It was the unanimous opinion of three dental experts that the teeth and jaws of the decedent were the teeth and jaws recorded in the records and x-rays as those of Danielle B. Forshey. A coworker of Danielle Forshey was further able to identify the rings removed from the severed hands as those worn daily by Danielle B. Forshey.

Detective Captain Henry Hague called an all-hands briefing of his Helvetia County Sheriff's Department Detective Bureau as soon as he had the autopsy and pathological correlation in hand. "I think she was tortured to death," he said, by way of kicking the meeting off, "possibly over a four-day period. Anybody got a better idea—or should I say, worse, in this case?"

None of the assembled detectives had one, better or worse, so Hague continued. "Take those jagged contour cuts in the breast area. It appears her breasts were hacked off before the maggots got to them. Though they go for soft tissue first— that's why most all the other soft tissue throughout the body is gone—those jagged cuts in the skin seem to say to me, and Salan concurs, that they were already gone." Hague picked up a pointer and indicated on a huge blowup of the body tacked to his briefing board. "See these stab wounds. Salan counted seventeen stab wounds to the chest and back area. However, he further states that they may not have been the cause of death and may not have been all the injuries. Though it appears most of the stab wounds and particularly the longer slashes were delivered from behind, very likely as she kneeled before him. The angle seems to indicate that she was kneeling facing him while he stood over her. The scoring on ribs six, eight, and nine seem to say she was also stabbed from the front. As you can see under magnification, rib six is cracked deep to the stab wound; so is eight. Rib nine bears three superficial stab wounds. These blows were very likely delivered while the killer was in some kind of frenzy, over and over, some of them delivered with extraordinary force, while others not nearly so. Possibly, he was spent by then, kind of just petered out at the end. Or, again just possibly, the slighter blows were part of the torture, while the deep thrusts were involved in the killing. That is, again, if she wasn't already dead from some other cause and the mutilation was upon her dead body." Hague laid the pointer across the top of his desk, consulted his notes. "Missing items: purse and contents, blouse, possibly peach colored, bra, shoes, and one earring, her glasses, large rectangular-oval, with heavy horn-rimmed frames. She never went anywhere without them. Our investigation indicates that she couldn't see ten feet without them, so they have to be kicking around somewhere too."

Hague laid down his notes, straightened, yet his lean whipcord body still seemed somehow crouched over his desk, ready to spring in any direction. "Now Badger over to LFPD has got the Linda Lou Craig case. I talked to Badger just a minute ago, but he doesn't seem to think Craig and Forshey are connected. Though the way they found Craig's clothes laid out last fall seemed to indicate the work of some kind of deranged individual too, Badger still strongly feels Craig was killed by his suspect Brown, the boyfriend, as the result of a passion murder. One little thing here: Forshey was facing east, Linda Lou Craig's clothes were laid out to point east. What that means if anything you can guess as well as I, but some of those hotshot young county prosecutors are saying something about Eastern religion or some such theory."

Hague smiled, his thin lips twitching under his neatly trimmed military mustache. Jankans, watching his captain closely, was again reminded of how much Hague looked and carried himself like a very proper British colonel, World War I vintage, just returned from India service. "I'm sure we will be hearing quite a number of some such theories as this investigation continues, voodoo, cult, sacrificial slaughter. We may even come up with one or two ourselves..." Hague paused, swept the room with gimlet eye. "Listen, speculate, but don't get carried away. So far it's just another mutilation murder, with possibly torture and a few other odds and ends like necrophilia maybe thrown in." Some of the detectives laughed a little, but Jankans thought it more a nervous titter than anything else.

Hague was continuing. "So Badger's got Craig, he sees no connection with Forshey. Now Denny Erickson over to University Police may have another coed missing, or he may not. A girl named Cindy Fall, it appears she's some kind of a flake, so she may just be missing. She was only reported two days ago, last seen by one of her boyfriends on the night of the twenty-seventh, the same day we found Forshey. So..." Hague leaned forward even more, his fingertips touching the top of his desk but receiving no weight; Jankans had the feeling his dapper little captain was preparing to vault his desk. "There may or may not be a pattern here. Chief Van Buren has still got six status-open cases out in Ghent Township left over from 'seventy-six, all found dead in the same general area where Craig's clothing was laid out. Of course, Forshey's body was not found in that area, so that might indicate there is more connection, if any, with Craig and the six status-opens than Forshey. But..." Again Hague paused, swept his rapt audience with glittering eyes. "...all we got so far is one body. One murder. Danielle Forshey. Killed, maybe kidnapped, could have been held elsewhere than the body site for up to four days, sexually abused conceivably, though the body was too decomposed for Salan to ascertain, sexual abuse and/ or mutilation very likely both before and after death. Tortured before, mutilated after. Maybe the sicko ate parts of her. Engaged in sexual acts with the body. Drank her blood. Who knows...but consider anything in this case. Overlook nothing. I feel we are looking for some kind of a madman. Sexually perverted, twisted, tortured. Compulsive. Compelled to kill, abuse, mutilate. I don't know just exactly what kind of a beast we got out there loose, but whoever he is has got to be got and got fast. For when they start this kind of psychosexual torture and mutilation and murder, they usually keep on and often. So get out there and get the filthy bastard!"

24

Vern Lukken drove home from work whistling. Swinging his Lukken Builders pickup truck jauntily onto his circular drive, he couldn't help but smile fondly at his gleaming new house, well-groomed yard, beautifully manicured flower beds. Not bad for a kid from New Hope. Now all we need is a few kids to fill it. The last thought invariably came bouncing along right behind the first.

Yes, that was about the only thing him and Bev didn't have going for them—married eight years and not a prayer answered so far, even though the doctors said there was nothing wrong with either one of them. Yet, for all their other successes, try as they did, they couldn't seem to pull this last big one off. Vern smiled, he couldn't keep from it very long. "Little baby, yeah, that's the big one."

This adjectival turn tickled him, he kept right on smiling as he walked up the cinder stone walk to his attached garage. Noticing the empty slot next to his Olds 98 Regency LX, he remembered today was the day Bev was to drop her little Volkswagen convertible off at Smoky's to get the fender-bender pounded out. He'd have to get after her about shutting the garage door, now that they had one with an electric eye. All she had to do was push a button, and she even forgot to do that . . .

"Ah, that woman," Vern said under his breath, but he was still grinning when he said it.

His perpetual grin started to shrink a little as soon as he got inside the garage. Blackjack, their cross-breed Lab-setter started yowling the minute he heard Vern's footsteps crossing the cement floor. As Vern opened the door that connected the garage to the breezeway, the dog bolted out past him and went skidding around the corner of the garage to lift his leg against his favorite spruce tree, already yellowing from his many visits. "Damn you anyway, can't you ever quit leakin' on that tree!" Here he'd paid forty dollars just to have that tree set this spring, built a stainless steel cyclone fence around his whole backyard just to give the mutt a place to pee in and—

That's funny, he thought, that dog's acting like it ain't been out all day.

Stepping into the breezeway, Vern yelled through the screen door leading into the kitchen, "Bev! Hey, Bev, didn't you let the dog out all day?"

There was no answer. He kicked some construction site mud out of his cleated steel-toed boots on the piece of angle iron he had sunk into the cement of the breezeway floor for just that purpose and stepped into the kitchen, yelling louder, "Sweetheart, I'm home."

She must be to the back of the house, he figured, noting with justifiable pride that, big as it was and tight as he had built it, nobody could never hear nothing unless a person was almost in the same room. Sniffing, he suddenly realized what he wasn't smelling: his supper. No food was bubbling away on the stove like there usually was, nothing was being kept warm in the oven.

Proceeding through the house room by room, calling her name from time to time, Vern worked his way all through the split level ranch, but couldn't raise her. He stepped out in the backyard, scanned it, called her name even though he could see she wasn't there. The grin gone now, he walked quickly back through his house room by room. Yeah, there were a few things that didn't seem quite right. At least, not for Bev, housekeeper that she was. Their bed wasn't made. There were some dishes still in the sink. Vern walked over and inspected the dishes more closely. They had egg on them, looked like breakfast dishes . . . Bev always rinsed them off as soon as they finished eating and put them in the dishwasher. Especially breakfast dishes with egg on them, he'd heard her say a hundred times how she hated to handle breakfast dishes if egg dried on them. . . .

Looked like she hadn't gotten back. The dog figures too.

That's why he was so worked up. Had to pee so bad. He hadn't been let out for his run all day.

Vern glanced at the kitchen clock ticking away atop the refrigerator, worry plowing furrows through his work-hard slab of a face: 6:43 P.M. He had left home at 5:45 A.M. for the construction site. Bev had still been in bed sleeping, but he had leaned over and kissed her good-bye anyway, just a little peck on the forehead. Not enough to wake her if she was really sleeping sound but enough to open her eyes if she wasn't, give her a chance to kiss him good-bye. She looked so cute lying there, her new curly hairdo sticking out all over like some kind of Afro. . . .

Vern reluctantly shook his head, steeled himself to think on the situation at hand. She must have taken her car to Smoky's Auto Body. Yes, that much she must have got done; it wasn't in the garage. Maybe she had driven it over there, dropped the car off.

Without realizing it till he was there, he had wandered from the kitchen into their bedroom. Was standing kind of half staring at their rumpled bed, then turning to look at himself in their bureau mirror without even knowing why. Looking down, he noticed a bus schedule on the top of the dresser. Yes, Bev had said she was going to take a bus home from the body shop.

Grabbing up the bus schedule, he tried to make sense out of the many tiny numbers and street names bisected by even tinier lines and dots. Realizing he was standing in semi-darkness, he stepped over to the large picture window that looked out into the backyard.

"What am I doing this for?" he slowly asked himself. "What difference does it make what bus she might have taken home if she's not even here?"

His eyes scanned their backyard. No, she wasn't out there by the barbecue pit either. No charcoal smoke was curling up like it did days when she surprised him by broiling T-bones and having a little party for just the two of them, tablecloth, cut flowers, candles, and all.

He turned from the window, stood looking at the rumpled bed. Suddenly, he wheeled and strode out of the master bedroom and down the hall to his auxiliary home office. He felt slightly better in here, more in command, surrounded by the paper tools of his building trade, estimates and contracts, bids and bills. Sitting authoritatively down at his battle-scarred desk, Vern crisply reached out and jerked the phone over closer to him and got right on it. "Mercy Hospital, this is Vern Lukken, Lukken Builders. Have you admitted a patient by the name of Beverly Lukken today? Ah, possibly it could have been a car accident, maybe sometime this afternoon?"

They hadn't, nor had any other hospital in the area. Vern then proceeded through the long list of their friends, calling everyone he could think of; none of them had seen Bev in the course of this day, she wasn't there now. He even called their church, St. Paul's, his steeled reserve almost giving way when Father Felix Gardina told him no, he hadn't seen Bev since confession a week ago yesterday. The jovial priest gently chided Vern for his and Bev missing Mass yesterday. Vern explained that they had been out of town boating with her folks, and maybe Bev had run back up to New Hope quick to see her folks, forgot to leave a note.

Fighting the words through the lump of fear that was fast filling his throat, Vern now called his in-laws long distance. "Pa," he asked Beverly's father, "Bev didn't drive back up there today, did she?"

"Why, no, Vern," Fred Ritski answered, anxiety immediately filling his voice too. "Somethin' wrong, Vern? It's past ten."

"I . . . no, I don't think so, Pa. It's just that I came home from work my usual time, around 6:30, Bev wasn't here, no note—"

"That's not Beverly, Vern," the tough old fighter said flatly, his voice ominous.

"I know it, Pa," was all Vern could manage.

"Where was she supposed to be today?"

"Home. Just take her car to the auto body this morning, come right home on the bus—"

"Did you call the auto body, was she there?"

"Closed. I don't know the home number, even the last name of the guy who runs it—"

Her father was too smart not to ask the next question. "Her car there, Vern?"

"Ah . . . no."

"Then she must have took it to the auto body . . . something happened to her on the way home."

"That's just about . . . the way it's starting to look—"

"Did you call—"

"Yeah, all of them, nothing doin'."

"The police?"

"Not . . . not yet."

"Call them, Vern."

"Pa . . ."

"Yeah?"

"Pa . . . do you . . . is it even possible . . . maybe you know her even better than me?"

"I'm ashamed of you, Vern. For even thinkin' such things about Beverly."

"I'm not, Pa. I'm . . . hopin'."

"Call the police, Vern," the tough old father of seven girls ordered. "I'll gather the folks. She don't show up by then, we'll be down there first thing in the morning."

But Vern Lukken still didn't call the police. Or the morgue. The only two places he could think of he hadn't. It was just . . . too much. It would be admitting something. Accepting something. The awful possibility Vern couldn't even allow himself to think, let alone face. The one Beverly's pa had hinted but couldn't quite bring himself to say either.

The possibility of the madman killer. The missing girls. The mutilated body found just last month. The other coed disappearing into thin air the day the Forshey girl was found. Yes, Vern Lukken was well aware of what had been happening in his town. His neighborhood. Why shouldn't he be? He lived on Elmwood. Linda Lou Craig had lived just three streets away on Drake. Bill Brown lived even closer, just about three long city blocks as the crow flies from where Vern was sitting right now.

Vern swiveled his chair to look out his office window into the impenetrable darkness of the undeveloped wild land that separated his house from Bill Brown's. He had even seen the kid around once or twice. Somebody had pointed Brown out to him as the boyfriend who was suspected of having somehow knocked off Linda Lou Craig. Remembering him now, as Brown had looked in person and on television last year when his girlfriend was first missing, Vern felt a little better. That pantywaist asshole didn't look like he could hurt a fly unless it

was open. Athletic as Bev was, she could probably take him
in a fair fight—

But then, a . . . gun . . . knife. According to the papers a
knife had been used on that Forshey girl—

But they were coeds. Probably all out prowling around at
night, just asking for trouble. She was Beverly Lukken. His
wife. The finest, purest, best woman who ever lived, just out
dropping her car off, shopping, whatever a woman does in the
middle of a bright sunny day. Not just his wife, his best
friend.

"God, no, she ain't got nothing to do with them other
trash!" Vern Lukken cried out to the ringing emptiness. He
was still staring out across his backyard through the wild land
toward Fauntleroy. He could see one car's headlights working
slowly along the quiet residential street—

"You do something to my wife . . . I crush every bone in
your slimy body!"

Vern's scream reverberated through his tightly constructed
home, jarred him back to his senses. He looked down at the
clenched fists that had built it, poised as though to smash the
pretty picture window to smithereens, casing and all. Get a
grip on yourself, Lukken, he counseled, you don't even know
yet something's wrong. Sure not somthing to do with this
Brown kid. Sure not something to do with Bev . . .

Vern sat in his darkened house all by himself till, finally, at
11:43, one big work-gnarled fist reached out and picked up
the phone. Even then, when he got the police on the phone, he
couldn't bring himself to state his case as clearly as he saw it
in his heart of hearts. He let Vern Lukken of Lukken Builders
do the talking. "Yeah, I . . . I don't see it totally as an emer-
gency. Yet. Of course, I'm still hoping . . . she's . . .
somewhere."

"OK then, sir," the disembodied voice from LFPD agreed.
"Don't worry, we certainly have no evidence of foul play.
Nothing's been reported. Like you say, it was broad daylight.
We'll just put out a 'BE ON ALERT' for her tonight. But if she
doesn't show up tonight, contact us again first thing in the
morning."

"Yeah, I . . ."

Vern let the phone drop. He didn't even know if it hit the
cradle or not, so he felt with his hand to be sure, just in case

she called. Switched off the desk light he had put on to make this last final call. Now he sat in total dark, his big hand just resting on the phone.

He never moved till daylight. How he got through that awful night, he'd never know. He didn't sleep, but yet in a way he did; it was like his mind and body both kind of turned to steel as he sat there. Redwood plank. Brick and mortar. His whole being just seemed to ossify in that chair, to construct a house of some kind of sanity around himself within which to exist through that awful night. For this was the first night Vern and Bev had ever spent apart since they were married.

He called the police again at 7:47 the next morning. But by that time he had been out searching the wild land between his house and Fauntleroy since bare daybreak. Officer Tom Strand of LFPD was there in three minutes, 7:50. Neighbors Don and Jeanne Elroy were with Lukken, looking just as worried as he was.

Strand obtained basic information of the MP and then proceeded to Smoky's Body Shop at 119 South Wren in Big Falls. There he spoke with Tommie Engel and Rich Shufeldt. Both men saw Mrs. Lukken at about 8:30 A.M. on August 14, 1978—the day before—when she dropped off her car and spoke to them briefly about what she wanted done. She couldn't have been there more than about fifteen or twenty minutes. Nothing about her struck the two men as being unusual. Neither of them noticed exactly where she went after she left the shop. Mr. Engel had the most contact with her at the shop and stated that she had on a dark colored top, possibly brown, and kind of a pinkish colored pair of shorts. Neither man could tell Strand whether or not she was carrying a purse or what kind of shoes she was wearing but were real sure of the shorts and the top, though not as sure on the colors.

Returning to the Lukken residence, Officer Strand found Vern Lukken and friends and family had already begun to search the area on foot. Vern rushed up to Strand, told him that one of his men, a Herb Felpel, employed as a carpenter by Lukken Builders, had seen Beverly at about 9:30 or 10:00 on 8–14–78. Strand then spoke with Felpel, who told him that he did see Beverly Lukken at the intersection of Oakdale Drive and Wilson Road. Apparently Felpel stopped his pickup truck for a few seconds and spoke with Beverly. This reportedly took place fifteen to twenty feet from Wilson Road on Oakdale, and at the time Mr. Felpel was on his way to Tigerton Lumber. His vehicle would have been facing toward Wilson Road. After talking with Beverly for a few seconds, he then made a left on Wilson and proceeded south to Tigerton Lumber. Mr. Felpel stated that Beverly seemed in good spirits at the time and nothing seemed to be wrong. The last he saw her, she was on foot eastbound on Oakdale. Mr. Felpel described Beverly as wearing some sort of denim outfit with full length trousers. These apparently were of the faded variety. He stated that she did have glasses on at the time, large oval-rectangular glasses with heavy darkish, brown or black, horn rims. Mr. Felpel didn't remember if she was carrying a purse or not.

Officer Strand didn't wait as long as Porath and Dinato had on Linda Lou Craig to call for help from on high. Then again, a lot had happened since New Year's Day, 1977. Nor did the powers that be wait quite as long to focus on the case. Deputy Chief Grout and Lieutenant Brant were on the scene within minutes of Strand's call at 9:35. Quickly agreeing with Strand's assessment of the situation as extremely suspicious, Grout and Brant set up a command post at Oakdale and Wilson and radioed Lieutenant Badger, to acquaint him with their suspicions and request him to send extra personnel so that a foot search could be initiated. Badger sent five members of the bike patrol and roared out right behind them.

"Good job, Strand," Badger told him, after Strand had quickly briefed him. "How has Chief Grout set you up for the foot search?"

"Started searching from the command post out. Sent some people on foot door to door. Start on Elmwood and Birchwood, fan out from Lukken's house on Maple, Oakdale, Elk Avenue. If nothing pans out, keep going."

"That's right, keep going. All the way, from Northland Highway to Lake Waupaca Road."

"I got a number of pictures of the victim from her husband, Lieutenant, to pass out to the searchers."

Badger nodded, looking closely at Strand. "I notice you referred to the MP as 'victim,' Strand—twice."

"I think she is, Lieutenant."

Badger nodded again, a worried look on his face. "So do I."

Strand directed Badger to the Lukken residence and, after meeting with Vern Lukken and his wife's parents, Badger and Strand began a systematic search of the home.

At 11:30 A.M. a police radio call came to Badger stating that a pair of eyeglasses had been found lying along Oakdale Drive by one of the searchers, Officer Grancelli, and were now in the possession of Detective Sergeant Brown at the scene of the find. They had been found about 100 yards east of Wilson Road and just off the south side of Oakdale, in the ditch. Badger and Vern Lukken rushed to the scene, where Mr. Lukken, tears running down his face, said that he was quite sure that the glasses were his wife's. Returning to the Lukken residence, Vern Lukken checked to see where his wife bought her glasses and produced a New-View business office billing with an address in Lind Center, suboffice in the Old Dam Mall, Big Falls. Tucker contacted New-View, Old Dam Mall, and advised an employee that he had a pair of glasses, delivery number 2361289, believed to belong to a missing person. The employee, after fifteen minutes, verified that 2361289 was registered to a Beverly Lukken, Little Falls. They were her glasses.

Badger replaced the phone and turned to Vern and Bev's mother. The father was still out searching. "How badly does she need her glasses, Vern?"

"She . . . she can barely see without them. That is, without them, or her contact lenses."

"Are they here?"

Mrs. Ritski left to see if she could locate her daughter's contact lenses somewhere in the house. Badger mulled over the seemingly coincidental similarities between the vision problems of Beverly Lukken, Linda Lou Craig, and, quite probably, Danielle Forshey. As he was not investigating the latter case, he was not certain of Forshey's actual vision problem, but from all accounts and pictures he had seen, she wore heavy, dark horn-rimmed glasses very similar to Linda Lou Craig's and the pair he now held in his hand.

Beverly's mother returned. "They don't seem to be here."

"She usually carried them in her purse," Vern volunteered.

"Even if she was wearing her glasses?"

"Yes, sometimes she would wear her contact lenses for a while, then switch to her glasses. She had trouble getting used to the lenses, they hurt her eyes. I asked her why she bothered. She thought I'd like her even better without... without..."

"What kind of a purse was she carrying?" Badger hated to keep after Vern, the man looked out on his feet, but, of course, he had no choice.

The mother, who appeared to Badger as a strong old-fashioned pioneer type of a lady—she had already told him she had borne and raised up seven other children besides Beverly, most of them on their way down to help search for their sister —stepped in to help her son-in-law out. "I already checked. The one that's missing, she almost always carried that one, it's a big brown canvas bag, with long straps. She went carrying it over her shoulder."

"Her wallet inside?"

Both Vern and Mrs. Ritski nodded. "What do you think it means, Lieutenant?" Vern asked, his face indicating he might have already guessed the answer. "Her glasses just laying along the road . . . like that?"

Badger decided to level with him. Vern Lukken looked to him like the type of guy who would rather know just about anything than be kept sitting in the dark; in short, Vern reminded Badger quite a bit of himself. Yet he pulled the punch a little. "Kidnap, maybe, Vern. It's just a guess, but maybe she scuffled with her abductor, her glasses got knocked off . . ."

Vern just nodded grimly. Badger had the feeling he couldn't trust himself to talk.

"Look at the bright side. Kidnap . . . isn't the worst. You might get a ransom call—"

"I'll pay anything!"

"I know you would, Vern," Badger said softly, "maybe the abductor does too."

The tiny receiver on Badger's belt beeped; another call was coming in. Some vehicle skidmarks had been discovered on Oakdale right near where the glasses were found. Not real distinct skidmarks, blending somewhat with the warmed asphalt this hot humid summer's day, but distinct enough to be isolated by painstaking Detective Sergeant Dale Brown, who had photographed them from various angles and was now standing by. "You think these skidmarks are related to the glasses, Dale?" Badger transmitted back.

"Hard to say, Floyd. Proximity is good. Glasses are only three feet from where the skidmarks end at the edge of the roadway, there's paint on the curb."

Badger didn't want to come right out and ask the question in front of Vern and the mother, so he just kind of hinted at it. "Any . . . broken glass, anything like that?"

"No. No broken glass, no blood, nothing."

"Do you think, the glasses, they could have been . . . ah, thrown that far?"

"Thrown? Oh, you can't talk—"

"You got it."

"Sure, depends on how fast the car was going at the point of impact."

"That is your best guess, then?"

"Yes. I think she was hit by a car. Her glasses knocked off, ended up there in the ditch off the roadway."

"OK. Thanks, Dale. Soon as I finish up here, I'll come down and take a look myself." Badger turned to the family. There was no point in trying to keep this from them either. He spoke quickly, not giving them a chance to interrupt, dwell unduly on what he was saying. "Skidmarks. They may or may not be connected with the glasses. I don't think hit and run," he said aloud, thinking more likely "hit and take." "There's no broken car glass, her glasses are intact, best of all, no blood. There are skidmarks on every street in town. These may have nothing whatsoever to do with your wife's disappearance. Right now we can't lock ourselves into anything. We don't know a thing for sure. All we have for sure are her glasses." Badger did some fast calculating. "Approximately a hundred yards east on Oakdale from where she talked to Herb Felpel. Between 9:30 and 10:00 in the forenoon. Broad daylight. Cars all over the streets; a hundred yards from Wilson, a fairly busy street. She takes her car to the auto body, probably takes a bus home—I got men checking on that right now—apparently walks east on Oakdale toward home, but unless either the guys at the body shop or Herb Felpel is dead wrong, she's already been home and changed her clothes—"

Heads jerked up, particularly Vern's. "Lieutenant, I don't think she ever came home."

"The guys at the body shop say she was wearing pink shorts and a darkish top. Your carpenter says it was some sort of faded denim outfit with full length trousers."

"That's right," Officer Strand verified, "and the guys at the auto body were real sure on the shorts. So was Felpel on the denim outfit."

Badger turned back to Vern. "She have clothes like that, either set?"

Vern nodded numbly, spreading big work thickened hands. "Both. All kinds of clothes."

Again Beverly's mother stepped in to help him out, laid her own work-strong hands on her son-in-law's bulging forearm. I'd hate to catch one of them meathooks in the mouth, Badger thought. Pride pulsed through the fear in the mother's voice. "Vern's a good provider. She could get anything she wanted, all she had to do was go pick it out."

Badger nodded. "Think you could go look through her wardrobe, see if something like either one of them outfits is missing?"

Mrs. Ritski nodded but not hopefully. "I'll try."

"Strand, you go with her."

Badger waited till both had cleared the door, turned reluctantly to Vern. "Vern . . . it almost looks like she hurried home, quick changed her clothes, started back out again, got a couple of blocks, maybe remembered she forgot something, changed her mind, who knows, started back toward home."

"But . . . why?" Vern asked plaintively.

Badger moved in a little closer to Vern, eyed him man to man. "Vern, think hard now. I know, no man likes to think it, but could your wife possibly be meeting some other man?" Vern's eyes hardened down to bloodflecked buckshot, but Badger had to continue, such was his job. "Who knows, maybe some stupid little nothing thing she somehow got herself trapped in, was even trying to break off, get out of—"

"No!" Vern was shaking his head all the while. His whole body shook. "No! No!" he kept saying, crowding Badger's words even faster.

"—but she agrees to meet this guy one last time, she doesn't have her car this day, so she agrees to meet him in his car at the intersection of Wilson and Oakdale—"

"No!"

"Against her better judgment. She goes there anyway—

gets there, thinks better of it, starts walking back home, sees
your carpenter, chats with him a few seconds, keeps on going,
the guy comes along, sees she's not at the intersection where
they agree, can even see her walking back home from where
he's driving on Wilson, gets mad, goes after her, goes skidding to a stop, tries to argue her into going with him, her
glasses get knocked off, she finally agrees or he forces her
into the car, she goes somewhere with him, now it's been
done, she's ashamed to come home, too ashamed to come
home . . . face you."

"No. No, Lieutenant, no. Not another word."

"No. No, I didn't think so either. But I had to . . ." Badger
spread his own big gnarled shotgun hands. ". . . lay it out
there."

"No, Lieutenant, not with Bev. That kind of thing . . . just
ain't in her. Right now . . . I wish it was . . . but it just ain't."

"OK." Badger nodded. " 'Nough said."

Now Vern nodded, eyed up Badger. "OK, now you tell
me, Badger. What do you really think has happened to my
wife?"

Badger took a deep breath, but even this was easier than
the other with a guy like Vern Lukken. "If she's the woman
you say she is, only one thing could have happened to her.
She had to be taken by force." Vern nodded again, held
Badger's eyes. "Let's only hope," Badger continued, "he
didn't use too much."

"You think it's . . . the same guy . . . that got them others?"

Badger let out a long slow sigh. Now it was his turn to
have trouble holding Vern's eyes. "Could be, Vern, could be.
Up till now, I didn't think . . . any of them were connected.
Now . . . Christ . . . I don't know."

Vern Lukken hooked his head toward his picture window;
out there beyond the wild land ran Fauntleroy. "This Brown
kid . . . it's no secret you've been after him since Linda Lou
Craig. You think it's him?"

"On Linda, yes. The rest . . . I got no connections—"

"Do you think it's him!" Vern's hands jumped with his
voice, both into fists. Badger would rather have been hit with
the last.

It was all he could do to hold Vern's blood-seeking eyes.

"Vern . . . Vern, if I knew it was him, I'd have took him a long time ago."

There'd be no stopping Vern now short of shooting him. He moved in close, reached out and grabbed Badger's arm in his own big callused claw. "You're not answering me, Badger. I asked you if you *think* it's him *now!*"

Badger thought a long while. Seemed like the whole year and eight plus months since Linda disappeared went zooming through his head. Here was a man who very likely had just lost his wife asking him point-blank the question. No, it wasn't asking now, it was demanding. This guy he couldn't equivocate with like he could with himself. This wasn't the press, a bull session with other law enforcement officials, the public at large who could be put off with a "No comment" or "That's police information" or "At this point, I'm not at liberty to speculate," so on and so forth. No, this wasn't even himself, who, hurt as he might be by his nerve-racking, heart-squeezing, doubt-breeding inability to "take" whoever "it" was that had done Linda and now maybe all the others, still had his wife and kids safe at home . . . at least, as far as he knew, they had been when he left home that morning.

"Vern, if I knew Bill Brown had done anything since Linda, even a lousy traffic ticket, I'd take him as soon as you get your big claw off me." Vern took the hint. His hand dropped away, but he didn't back off. "If I thought he was responsible for Forshey, I'd have him under surveillance night and day—I'd scrape up the men somewhere. And if I couldn't some other cops would, the WSP, Helvetia County, whoever. They got everything I got on him. And, if they don't, all they got to do is ask. This ain't the dark ages; we got all kind of electronic gadgets now. We pass this kind of info on suspects back and forth every day." Now Badger moved in the last half step separating him and Lukken. This was his territorial imperative. He tapped one of his own big fingers on the even bigger chest. "You don't see none of them arresting him either. Even tailing him, unless I request it. Shit, those other cases ain't mine. Only Linda. And now this one—Vern, I just got here two hours ago. Man, I'm human too. I only got two arms and two legs, one brain, one heart. So many men to help me. But I'd find a way. If I thought that slimy little psalm singer was responsible for more than Linda, I'd find a way."

Vern Lukken just nodded. He understood a man like Badger. Just like Badger understood him. "If Bev . . . is gone . . . and he got her . . . don't get in my way."

"Step lively then, Vern. Because, if I find that out, it'll take some fast stepping to get to him before I do."

25

The midafternoon sun bounced off the hood of Marley Walton's new GMC pickup, dancing red-orange-green ingots melted off the glossy green surface, sparks arcing back against the windshield. It reminded him of when he used to work in the foundries. He was a helluva lot better off now just putting the cars together at Chevrolet, particularly now since he'd made foreman. If only he could shake this godawful toothache. The whole left side of his jaw hurt. If he didn't hurry up, he'd be late for his three o'clock appointment too. He only had a few minutes left, but it was tough going trying to make time down River into this glaring sun. He wished he'd remembered to bring his sunglasses. His left hand reached up and snapped the sun visor down. By crouching and peeking just along the leading edge of the visor he could see better but not great. Another car was coming toward him along the two-lane residential street. Coming up on the right was a new house, the yard hadn't even been seeded in yet, the front door was opening and—

My Lord, was it a mirage! It didn't look like the young girl had any clothes on. No, he blinked his eyes, she's behind some bushes now, squinted, yes, she had no clothes on. Except a necktie around her neck. She's running across the dirt yard toward the street. There's something wrong with the way she runs. Her arms, her hands are tied behind her back. Out in the street toward me—"Watch out!"

Marley Walton didn't realize it, but he had been braking his truck ever since he saw the front door open, so he got it stopped in time. He had seen her mouth working while she

213

was running across the dirt yard. When the tires quit squealing and she was beside his open passenger side window, he could almost make out what she was saying. Almost, but not quite. He didn't know if it was just because she was so hysterical or because he was so welded to the blood coming out of her mouth and smearing down the front of that naked young body.

"Help me!" he heard now. "Help me! There's a man in there trying to kill my little brother!"

Marley Walton jumped out his side door. By this time the other car that had been coming toward him was alongside. "Cover her up," he directed the startled face, "get her in your car." That said, Marley Walton jumped back in his pickup, spun his truck into the new cement slab drive, slid it to an angled stop directly behind the older brown Chevrolet Impala, blocking it off if it needed to be. Though the naked young girl had said nothing about it and he hadn't had time to ask, Marley Walton somehow felt that this brown 1974 Chevrolet Impala didn't belong in front of this new house on this new cement slab circular drive. "STP-500, STP-500, STP-500," he kept saying over and over to himself as he ran toward the front door. Suddenly he caught himself, what if something should happen to him in there? "The license number!" he yelled back over his shoulder to the other man who by now had the naked young girl in his car—another passing motorist had stopped, two women were running toward the scene—"STP-500," Walton hollered, "write down the license number. STP-500."

The front door was opening. Just as he turned back from hollering the license number and was about to jump up on the steps, the front door slowly opened and a young fellow came hesitantly out onto the two-step poured cement porch. Walton felt his body start to go into a springing crouch. His hands, fingers curled halfway, worked out in front of him. He'd always been kinda brave; this was no time to stop.

"Is there a little boy in the house?" he heard his voice ask. Yet, even as he assessed his own courage, asked the question, he was assessing the other. Slender, I got him there. I don't see a weapon but he's kinda got his hands down behind his body, maybe one in his pocket—might be a knife or something in there. No doubt he's the one, there's blood on his green T-shirt, pants—

"Yes, I guess so," the slender young fellow with the medium length hair falling haphazardly forward on his forehead answered in a fairly calm but rather high-pitched voice.

"Where is he?" Walton asked, trying to keep his voice just as smoothly calm, all the while working in a little closer to the slender young man on the porch.

"He's upstairs." There was something else goofy about the guy. Yes, the sunglasses he was wearing, they were teardrop shaped, more like the kind a girl would wear—

"Is he all right?" Walton asked almost casually, carefully, for he had one foot on the bottom step now.

"Yes, I guess he's all right . . . why shouldn't he be?" It appeared to Walton that the young man's body tensed when he asked that question, might be gathering itself to leap off the porch.

"I don't know," Walton answered casually, gathering the strength in his anchored springing leg, "I want to see him. You better wait right here until the police get here—"

The young man leaped by Walton as he grabbed for him, breaking away with an astounding show of strength and agility, was in his car and slamming the door shut before Walton could gather his bigger slower body and sprint after him. Walton grabbed hold of the car door handle and tried to jerk it open but the young man already had the door locked and the window rolled up. Still pulling on the door handle, Walton swiveled his head quickly to see if he could sight a rock or anything handy with which to smash in the window and get at the young man. It occurred to him that, if it was a gun the young man was concealing, now would be a perfect time to take one through the back of his head. The engine of the brown Chevy snapped alive, the car jerked backward in a sharp semicircle, banging into Walton's lower body enough to knock him off balance and send him tumbling into the dirt hole of the doughnut driveway. Scrambling to his feet, Walton watched the car gun forward straight at the house then veer at the last moment around the basketball pole erected off the end of the garage apron, go plowing across this freshly seeded half of the lawn, heading back toward the driveway. Walton, realizing that the young man had in mind to intersect the driveway again behind his pickup truck and thence out onto River Road, ran kitty-corner behind his truck, leaped forward, wildly grabbing at the passenger side door handle of the speeding brown car hoping this one would be unlocked. Though he knew it was futile, even foolishly dangerous—the brown Chevy was rocketing past—Marley Walton just had to make this one last desperate try to stop the young man from escaping.

But this time he physically failed. Walton bounced off the side of the speeding car and lay once more in the dirt watching the brown Chevy STP-500 hurtle across the driveway, over the ditch and culvert, take off south on River Street. "STP-500!" Walton screamed again in the general direction of the people huddling around the car containing the bloodied young girl. "Call the police!" Then, turning back and running toward the house, he saw a sight even more ghastly than the bloodied girl, for she had always been moving, running, right from the time she came out the front door. Now came a young boy, crawling, inching his way, his bared upper body gleaming richly red in the bright hot sunlight, torturedly sliding himself along in his own blood till he finally stopped and just lay there half in and half out the still open door. Just lay there, very still, balancing on the threshold.

Badger and Jensen were on their way to Smoky's Body Shop to backtrack Beverly Lukken's bus route. They had come up with an MTA driver who was pretty sure he remembered her being on his bus between nine and ten Monday morning, August 14th, the day before yesterday. It was 3:14 P.M. Badger automatically glanced at his wristwatch when the all-points bulletin started crackling through the unmarked squad car's police radio. "All cars, all cars, be on immediate lookout for 1974 brown Chevrolet Impala, license number STP-500, that is Samuel Thomas Peter 5-0-0—"

Damn, that sounds familiar, Badger said to himself as first the letters then the digits dropped one by one into his memory bank. "Brown!" he almost screamed. "That's Bill Brown's car—"

"—last seen heading south on River Road, Mesa Township, Portage County, at high rate of speed. Subject driving car white male, slender to medium build, brown medium length hair, approximately five foot eight to five foot ten, early twenties—"

"That's him," Jensen said quickly, tersely, afraid to break the radio flow.

"—wearing tan or brown pants, green pullover short-sleeve polo-type shirt, possibly bloodstained, subject fleeing

stabbing and rape scene, subject considered extremely dangerous, very likely armed with at least a knife—REPEAT—This
is Portage County Sheriff's Department calling all cars, all
cars, immediate alert. Stabbing, rape, just went down, suspect
fleeing scene south on River Road, Mesa Township, Portage
County in brown 1974 Chevrolet Impala, Samuel Thomas
Peter 5-0-0—BULLETIN—car traced, registered to a Bill
Ray Brown, 1546 Fauntleroy, Little Falls—"

"He's coming home," Badger growled, thumbing in the
transmit button of the mike he already held in his hand. "Portage County, this is 691, Lieutenant Badger, LFPD. We have a
history on your stabbing/rape just went down. We know the
suspect, we will attempt to intercept."

"Very good, 691, what are your plans?"

"Stakeout . . ." Badger suddenly stopped himself. "Negative, Portage County, let me set the trap first, then I will advise."

"What? Come again, 691, I do not read you—"

"Subject we seek extremely devious, Portage County.
Complex history, may have access to police band."

"I read you now, 691. Advise when possible, necessary."

"You got it." Badger slammed the transmitter back in its
cradle, hissed at Jensen through clenched teeth, "Head for
Fauntleroy . . ." Yet, even as he said it, he instinctively felt he
was wrong. No, not this time. This time I think he'll be running to his new mama. "Strike that, we'll take Algonquin,
Sarah Fortunato." Snapping the transmitter back up, Badger
radioed home. "Little Falls dispatch, this is Badger, did you
monitor Portage County/691?"

"You bet" came back the excited informal reply.

"Stakeout, all available cars. 1546 Fauntleroy; Little Falls
State Bank, Marion Branch; his grandparents' home on Jefferson—check Watchdog Surveillance, see if he's slated to be at
work this evening, if so, where—stake that too."

"Roger, will do. Where will you be, 691?"

"Cruising," Badger snapped. Yes, his bones spoke surely
now. It was 3:17, Bill will come to Sarah. Sarah would be
getting off from work at the bank very shortly, probably 4:00,
4:30. It would take Bill an hour or so to drive from that location in Portage County to 4312 Algonquin no matter how fast
he drove. That would give him time to get into her empty
apartment, get the blood off him, change clothes before she

got home. "Christ," his skeptical police mouth breathed aloud, "I hope I'm guessing right. I sure want to be the one to take that psalm-singing sonofabitch."

"Me too," Jensen muttered, taking a corner on two wheels.

Badger figured if Bill was coming from Portage County he would drive down Algonquin from the north, so he directed Jensen to park around the corner to the south on Locust Avenue. Here they had a good sight line diagonally across the lawn to where Bill invariably parked along the curb directly in front of Sarah's apartment building. It was only a hundred feet or so, and their unmarked police car was further obscured from Bill's projected perspective by an intervening maple tree.

"Leave the motor running," Badger muttered, reaching out through his open window to position his side rearview mirror so he could see south on Algonquin, just in case. "Keep an eye behind us too," he cautioned Jensen.

Jensen pulled his Brewers baseball cap down low over his brows and lolled back in his seat, eyes sweeping Algonquin when he wasn't watching Locust behind. Badger slouched down along his door, cheek resting on the window frame, one eye on the parking spot in front of 4312, the other flicking occasionally south along Algonquin. Badger was wearing his Chicago Cubs cap. A passerby could very easily mistake them for two weary drunks just back from the ballpark.

They didn't have to wait long. A chocolate brown Chevy slid into Badger's rearview mirror. He knew it so well he didn't even bother trying to read the inverted license number —"Here he comes," he hissed, not moving. "Behind us. Don't move. Soon as he goes by, slide low in your seat, call for backup." Badger watched the chocolate-brown Chevy Impala grow ever larger, watched it finally fill his entire rearview mirror, a part of him thinking how totally right it was that, even now, Bill was coming from the wrong direction.

The chocolate-brown car slid out of the ninety-degree mirror. Badger listened to it go by, so close he probably could have reached out and touched it, was aware of soft gospel music gently wafting out the other's open windows.

Now Bill's car moved into his naked sightline, proceeding away from him. Badger watched it jockey into the hoped-for parking space, half-heard Jensen's terse radio communication.

Waited till he saw Bill's brake lights blink off. "Let's go," Badger growled, "church is over."

Jensen idled around the corner, slid in smartly behind the brown Chevy. Bill was just getting out of his car, busy locking his doors, didn't even look back in their direction. The two cops hit the asphalt running, bent over, pulling out weapons as they dashed the two car lengths. Now Bill started to turn toward them. "Freeze!" Badger snapped, jamming his revolver into Bill's ribs.

"What . . . ?!" Bill said, turning so as to roll away from the gun barrel.

"Don't move!"

"What . . . why are you doing this crazy—" Bill actually started to move away, take a step toward the apartment building.

"Stop, you sneaky creep, or I'll blast you on the spot!"

Bill stopped, a look of abject disgust filling his face, shook his head the same way. He looked from Badger to Jensen, glazed eyes sliding down to their out-thrust guns. "You . . . dopes."

Badger's gun hand came up. He had all he could do to stop himself from pistol whipping that sneering arrogant face. He might not have been able to, but just then squad cars came sliding in from all angles. Atwell was there, Poulous, Dinato, Porath, half of Uniform. Badger vaguely wondered who was minding the store. All ringing Bill, circling him like a pit bull, guns thrusting at him, hands grabbing for him, twisting him around, jerking his hands up behind his back, Bill sputtering protests all the while. "Why?! I insist! My right to know. You must tell me why—"

"Here," Badger directed, stepping forward to take the cuffs out of one of the young uniformed cop's hands. "Here, let me do that."

He did. Cinching the cuffs down so tight on those slender, almost girlish wrists, Badger hoped he felt some bones give. He was somewhat satisfied to see Bill's eyes tear, the sudden pain swallowing the bullshit innocence in quick sucking breaths. "Like that, pretty boy," Badger sneered low in the dainty ear—he had a fearsome impulse to bite it off—"that feel a little bit like what you did to Linda's neck?"

Badger felt Bill jerk like he'd just been stuck with a cattle prod. Watched his eyes slowly widen, clear, focus. He had the feeling Bill was only now really seeing him. "You . . ."

"Yeah, it's me, baby. Your old buddy, Badger."

Bill's eyes widened even more. Finally nodded his head, just once. "Sure, that figures. You're finally framing me for Linda's disappearance."

The
Indictments:
Part 4

26

The arrest of Bill Ray Brown for the criminal assault and rape of fourteen-year-old Dawn Mathews and the attempted murder of both her and her twelve-year-old brother, Johnny, caused some quick rethinking by law enforcement officials of all outstanding murder and missing persons cases in the Greater Big Falls area. Chief among those law enforcement officials involved was Prosecutor Michael Hunt, titularly in charge of all crimes prosecuted within his jurisdiction, Helvetia County. Having assumed the mantle of office at 12:01 A.M. January 1, 1977, possibly within minutes of the time Linda Lou Craig became a missing person, Mike Hunt often had cause to reflect on the irony that his reign as a tough law-and-order prosecutor and the baffling disappearances had commenced at virtually the same exact time. The disappearances hopefully ended, for it now appeared to Mike Hunt that the series of crimes had been most likely committed by one man, and that man was Bill Ray Brown. He was almost certain that Bill Ray Brown had somehow done away with Linda Lou Craig New Year's Eve, 1976–1977, then either took an eighteen-month sabbatical from murder or had killed in other areas—there were girls who had disappeared under like circumstances in neighboring towns, including two coeds from the University of Wisconsin at Iola. Then, setting up his grisly operation once more in the Greater Big Falls area during the summer of 1978, he had killed or otherwise caused to become missing Danielle Forshey, Cindy Fall, maybe, and Beverly Lukken, culminating with his botched job against the Mathews children in Portage County.

Hunt worked late into the night that Bill Brown was arrested, making sure this latest piece fit the rest of the puzzle.
There was no doubt in his mind Brown had fully intended to
murder/mutilate Dawn Mathews very much as he had Danielle
Forshey. The only thing that stayed his butchering hand was
the interfering chain of events. Her little brother Johnny's arrival in the house just as Brown was in the process of throttling Dawn. Then the arrival outside the house of Walton
closely followed by Mesa Fire Chief Day. Hunt believed that
Brown very likely had either seen or heard Walton and later
Day outside the house and realized his only hope of escape
was just to leave Johnny Mathews, hopefully for dead, and try
to bluff his way out before the two men came in the house and
saw what had really gone on in there.

Yes, that was the way it looked to Mike Hunt, high in his
office overlooking Big Falls—fairly open and shut. Now that
the case was finally open, it was left to him to shut Brown
behind bars. Hang him if he could. At this first-night juncture,
mad dog Brown safely ensconced in the Portage County jail
awaiting arraignment tomorrow morning, Mike Hunt wasn't
all that much interested in the why of Bill Ray Brown committing these seemingly senseless acts. He still had to put
together the what and how, find something to prosecute him
on. Certainly, it wasn't lack of interest on his part. He was as
intrigued by the "why" aspect of the shy young "Christian's"
reign of terror as the next man. It was just that he probably
had less time than even the average citizen to speculate on this
new Jekyll and Hyde awaiting trial. Of course, his office
didn't even have the job of prosecuting Brown on the
Mathews assaults; that fell to his counterpart, Clarence Martin, of the adjoining county, Portage. But it still followed that
he would be the one left with cleaning up the bigger mess, the
Craig/Forshey/Fall/Lukken disappearances and/or murders in
his own Helvetia County. And only Christ knows how many
more.

Continuing to sift through the police reports on Craig, Hunt
reflected upon his prior position on the Craig case. He, along
with most everyone but Badger, had leaned toward an actual
disappearance at first, under her own power, but quite probably aided and abetted by her boyfriend, Bill Brown. For quite
a while, much of his office effort was directed toward The
Path, the farout religious group—Hunt's information seemed

to indicate that the Craig girl might have hooked up with their main camp in Iowa—and the thought that The Path had successfully swallowed her in their brainwashed program, had sent her on her way proselytizing for them. Possibly, with her strong background in French, she might be in their language missionary program, conceivably in the Montreal area, or France itself. The Path tries to break down family ties and with hers apparently already somewhat severed through her parents' divorce, she had seemed a likely prospect.

Then his office had done an analysis of Linda Lou Craig's letters and diaries, of Bill Brown's writings to her. There were some very weird things here. Hunt felt it even now as he reread them. References by both of the almost obsessively religious young people to such phenomena as daily encounters with God. Bill Brown wrote to her from his 1976 summer job on Oyster Island that he and God had borrowed a ten-speed bicycle this fine summer day and the two of them had gone bicycling all around the island, talked, and written letters together. Then there was "The Miracle Letter," as it came to be known in his office. Bill wrote to Linda, again from Oyster Island, that he had been climbing on cliffs and had slipped and dropped at least 100 feet onto a pile of sharp rocks. But, just as he was about to be hoist on these earthy petards, it seemed like a hand reached out and caught his hurtling body, so he settled in without a scratch. "Linda," Bill felt obliged to add, "I know this sounds insane, but first I was scared like hell, but then I heard a voice inside me say, 'It's not your time yet.'"

Hmmm, Hunt wondered, "scared like hell" . . .

Both Linda and Bill regularly wrote letters to Jesus. Linda noted in her diary, "He planted the seed in me." A school of thought had taken that to mean that she was likely pregnant, but Hunt himself felt that the allusion was more Biblical than physical. More likely something to do with the seed of a particular faith, one eschewed by Bill, maybe even the "seed" of her subsequent running away.

There was a fanatically religious letter Bill had written to Mrs. Craig, Linda's mother, also in 1976. It was cluttered with jagged crosses, exclamation marks, childish squiggles and curlicues, ringing perorations to God's glory, so on and so forth. Sad, sick, weird, Hunt thought, massaging tired eyes with both forefingers, letting the fingertips slide down over his aquiline nose, stroke his jaunty, jet-black mustache. Why, in the name of God, would a normal young man write a letter like this to his prospective mother-in-law? "Because he ain't normal, that's why!"

Hunt's mind strayed to his last visit with Mrs. Irene Craig. That poor woman would never be the same. Neither would the Forsheys, the Falls, the Lukkens . . . something started ticking in his head about the Bev Lukken case, something maybe he should do, should have done already, but what?

Unable to translate the ticking into thought, he took another swig of his cold black coffee, went back to work. Maybe now he could at least give Mrs. Craig and the rest of the survivor/victims their pound of flesh—a small enough return for a life.

Glancing through other kindred correspondence, Hunt noted the statement Linda allegedly made to her cousin, Crissy Hogan. "Bill is not enough of a man for me. I would have to wear the pants in the family." The cousin further noted that Linda had once characterized Bill to her as a "little itty bitty boy." Bill was constantly referring to certain passages in the Scriptures, certain verses: 1 Corinthians, verse 13; Psalms 84:11. Hunt read, "Life, shall in perpetuity, remain centered around and in Philippians 1:21 and Galatean 5:22-23; growing and growing; serving life; on all that is all."

Hunt shook his head, dumbfounded. Then this guy goes out and murders! Hacks people up? Rapes and assaults innocent children?

He reminded himself again to get ahold of a Bible and look up these passages.

Hunt continued glancing through the mound of data on Craig/Brown. Tried to correlate all they had done throughout the investigation, particularly his office: The Path investigation, pursued them all the way to their U.S. home office in St. Louis, Missouri; The Jesus People, U.S.A., headquartered in Chicago; The Way International, also Chicago; Hare Krishna; The People's Temple, Jim Jones's outfit, on and on. Why all these farout fanatical religious movements springing up all over creation? Scientologists, the Moonies—had Linda Lou Craig run off and joined them? Why would decent, well-educated, young Americans in ever-increasing numbers continue turning to these types of organizations to try to find whatever they think is missing in their lives? Why would a young

American want to spend his or her life panhandling for some South Korean madman?

Take Bill Ray Brown himself. Why was he so fanatically religious? What did he need that much religion for? Linda Lou Craig? She seemed to be inexorably drawn back to Bill Brown, no matter what she apparently thought of him. She kept coming back to a man she herself characterized as a "little itty bitty boy," not enough man for her. When she was away from him, she seemed able to see him clearly enough. But as soon as he got physically close enough to get her back in his clutches again, there she was following him around like some brain-washed Moonie, mouthing his warped religious platitudes.

So what was their actual sexual connection, if any? She wrote in her diary about feeling guilt for allowing herself to be involved sexually with him, letting him go too far. But how far is far to them? French kissing? Then, on the other hand, she wrote of him trying to force her sexually. Yet "He's not enough of a man for me," "Can't even kiss right," "Doesn't know when to kiss or not."

Hunt shook his head again, let the words slip slowly out. "None of these people are too tightly wrapped."

Then after the hunters found the clothing laid out the way they were, his office had become convinced Linda Lou was the victim of a ritual killing. Again, many scenarios had been constructed but, eventually, all of them played out too. Linda Lou Craig had slid again to the back burner.

Then Danielle Forshey disappeared in June, two months ago. Hunt had automatically said Bill Brown did it, but this time the police had disagreed, particularly Badger, the cop who should know the most on Brown. Cooperation between the various agencies broke down again, everybody going his own way.

There's some connection between Forshey and Lukken, his mind ticked . . . but what?

Mike shrugged, continued turning papers, pictures, clippings, transcripts, depositions, affidavits, a veritable mountain of fact, half-fact, nonfact, guesses, theories, bullshit! Seemed like everybody who worked on these cases had a different opinion, their own jealously-guarded scenario. When Cindy Fall disappeared, Hunt had requested a meeting of all agencies to share information. This had met with some reluctance, even then. He finally had to threaten to take the investigations on all the disappearances and the Forshey murder away from local agencies and turn them over to the State Police unless cooperation ensued. An all-hands meeting was finally held in July, last month, dealing with all unsolved female homicides. All names and info on board and everybody to share whatever they had. There were other good suspects. It soon became apparent that not all agencies were uniform in their suspicion of Bill Ray Brown or that he had killed them all. Yet, he remained the prime suspect on Craig. There appeared to be no connection between Brown and Fall. One police agency, the University Police, firmly believed she had run off. Also, Fall was different from the other three in looks. Craig, Forshey, and Bev Lukken all pretty much looked alike and were roughly the same size. All wore the same kind of large oval-rectangular horn-rimmed glasses. Hmm, yes, that may be as good a connection as any, Hunt mused as he stared down at the faces of the young women spread out on his desk before him.

That brought Hunt up to date. Bev Lukken day before yesterday, Brown's arrest for the Mathews assault late this afternoon. Now, naturally, everybody was convinced Brown had done them all, for miles around. But still not one single stitch of physical evidence. Not even hard facts. They now knew Brown had the capacity to commit the kinds of crimes under investigation—if he, in fact, had committed the Mathews assault—but unless Brown started singing and supplied some facts himself, they were actually no further ahead on Craig, Forshey, Fall, and Lukken than they had been before the Mathews assault.

Hunt then pondered the missing items, "the cache," as he and his boys were beginning to characterize them. It appeared that some small items were missing from every one of the victim's personal effects. Of course, they weren't certain on Linda Lou Craig, having only found her clothing and purse. Her so-called missing items could still be with the body, but Hunt's hunch was that her glasses and engagement ring were part of the killer's cache too. Missing from Danielle Forshey had been one earring, her purse, shoes and glasses, upper body clothing. With Cindy Fall, there was no body, no anything, no clues, background and life-style different from that of the other missing women—no glasses worn, no look-alike.

Again Hunt was tempted to lift her out of his composite file completely, but, at last thought, left her file with the others. Beverly Lukken's purse was missing, glasses were found in ditch along roadway. Maybe killer had them too but somehow dropped them?

There's something about Lukken . . . Forshey . . . Lukken.

Yes, definitely, glasses seemed to play some kind of connecting role between the three victims. But Dawn Mathews had not worn glasses. If Bill Ray Brown only attacked women wearing glasses, females ranging in age from nineteen to thirty, why had he attacked fourteen-year-old Dawn Mathews without glasses?

Turning back to the Brown file, Hunt plunged once more into its voluminous depths, scanning through to the bitter end. A seemingly inconsequential statement just taken by Badger that very afternoon from Brown's current girlfriend, Sarah Fortunato, caught his eye. Badger was questioning her as to Brown's activities on the two days prior, leading back to the Beverly Lukken disappearance. Sarah Fortunato had stated that Brown had spent the afternoon of the fifteenth, Tuesday, yesterday, the day between the Lukken disappearance and the Mathews assault, "going to Sears to buy a new lock for his bedroom door . . . and returning to his parents' home at 1546 Fauntleroy to remove his old bedroom door lock and replace it with the new one." His sister, also home at the time, had observed her brother at his locksmith work.

Now why in the world would a normal guy be so concerned about changing locks on his bedroom door in a home he shares with his parents and grown sister—a normal guy who has a divorcée girlfriend who has her own apartment, with two little kids, ages three and five? Now if he was changing locks on that bedroom door, maybe the old one wouldn't lock, they didn't want the little girls walking in on them, that would make some sense, but in his parents' home? Hunt reached for his interoffice phone, buzzed Assistant Chief Prosecutor Jim Barry, logging a little late work himself. "Jim, I want to search Bill Brown's house tonight. His parents' home, 1546 Fauntleroy Lane. Concentrating on Bill's bedroom. An all-agency search. Give them all a chance to send some men, so we don't get any stupid backbiting bullshit on this one. And tell them . . . if there's a leak on this, I'll personally hunt that person down and run him out of the county!"

"You're not talking about tonight-tonight, are you, Mike?"

"You betcha."

"Checked your watch lately? It's way past midnight."

"It is?"

"You betcha. I've got to get ahold of, let's see, that would be Little Falls, Judge Wally Seefeldt, get him to sign a search warrant, order of suppression—"

"Dammit all," Hunt swore in mild frustration. He knew all about due process. "If we could just once move on something as soon as we thought of it. Of course, the family's probably got it all cleaned out already—"

"What you looking for, Mike?"

Just that very second, just as he was about to answer this other question, just standing there holding the telephone in one hand, his other resting on Prosecutor Salan's autopsy report on Forshey—he might even have been subliminally re-reading it as he talked—the other thought that had been ticking took. "Lukken could still be alive!"

"What? What the hell are you saying, Mike—"

"Beverly Lukken could still be alive! Salan, Hague thinks maybe Brown kept Forshey alive for possibly four days, maybe torture . . . Jim, he only got Bev Lukken two days ago . . . bought a new lock, changed locks on his bedroom door."

"What . . . what the hell *are* you saying, Mike?"

"Nah, it's just too . . . crazy, but, God, this whole thing is. Jim, his folks were gone up north sailing over the Father's Day weekend, the house was empty, some people here think he might have kept Forshey alive there part of the time."

"OK. I see what you're driving at, but they're home this time. It happened on a Monday, everybody's there, the sisters, the folks—"

"Well, forget about them being there. She could still be alive—maybe we can still save her. You work on the search, set it up for as soon as possible. I'm going to call Knutson, ask him to go out to the Portage County Jail, talk to Brown, ask him!"

27

Ken Knutson had been eating dinner when the first call came —the one that really blew his mind. Leona Brown frantically screaming something about Bill having been arrested by Badger on some trumped up charge—framed, Leona kept screaming, for something that supposedly happened out in Portage County. That Ken should go out to the Portage County Jail right away!

Ken did. "Excuse me, hon," he had said to his wife Mary and left his half-eaten dinner—she was used to that. Hauled ass for Portage County.

But Bill was nowhere to be found when he got there. Though it was past eight and he should have been by this time—according to the printout he had been arrested at 4:47 in the afternoon. Ken smelled a rat. "Where you got him stashed?" he asked the only person around with any rank at all, a deputy sheriff by the name of Mahew. That in itself was suspicious, made a lawyer almost believe that the top brass were elsewhere, doing something else.

They were—at the Mesa Township Fire Station, grilling Bill. At Badger's request, Ken guessed. Piecing the story together from what Mahew grudgingly told him and what was coming in on the ticker, it appeared that Bill had been arrested by Badger and half the LFPD at his new fiancée's house for some alleged assault and rape that had occurred out on River Street in Portage County earlier in the afternoon. After a quick look-in at LFPD, Bill had been spirited, along with his car, to the Mesa Township Fire Station and had been there ever since. Why? That was simple enough, as far as Ken was concerned.

This was a hands-across-the-border job—county, that is, Portage and Helvetia. Very likely every top cop of both counties was out there right now giving Bill the third degree, grilling him on every murder that had gone down in the last ten years.

It stunk to high heaven, smelled of police complicity and duplicity. Unable to get Bill on Linda and now faced with the recent rash of murders and disappearances, the police had linked hands and rigged some kind of hit where they could pull Bill in and grill him for a couple of hours before his attorney could step in between them.

Ken was boiling. "You call your boss or Badger or whoever's behind this and tell him that he better get my client down here and book him or let him go or whatever the hell you're going to do and damn quick! Or I'll sue both counties for false arrest, false imprisonment, infringement upon civil liberties, and every other damn thing I can think of!"

That did it. The right call was made. Bill showed up at the Portage County Jail within minutes. Ken was even more incensed when he found out who had turned in the call on Bill —Fire Chief Day of the selfsame Mesa Township Fire Department. Talk about coincidence. Bill and his car are tucked away in the very same fire station of the chief who had pulled the alarm on Bill at a residence within his jurisdiction —the whole thing tucked away for Badger out in the hinterlands. If this didn't smell of intercounty and interdepartmental collusion, his name wasn't Ken Knutson!

Particularly after talking to Bill—he didn't have any more idea of what he was being charged with or held for than the man in the moon. According to him, he had just left work, spent the afternoon shopping at a couple of stores for a birthday present for Lori, one of his new fiancée's little children, was just heading for her apartment when Badger hit him.

Ken thought that over now, as he drove back out to the Portage County Jail in response to Mike Hunt's weird request. The only thing that had gotten him out of bed at this unearthly hour of the morning was the urgency in Hunt's voice, the real belief he obviously held that Bill had had something to do with the disappearance of the Beverly Lukken woman.

"It just doesn't make any sense." What would the Bill Brown he knew be doing running around in broad daylight, attacking married women and teenage kids?

But he also knew Mike Hunt. And the Mike Hunt he knew wasn't one to jump to idiot conclusions.

Ken thought on this as he drove. Maybe he didn't know Bill Brown. After all, he hadn't had all that much to do with him since the initial flurry over Linda Lou Craig had died down. Other than an occasional conversation with Fred over his fee and a lovely letter and Christmas card from Bill, he hadn't had all that much contact with Bill and his family in the last year and a half. Maybe there had been some drastic change in the kid he hadn't perceived last evening. Maybe Linda's disappearance and all the resultant flap had somehow unhinged him, and he had snapped and gone off on some kind of goofy kick.

Nah, Bill had seemed just the same as ever last evening. Confused, yes, who wouldn't be, but there was sure no sign that he had been engaged in anything criminal, that day or any other—at least, as far as Ken could tell. And he didn't consider himself any idiot either. He always figured he could tell when a client was telling the truth. Yes, this whole thing still stunk of some kind of foul fish or fishy fowl. Even if Hunt was involved . . . shit, for all he knew, the whole thing might be Hunt's idea! He was the one on the big spot about the disappearances/murders, his was the head the mob would be screaming for if something wasn't done soon, a body dragged forward to pay for all the other bodies.

It did make sense. Maybe the frame was on. Don't think it still doesn't happen, for it does. Particularly when a redneck cop like Badger is convinced a mark has already killed once, he'd have no compunction whatsoever about roping Bill in on something else to get him for Linda. Of course, something had happened out in Portage County. Those two kids were undoubtedly hit in some way by somebody. The cops wouldn't stoop to rig anything that drastic, but they sure as hell would conveniently drop Bill into it if they thought they could gain something on the murders by doing so.

"Surely, they can't now be looking at Bill for all those . . ."

That was some kind of madman nut—the way this Forshey girl was found all hacked up.

Ken shuddered, gripped his steering wheel a little tighter. "No way." Swung into the jail parking lot. Dawn was just checking through dirty gray clouds. There were still plenty of high-powered looking official cars in the lot, but Ken didn't see Badger's or any he recognized from LFPD—or the Helvetia County Prosecutor's Office either, for that matter. Maybe I'm getting paranoid, he thought.

Bill had been sleeping peaceful as a babe, was still rubbing his eyes childishly when the turnkey led him in. He didn't seem to even know what Ken was talking about. "You mean . . . this woman . . . that disappeared a couple of days ago?"

"Yeah, Bill."

"How would I know what happened to her? Where she might be now?"

They were standing, just the two of them, in the jail visiting room. It was the break of day, another hot humid day by the feel of it already. Sunlight creeping through the steel-meshed window fumbled over Bill's face. Ken had the feeling the sunlight was as hesitant about coming back within this dark dank building as he had been. I was afraid of what I might hear, he thought. But now, once more, looking at Bill's youthful unblemished face, his clear, blue, innocent eyes, he felt much better—not great, mind you, but considerably more relieved than he had been last evening when Leona's call came.

His mind already back on that one, he asked that question again. "So, Bill . . . ah, forgetting about this Lukken woman —your position on yesterday, this alleged assault and so forth they claim you committed upon the two Mathews children. You had nothing to do with that either?"

Bill shook his head slowly, never dropping his gaze from Ken's. "Man, that whole thing is . . . weird! Like I told you last night, all I do is punch out from work, change clothes, go to Sears and Woolworth's looking for a birthday present for Lori, am over to Sarah's house by just a little after four—she wasn't even home from work yet—Badger jumps on me and arrests me! How can I do all they're claiming in just that little while? Drive out here to Portage County and back? When I know I went shopping for a birthday present for Lori. If they would have just taken me over to Sears and Woolworth's and let me show them the people that would remember me this whole mess could have been cleared up before it began."

"It's too bad you didn't actually buy the present for Lori," Ken reiterated, as he had a number of times last night.

"I couldn't find anything I wanted. That's why I went to

both stores. Went looking for Sarah to check with her first. Shucks, I was all over Sears, in every kid department in the store. If they'd only use their common sense and listen to what I keep telling everybody and really try to hear what I keep saying, this whole thing would be all over. It's just like with Linda. All they want to do is harass me. Badger, that... fool. Boy, would I like to really tell him what I think of him, right to his face. Some day I'll show him, just you wait and see, really show him! Yeah, if him and some other people would ever stop and really hear what I've been trying to say all along... They're just trying to frame me, use me for the whipping boy for all their mistakes they been making all their lives—"

Ken was forced to interrupt Bill. He had promised to get right back to Mike Hunt on his farfetched theory that Bill might have the Lukken woman stashed somewhere, been keeping her alive for some kind of kinky sex/torture. "Bill, I absolutely have to go. Get back to Hunt on his wild-eyed theory." Ken smiled to soften even the suggestion. "About you and your supposed kinky MO. I've got to be in court on another matter at nine, hardly even have had time to find out what that's all about—"

"I understand. Hey, I'm just so darn glad to see you. I'm starting to think you're just about the only really sane person left out there... 'cept my family, of course." His eyes clouded momentarily, or maybe it was just the sun outside ducking under its own morning cloud; the forecast called for more thunderstorms. "Ah, how... how'd they take it, when you spoke with them last night?"

"Outraged, like us. Up in arms. They'll all be out, soon as the powers that be let them see you."

Bill nodded, but didn't seem quite satisfied with Ken's answer. Finally he asked, "Gramma and grampa... they coming too?"

"I'm sure. I'll make a special effort to make sure—"

"Oh, I'm sure they'd be coming anyway, soon as they can. You think they'll all be here for my arraignment?"

Ken kind of wondered why he would want them there for something as painful as an arraignment could be—that is, of course, if Portage County was actually planning on continuing this charade and actually booking Bill. "Bill, I don't think that will be open to the public—"

"They're not public, they're family."

"Well, even family . . . alright, I'll see what I can do."

Bill's eyes brightened, out from under his cloud. Sure, Ken understood now, the Browns were a deeply connected family, wholly committed to each other. Bill would need their unalloyed support at just such a time as this. Almost as though divining Ken's thinking, Bill suddenly smiled his shy little smile, giving Ken the warm feeling that he was being included within protective family circle as well. Bill's words made him know for sure. "Ken . . . you . . . you'll be there for sure, won't you?"

Ken extended his hand. "Of course." They shook, then, hands still connected, Ken added, "Bill, I told you almost two years ago, the first day you came to my office, I wouldn't let them railroad you. I haven't changed my thinking any."

Bill squeezed his hand in return. "Thanks, Ken. I knew all along I could always count on you."

28

Badger was in his office early the morning after Bill Brown's arrest. The same warm sticky sun shone through the lifting haze down upon him. Dammit, he thought, his bared forearms already sticking to his desktop, is this devil heat wave ever going to end?

He let his head slip forward on his arms, worked his nose into the slippery crack between his wrists. He could just as well have stayed here all night, for he hadn't slept a wink at home. After the initial euphoria of finally nailing Bill Brown had worn off, there had come the other thoughts, feelings, just about the time he was supposed to finally get some sleep. He had blown it. He had let a killer he knew in his bones to be a killer slip through his fingers to kill again! And again! And again! God only knew how many times.

Badger slowly lifted his head, no sleep slept in such thoughts, feelings. And, now, yesterday . . . this . . .

Looking down at the bulldog edition of the *Times Union*, Badger read the headline one more time. EX-FIANCÉ OF LINDA LOU CRAIG ARRESTED FOR ASSAULT, RAPE! He read on, for probably the tenth time: "Bill Ray Brown, 1546 Fauntleroy, Little Falls, was scheduled for arraignment later today . . ." Badger skipped the newly familiar, his eyes drawn magnetically to the familiar old. ". . . but police said they couldn't legally question Bill Brown about the disappearance of Linda Lou Craig, first of four Little Falls women whose disappearances have mystified mid-Wisconsin law enforcement officers."

Badger slowly shook his head, asked his empty office

plaintively, "What in Christ's name are we going to do about some of our laws? The exact right time to sweat him on everything is just exactly when you catch him cold on something else . . ." He dwindled off, helpless, didn't even like the sound of his own voice.

Or the look of his name. ". . . arrested by police stake-out, commanded by Detective Lieutenant Floyd Badger of LFPD . . ." He had no feeling of pride as he usually did. ". . . little thus far is known as to the motive for the vicious attack on the two youngsters, but there is some indication that the suspect, who worked as a store detective for Watchdog Surveillance, had been involved in an argument with a female supervisor at work shortly before the attack took place, and some theorize that may have triggered the violent outburst. The argument reportedly ensued over Brown's refusal to guard the adult magazine section."

Badger sniffed. Why don't they just come out and say it, "pornography."

". . . Portage County Prosecutor Clarence Martin is preparing four felony warrants . . . two counts of assault with intent to murder . . . one count of criminal sexual conduct, first degree, involving a weapon and penetration . . . one count of breaking and entering an occupied dwelling with intent to commit a felony."

"No," Badger assured the pretty young man modeling police-issue coveralls all over the front page of the *Times Union*, "no, my pretty, I'm gonna have to fix you up with something a little fancier than that, say, murder one!" He reached out and yanked down the Beverly Lukken file. Here was the case he would have to nail Brown to his cross on. But he couldn't make any mistakes, would have to make sure he didn't overlook anything as he may have done on Linda. For this time he knew for damn hundred and ten percent sure who the killer was. Frig it if what they say don't match with theory or handbook or precedent or psychology or anything else. I know Bill Brown somehow, somewhere, killed Bev, and that is the way we are going to work. I am going to have me a piece of Brown murder-one ass—

Quit your damn raving and check first where Brown was at the time of Bev Lukken's last known sighting, by Herb Felpel on Oakdale, between 9:00 and 10:00 A.M. Monday morning.

It was 8:05. Jensen should be in his office. He picked up

his interoffice telephone. "Cliff, take somebody and go out to Watchdog Surveillance, 1720 Wolf Road in Ghent and see if you can find out Bill Brown's activities for the morning of August 14, Monday."

"Between 9:00 and 10:00 A.M. perchance, Lieutenant?" The smug voice of Jensen came back.

"Yeah, just for the helluv it."

"You got it."

Bill Brown's work sheet for Monday, August 14, indicated that he was supposed to be at work at 10:00 A.M. at Bookland in Big Falls.

Racing back to Big Falls, Jensen picked up Bill Brown's time card for Monday, August 14, at Bookland: 11:28 A.M., the mechanical printout read. Scribbled in the margin, presumably in Bill Brown's handwriting, were the words, "Due to flat tire."

"That gives him the time," Badger said, when Jensen phoned in. "Now all we need is for someone to place him at the scene."

Hanging up on Jensen, Badger buzzed Detective Sergeant Mahew. "Mahew, buzz out to the Mesa Township Fire Department garage. The Portage County Sheriff's Department and the WSP Crime Lab are out there searching Bill Brown's vehicle. I want you to specifically note the condition of the tires. Particularly in reference to whether or not it appears any of them had been changed as recently as the morning of August 14, Monday. Check closely the spare tire, the jack, condition of spare tire. Is it flat, inflated, dirty? Has it been removed lately? Check the lug nuts on the four rolling tires. Have they been taken off lately? Check the tools, everything. It is extremely important we find out whether the spare has been out or any of the tires removed or replaced on the morning of the fourteenth, Monday. Take your camera."

"Don't you worry, Floyd," Mahew said soberly. "I'll get it all."

Badger was right this time. According to Mahew's report, hand delivered by Mahew himself later in the morning, "... the spare tire was not flat, did not appear to have any recent work done on it, concerning the type of work that might have happened if it was flat recently. Also the jack underneath the spare tire, the top side of the jack was extremely dusty and did not appear to have been handled recently. Concerning the tires and wheels themselves, after State Police pulled the hubs, I did photograph all four (4) tires. These photographs will show that the tires were extremely dusty. The nuts on the tires were extremely dirty, and it is my opinion that these tires had not been removed from the vehicle recently."

Thank you, Mr. Mahew, Badger said to himself as he carefully laid Mahew's report on top the newspaper photograph of Bill Brown. He placed the sheet of LFPD monogrammed paper carefully just over the bare feet of the ex-marching band member, who still looked for all the world like some well-groomed, sweet-faced innocent teenager even in PI overalls. If this were the movies or television, the cops flanking him would be the bad guys. "By the time I get through with you, sweetie, you gonna be all papered over with just such hard evidence. I'll work up from the bottom, cover your head last."

Later that afternoon, Jensen followed up on a tip that had been called in on the phone recorder set up at the Vern Lukken residence by a Sally Rivenburg, 1602 Elmwood, a neighbor of the Lukkens, 1600 Elmwood. Mrs. Rivenburg claimed that at approximately 10:00 A.M. on Monday morning, August 14, 1978, she observed a goldish colored vehicle drive slowly down Elmwood, turn in front of her house and proceed back westbound on Elmwood to Birchwood and north on Birchwood until she lost contact with the vehicle because it left her sight line. Mrs. Rivenburg stated that what drew her attention to this vehicle some three days after the incident was that the picture of Bill Ray Brown shown in the *Times Union* on this date looked very much like the subject she observed driving the vehicle.

Mrs. Rivenburg said she would place herself available to be hypnotized if it was felt such a session would further sharpen her remembrance.

29

At 8:00 P.M. that night, August 17th, 1978, twenty police officers with drawn guns descended on the Fred Brown residence without a warning. Surrounding the home, they moved in quietly, stealthily, from all angles. Badger, task force commander by virtue of territorial imperative, hammered on the front door with the butt of his revolver. Fred Brown opened the door a crack, and Badger thrust the search warrant in his face and growled, "This is a search, Fred."

The search concluded the next day at 1:45 in the afternoon. The twenty officers went through the Brown home from stem to stern, basement to attic, wall to wall, overlooking nothing. Overturning everything, so far as the Browns were concerned. Tearing apart beds, emptying garbage cans, crawling in cupboards, taking up loose carpeting, running snakes in toilet flush lines, whatever they felt they had to do. When they finished their eighteen-hour search, the house was a shambles.

Many personal family items were seized. Prior to their seizure they were photographed in their location, then marked, tagged as evidence. All items were seized by Mahew for LFPD. Minor family skeletons were exhumed, some fairly curious adult reading/viewing material found tucked between mattresses—curious only in the sense that they were found between the mattresses of this professedly highly moral, deeply religious, moral majority American family.

But they didn't find what they came for. No killer cache was found behind Bill's shiny new bedroom lock or anywhere else in the house. Nothing that appeared to be of real significance was found, with the possible exception of a curious Bill

Brown painting depicting an electrified Lord, a muscle-beach Devil, flanking a lowly man in the middle. The Lord's eyes had tiny glowing crosses superimposed on the pupils.

There was something a little curious about the handcuffs too. A pair of shiny clean handcuffs, issued to Bill for use in his role as store detective by Watchdog Surveillance, reposing in the top drawer of his bedroom bureau. Still in their issue box, but apparently without keys, for there were none in the box and none could be found elsewhere in his room—or anywhere, for that matter.

30

Badger didn't think the search was a failure. He had been inside Bill's house—their house—through every nook and cranny. He had pawed over their possessions, dug through their debris, smelled their dirt, saw what they liked, imagined the rest. He noted what wasn't there and took that into consideration too. He had always figured he could tell a lot about a suspect by seeing how he lived, particularly his or her bedroom. That's where the story begins, many times where it ends too. What goes on between the sheets invariably has some bearing on what fills the file. He just kind of liked to stand idly in a suspect's bedroom, eyes slowly traveling over the furniture and fixtures, imagine what he does when he finally gets to bed and pulls the covers over his head. Give him or her enough time for whatever they had to do, and strip the bed down for evidence. Check the mattress stains closest, they were the hardest to wash out. Look inside the mattress; that's where many secreted their most precious possessions, and he wasn't talking money. What they needed to get it on, as his kids would say. Dig through the box springs, he had found many a goody over the years in them too. People never ceased to amaze him, what lengths they went to to get past a simple little thing like sex. Maybe it was just because he was so straight himself.

He left the Brown house more convinced than ever that they knew more than they were telling. Though there was no murder scrapbook per se, virtually every newspaper that had anything in it about Bill and Linda had been found somewhere. As he sifted through the physical findings and his own deductions, Badger found himself humming, "Sex and Murder, Sex and Murder, they go together like a horse and carriage, Dad was told by Mother, you can't have one without the other."

No, the Browns were not quite the pair of goody-two-shoes they wore to church. He didn't know exactly what it was, but there was something about them that had made his skin crawl. They hadn't found anything rock hard in the search of the house, but the soft stuff showed sand in the foundation. For all their churchy mouthings and holier-than-thou attitudes, he just hadn't felt close to Jesus in that house. Now he hadn't been to church so you could notice it since he was a kid, but damned if his own house didn't feel holier. That, of course, was due to his wife—she held down that end for both for them—and the kids, particularly the little one. The oldest one was more like him. He said a short prayer, his brain fumbling for the unfamiliar words, prayed neither one of them would turn out to be a Bill Ray Brown.

Yes, something was rotten in that house. What was it he was smelling? Which one held the rot, besides Bill?

Give Fred a platform, and he'll talk himself to death. Leona's troubled conscience shows in her eyes. The girl Elizabeth knows something too. Badger had sensed that just being in the same room with her. But now they're all stonewalled behind Knutson like Bill was before. How to smoke them all out in the open? Maybe this guy Hunt could give him some kind of hand there.

Meanwhile, maybe I can smell something through the grandparents, the girlfriend, Sarah Fortunato. Just keep pounding away on what he had, digging for more, all the while circling the wagons tighter and tighter around the Brown family, working closer and closer toward Bill's head.

On the twentieth, Badger and Jensen finally found a Brown that would talk to them, Earl Brown, Bill's grandfather. He let them go through an abandoned building that he owned on Quince Street, but nothing was found there, no bodies, no killer cache. Earl happened to mention that he had last seen Bill early Monday morning. Badger asked him if he could tell him more about that, but Earl said he would have to speak with his wife first.

Apparently, this was agreeable with grandmother, Joyce

Brown, as she called in to the station and told Badger that they could come to the Brown home on Jefferson at ten o'clock the next morning which he and Jensen did. Badger was impressed by their solidly built, old-fashioned, turn-of-the-century brick home. It was like many in this older section of Big Falls, peaked and gabled roof, higher-ceilinged, solid oak framed doors and woodwork. Though nominally in town, their home still retained a kind of country feeling, a much different feeling than he had felt in the younger Brown ranch-style home on Fauntleroy with its newly planted shrubs and maybe ten-year-old nursery trees. Everything seemed so temporary there, transitory, squeezed in suburbia development, yard and garage choked with vehicles of every shape and description, family, recreational, escape. Badger's thoughts went back to the search of the Fred Brown home, the curious items tucked between mattresses, pushed far back in dark corners. We wouldn't find any of that here, he thought.

Speaking with the kindly-appearing, white-haired couple, Badger and Jensen learned that Bill had been to their house in the early forenoon of Monday, August 14, the day Bev Lukken had disappeared. Had brought them a phone message from some old friends because their phone was out of order at the time. Bill had arrived at approximately 8:15 A.M., given them the message, chatted a few minutes, and taken some tomatoes Joyce had proudly grown in her garden and wanted to send along to share with Bill and the rest of the family.

"How long did Bill stay, ma'am?" Badger asked.

"Oh, just a few minutes."

"How . . . few?"

"Three or four. Just out of his car and in the house, picked up the tomatoes, out the door again—he had to get back to clean up and change for work."

"Is that what he said?" Badger asked, looking at Earl Brown to see if he might have something to say too. Earl didn't have the chance, his wife answered for him. "Yes. Bill is like that, neat as a pin. Always on the go. There's never enough hours in the day for a boy like Bill," his grandmother stated proudly, adjusting her flesh-toned, horn-rimmed glasses with her free hand. She tended to speak with the other. "Always the nicest, sweetest, finest boy you'd ever want to see. Never gave us a speck of trouble a day in his life. Wouldn't hurt a fly. Why, one time Earl and Snuffy—"

"Snuffy?"

"Oh, that's what we still call Fred, have ever since he wa a little boy. Anyway, they wanted to take him out huntin, back when we owned the farm up near Split Rock—" Badge nodded unthinkingly, he'd walked over every foot of that farm looking for Linda. "—but Bill wouldn't have anything to d with hunting. He doesn't even like to handle a gun. Isn't tha right, Earl?"

Earl nodded obediently. No, Bill prefers knives, Badge thought.

"I remember one time when Bill accidentally killed a bird," the grandmother continued. "He couldn't have been more tha about five then. Why, land's sake, I thought that boy woul never stop crying, he felt so bad about it, didn't he, Earl?"

"Yes, that's true enough," Earl started to confirm, but thi time Badger interrupted him.

"How'd he kill the bird?" He was looking directly int Earl's eyes. Badger wanted him to answer this question Whether for that reason or that the sharp suggestive questio temporarily befuddled Bill's grandmother, this time she al lowed her husband to answer.

"Why, I . . . golly, I'm not sure I even remember, if I eve knew." It was Earl's turn to adjust his glasses, lifting them hair to gain a better bifocal view of Badger. Earl's glasse were even more old-fashioned than Joyce's, lenses suspende from dark horn-rims extending over flesh-colored nosepiece t stainless steel ear straps. "I reckon it was what most kids us for something like that, a BB gun—"

"At five? A boy who doesn't even like guns?" Badger cu in.

"No, I guess—" Earl started to say.

"We have no idea," his wife answered. "It's been so lon —Bill was born here, you know. Right here in this house Snuffy was away in the Navy. Leona stayed right with Bill and us until Snuffy came home a year later. Then, o course, it took them a while to get settled, get Snuffy a decen job. He was forced to work all kinds of terrible nothing job there at first, certainly no way to treat a deserving veteran Leona was a kindergarten teacher then, making good money taught until Bill was four or five years old, I forget just which now . . . then she quit work, Snuffy wanted her to quit. I can' just place the reason for that in my mind now either, but now she just stays at home . . . keeps her closer to the kids, I guess. Bill was here with us most all the time those first five years, till they finally got their house on Fauntleroy. Elizabeth was born . . . what a perfect little boy. A woman couldn't ask for a more perfect little boy. Much easier to handle than even my very own little Snuffy. He was always getting into something when he was Bill's age. I made up my mind . . ." She seemed to forget momentarily what she had made up her mind to do so long ago, the bright blue eyes lost behind thick obscurant prescription glass in their own private remembrance of things past, her firm jaw set firmly, head cocked questingly a little to one side. Just then Badger was struck with the family resemblance—how much her son Fred looked like her, and, through Fred, Bill.

The Brown family prototype suddenly snapped out of her age-old reverie and exclaimed as though she had never missed a beat, "But Bill . . . why Bill . . . he was always just . . . perfect!"

Badger stood up, he was suddenly feeling very uncomfortable. "I'm sorry, but I'm afraid we have to get going. Business is, ah, very pressing these days, you know."

"Yes, I'm sure it is," Joyce Brown agreed amiably. Earl got up to say good-bye.

"Incidentally, what was Bill wearing when he stopped by with your message Monday morning?" Badger asked. They were seeing him out the door.

The grandparents looked at each other, both shaking their heads. "Why, I don't have the foggiest. Do you, Earl?"

Earl didn't.

Jensen barely had the squad car in gear before he exploded, "Jesus, Lieutenant, did you get the funny feeling that they didn't even know Bill had been arrested?"

Badger thought awhile. "I got a funny feeling alright . . . that she was trying to tell us something."

"Like what?"

"Beats me. I don't think she even knew."

Jensen drove another block, hung a right on Lincoln. "Seemed like damned nice people, didn't they?"

Badger nodded. "The salt of the earth. Every kid's idea of what grampa and gramma should be like."

"He didn't get to say much, though."

"No, she does the talking in that family. Of course,"

Badger reflected, "that's about par for the course." Actually, to tell the whole truth, the elder Browns weren't all that different from his own folks, but he didn't mention that to Jensen.

Jensen suddenly exploded again. "Boy! Then to end up with something like Bill!"

Badger found himself shrugging. "Oh, I dunno. She still seems mighty proud of him."

Jensen quickly glanced at Badger to see if he was kidding. He couldn't tell; Badger was slouched back against the seat, his eyes closed. "I mean, you meet grandparents like them. Then there's Fred and Leona . . . I mean, Fred can really piss a guy off, his mouth never stops, but, I mean, he's reasonably normal. You can't really blame a man for trying to protect his son. Got a good job, decent house, seems to take good care of his family, they all go to church together on Sunday. Leona would probably do or say most anything to stick up for her boy, but that's pretty normal for a mother too, I guess . . . I mean, you take a kid like Bill Brown, this good solid background—"

Badger couldn't ignore that. "Fairly solid, Cliff. I'm starting to see a few sand spots in that rock-ribbed foundation."

"Alright, fairly then, but a helluva lot solider than most of the dudes we deal in. I mean, he went through one of the best school systems in this state, graduated," Jensen said, "psych major from UW. What the hell gets into them? Where'd they go wrong? What for? Why? I believed his gramma. Bill probably was just about the sweetest little thing since apple pie. What happened to him? When did he quit 'minding'? Why?"

Badger still didn't answer. Tired as he was, Jensen was more than starting to get on his nerves with his incessant harping on the "why" of Bill Ray Brown. He was tired enough of listening to himself ask himself that question without having to listen to Jensen ask it too! Besides, right now he was trying to concentrate on Bev.

Say we accept the fact Bill attacked Bev at the spot where her glasses were found, at the end of the skidmarks. And had driven her away in his car to do Chirst knows what . . . and been back to punch in at 11:28. So, if he hits her at, say, 9:50, punches in at 11:28, he's got one hour and thirty-eight minutes to confront her, attack her, do whatever, and dispose of the body. What is this guy, a magician? With Linda he kills, disrobes, does whatever, lays out the clothing in Ghent Township, gets rid of her somewhere else so good we can't find her in over a year and a half—all in supposedly two and a half hours. Now Bev!—what's he do with her? Cover her in his car with a blanket while he's at work? Take her in to work with him? Lock her in his bedroom? It almost seemed impossible to have dropped off her body somewhere they couldn't find it searching as they were, ground and air, in that length of time. His time cards show that he worked two more four-hour shifts the rest of Monday. Then where does he go? Does he have Bev hidden in his car, take her somewhere that night and hide her, dead or alive?

If he did, that would give him almost unlimited time and range. According to his work schedule, he's got the next day, Tuesday, off. That gives him all day Tuesday too, to do whatever to the body and get rid of it. What does he do Tuesday night? Wednesday? Before he comes to work from ten till two at Bookland?

From there, he goes out and hits the Mathews children. We get his car an hour later, guard it all the way to the Crime Lab. They take the frigging car practically apart, piece by piece this time. And what do they find? Half his wardrobe in the trunk. A piece of brown material, a section of knotted clothesline rope, and a piece of black plastic. Theorizing aside, they could mean anything or nothing, for there was no blood on them. No blood anywhere in the car. But even more amazing, bloody as the stabbing of Johnny Mathews was, there was no blood on Bill's person! Even under his fingernails! And the Crime Lab had scraped, swabbed, dug through him minutes after his arrest, as thoroughly as they had his car the next day. What is this, Badger raged, black magic?

A weary sigh escaped him, loud enough for Jensen to glance over. Maybe the vacuuming of the entire car the Crime Lab had gone back and done on the nineteenth would bear some fruit. Examinations of the sweepings already done showed the presence of much soil, plant material, insect parts, assorted paint chips, minute pieces of glass, small pieces of paper and numerous hair samples. Maybe the "numerous hair samples" would match some victim's head or body this time. Danielle Forshey's, maybe. If just one of those hairs came from Danielle Forshey! If he could only find Linda or Bev!

Damn, Badger said to himself, for likely the ten thousandth

time since the accursed Bill Brown had so piously blasphemed his life. What is this guy? Mad genius? Evil scientist? Luckiest bastard who ever drew breath? Where are the bodies? Why can't we ever land some hard evidence on him!

". . . so what do you think, Lieutenant?" the indefatigable Jensen was asking him. "What do you really think Bill was like as a kid?"

"He still is," Badger grunted wearily.

"Seriously?"

"About the same as now."

"You mean, like a born killer?"

"Something like that."

A perplexed look sort of frightened over Jensen's normally open optimistic face. "Jesus, I didn't know there was such a thing!"

"Neither did I. But I hadn't met Bill Ray Brown then."

31

On August 22, Atwell and Jensen escorted Natalie Flowers to the office of hypnotist Orson Frankfurt, hoping that he might aid her in remembering just exactly what it was she had seen the morning of August 14. She was the lady who had called the Lukken tip line in the middle of Tuesday night, August 15, to report that she had been driving near the intersection of Oakdale and Wilson at approximately the time of Beverly Lukken's disappearance and had observed a vehicle she described as goldish in color stop at Oakdale and Wilson with a subject standing alongside the vehicle. Jensen had gotten back to her promptly, the next morning, August 16, but at that time Mrs. Flowers sounded very uncertain as to just what she had actually seen. So, other than ascertaining from her that she would be willing to undergo hypnosis to recall the incident, Jensen had pursued her no further than to arrange this session with Frankfurt. Then, that afternoon, Bill Brown was arrested for the Mathews assault, so the cryptic Flowers tip had been more or less lost in the mad shuffle—but not forgotten.

Two of the three interesting things Natalie Flowers had said in her one sentence was "a goldish colored car" stopped at the intersection of Oakdale and Wilson at "right around ten o'clock in the forenoon." Both time and approximate color of the car were right. Interestingly enough, as Jensen had remarked to Atwell on their way to pick up Flowers, both Sally Rivenburg and Natalie Flowers had described the car they noted that morning as being "goldish" in color. Though Bill Brown's car was chocolate brown, Flowers having seen it the same way as Rivenburg caused Jensen to believe that both ladies had, at least, seen the same car and were struck by something "strange" about it. This was particularly true in Natalie Flowers's case, or why would she have called in about it in the middle of the night, Tuesday, August 15—some sixteen hours *before* Bill Brown was arrested? It was one thing for neighbor Sally Rivenburg to "see" a "goldish" car in the vicinity after Bill Brown's arrest and the subsequent media publicity about him and his car, another for Natalie Flowers before the fact. Certainly, there had been plenty of publicity about Bev Lukken being missing, her glasses found on Oakdale off Wilson, so on and so forth, but there had been none about a "goldish colored car stopped alongside the intersection of Oakdale and Wilson right around ten in the forenoon."

What the hell, both detectives agreed, it was worth a try. Maybe the woman had seen something. Even though the site she had mentioned in her one-liner was a little off—by this time there was little doubt in any official mind that Bev Lukken had been snatched where her glasses lay at the end of the skidmarks—maybe this Flowers lady had seen Bill Brown doing something or other outside his car before he turned down Oakdale. For that was the interesting third part of Natalie Flowers's abrupt message: ". . . and somebody was standing alongside the car." If that "somebody" turned out to be Bill Brown, that would place both him and his car within 300 feet of the attack site, at just about exactly the right time of day. Within minutes of that time, give or take, Herb Felpel had watched his boss's wife continue eastward away from Wilson on Oakdale toward her home.

Natalie Flowers turned out to be a very nervous lady. It took some time for Frankfurt to settle her down, but once he did she slid under hypnosis quickly. She recounted what she had been doing prior to leaving her home on Elk Avenue to drive to meet her husband at 10:00 A.M. She said she was running late because of a telephone call from one of her daughters, turned onto Wilson, saw a "goldish" car that became tan or even brown when she remembered that it was viewed through sunglasses, saw what she felt to be a "guy trying to push a girl" into the car. "He was trying to hurt her, he was hurting her!"

She slammed on her brakes, skidding to a stop with her car ranged right alongside the by-now brown car, was looking through the brown car's open windows at the struggling couple. He had her by the "arm muscles, squeezing hard, he is hurting her, she had an awful scared look on her face, she is struggling back, trying to get away...there's something wrong with her too, she can't do much either, her hand comes up in his hair, she grabs a handful of his hair...he's pushing her in backwards on the front seat, her hand is up pulling yanking his hair, there's something on the dash, a pencil no yes that too but a book a black book a black book ablack book ablackbook—"

Frankfurt brought her out of it then. She appeared to be in such an extreme state of emotional agitation that he feared for her well-being, didn't dare continue without a medical doctor or mental health expert present.

32

The next day, Badger personally hustled nervous Natalie Flowers to a trained forensic psychologist, Dr. Tony Grancelli, Department Psychologist for the Wisconsin State Police. On closer reflection, there were a number of things about the Flowers testimony, if he could call it that, that bothered Badger. For big starters, there were logistical problems. She insisted that what she had seen took place directly at the intersection of Oakdale and Wilson, in the far right turning lane to be exact, not 300 feet down Oakdale where the glasses were found at the end of the skidmarks. Of course, that could be accounted for any number of ways, simplest of which would be that Brown did snatch Bev Lukken at the intersection of Oakdale and Wilson, then sped down Oakdale and, for whatever reason, threw the glasses out the window—forget the skidmarks. Or remember them—she's still struggling within the car, grabs at the steering wheel or something like that, the car's heading for the ditch, he slams on his brakes, her head bounces against the open window frame, her glasses fly out. That one kind of stuck. But what about Herb Felpel then? Badger believed Herb all along. He was the kind of witness a cop could take to church. If Herb said she was *already* walking *on* Oakdale toward her home when he pulled away to turn on Wilson, she was. How, why, would she turn around again and walk back to the intersection after Herb pulled away? It was already very close to ten o'clock, Herb thought. Natalie Flowers came along "right around ten o'clock in the forenoon." Badger had traced Bev from Smoky's auto body shop. She rode the bus, walked through the Old Dam Mall, along

Northland, up Wilson, turned right on Oakdale, walked into Herb coming toward her on Oakdale—but, just a few feet from the intersection, just "five, ten feet or so," Herb had said. Certainly, Brown could have come along just seconds after Herb turned the corner, pulled into the far right turning lane, called to Bev, she walked back. That way she would end up alongside his passenger side. He gets out and comes around the car—

Badger glanced over at the forty-year-old woman seated on his car's passenger side. She was still nervously working her fingers into little knobby circles, systematically working through one hand then starting on that one with the other. I just don't believe it. Sure, I believe her, parts of her, but I just don't believe "it." Bev was on her way home. There's something a little wrong here. But then what about the two different sets of clothing she supposedly was seen wearing? Two completely different sets, if one is to believe both Herb Felpel and the men at the auto body. Badger was tempted to ask Natalie Flowers right now if she could remember what the woman she saw struggling with the man was wearing, but he checked his tongue, decided it better that he not go into any of this right now, let Grancelli do it under hypnosis, she was nervous enough now as it was.

There were a number of people already at Dr. Grancelli's office when Badger arrived. Atwell was helping Inga Swenson from the Big Falls Public Information Department set up the recording and videotape equipment. If Mrs. Flowers couldn't just come right out and tell them what it was she had seen that was affecting her so deeply, capturing her terror-stricken anguish on videotape might later prove helpful, in various ways. Also, if she did have something indictable to tell and told it, it would be all there forever, both audibly and visually, just in case they couldn't get her to tell it a second or a third time. Obviously, at least under present law, they wouldn't be able to hypnotize her on the witness stand.

Lieutenant Harold Smith of the Little Falls Police Department was also there, sitting fairly unobtrusively off to one side, large artist's sketch pad on one knee, numerous pastel crayons on the desk beside him. LFPD's resident artist, his job was to make a composite drawing of the male subject alongside the brown car if Grancelli could get Flowers to describe him in detail. As a matter of fact, as far as Badger was concerned, that was the primary reason for this second hypnotic session. Unless they could get a make on the man, piece him to Bev, what Natalie Flowers may have seen would not mean a whole helluva lot, no matter how interesting.

Dr. Grancelli began as Frankfurt had, just talking to Natalie, attempting to obtain some background information, what she had been doing that morning around the house, the events of her day. She was to meet her husband at approximately ten o'clock to take his paycheck to the bank—

"My God, is it ten already!" she suddenly blurted.

It was, she ran out and jumped in their car, a Thunderbird, wheeled out the drive, down Elk Avenue, turned right on Wilson, heading north, driving hard, very aware of being late. She didn't like to displease her husband, particularly just as he was leaving for a long haul, then their anniversary was coming up later in the week too, on the nineteenth, she hoped he'd be back in time for that. . . .

What was that? The brown car is stopped there on the east side of Wilson Road just before the intersection, there's a scuffle going on, the white man is still trying to push the white girl into the brown car—

"Watch out!" Natalie Flowers suddenly screamed.

"Watch out?" Grancelli asked calmly. "Why watch out?"

Natalie's hands were out, fingers clutching the steering wheel of her T-bird, knuckle-popping white. Apparently Grancelli's calm question had the desired effect for her hands slowly came back down into her lap—she was lying on her back—and her voice returned to past tense. "A car . . . another car . . . pulled out in front of me."

"Pulled out? From where?"

"Why, from the intersection . . . I guess . . ."

"What did you do?"

"Slammed on my brakes. Slid to a stop."

"Where were you then?"

"Right beside the brown car . . . yes, now I'm right beside the brown car I was watching before the other car pulled out in front of me maybe I strayed over the line I'm looking right through the windows of both cars now I can see them real well real well—"

"Stop. Stop right there, for now, Natalie," Grancelli said kindly but firmly. "You can see the car."

"Yes, I can see the car."

"Just the car, Natalie, just the car."

"Yes, just the car."

"Very good. You're doing fine, Natalie, super. Describe the car for me, please, Natalie, what color—"

"Brown. All brown."

"The interior too. Can you see the interior of the car, Natalie?"

"Yes, I'm looking right through the windows—"

"Yes, what color is the interior, Natalie?"

"A kind of brownish too... lighter... yes, lighter, tan... yes, that's the tan part, the sun is shining so brightly on the windshield, there's a little something laying on the dash, some kind of a small object laying on the dash, maybe it's a reddish pencil..."

"Natalie, come back outside the car for just a second, would you, please. How many doors does the car have?"

"Ah... two. Yes, two."

"What make of car is it?"

"Make?"

"Yes, make, model, which car company makes this car?"

"I... just don't know makes of cars very well."

"Fine, that's all right, neither do I nowadays. Is it bigger than your Thunderbird?"

"No."

"Smaller?"

"Yes. Yes, it is smaller..." Natalie Flowers's head moved from side to side but her eyes remained closed. Somewhere behind those closed lids she was comparing the relative lengths of the two parked cars. "Yes, even though our windows were almost matched up, I was looking right through my right-hand side window through his open driver's side kind of kitty-corner through the right-hand corner of his windshield. I wasn't quite even with his windows, maybe back a few inches, four or five, my T-bird was still even in front, a little longer in the back."

"Marvelous. Just marvelous, you're doing outstanding, Natalie. Is it shaped like your T-bird?"

"No, not at all."

"What kind of car is it shaped like?"

"Gee, I just don't know cars... I sure wish I could tell you, sir, Doctor, but I'm afraid I don't know cars very well."

"Now, don't you worry about that, Natalie, you're doing

exceptionally well. Pull back a little, Natalie, we're too close to the car maybe. Let's say we're not even stopped yet, you're still driving up Wilson toward the parked car, you're still seeing it from a distance, you've just turned off your street—"

"Elk Avenue."

"Yes, thank you, Elk Avenue, onto Wilson, just first seeing the car, coming closer, looking at it close."

"It has more of a square back."

"It does. Marvelous."

"The license plate is in the bumper."

"Excellent. What is the number?"

"Number . . . ?"

"Yes, the license plate number. Could you give it to me, please?"

A lot of collective breath was being held in that room, all eyes strained forward toward those closed ones on the couch, eyelids fluttering, occasional rapid eye movements discernible, her entire face now scrunched up in an intense effort to see that license number somewhere still there on the backside of her brain. "K . . . L . . . M . . ."

Grancelli glanced quickly at Badger, who shook his head negatively. The letters he was looking for were STP, Samuel Thomas Peter before the numbers 500.

"Numbers, Natalie?" Grancelli asked, as though divining Badger's thinking. "What numbers follow those letters on this license plate?"

"Numbers . . . I . . . don't know . . . I'm sorry—"

"Now, don't you go worrying about that, it's not all that important right now, but if you should happen to remember them later would you be so kind—"

"Surely. Certainly, Doctor."

"Is there anything else you can tell me about the car? Any little detail at all?"

"No . . . not from this distance—"

"You're getting closer again now. Can you tell me anything now that you are getting closer?"

"It has chrome strips around the door windows."

"Good. Very good."

"Yes, I'm much closer again now . . . right alongside looking back inside . . . the door lock . . . it is one of them kind where you have to lift up on the handle to open the door."

"You mean the kind that has the handle enclosed in the arm

rest? Where you have to curl your fingers down under to pull up on the latch with your fingertips?"

"Yes!" A pleased smile spread over Natalie Flowers's tired drawn face. "Yes, that's it exactly!"

"Excellent. I can't tell you how well you're doing, Natalie. How proud we are of you." Grancelli was speaking softly but quickly, bending forward in his chair over her, his hand reaching out to take hers. "Natalie, I want you to see them again now. Through the car windows like before, but you are not to be frightened this time."

"It isn't just that I'm frightened, sir," Natalie interjected piteously, her voice suddenly assuming a saddened forlorn tenor, "not just that I'm frightened."

"What . . . what else is it, Natalie?"

"I . . . I should have done . . . some . . . thing." She moved her head back and forth slowly, her eternal debate still going on. "No, I . . . I just sat there. Watching. I didn't even . . . blow my own horn." A single tear came creeping from out the fluttering lid, dirtied itself on her mascaraed lash, slid into the worry river beneath her eye.

"Natalie, dear, you mustn't be so hard on yourself," Grancelli started to assure her.

"Maybe that's it, Doctor, I . . . I haven't been hard enough on myself."

"Nonsense! You did just exactly what 99 percent of the populace might do under the same circumstances. Besides that, you were very likely paralyzed with fear, terror-stricken—"

"Yes, I'm afraid . . . deathly afraid . . . he'll find out who I am, come after me too."

"Come after you? I see, you saw something more than just two people scuffling?"

"Yes." Natalie nodded quietly. "Yes, I saw . . . more."

Badger suddenly thrust his finger in front of Grancelli's face, pointed vigorously at Lieutenant Smith, mouthed "Composite! Get the composite!"

Grancelli understood. "Yes, I understand, Natalie, but I don't want you to tell me that just now. Just now you're seeing him, this young white man for the first time. You're just coming up on the car, you're seeing him real clear there alongside the brown car—"

"Yes, I'm seeing him," Natalie said softly, a long low

shudder ravishing the rest of her face, "very clearly . . . very clearly."

Lieutenant Smith sat up stiffly, a dark charcoal crayon poised in his fingers.

"Please describe him for us."

"White . . . man. Young . . . just about twenty-five years old. Medium brown hair. Blue eyes. No glasses. Wearing a white T-shirt." The words kept coming from her, old tired air slowly seeping from a child's punctured balloon. "Medium height. Kind of slim. Not really muscular but plenty strong enough. Not fat. No, not fat, he had that lean and hungry look. His hair could be kind of nice-looking, but now it's all messed up. Lightly tanned face . . . a nice face, it could be, but now it's all messed up too . . . cruel . . . mean." The only sounds other than the slowly seeping words were the "swish-swish" of Smith's charcoal outline crayon, "swish-swish." "I'll never forget that face till the day I die. It could be . . . almost pretty . . . there was something kind of like the girl's face in his too, but now it was all warped and twisted out of shape, his own mother couldn't even stand to look at it now. It . . . it belonged to the devil."

"Could you be a little more explicit, Natalie?" Grancelli interposed softly. "Were his cheekbones high, prominent, for instance?"

"Yes . . . and no. Just the way they should be on a pretty face, I guess, if it wasn't so twisted out of shape. Not too high, not too low, just somewhere there in the middle, average."

"His nose?"

Natalie Flowers nodded again. "Average. All his features average, just about what they should be for a good-looking young guy."

"His hair, did he wear it long?"

"No, average. Medium length, nicely trimmed I would think if he ever stopped jerking himself around so much and it got a chance to lay down."

Lieutenant Smith looked up—he had been crouched sketching feverishly as she talked—now pointed his crayon at Natalie, indicating that he wished to show his sketch pad to her.

"Natalie, I want you to continue focusing on this young man beside the brown car, but when I count backwards from five to one I want you to open your eyes and look at the sketch Lieutenant Smith has made. Could you do that, tell him if you think his composite sketch looks at all like the man you saw?"

Natalie grimaced noticeably, but she nodded her head. "Yes, I can make myself do that."

Lieutenant Smith sort of hopped forward, crouched over his sketch pad, held it in front of Natalie Flowers. She looked at it point-blank for some seconds, finally nodded her head slightly. "Yes, that's fairly close to him . . . but . . . his hair was a little fuller, more messed up."

Smith made the necessary changes, Grancelli counted forward to five again, the hypnotic session continued, stopping and starting a total of four times while Smith conferred with Flowers over the composite. After, the last occasion, Natalie said, "It looks real good. Real close to him, except he had a meaner look on his face and his hair was still even fuller and more messed up." Smith let the composite go the way it was though, as he felt that Flowers might be over-stressing the hair and contorted face aspect, possibly because of her emotional turmoil when viewing the subject.

In any event, based solely on Natalie Flowers's incredible memory under hypnosis, Lieutenant Smith had ended up with a remarkable likeness of Bill Ray Brown. Of course, neither he nor anyone else told Natalie Flowers that.

Now Grancelli was trying to get a description of the white female out of Natalie. She remembered that the woman was wearing a black top, something like a polo shirt, with blue shorts and brownish sandals, substantially corroborating the men at the body shop except as to the color of the shorts. That the woman had reddish brown hair but her hair was so messed up, "flying all over her head," that she could not see her face very well. That she was "about as tall" as the white, "younger" man she was scuffling with. That the woman had nail polish on her fingers, she saw that when "she flung her hand up, grabbed ahold of his hair . . . but then her hand kind of . . . let loose . . . fell away . . ."

Suddenly, Natalie Flowers stopped talking. Just lay there on Grancelli's open-sided fainting couch, her head propped up on the raised end portion. Her eyes were still closed, but Grancelli had the feeling that she was straining to see through them. Then, as suddenly as she had stopped talking, her body went limp. A weak little piteous sigh escaped her lips. She licked them with her tongue, swallowed heavily once or twice. Her breathing slowed. These were physiological changes indicative of deep stage induction. Grancelli was debating using a lightening technique, bringing her up on an escalator, elevator, something like that, when she spontaneously began to weep. Leaning over her, he could see the tears come pushing their way out from behind her compressed lids. She seemed to have no sense of it, just lay there silently weeping. There was no rocking of her body, just the tears groping their way out from behind those locked lids to trickle unceasingly down her cheeks.

Grancelli glanced at Badger, Atwell, Smith, Swenson, they back at him. Grancelli had cautioned them not to speak while she was completely under, but it was unlikely any of them would have found anything to say with or without his proviso, for there was such a silent, sad, lost, dispossessed quality to her weeping that it was not to be trammeled. They merely waited. All seeming to know that they were dealing with something far greater than any of them—quite likely, even Natalie—understood.

"The black book is a knife. It was laying there on the dash. When he got her pushed backwards in the car, his hand reached up and took the knife by its black handle and held it high over her. The silver blade gleamed in the bright shiny sun. The silver blade is long and gleams bright in the sun. He is holding it high over his head."

The words ceased as suddenly as they had begun, only the incessant, sad, silent tears remained.

"Natalie," Grancelli finally had to say, "is there anything else you . . . anything that would make you feel better if you told?"

"No," Natalie answered simply, "the black book is gone now."

33

Hunt was being moved closer to the big spot. He was aware of it even as he sat there at the head of the table listening to all the cops presenting their facts, theories, possible scenarios, but still not a single stitch of hard physical evidence.

It was almost becoming uncanny. Almost? It was! Here they had half of Wisconsin law enforcement working on one single punk who, dependent on the last man talking, had committed anywhere from four to take a wild guess of the unsolved female disappearances in half the state over who knows how many years, and they still had not one single stitch of hard physical evidence.

Hunt shook his head to some particularly farfetched theory, hardly hearing what it was or who was saying it. Believe it or not, they had precious little solid circumstantial evidence either. Good as the Flowers testimony appeared, the composite drawing a dead ringer for Brown, eye-witness testimony procured under hypnosis was still inadmissible in the state of Wisconsin. The Crime Lab report on the skidmarks on Oakdale indicated that they could have been made by Bill Brown's car, along with every other vehicle with a wheel base of 62 by 112 inches. The fact that identical skidmarks were found on Oakdale after Beverly Lukken disappeared and on the driveway of the Mathews home as Brown hurriedly sped away from that crime would help some, particularly before a jury—especially a grand jury. The Brown family still would not talk to law enforcement. They could expect no help from that end unless they forced it. Sarah Fortunato might know something, but she wouldn't say anything of value. Hunt had the feeling that she might know something of value, whether she herself recognized it or not. Subpoenaed before a grand jury she would have to talk. Then it would be up to his office to evaluate it, see if there was anything proceedable there. It could very likely help with a psychological profile of Brown, but Hunt had never heard of a killer hung on his psychological profile.

Nehring from the Crime Lab was talking now. Yes, he had found minute quantities of blood in the lock mechanism of the Bill Brown Watchdog Surveillance handcuffs procured from his bedroom during the search of 1546 Fauntleroy but not enough to type. It was Nehring's firm belief that there had been a copious quantity there, but that the handcuffs had been thoroughly cleaned, very likely taken apart and thoroughly cleaned. It was an interesting theory, but nothing to take to court. Even more interesting was Salan's fervent belief that the blood was Danielle Forshey's, that Bill Ray Brown had used the handcuffs as a guide in cutting off her hands, thereby the nice, clean, neat surgical separation. Hunt went along with Salan on this. It would explain the missing keys. Brown couldn't unlock the cuffs, so he had to cut them off, knowing they could very easily be traced back to him. Maybe Brown was no evil genius like some were postulating, but he was certainly no dummy either. At the very least, he appeared to keep his head at all times—most times, Hunt corrected himself, he hadn't with the Mathews assault. Curious crime, that, he thought again now. It just didn't quite fit with his other hits; it was sloppy, and these kind of killers usually don't mess around. When they hit, you're dead. They rarely leave victims around to talk later. Broad daylight too, just like Lukken leading up to the Mathews kids, just two days before. Is there some kind of message here?

A debate on the "Fallen Angel" painting was raging now, the Bill Brown painting also seized during the search of his parents' home. Others at times had entitled it the "Avenging Angel," but if that title was also supposed to refer to Bill Brown it made little or no sense to Hunt. Brown was no angel —fallen, avenging, or otherwise. He was just another kid caught somewhere in the middle, between Christ and the devil, just like the painting showed. Shit, Hunt thought, Bill Brown knows who he is; he painted the painting. Beset by devils and christs yes, but they are of his own kind, his own making—lower case. With more than a little help from a few others.

Hunt caught himself. What I'm being paid for is to prosecute, not theorize. They all wanted to see a little Bill Ray Brown blood for a change. And he was the man everybody was looking toward to feed it to them.

Looking toward him right now, to be exact.

Hunt cleared his throat, stalled for a little more time. Brown was already in jail for Portage County; he wouldn't be hacking up any more females up there. Maybe it would be best to just wait to see what happened in that trial. Who knew what might come out of that. Maybe the Forensic Center could crack him on the murders when he went up there for evaluation. Maybe in the hands of a skilled psychiatric interrogator the truth would come out. "Yes, Dr. Grancelli, what was that you were saying about the painting; I didn't quite follow you?"

"In reference to what, Mr. Hunt?"

"You mentioned that there was a great deal of hostility in the painting and that you felt that anyone who would paint such a picture would derive pleasure from hurting? Can you describe the depictions in the painting that made you react thusly?"

"Well, if I remember, there are three graves, which would suggest three bodies, and presumably that he was in some way responsible for those three bodies, which to me would mean having taken life, having hurt. Obviously, it's the ultimate hurt to take another person's life. There's also, if I remember correctly from the painting, evidence of a conflict between the forces of good and evil. Next to the angel we found the symbol, the one side is similar to the devil's pitchfork. I think it represents the draining of blood. Jesus had blood on each palm. All of these things suggest to me stabbing, that the pain would have come about not from an instantaneous death, the termination of life, but by some kind of agony in the process of dying."

"OK." Hunt nodded. "I'll buy some of that. But, if I remember the painting—where is it now, by the way?"

"The Crime Lab," chemist technician Twetan answered, "we're trying to analyze the oils to see if they were all applied at the same time."

"That's just exactly my point. If I remember correctly, and

I think I do, the painting was painted long before he, theoretically, began murdering."

Badger spoke up. "Seventy-five. The date on the back says 1975. He's twenty-two now, was born December 27, 1955, would have been nineteen that summer vacation when he supposedly painted it, had just turned twenty-one when Linda, ah, Linda Lou Craig disappeared New Year's Eve, 1976–1977."

"Thank you, Lieutenant." He was thorough, he'd have to say that for him. On sudden impulse, he asked Badger another question, seeing he had been so Johnny-on-the-spot with the last answer. "Lieutenant, do you think that is when Bill Ray Brown began killing?"

Badger's head snapped up, even higher than it already was. "Sir?"

Hunt began patiently reasking the same question. Halfway through Badger stopped him. "Oh, I heard your question alright, Mr. Hunt, but if you don't mind, I'd like to reserve judgment on that answer for the time being."

Hunt nodded. "Fair enough." Smiled at Badger to let him know he understood. "For that matter, so will I." A few people laughed, knowingly or otherwise. "So, getting back to the painting—which, by the way, I refer to as 'The Man in the Middle'—is there any real evidence, other than speculation, that it was not completed in 1975, but over a period of time . . . as—I've heard speculation—additional victims, that is, graves, were added?"

Twetan shook his head. "Unfortunately, I'm afraid we don't have that kind of technology yet at the Crime Lab. At least, we haven't been successful with the preliminary tests we've conducted so far. But, if we fail, there may be art experts who can tell us."

Hunt nodded. "Yes, I'm sure they can tell us if the oils were applied over a period of time, but I doubt seriously if they can pinpoint the application of such dates as, say, New Year's Eve, 1976–77; June 14, 1978; June 27, 1978; August 14—"

Everyone was already laughing, so he didn't bother continuing. Decided it was the perfect time for adjournment. No, he wouldn't be indicting Bill Ray Brown today. Not on the kind of evidence before him on this table. Not when police and legal brains were reduced to speculating over content and date of a half-assed painting as evidence for issuing indictments for murder. What would a good defense attorney like Knutson do with that bill of particulars—after he got through licking his chops? No, he wouldn't be issuing indictments today, but, maybe . . . maybe . . . grand jury. On the way out, he nudged Badger. "Let's meet again tomorrow, take a closer look just between ourselves and Grancelli at your Flowers testimony and her composite drawing." Badger nodded. "Good, same place, say, one o'clock?" Badger nodded again.

Badger had barely cleared the conference room door when Jensen came running up to him. "Natalie Flowers just called, very upset, crying like crazy!"

Badger rushed to the Flowers residence on Elk Avenue. She was waiting for him at the door, the *Little Falls Daily News* in her hands. "It's him! It's him! You printed our drawing of him in the newspaper! He'll come to get me now! My daughter! All of my girls!"

Badger tried to lay his hands on her soothingly, talk her down a little, at the same time see what was in the paper she was waving around frantically. "Now, Natalie, please. Mrs. Flowers, try to calm yourself. I don't know what you're talking about."

A teenaged girl, apparently one of her six daughters, was also there trying to calm her. "Mother, please, the man is here now, try to stop and tell him what you're so excited about—"

"You shouldn't have done it! You lied to me. You promised me you wouldn't let anybody else but you guys see our drawing, but now you printed it in the paper, and he'll find out who saw him and come and stab me and all my girls—"

Badger grabbed ahold of the newspaper and Natalie Flowers simultaneously. "Mrs. Flowers, I did no such thing. Here, settle down, let me see—"

"See!" Natalie Flowers said, stubbing a rigid forefinger against the picture in the newspaper.

"That's not our composite, that's a photograph of—"

"It's him! The man I saw beside the brown car!"

"Yes, it's him alright. Not our drawing, but it's him alright. Bill Brown."

34

Bill and Ken spent a good deal of time together that Christmas season. In truth, Ken very likely spent more time with Bill and the Brown family than he did with his own. Of course, he told himself, he didn't really have much choice in the matter. Bill's trial was coming up fast, and a good lawyer has to do whatever he has to do to adequately protect and defend a client, particularly an innocent one.

But then, the holiday season was not all that different. They had been spending quite a bit of time together all along, ever since Bill was arrested. Having his normal workload at Walcott, Barry, Anderson, Washburn and Knutson to more than occupy his weekdays, weekends became the time to set most else aside and really concentrate on Bill. It wasn't the "Mathews Assault Case" or the "Mathews Rape Case" or whatever the media and others in his office referred to it as; to Ken it was always just "Gee, I'm sorry, hon, I've got to go out to Portage County and see Bill."

Sundays became their special day. Sunday mornings during the period, Bill—or Ken, too, for that matter—would normally have been in church. Bill longed so fervently to be once more seated between his mother and father in the Brown family pew at their beloved St. John's Lutheran Church that he just could not force himself to attend services at the makeshift jail chapel; it seemed a sacrilege somehow.

Not that he needed any more religion. Even Ken suspected that was becoming too much of a good thing. He carried his Bible most everywhere he went, read it at the slightest opportunity—the other inmates thought him "weird," avoided him.

But then, what difference did that make to Bill? He was just darn glad that they did. That alone would have been reason enough for carrying his Bible, given to him by Grampa and Gramma Brown for confirmation, for he didn't like the looks of his fellow inmates, no way! "Some of those guys scare the living bejeesus out of me" was the way he put it to Ken one Sunday morning while they were visiting.

Ken thought on that word now as he drove along, "visiting." He always used it with people, even when what they were really having was a very serious business conference. But with Bill it almost always did seem like they were merely "visiting"—like two old friends, maybe, but more like an older brother going out to see his little brother who got himself in some kind of stupid scrape. It was just a matter of time before big brother worked things out for little Billy. Now you just be a good boy and mind your manners until I get back, and I'll bring you another hamburger. And if you're super good, I'll bring a Coke and french fries, too.

Ken automatically glanced down at the briefcase lying on the car seat beside him. If those guards only knew that just about all it ever contained was a bag of McDonald's "munchies," as Bill called them. But they almost had to know. By this time his briefcase smelled more like a McDonald's oven than a McDonald's oven. A few more trips out to visit Bill, they'd be calling him Ronald.

Ken allowed himself a small grin, even though he sure didn't feel like it. A couple of things he had just found out about today were nothing to grin at. He almost wished now he hadn't pushed Portage County so hard to declare evidence—it would make for a happier holiday for all hands. Maybe he shouldn't even tell Bill till after the New Year's, just try to forget about it till we all go back to work next year . . .

Why not? he shrugged. What earthly difference would it make? Probably neither of them is true anyway. That's one thing Ken had long since learned in this business. *Never* take a piece of evidence prima facie, particularly if it comes from the other side of the courtroom. Shit, that's all the one was anyway, bullcrap! No way in the wide world Bill would ever say anything like that to anybody, much less some inmate asshole just happens to be in the next cell. Just up and spill his guts to the first ununiformed face he sees! After just leaving me a few minutes before down in the warden's office, warning him not to talk to anybody about anything. No way! There was just no way the Bill Brown he knew would say something like that, even if it was true, to a perfect stranger. Some conniving little weasel con artist trying every trick in the trade to curry favor, sell info for a transfer, short time, whatever his lying twisted needs were. The whole thing so blatantly bullshit, Portage County should be ashamed to present it as evidence under any name. Unless, of course, in their desperation, they set it up themselves. Run in Jarre. Poor bastard is just repeating back what they whispered in his ear. Or how else would a guy like him know enough to refer to Linda Lou Craig in the same breath as the Mathews kids?

Ken compressed his lips; it tasted like he had bit down on an anchovy. He semi-shuddered, involuntarily shook his head. "Nah! No way! That just isn't Bill Brown."

But . . . why? Why would Portage County try the tired old jailhouse confession ploy that they don't even need if they have all they say they do . . . unless . . . unless it isn't Portage County at all. It's Helvetia County, Hunt's office. Sure, they got a whole lot more to gain by trying to connect Bill with Linda through a statement like that than Portage County does. They're desperately trying to drum up something to indict Bill on. Just like their secret grand jury that the whole town's talking about? SECRET PROBE WILL ATTEMPT TO LINK BROWN WITH MISSING WOMEN. Sure, Helvetia County set up Portage County to set up Jarre to set up Brown on the murders.

Ken was so engrossed in this other slippery twisting road that he damn near drove off his own. The right front tire dropping off the narrow shoulder jolted him back to some kind of reality. This was not a night to be running into a snowbank, setting out here in the middle of nowhere in fifteen-degree-below-zero cold.

Would Hunt be a party to something like that? he asked himself warily.

No, came back the immediate answer, but some of his men might. Jim Barry might. Since they roped together their grand jury, he and Badger had become thicker than thieves. Ken had word through his Grapenuts Flakes that Badger and Barry and Mrs. Craig had been seen huddled over breakfast at Simpson's a couple of weeks ago, the day the secret grand jury kicked off on Brown, the day Badger and Mrs. Craig so secretly testified. They could have been plotting something new then—

C'mon, Knutson, Ken told himself disgustedly, you're starting to think like Fred. According to the deposition, this whole thing with Jarre took place the night Bill checked into the Portage County jail, long before the grand jury ever started sitting on Bill—but, not necessarily before the idea was conceived. There's been pressure on Hunt to do something about the disappearances/murders for months, the public's been howling for him to indict Bill on them ever since the boy was arrested on Portage County.

Yes, it's all still possible. Anything is.

But, then, carrying that logic to the extreme, Ken had to also suppose that Jarre was telling the truth, farfetched as that might sound, that it had happened just the way the deposition read. But . . . but . . . "That's preposterous!"

Ken glanced down at his briefcase again. Jarre's deposition was in there, alongside the bag of munchies; he hoped it was getting as greasy as greaser Jarre.

Jarre properly disposed of, Ken forced his mind to consider the other matter. Now that was another, entirely different kettle of fish. Ken grimaced. A pail of worms. The state claimed they had a print from inside the Mathews house that they could call—a fingerprint, Bill Brown's fingerprint.

Ken sighed. That was a biggee. Not a half-assed Portage County fingerprint maybe thumbed up for the occasion, but a Wisconsin State Police/Bill Brown fingerprint. Lifted from within the Mathews house, on the inside of the front door by the Crime Lab and called by the Crime Lab. Just today.

At least, Ken just got word today. The Crime Lab had called it months ago. Hunt had to know about it since day one. Its existence probably had a lot to do with him throwing it all before the Grand Jury. What else did Hunt know that Ken didn't?

Funny thing, he still trusted Hunt. There was no reason not to. Hunt was under no obligation to tell him anything at this point. He was not going to trial against Hunt in Helvetia County . . . at least, not yet.

Could Bill be guilty of something?

Ken felt his head involuntarily automatically instinctively shake itself no. "No! No way!"

Even as he heard himself say it, Ken knew, of course—he was a good lawyer too—that that wouldn't be the end of that. He would have to think on that some more too, plenty more. It was just that . . . he didn't want to. He just didn't want to, not tonight, not New Year's Eve.

You know, he thought sadly, I guess . . . I guess I just don't want this guy to be guilty of anything. Those other guys I've defended—murderers some—that was alright. Not alright, of course, it's never alright, you know I don't mean that, but they were different. They were . . . murderers.

His car had stopped in front of the little Portage County jail. Ken sighed wearily, got out, reaching back in to grab his briefcase. Suddenly, the subzero air hit him across the forehead, the icy fist staggering him. He felt dizzy, as though he might even faint. That's just the opposite, he thought. Cold air like this is supposed to wake you up, make you think more clearly. I just want to sit down in that snowbank and close my eyes, go back to sleep.

But he didn't. Ken Knutson just took a firmer grip on his briefcase and ducked his head into the rabbit-punching cold and strode purposefully into the Portage County jail. As always, the first thing he noticed was the Beverly Lukken 10,000-dollar-reward poster tacked to the foyer wall. Gimpy, the regular night jailer, was on duty. Whether he smelled the contraband McDonald's munchies or not was, as they say in law, a moot point, for right then Ken could care less, maybe even less than Gimpy, sprightly stepping alongside Ken's longer, more purposeful stride but keeping up. That took some doing for Gimpy as he had only half a leg on one side, the rest left dangling from some barbed wire on his only trip to the south of France. But Gimpy was still cheerful. He greeted Ken familiarly, used to seeing him come to his place of night business. He hopped along with him down the corridor till they got to the maximum security section—Max. as they called it—where he turned Ken over to Charley.

"You going to be here about the same time as usual, Mr. Knutson?" Charley asked.

"Yeah, about two hours, Charley."

"OK. You know the rules."

Ken nodded, walked on down to the "lawyer" cubicle isolated in the basement bowels of the decaying old concrete structure. Ken shivered. It was even colder and damper than usual down here tonight, the annual Wisconsin permafrost starting to completely penetrate the uninsulated walls, rime them with cold sweat. He set his briefcase on the single narrow desk, took the chair facing the double steel door. There were no windows in the room, just an eight by ten or so cubicle of solid concrete and steel, a desk and two metal folding chairs. Nothing else.

"Man, how would you like to live the rest of your life in something like this?" Ken asked himself, as he invariably did every time he sat waiting for the Max. guard to bring Bill. His answer was always the same too: "I'd go stark raving bananas."

His voice sounded funny in the cubicle tonight, almost like he was testing, testing, to see if it was still there. He would have checked that out even more thoroughly, but just then the double steel door creaked open and Charley ushered Bill in. "Here's your little saint, Counselor," Charley said, delivering his stock speech, "Bible and all. I'll be up in Max. Just knock three times if you need me." Ken nodded, Charley had his little chuckle, shut the double steel door behind him. Ken could hear the big slide lock rasp into place. Chuckle away, Charley, Ken thought, a man could rot in here before you'd ever hear him knocking.

Bill was standing there eyeing him up. That wasn't unusual. He never moved or did or said anything until the guard cleared the scene and had locked the door behind him. That now being the case, Bill went into his little routine, checking the cubicle thoroughly for bugs—the Watergate kind, not cockroaches. This little paranoia of Bill's seemed to Ken to get worse with each visit. Tonight he was looking under the desk, checking the double steel door to see if it was completely closed.

"Bill, why do you do that?"

Bill looked up, his eyes startled, as though it had never really occurred to him either, yet he continued, giving the door one last unshoveable shove. "People in here claim they always try to hear what we say to our lawyers," he finally said rather lamely.

Ken just nodded, more aware of the "we" then what Bill had said. It was the first time Bill had ever included himself as one of the inmates. Bill headed directly for the desk. Ken knew what he was after, so he opened his briefcase and took out the McDonald's bag, very aware of the Jarre affidavit and

Crime Lab fingerprint statement clinging close, the big letters WISCONSIN STATE POLICE blaring across the top. With a not too casual move, Ken turned over the Crime Lab report with one hand and fished out the McDonald's bag with the other. Bill noticed nothing, he was diving into the munchie bag, oohing and awing over its contents.

Ken just stood there, watched him eat. A feeling of sadness slipped onto him so deftly, he literally shrugged to shake it off. "You like those munchies, don't you?"

Bill merely nodded, his mouth too full of Big Mac to answer. How sad it is, Ken thought. That's what he should be doing every night—out with the kids, hitting the drive-ins, going to the movies, not stuck in this dank hole with me. Particularly on New Year's Eve.

Ken glanced at his wristwatch, 11:32. Bill noticed his move. "What's the matter? You in a hurry?"

"No, we got the usual two." He hadn't planned on bringing it up unless Bill did, but something made him. "I guess you remember what night this is?"

"Sure, New Year's Eve," Bill responded just as casually, ripping open one of those little McDonald's salt packets, sprinkling his french fries. Ken remained aware of Bill's hands, how quick and sure they moved, spearing a french fry now, stabbing it into the blob of catsup, snaking it into his mouth. Funny, Ken thought, the rest of him moves much slower, more laid back, except his mouth. That moves fast too, when he chews. He's a greedy eater . . . there goes his hand again, spear, stab, catsup blood, chew chew. "Bill, we got a couple a . . . ah, minor problems."

"Yes, what's that?" The hand was arrested in mid-air now. He always wore his fingernails a little long for Ken's taste, none too clean either.

"Let's go over this a little. I'm not too worried about the visual IDs. This Walton guy who's supposed to have seen you coming out of the Mathews house—the dumb cops used a photograph of you from the newspaper on him—I think I can blow him off the stand by claiming they tainted his mind, contaminated his ID."

Bill nodded, back chewing hungrily again. He'd heard all this before, knew all the words, the courtroom jargon, lawyer patter. Suddenly Ken was a little annoyed. For some reason it irritated him that Bill just kept wolfing his munchies down, scattered McDonald's wrappers all over their little narrow desk, even one on top of his briefcase.

"Aren't you kind of wondering why I'm out here tonight?"

He didn't even stop chewing. "Well, yeah, kind of. I thought maybe you . . . just kind of thought I'd be lonely. You came out Christmas."

"Yes, that's one of the reasons—"

"Say, I don't know if I thanked you enough for the Christmas present. The guys here can't believe my lawyer brought me a multi-band radio."

"You thanked me enough, Bill."

"Well, I'm thanking you again. That's a super radio. I got Del Rio, Texas, the other night—take it under my blanket with me and listen low all night if I can't sleep too good."

Ken grinned. "Yeah, I used to do that myself when I was a kid. I got this new radio for Christmas once too, used to hide it under my covers most every night, see what faraway stations I could get, Del Rio, Clint, The Blue Room atop the Roosevelt Hotel, New Orleans—one time, a real clear night, I guess, I even got Hawaii."

"Nah, you couldn't get Hawaii."

"I swear I did . . ." Ken suddenly stopped talking, cocked his head. "Maybe I didn't. Maybe that's just in my head, some kind of fantasy."

They were both laughing by now. "Shoot, I don't even think it's logistically possible to get Hawaii from Wisconsin on a regular radio, certainly not before satellites," Bill added.

"No, I guess not," Ken admitted, "must have just been another one of my pipe dreams. You say you're not sleeping nights?"

"Oh, not every night. I don't want to make it sound worse than it is."

Ken leaned over the desk a little closer toward Bill, put on his reading glasses. "You are looking a little peaked. You're not sick, are you?" Now that he had his glasses on, Ken could see that Bill didn't look that good at all, had kind of changed in appearance somehow. There was a harder edge to his features, his lips dragged a little petulantly at the corners, his eyes were deeper in their sockets; they stared out rather owlishly at Ken as he took his inventory.

"Sick of being in here. Ken, when are you and Dad going to get me out?" Bill suddenly blurted.

Ken had to blink his eyes but forced them to stay on those deep blue eyes. Yes, even the color of his eyes seemed to have changed, deepened, even more like Fred's now. "We're working on it, Bill. Believe me, your folks every day, me, every day I can possibly spare—"

"So what's Dad been doing about it?"

Ken shook his head with wonderment. "Everything you can possibly imagine—he even dragged me to see a psychic. You know what she said?"

"No. I don't believe in them anyway."

"You'll want to believe in this one. She told us not to give up hope, that you would ultimately be vindicated."

Bill laughed, a sharper, more biting laugh than Ken used to hear. "Ultimately! When's that mean?"

Ken ignored that, hurried on. "We also went to Milwaukee one night, visited with a lady whose son is still in The Path. We . . . ah, wanted to know if a person could be, ah . . . instructed to commit a crime."

"Instructed . . . what kind of talk . . ." The puzzled frown slid into disbelief. Bill's eyes glinted tiny blue sparks. "You . . . Dad . . . actually think I did . . . something?"

"No, no, but a good lawyer has to take a look at every possibility, no matter how farfetched."

"Well, that sounds about as darn farfetched as you can get. You mean, like 'programmed' to kill, something like that?"

"Well, any kind of crime, whatever. You know we used to think maybe they brainwashed Linda."

Bill laughed, the bitter edge was there again. "Maybe I still think that. Somebody must have done something to her to make her run away like that, just leave me sitting here holding this miserable bag. Shoot, who knows, maybe they did brainwash me too, and I don't even know it! Somebody programmed me to end up sitting here in the middle of the night like some kind of common criminal. Somebody else has been whispering in my ear all my life, 'instructing' me to go out and do this and that, testing my soul like Christ on the Cross, so I have to be crucified too before I get 'ultimately vindicated.' Shoot, who knows, maybe . . . maybe I don't even . . ."

Bill just sat there staring Ken right straight in the eye, his hands still spread palms up. Ken almost expected to see the nail holes there, but there wasn't any blood. He hadn't planned this either, but the words came. "Bill, the name James Jarre mean anything to you?"

The Christlike hands came slowly down to rest palms up on the narrow desk between them. Ken watched with fascination as the fingertips began to slowly curl. "James . . . oh, Jamie. Yeah, he's in Max. 11, right next to me. Why?"

"You do much, ah, talking with Jamie?"

Bill shrugged. "Here and there, as little as I have to. He's not exactly my type of guy."

"You talk to him much the first night they brought you in?"

Bill's eyes narrowed, the pupils seemed to shrink. "What . . . what you getting at, Ken?"

It relieved Ken to be able to look down at his briefcase, tap it with his finger. "The Portage County Sheriff's Department took a deposition from Jamie. He claims you more or less confessed to him the first night they brought you in here."

Bill's eyes went round, his whole face gave a little jerk. Ken could only characterize his look as one of utter amazement. "Confessed! To Jamie Jarre! What!"

"What?"

"Confessed what?"

The words were burned in Ken's memory. "That if you had done away with the Mathews kids like you had your fiancée, you wouldn't be in this trouble now. That's not verbatim, but close enough."

Bill's mouth worked, but no words came out. He could only make little huffing sounds. There was absolutely no doubt in Ken's mind that his amazement was genuine. No man is that good an actor. Ken reopened his briefcase, took the affidavit out and slid it across the narrow desk under Bill's eyes. He still hadn't changed his position, his hands still lay palms up, the fingers curled more by now. He just crouched there that way, read the single-paged affidavit without looking up once. Ken studied his face. The tiny first wisps of a mustache strained forward along his upper lip; Ken could discern a hopeful outline arcing from either nostril to the upper corners of his lips. You know, he thought, surprised at his own amazement over such a simple fact, this is the first time I ever looked at Bill through my reading glasses. His nose is broader than I thought it was too, none of his features quite so fine.

"Bullcrap!" Bill suddenly said, still looking down at the affidavit. It appeared to Ken as though Bill had finished reading it once and was starting over again. "Nothing but plain unadulterated bullcrap."

"That's the way I see it too," Ken concurred quietly.

"That lying little weasel. I know him by now. He's just angling for short time. Been reading the papers about me, watching the news."

"Check the dates," Ken said. "He went down the very next morning, according to them, before he could have had an opportunity to, ah . . . have obtained, ah, some of that information."

Bill didn't even bother looking up. "Yeah, according to 'them,' but even that's bullcrap. The only part that's true is that we did watch it on television. It was all over the news that night that I had been arrested for this bullcrap Mathews thing . . ." Now Bill's eyes came back up to reengage Ken's. By now they were very normal in appearance, almost . . . pleased. Yes, that was the only word Ken could think of. There was almost some kind of pleased look in Bill's eyes now, but it passed over in a hurry, was gone by the time he got to Linda's name. "They kept referring to me as the boyfriend of the missing Linda Lou Craig. I'll never forget it. In fact, every time they would tell something about those poor Mathews kids and my being arrested for whatever I was supposed to have done to them, the next line would be that I was the boyfriend of Linda when she disappeared." Bill glanced down at the paper again, shook his head sadly. "This is typical jailhouse politics, Ken, scratching and clawing for favor. I'm surprised you even took it seriously."

"I didn't," Ken countered, trying for a lighter soundtrack in his voice, "my sentiments almost exactly."

"Stupid jerk! Now you see why I'm getting paranoid, living day and night next to a stupid jerk like Jamie Jarre."

"You won't be after tonight. I've requested Sheriff Mork to either move you or Jarre."

Bill tried to smile. "While you're at it, why don't you just request him to move me all the way right out of here."

There was no point in stopping now. "Bill, we could be in bigger trouble than Jarre."

"Oh." The eyes narrowed again. "How so?"

"They got a fingerprint."

Eyes narrowing more, just slits and glittering pupils now

—Ken thought of a dope addict he represented once. "Fingerprint . . . whose?"

"Yours. At least, they claim it is."

"Who? Badger?" Cat eyes in the dark—no, a tiger backed into a dark cave—

"No, not Badger. State Police. Crime Lab."

Bill kind of nodded, his eyes settled somewhat. Ken had the eerie feeling that Bill could kind of accept that, so long as it wasn't Badger. "Where?" he asked, almost as an after-thought.

"Inside the door."

"Which door?"

"The front door."

Bill's eyes flared wide now, a different kind of glitter. "No, where? Where?"

"Oh, the Mathews house."

"Ken, were you trying to trick me?"

Bill's eyes were different now. Ken had never seen eyes like those before. There was no description. They stopped his mind. Ken could think of Bill no more. He felt fear for his own safety. "Trick? Me trick—"

"Yes, you!" Bill snapped. "You tried to trick me into knowing the door."

"Bill, settle down, I just didn't think. I just assumed you'd understand I was talking about the Mathews house."

"Understand! You dare ask me to understand! I understand nothing! I know no house! You're just like all the rest of them, like Badger! Always trying to trick me—"

"Bill, please, I'm not like those. I'm your friend, probably the best friend you got in the whole world—"

"No—"

"Yes. Not just your lawyer, your friend. Friend. I'd never try to trick you, I know you're innocent. I fight day and night for you, your innocence. Your family, they call me all the time. Fred—"

"He's no friend."

"He certainly is. Probably the very best one you have."

"No . . ." Bill said, but the cold killing edge was gone from his voice now, the agate eyes were back in their cage, his features were becoming Bill's again, the strange yellow-red color draining from his skin. Suddenly, he slumped forward,

his head falling forward so rapidly Ken had the flicking image
of it having been momentarily cleaved from his shoulders only
to snap back on again before his forehead hit the desktop.
Only his hands kept working, the fingers continued to curl,
clench, constrict, seemingly of their own volition, the
chicken's body still fighting for life or death after he had lost
his head. "No," the strange voice mumbled, "no, grampa,
gramma, mama . . . mama, gramma . . . gramma mama . . .
mama . . . gramma . . . ?"

"They always ask for you, Bill. Of you. Grampa, gramma,
mama—if it's not one calling me, it's the other. One calls me
up to tell me this, then the other follows with that . . . " Ken
tried to chuckle; it came out a hoarse choking strangulated
squeak. He knew he was babbling, but it seemed to be working. "It's kind of like they're all fighting over you, Bill. All
wanting to be sure they let me know how much they love you.
Make sure that whichever one talks to me last had got the best
scoop. Me . . . me, I guess, I'm supposed to be the protector
. . . minister . . . priest . . . for you . . . all of them."

Ken heard his voice dwindle off, but for the life of him
couldn't think of another word to say. It was as though he had
somehow said it all, all he had to say. His mind wouldn't let
him say any more. It was too busy fending for itself. It had to
consider its major concern. He had to think of survival, if it
came to that. What did he have to work with if the awful thing
that was crowding his mind was true? He was no physical
fighter, never had been. He was the little bright kid with the
big books. Though Bill was no taller than him, maybe just a
few pounds heavier, Ken could feel that he would be no match
for him. This was not any kind of intellectual process. He
knew it in his bones, could feel it in every fiber of his body,
taste it in his mouth.

Time stood still. Yes, Ken knew what that old cliché meant
now too, for time stood still. For all Ken knew they sat thus
transfixed for five minutes, ten minutes, a half hour . . .
eternity. Ken, the one, the lawyer, protector, minister, priest,
frozen on the edge of his hard, straight-backed jailhouse chair,
staring at the working, curling, air-clawing fingers. No longer
looking at the other, Bill, seeing him whole, just those severed
hands. There was absolutely no sound penetrating to them in
their concrete steel cubicle. Not even the sound of breathing.
No sound.

Then faintly, oh, so faintly, came sound to them. Somehow it trickled its way down through those two-foot-thick concrete walls and double steel doors. Music, faint thin strands of music, tiny tinny yelps, trembling howls, words, almost words, "Happy New Year."

Bill started to cry. The fingers stopped working, quit clawing the dank futile air, seemed to grow back onto the wrist naturally, came up to cradle his face. Ken wanted to get up off the edge of his chair and go over and at least place his hands on those bowed wracking shoulders, but he decided to let well enough alone for now. So they just sat there that way, time standing still, until their jailer came back to let them out. Charley from Max.

"Bill," Ken said softly, when he heard the heavy push-bolt rasping against the outer steel. "If this other stuff is true, the only street left is insanity."

Walking out through the jail foyer, all Ken could see was the reward picture of Beverly Lukken tacked to the wall. It seemed to take up the whole wall now, grown ten times bigger in those two long hours. My God, Ken's mind screamed, could he have done this too?

35

"So what do you make of all this, Doctor?" Ken asked Dr. Wolfgang Mueller, indicating the numerous papers and charts and psychological tests strewn over the consulting psychologist's spacious, modern, Scandinavian-style desk. They were in Dr. Mueller's private office at Crisis Counseling Center, Orahula, Wisconsin, of which Dr. Mueller was president and co-owner.

Dr. Mueller picked at his beard thoughtfully. "Very, very complex. As I mentioned, I conducted a clinical interview and administered three tests, the Bender gestalt, Rorschach, and thematic apperception tests. Here, let me show you. I gave Bill the Bender gestalt test first. It's a series of geometric designs, nine in all. You tell the individual that you are going to show him some pictures, and you want him to draw them on a piece of paper as he sees them. The test itself serves two purposes. One is a fairly good screening for organic brain damage, but a more important use is in the question of person-ality." Dr. Mueller picked up the single piece of test paper, held it up to Ken. "Now look, the most striking characteristic of Bill's rendition is its meticulousness, its compulsivity, in the sense it was done with great care, with great diligence. It was constructed tight, and all the figures in fact are on the top half of the page, which indicates kind of a bunching, constric-tion, more than what you would normally expect. The other most striking characteristic of Bill's rendering—look here, on the back, almost all of the figures show through. This is indic-ative of more than usual pressure applied. From a psychologi-cal standpoint, this coincides with the issue of anger and

282

what's done with anger. So here we have a very constricted Bender, but given its constriction is a tremendous amount of anger. What comes through clearly is a bound sort of presentation with underlying anger and rage. An analogy would be sort of a coiled spring where, if you wind up a spring until you can't anymore, on the surface it looks compact and tight, but the potential for release of the spring and the kinetic energy of that release and its consequences must be considered."

"I see," Ken said, for he did. Dr. Mueller was describing almost exactly the Bill Brown Ken had been seeing of late, all from a single sheet of paper.

"Given the compulsivity," the compulsively thorough psychologist continued, "there are some errors, there are some erasures, which again in the framework of the compulsivity are indicative of losing some control. Now these figures are very simple. Okay, a child of, oh, ten or twelve can reproduce them fairly accurately. So, given Mr. Brown's tremendous attempt to be controlled, careful, and meticulous, what comes through is his lapses in that as well as the rage which I mentioned before."

"Is there any time constraint insofar as his duplicating the various geometric designs?"

"No, he's allowed as much time as he cares to, to duplicate each one. Same with the Rorschach. Now this test is purposely ambiguous. The ambiguity enables the individual to try to make some sense out of it. That's not to say that there are not some standards in terms of usual responses and normal kinds of responses, but this particular test gives a very rich flavor of the individual if you look at the test in its entirety, and the individual has to come from within to make sense of rather ambiguous stimuli."

There was no doubt about that. The card Dr. Mueller was holding up to Ken looked like a chicken had run through spilled ink just prior to stepping on the card. "Looks like just an inkblot to me."

"That's because they are," the poker-faced doctor admitted, the hint of a smile creating a ripple effect through the lush growth of beard around his mouth. "A series of inkblots, sometimes colored ink, sometimes just black ink, made pretty much as you might if you took some ink and put it on a piece of paper, fold it in half and open it. They were devised in the twenties by Herman Rorschach and have been used ever since."

"How many cards are there?"

"Ten. Though all are important in reaching my diagnosis, I would like to comment on two particularly at this time, four and seven." Mueller slid his hand into the mound of Bill Brown psychological detritus clogging his desktop and magically brought forth the right card. "Card four in psychological jargon is known as the father card, because it tends to generate responses indicating relationship to the father. Again, there's a relatively long delay. The guardedness. Here's the tightness. Has a puzzled look. Turns it around and says, 'This looks like petrified wood. I've collected rocks and things, and I have at home, at least I believe I had—my father used them for some rock gardens.'"

Ken stared up at Mueller, he stared down at Ken. It was almost uncanny the way Mueller could assume the flavor of Bill Brown when answering on his behalf, not only in vocal inflection but cadence, body English. Suddenly the hulking psychologist would shrink to a bargain basement Bill Brown with just the turn of a word. Equally impressive was his seeming ability to remember almost verbatim Bill's responses, only occasionally consulting a dog-eared set of note cards he had obviously taken to conjoin with each Rorschach card.

"I asked him again what is it about the picture that makes it look like petrified wood, rocks. Nothing about the picture, per se. It's what I recollect. I compare the two." Mueller gave his quick curt nod. "Okay, he's losing the stimulus again. This is a measure of internal control in an ambiguous situation, and in a situation that is generating some internal tension, and he's losing it in getting very idiosyncratic, putting in more and more of himself. A very unusual response to this card in terms of issue of father and self-perception. Can you imagine seeing someone that you've been involved with all your life as a petrified piece of wood or rock?" he suddenly asked Ken.

"Why, ah, no," Ken finally answered. It took him some time to break from the colloquy Mueller had been having with the omnipresent Bill Brown and realize the psychologist was speaking to him directly.

"The absence of feeling, the absence of relationship, the distance, the closed off quality to that."

Ken didn't know whether Mueller was still speaking to him

or Bill, so he said nothing. He waited, but Mueller said no
more about the father card either. Apparently there was nothing more to be said.

Instead, Mueller fished another card out of the pile. "Card
number seven, we call it the mother card. He tells me it gets
stranger and then he says, 'Not really, just looks different.'
Again he turns it around several times. He blinks and shakes
his head, puts it on the edge of his desk to look at it, like
this." Mueller propped the card up against an antique inkwell
on his own desk, as far away from himself as the card could
be and still remain on the desk. "He's having difficulty. He's
trying to be cool. He's trying to be controlled. He's trying to
be on top of it, but he's having difficulty."

"Yes?" Ken asked with hushed voice, staring up at Mueller
like his round unblinking eyes were the screen of a murder
mystery and he was about to find out "whodunit."

But Mueller wasn't about to be hurried. "A two-minute
delay—very unusual. And he shakes his head, puzzled. 'Let's
see, I've done some antique collecting with my dad. Not too
much with my girlfriend. It looks like an old rusted horseshoe
in terrible shape. I can't say 100 percent, but that's what it
looks like.'

"I asked him to explain that. He said, 'You can tell by
looking at it it's been exposed to the elements, and it no longer
looked like a horseshoe exactly. It's decayed.'"

Ken didn't quite know why, but a shiver danced up the
back of his neck, pirouetted through the short hairs. Mueller
laid card number seven down gently, carefully aligned it with
its sister cards. Ken was struck with the symmetricality of
Mueller's row of cards, when juxtaposed with the seemingly
haphazard jumble he had retrieved them from.

"Now this card typically reflects the individual's relationship with mother, his relationship with women. You recall
men are petrified rocks, without feeling, stones. Women are
decayed. Women are defective. Women are decomposed.
There's an absence of any warmth in Bill Brown's response.
There's a reflection of almost a looking down at this diseased,
decayed, decomposed horseshoe, but it's not the horseshoe,
it's women. It's mother."

Ken found himself nodding, even though he didn't really
want to. He couldn't help but think of Danielle Forshey, even
while he was assuring himself this was merely psychological

projection. It had nothing to do with abject reality. After all, Bill had loved Linda, still did, while striving for a love as lasting with Sarah. And, surely, he didn't feel that way about his sister Elizabeth. It was easy to see how fond Bill was of her. His grandma, Joyce, Leona—surely he didn't view his mother as diseased, decayed, defective, decomposed. This was just some more of the usual shrink cant, he did "it" because he hated his mom. Ken was beginning to wonder just how sharp this Mueller was, maybe he had overestimated him. He continued to be eerily fascinated by Mueller's physical movements, the deft sure way his disproportionately small hands could dive into the clutter and come up unerringly with just the card or note he sought. Ken was equally fascinated by the almost magical transformation of clutter to straight-line symmetry, couldn't help but wonder if he wasn't using this apparent obsession with extraneous trivia to keep from really focusing on what Mueller was saying.

"I think you can start to get a feeling for where he's at in relationship to people, and the kind of relationships he has. This man *is* programmed. I interviewed him at length. There's the transcript, it's all in there too. This man has had a lifelong program which deals with the issue of religion in terms of goodness of the word and rightness, and on the surface he seems a very articulate, thoughtful, bright, seemingly kind individual. Now that's fine if you don't look any further, but underneath this, the explosions, the loss of control, the rage that's in this man, that's buried."

Ken had a sudden image of himself buried in a concrete-steel catafalque, sprinkled with salt, smeared with catsup, spewed with crumbs, crunchingly chewed, mummified in orange and black McDonald's wrappers. He shook his head so noticeably to rid himself of the tremor-making image that Mueller thought he was taking issue with his prognosis.

"I'm telling you, that is this man, Bill Brown."

"Oh, I don't doubt what you are saying. That is, it's a little difficult to take something like this all in at once, after knowing the other Bill for over two years now."

The wry breeze tickled through Mueller's lush beard. "We'll get to that too. When I asked him how it was going at the jail, what brought him there, he didn't know. He had been charged with a crime, no recollection, no understanding, can't figure it out." Mueller paused for emphasis. "For half of him,

I think that's true. I think he doesn't know. He doesn't know the existence of the other half. He doesn't know the existence or isn't allowed or never had been allowed to know the existence of his feelings, particularly angry feelings."

"I think . . . yes, that's quite true."

"Certainly, I'm sure it is." While he spoke, Mueller deftly scanned paper after paper from the interview pile, arranged them too in symmetrical stacks. "Now normal people, if you are raised well and you are kind of developed well, we know when we are angry. We know what to do with it. Hopefully we are taught that it's allowed. You don't go around punching people in the nose, but hopefully you feel some anger and you can say to the people in your life, 'I'm angry with this. You said this or this.' And they say, 'Joe, I didn't know you were angry.' You have discussions about it. And it's okay to have feelings, it's developed, it's okay to have sexual feelings. There are times it's perhaps not proper to act on those feelings, but they are normal. Okay, it's healthy.

"This guy can't have feelings. It's against his law—their law. He can't consciously be aware of feelings except that everything is nice and everything is good and everything is gentle, and the world is beautiful and I love everybody."

Ken merely nodded. He was afraid to speak, the sick sad feeling was there. He knew it would show in his voice.

"After the testing was all over, I said to him, 'When did you get angry?' And his first response was: 'I never get angry.' And I said, 'Never?' And he said, 'Oh, yes, I got angry once at my father, but it was only because I loved him. It was only out of love.'" Now it was the psychologist's turn to hesitate. It was starting to sound in his voice too. "How sad. It will be interesting to find out what his early childhood was really like."

"I . . . I've come to know his folks really well—that is, what I have come to believe is really well. It would be difficult to believe that they are not what they appear to be."

"Difficult, yes, but not impossible. That is one of the first things one learns in my business, nothing is impossible. Not of people, or done by them." Mueller tapped one of the stacks. "The issue is here. It takes a lot of doing to make the Bill Ray Browns of our world. They are programmed. You throw the right ingredients in the right pot, and you invariably get the same stew. It has almost become a formula."

"What is the stew?"

"I'm only the psychologist, you're the lawyer. I can't deal with criminal particulars at this stage. He has told me nothing; I can only give you his profile. But be aware of this. If someone can't get angry or be aware of anger and you can't verbalize it, what do you do with it? You stuff it. If you are told it's wrong, it's unacceptable, if you can't talk about it, whatever, you stuff it, and you stuff it, and you stuff it, and you stuff it. Anger doesn't go away, doesn't go out through your pores, doesn't leave by osmosis if it's not dealt with. And if it's not dealt with, it stays.

"Now that's bad for the average person, and that's how you get ulcers, and you get migraine headaches at times, and that's how you sometimes somaticize feelings if you stuff them in. You get tense trying to keep them under control.

"But when the rage and anger is enormous, what do you do with it? Where does it go?" Mueller swept both hands over his by now nearly rearranged desk, almost everything stacked neatly or deftly filed, laid out in a long multicolored line. "Well, in this man it's buried, like a bomb. And he doesn't hear it ticking. He can't say to himself, 'Hey, it's there, and it's better to do something about it.' He's got to keep shutting it off and shutting it off and shutting it off. You can't do that forever, nobody can. His defenses against it, his difficulty with it, the way he restricts it and compresses it, these are not your neurotic styles, this is psychotic."

Ken nodded. He had to. The feeling within him of Mueller's rightness was too great to any longer stifle that nod. "Doctor, Doctor, I sent you to him, as I believe I told you, to test him, for you to attempt to ascertain whether or not he might be criminally responsible, had the capacity within him to commit the type of crime he is charged with —"

Mueller nodded curtly.

"Therefore, what crime, or types of crimes, could a man with his profile . . . what —"

"Whatever."

The abruptness of Mueller's answer momentarily puzzled Ken. "What . . . ever?"

"Whatever," Mueller repeated. This time Ken understood, so he pressed no further, neither did Mueller elaborate. Instead, he placed each hand on twin stacks of Bill Brown data and leaned forward toward Ken, owlish eyes seeming to almost protrude over his tucked down reading glasses, his general demeanor even more serious than before. "There's one other issue, and that is I'm convinced that he is not aware of certain things consciously. There are parts in him that he has hidden from himself as well. There's a split. There's a good part, there's the angel, the good guy. The good guy goes to choir practice, interested in religion, even the ministry, interested in law and order. This is the good part. And then there's the ugly, explosive, dangerous, rageful part, the devil."

"The . . . devil?" Ken couldn't believe his ears, was starting to think he had somehow been spirited out of Mueller's stylishly modern office and into some movie like *The Exorcist*.

"The devil," Mueller calmly repeated, albeit grimly. "Good and evil, angel and devil, call it by whatever name, I think two distinct divisible selves reside in Bill Ray Brown."

"Like Dr. Jekyll and Mr. Hyde."

"Something like that. I mentioned to you the thematic apperception test. His is rife with indications of the splitting of self. There are themes of splitting. I won't dig them out now, but in both card number four and eight he sees two men. It goes on and on. He sees crosses that aren't there in some pictures, weapons that aren't there in others. Things are fuzzylike to him, he keeps saying—dreamlike. Other cards, he talks about meditation. People are meditating. The flavor of the hypnotic state. I believe he experiences things at times in a hypnotic kind of state, personally, internally in a dreamlike state. I'm convinced that, when his rage is triggered, it becomes a fugue state. There's a disassociation from the good guy, from the controls, from everything is okay, and there's a driven kinetic like that spring that unwinds. It's like going, aha, no stopping it—no attempt to stop it by the other side. But once the trigger is flipped, once the door is opened, swish, out comes the rage, the anger, tremendous anger, long strange anger all of his life."

This was blowing Ken's mind. He could do little more than sit and stare at Mueller. Yet, way down in his own deep below, he already knew there was some truth in what Mueller was so earnestly saying, by whatever names.

"There are constantly reoccurring themes of 'religion means good, darkness, bad.' There's a flavor of the occult, of Heaven, Hell, good, bad, angels, the devil, opposites, splitting between the two. You do not get that kind of thing from your average person. What you get from Bill Ray Brown is what is coming from inside him. So I arrived at two diagnoses. First of all, he's psychotic through and through. Second of all, there's an imposition on the psychosis of multiple personality. There's two sides. There are parts that are excluded from the other, and in consciousness, the psychosis is through and through, and the only difference in the parts of the multiple personality is there's a control to one. As long as there's no rage, as long as there's no stimulus, as long as there's no triggering, he's quietly subdued, crazy."

"Crazy?"

"Crazy. Both selves. Sides. The other side is he's crazy but not quiet and subdued. Violent, explosive, like a railroad train trying to put on the brakes that you can't. This train has no brakes."

"Crazy?" Ken heard himself asking metronomically.

"Crazy," Mueller repeated quietly, "both sides." Mueller dropped his eyes from Ken's, surveyed his desk, found one thing not yet in place. The number ten Rorschach card had somehow got stuck under the thematic apperception test binder. Mueller speared it out now and teetered it at the end of that long multicolored line, half on and half off the end of his desk. Ken watched, waited, even held his breath, but the card somehow did not fall.

Mueller waited to be sure, then looked up at Ken, an impish smile rippling his beard. "I think that's all."

"Yes." Ken nodded. "I would think . . . so."

36

On February 6, 1979, Bill Ray Brown was evaluated at the Wisconsin Center for Forensic Medicine, to determine whether or not he met the criteria of the State of Wisconsin as to criminal responsibility. After a ninety-minute interview conducted jointly by psychiatrist Clyde Klutz and psychologist Bruce Petty, they concluded that Bill Ray Brown was not mentally ill at the time of the crime and therefore clearly criminally responsible for his behavior, should he be found guilty of the Mathews rape and assaults.

On February 12, Bill Ray Brown was transported under guard to Crisis Counseling Center to be questioned by defense mental health experts Doctors Franz Wendel and Ashley Cantwell as to his involvement, if any, in the Mathews rape and assaults. After preliminary interviews, which revealed little, Bill Ray Brown was injected with seven-and-one-half grains of sodium amytal, a drug reputed to reduce inhibitions and help free up repressed memories. Under sodium amytal, Bill Ray Brown confessed involvement in both assaults though not the rape per se, maintaining that he was under the delusion that the Mathews children were "satanic occult evil demons" which he felt compelled to attack before they attacked him. Prior to this "attack," Brown recounted how he had been "traveling unknown roads, hands feeling glued" to the steering wheel of his car, had been drawn to the Mathews home because the house "glowed red and yellow spots." He further recounted how he had stopped while in flight from the scene of the crime and changed clothing and carefully washed the blood from his being with a jug of water he kept in the trunk of his car, then disposed of the bloodied clothing, jug, and knife used in assault. Shortly thereafter, "the whole ugly world returns to God's beauty," and he finds himself "driving to his fiancée's house, thinking about buying one of her little daughters a birthday present." Then he is arrested.

Bill Ray Brown's confession was essentially an elaboration upon a scenario he claimed to have dreamt during the night of February 9, and detailed in a letter to Attorney Knutson the next day, February 10.

After gaining this information, Doctors Wendel and Cantwell attempted to get Bill Ray Brown to admit involvement in the murders/disappearances, but were unable to do so.

On February 21, 1979, the grand jury indicted Bill Ray Brown for the murders of Linda Lou Craig and Beverly Ann Lukken. The case was remanded to Little Falls District Court.

On March 5, Judge Elmer Peterson ordered that Bill Ray Brown be brought before a jury of his peers at the Portage County Courthouse on the thirtieth day of April in the year of our Lord nineteen hundred and seventy nine, to answer charges that he criminally raped Dawn Mathews and assaulted with intent to commit murder both her and her little brother Johnny Mathews.

On March 17 through 19, Bill Ray Brown was returned to Crisis Counseling Center for further interrogation as to his possible involvement in the murders/disappearances. Though subjected to several protracted sessions, some including sodium amytal, he could not—or would not—provide Doctor Ashley Cantwell or Franz Wendel with information linking him to any of the unsolved cases.

On May 7, after six days of trial, Bill Ray Brown was found guilty as charged on all three counts: the criminal rape and assault with intent to commit murder of Dawn Mathews and the assault with intent to commit murder of John Mathews. Though Ken Knutson and four defense mental health experts mounted a persuasive argument that Bill was insane and therefore not criminally responsible for his acts of August 16, 1978, the Portage County jury rejected their no guilty by reason of insanity plea and found for the prosecution after deliberating only 110 minutes.

Bill was sentenced to thirty to fifty years on each count, sentences to run concurrently. He would be eligible for parole in thirteen plus years, counting time already served. There were those who thought Judge Peterson was of the opinion that Bill would be less likely to be paroled prematurely on a fixed-year sentence as opposed to life imprisonment and that was why he opted for thirty to fifty, but, as no one was really privy to the judge's thinking on the matter, it remained just that, speculation. Whatever the judge had in his mind, the imminent trial in Helvetia County on the Linda Lou Craig and Beverly Ann Lukken murder indictments hung heavy over the proceedings, conceivably influencing as much as the case at hand the participants' actions. This included those of the babyfaced young man standing stiffly as the sentence was read out over his head, displaying no discernible emotion, no last-second outcry as the years were tolled for him, no eleventh-hour plea for mercy and understanding.

"Have you nothing to say?" Judge Peterson asked.

"I am sorry," Bill offered meekly.

"We're all sorry," the judge agreed dryly. "I think you have some serious mental problems. I think you would have killed both victims if fate had not intervened. I recommend psychiatric treatment while he is in prison," he continued, turning his head slightly to be sure the court recorder caught this. Then he squared off again on Bill. "I suggest you take full advantage of the opportunities afforded you in this regard. You will be dispatched forthwith to the Reception and Guidance Center at Elsinore Prison."

37

But this day was not over, merely moving toward night. Ken walked slowly along spring-bursting streets toward the Holiday Inn, the "guilty" verdict chirping louder than the gamboling robins. It had just finished raining, a quick pounding spring rain, now the air was clearing. Is there really justice in all this? Ken asked the lovely spring day, waning now into deep purple and lavender-brown, painting pink and orange sunstrokes across the western horizon. What the hell was this trial all about?

It seemed now to have been only a gigantic waste of time and effort. Some kind of way station on the road to their final destination, the murders/disappearances, a means to get Bill locked away while they picked and pulled at him, for those like the robins were the angleworms—why do they crawl up out of the ground after a rain? he now wondered. Are they just living to be eaten? Seems like they only expose themselves a few times a year, after soaking rains . . .

But Bill was no worm, and Hunt no robin. Neither was Badger. Both of them had been sitting up there on the back benches, just waiting for Bill to get his on these three counts, so they could start pecking away at him for the next. Hunt had already approached Ken on some kind of plea bargain if Bill would plead guilty on Craig and Lukken and lead them to the bodies—that is, of course, if Bill got the guilty axe on Mathews.

Now he had. Hunt must have been pretty damned sure, Ken realized now, for he had moved in right across the courtyard from him . . . waiting.

So had Badger, along with half the law in central Wisconsin. The local Holiday Inn was crawling with investigatory and prosecution people, showing up at the trial to study Bill like some rare specimen under glass, see what kind of defense Ken would throw up in his behalf. That's probably why Hunt is here, Ken muttered to himself, so he'll know what to expect when we go to trial on Craig and Lukken—if we go to trial. Obviously, Mike doesn't think he can get a conviction on what he has or he wouldn't be down here staring over my shoulder. Of course, now that Bill already had thirty to fifty. . .

Guilty on all counts, not mentally ill, and therefore criminally responsible, the jury said. Just like the prosecution and their toadies, the Forensic Center, had maintained. Now that was criminally irresponsible! They spend a total of maybe three hours with him and jump up on the stand and flatly state the kid is damn near perfectly normal and knew exactly what he was doing! And the jury believed them—because they wanted to. After two solid days of defense experts telling them, showing them, how the kid was stark raving loony on the day he hits the Mathews children, Prosecutor Martin trots out the Forensic Center for what seemed like twenty minutes and the jury nod their heads and say, "Sure, we knew it all along, the dirty little worm is just malingering. Lock him up and throw away the key. We can't take a chance on such as he."

Well, there's certainly truth in that, Ken had to admit. I didn't argue that he shouldn't be locked up somewhere, but not Elsinore Prison. A guy like Bill shouldn't even be put through the regular jury trial system—it's a farce. We choose up sides, then they choose up sides. We argue our heads off before a jury that for the most part hasn't the foggiest idea what we're talking about. Then at the end of all our sociopsycho gobbledygook, the judge wakes the jury up to read his charges to them. Tells them that, if they decide Bill is not guilty by reason of insanity, he will be sent back for another evaluation to the very same Forensic Center that has already testified they found him sane. Stresses to the jury that if they again find him sane they will have to release him back on the streets in sixty days. Now, that's real insanity!

Ken kicked the head off a dandelion. How can you expect any jury to find NGRI after listening to a judge tell them that? Dammit, we have to find some different way to deal with the person accused of psychosexual crime right off the bat. They should be put through an entirely different judicial process. Forget about the twelve men good and true—that's fine when you're dealing with horse stealing or cattle rustling, but not these deeply technical, highly sophisticated psychosexual matters. We need experts judging them too! The average judge does not truly understand the sociopsycho testimony being offered up either. What we need are some real experts hearing these cases. Say a panel of six men or women, maybe one to each judicial district. Real experts, unbiased, unpartisan, truly learned mental health people trained to sit on these cases and only these cases, day after working day.

Sick men such as Bill should be sorted out from the general criminal populace and only tried before these examining bodies, who would not only receive history and take testimony from all ancillary sources, but also from the defendant. Yes, Ken asked himself, even nodding as he did so, "How can a jury of any sort be expected to pass on the sanity and criminal responsibility of a person they've not heard one word from?" It's not their lawyers who are being judged. Not their mental health professionals, no matter how good or bad or what they say. Any defendant choosing to plead NGRI *must* get on the stand and testify on his own behalf. If he is capable of doing so and does not, then neither he nor his lawyers or mental health experts truly believe him to be mentally ill and not responsible—

That stopped Ken dead in his tracks, long enough for a particularly big robin to finally yank a particularly tough worm out of a particularly small hole. Did I say that? I, who just went along with Bill and our mental health experts, and didn't put Bill on the stand? I . . .

Maybe we didn't really believe enough ourselves that he was mentally ill and not responsible. Maybe that's why we lost the trial. We couldn't match Prosecutor Martin's passionate conviction. We didn't dare risk our own man on the stand, he'd seem too sane, too cold-blooded, too callous—

Nah, Ken interrupted himself disgustedly, flicking an annoyed hand at the big greedy robin yanking away on another stubborn worm. Nah, we just were so sure we already had it won, we didn't want to risk upsetting the loaded cart by putting him on. Would have won too, if it hadn't been for the Forensic Center and the judge's insane charge to the jury.

Was that it? Was that really it?

"Bullcrap," Ken muttered angrily, scattering the flock of worm pullers as he briskly turned into the parking lot of the Holiday Inn. "Do like I say, those decisions would be out of our hands, we shouldn't have them anyway. The temptation is too great to play God.

"I'm still stuck with him though."

He stumbled over a spring-sprung crack in the asphalt, quickly looked about to see if anyone had heard. There was only one other man in the parking lot, wandering around way over by the building. He looked vaguely familiar. I'm even more beat than I thought, Ken admitted. Maybe I should just drop off this case and spend more time with Mary and the kids—

There, he had thought it again. But . . . maybe it was just plain fatigue, defeat. No, he wanted to be rid of Bill, finally, once and for all, rid of Bill Ray Brown. "Rid of him!" The worm.

Ken did stop now, just stopped and closed his eyes, threw his head back to stare through kindly closed lids at the high blue sky and the heavens beyond. Stood listening to the gentle sounds of spring. How peaceful it was. Without Bill Ray Brown.

Why not? Why not just do what the jury had done—the judge and the jury and the Forensic Center and Martin and all the rest? There! There, damn your sad sick eyes, take thirty to fifty and get out of sight. Go pick your dirty rotten sores in the dark somewhere—Elsinore Prison. Let me go home!

Yes, why not? Just stand here with his eyes closed and hear only the spring sounds and smell only the spring smells. Forget about Bill. Good-bye, Bill. Yes, after he had heard and smelled and forgotten enough, he could just open his eyes and step forward into the Holiday Inn like a regular American human being, have himself a nice long luxurious swim in the heated pool, belly up to the bar for a few Chivas Twists, wallow through a T-bone and fries. Forget about Fred and Leona waiting inside to share the post-guilty supper of hemlock and ashes, start planning the appeal, dream up some new miracle for the murder trials. "Pack my bags!"

Why not? Sure, just quick pack his bags and jump in his car and pound back down the road to Little Falls and Mary and the kids. Shit yes, sure, of course it could be done, who

was to stop him. It was only barely getting dark. If he really
hurried and stepped on it he could even be there in time for a
late supper, particularly if he called ahead and told her to keep
it warmed up.

He smiled then, his eyes still closed, thinking of the old
dirty joke, the one about the guy who called home and told his
wife to keep his supper warm, she said—

"Excuse me . . . Mr. Knutson?"

Ken squinted through the dusk, it seemed like there was
also some kind of film hindering his vision, saw that the man
was young, about his own age . . . yes, it looked like the foreman of the jury.

"Yes, it's me, Knutson."

"I . . ."

"Yes?"

Still the man hesitated, he seemed as uncomfortable about
the meeting as Ken. Yet, why should that be, Ken wondered.
They were not supposed to be adversaries.

"I don't wish to quarrel with the verdict," Ken heard himself say, "but could you tell me how you reached the verdict?"

The young foreman took a half-step backward, then leaned
forward to peer through the failing light long into Ken's eyes.
"We didn't know . . . what else to do with him . . ."

That was all the man could get out. Tears suddenly rose in
his eyes, and he quick turned his open prairie face away from
Ken. Ken dropped his briefcase, patted him on the shoulder
forgivingly.

"Don't feel bad. None of us do."

All was dark on the western horizon now, only a few
streaks of blood red remained to show where the day had
gone.

But this day was not over, merely moved into night. Fred
and Leona were waiting for him when he entered the defense
headquarters, a suite of rooms taken over by Ken for his office
and lodging during the course of the trial. Momentarily taken
aback by the sumptuousness of the supper they had spread for
him over combination desk and dining room table, he just
stood there inside the door staring incredulously at the many
and varied dishes. It looked more like a banquet for a con-
quering hero than the crushed loser, he thought, adding to
himself wryly, "Maybe I ought to call Martin to share it with
me."

But after a couple of Miller Lites the food started looking better so he ate the best he could, which was pretty well, seeing as how, he just realized now, he'd barely eaten a thing since the night before. Fred joined him, did fairly well himself, but nothing like the trencherman he could be on another occasion. Leona ate practically nothing, though the men urged she do so, contenting herself with "picking," while she flitted nervously about serving "her men."

They tried talking about everything but Bill and the trial, but it was no use. Ken could see that Leona wanted to say something about something. She kept giving him that look. Often he would look up to find her eyes on him, but then she would quickly look away, busy herself by passing him the same plate she had two minutes before. She seemed to be just waiting for him to lay his fork down and push back from the table, so he did.

"Ken, Bill almost tried to kill Elizabeth once."

Ken thought he was hearing things, just sat there with his full mouth open.

"Leona, what in the world are you saying—" Fred started to say.

"Fred, you sit right where you are!" Leona said fiercely, as though Fred had actually been getting up to try to stop her. But as far as Ken could see he hadn't moved a muscle since his head had snapped up along with Ken's. "I'm going to tell this now and don't you say a word till I finish. One day we were all going to take a nap, not all, just Beth and Bill and I, we were the only ones at home. I laid down on the sofa in the living room, Beth in her room, Bill . . . well, I thought Bill was going to lie down on his bed and take a nap too . . . I did, I fell asleep, the next thing I heard a . . . gurgling sound, the walls are thin, it only happened through there."

Leona waved a hand in the direction of Beth's bedroom. She was right back there in her living room, something had shocked her awake, her habitually lugubrious face twisted with terror as though she somehow knew her worst fears were being realized. "It was such a strange gurgling sound, I've done hospital volunteer work, I'd heard sounds like that before, a person breathing through their own blood, sucking air and blood through a hole in their throat or chest, I got up and went where the sound was, Beth's room . . . Beth was lying on her bed, unconscious, her whole head blood, Bill standing over her with a jewelry box in his hand, his face deathly white, not saying anything, just standing over Beth looking down at her.

"I hurried to stop the bleeding, ran to the bathroom and got a cold wet towel to wrap around her head, got the blood stopped away enough to see that her head was not crushed in, it was just a deep laceration. Bill just stood there while I was quick doing all this, his face deathly white, clutching the jewelry box between both hands like he was in a daze or something . . . I finally said . . . 'Can't you do something to help . . . !' Here I was running back and forth to the bathroom, the blood kept coming, soaking through my towels, the whole bed, trying to get it stopped, close up the wound, I wanted to call a doctor but I didn't dare . . . leave her . . . somehow, Bill was in the kitchen, I don't know if he just went by himself or I pushed him there, over there by the door, just standing there still clutching the jewelry box, I was going to throw the bloodsoaked towels and sheets into the washing machine, it was late now, I had gotten the bleeding stopped and the wound dressed, I had sedated her, she was resting easy, that's one of the reasons I quit working, so I could be home and watch my kids closer if anything ever happened, I looked over at him just standing there clutching the jewelry box . . . I got mad then, real mad, maybe the maddest I ever been, at least, at him . . . I jumped at him, grabbed him by the arm like this." Leona grabbed her own left forearm in her right fist and squeezed down hard, her face contracting viciously as she hissed the words. "Don't you ever do anything like that again!"

Leona's eyes clung to Ken's as they had throughout her entire telling. Now he watched the wild mother anger drain slowly from her face, slide down on past her normal melancholy to be replaced by something altogether new. A look began to take dominion of Leona's mobile face—yes, that was the only way Ken could express it to himself, the eerie mask settling over the woman's face did not seem to him to come from within her alone, but to be placed upon her by forces she could not understand or control. It was one of abject fear and yet wonder, fascination and repulsion, the combination of which she had not the wherewithal within to completely feel or totally understand. "His arm was like steel. There was something . . . still . . . going through it."

"You could still feel his . . ." Ken sorted through the more appropriate words till he came to "fervor?"

"Yes." Leona nodded, she knew, she had felt that arm. "It . . . was still there. I was almost . . . I was afraid to hang on to his arm . . . but I felt I had to. You know . . . he had such a look on his face . . . I almost . . . I thought he might want to do something like that to me too. I didn't know what to do, run out and get the neighbors, call the cops, tell Fred, get help . . . somewhere . . ." She just dwindled off.

Ken felt very attuned to her, had become almost feverish as Leona blurted out her bloodcurdling tale in what was becoming her customary manner of address of late, apparently controlled on the outside but close to cracking inside. Is it just my fevered imagination, Ken asked himself, or is she trying to tell me something even beyond this? Maybe even beyond her own capacity to know and understand—or, mine?

"Leona. How come . . . you waited to tell me this now?"

"That other young girl, Dawn Mathews . . . all through this trial I sat there thinking of Bill and Beth, what he had done to her that other time. She even reminded me a little of Beth when she was that age."

"How old was Bill then? And Elizabeth? When did this happen?"

"When Beth was about the same age as Dawn, thirteen, fourteen, yes, she must have been fourteen. She had just started high school, was starting to date outside a little bit for the first time. We didn't like that much, we felt she was too young to be dating, even if it was just going to the movies and church things, particularly with that one boy. They went around saying they were going steady, you know, how kids do nowadays, they don't even know what the words really mean. What was his name again?"

"Junior Simpson," Fred interposed grimly.

Ken wasn't paying too much attention to Leona running on about Elizabeth, his head was working on Bill. "So if Elizabeth was, say, fourteen, Bill is five years older than her. My God, he would have been nineteen already. He was already out of high school, in his first year at UW."

The parents just stared back at him, not seeming to realize the significance of this. "My God, don't you see what I'm driving at? A nineteen-year-old college student hitting his little fourteen-year-old sister over the head with a jewelry box.

Might have killed her had you not been there, Leona . . . Fred, don't you see how bizarre that is? Doesn't that tell you something? I mean, maybe some brothers hit their little sisters. I don't know, but I can't visualize hitting mine over the head with a jewelry box as she lay sleeping."

Ken sat with his hands spread wide, waiting for their answers.

"Don't look at me," Fred finally said. "I was at work, I didn't even know about it—"

"Did too!" Leona snapped.

"I mean, sure I came home and saw she had her head all bandaged up, but I never exactly heard how it all came to be—"

"How did it come to be, Leona?" Ken asked her directly. "Why did Bill attack Elizabeth?"

She met his eyes, but not completely. "That . . . that's one thing . . . we've never been able to figure out."

"Probably just one of those brother/sister arguments that got out of hand—" Fred offered quickly.

"You heard no argument, Leona," Ken corrected. "It was the gurgling sound that woke you."

"No. Yes. It . . . was just like I told it."

"I've always thought a whole lot more was made of it than had to be," Fred continued, as though not interrupted. "Her head was healed up in no time. She hardly missed a day of school."

"Who all made a 'whole lot' out of it?" Ken asked, still directing his question to Leona.

"Just in the family. We never let it out of the family. But Elizabeth kept after Bill for months, kept reminding him of what he had done every chance she got, every which way she could, throwing it up to him. I finally had to get after her a little, said to her, 'Beth, can't you let up on that, just try and forget about it.'"

Ken just sat there shaking his head, looking from one parent to the other. "Why in the world . . . God's name . . . didn't you tell me this before? Don't you realize how sick this is? He is? I might have been able to use this to save him from prison, get him the treatment he needs. Now . . . it's too late."

Ken got up, tossed his napkin on the cluttered table, turned and walked out the outer door, continued on down the hallway till he got to the far left-hand wing of the Holiday Inn. He knocked on door number 101. "Mike," he said, when Hunt opened the door, "can I come in? I think . . . he did 'em all."

Resolution:
Part 5

38

Knutson's belated discovery opened no magic doors for Mike Hunt. He still had to prove that "he did 'em all." But it was the first major chink in the heretofore impenetrable Brown murder defense and opened the deal door. Hunt had tried everything he could think of short of plea-bargaining, and now he was. He just didn't feel he could take the chance of going to trial on what he had.

Facts remained facts. Not one piece of physical evidence had yet been found positively linking Bill Brown to the deaths of Linda Lou Craig and Beverly Lukken, and the only direct evidence of Brown's participation in any of the crimes came from an eyewitness whose memory had been refreshed by hypnosis. In the one reported Wisconsin decision dealing with a homicide prosecution where no body or body part was recovered, the Supreme Court said, "We think under the authorities cited, it should be held that the People have failed to show beyond a reasonable doubt that the defendant is guilty of manslaughter." Further, in the most recent appellate court decision involving the attempted use of evidence obtained through hypnosis, that evidence was deemed inadmissible. There had not been a single reported Wisconsin decision combining and resolving both the no-body and the hypnosis issues presented by the Brown case. The Forensic Center and Feo Sakarov, the top psychologist at Elsinore Prison, agreed that it was highly unlikely that Bill Brown would ever divulge the whereabouts of his victims' bodies unless he was somehow prompted to do so. And in this day and age, the law does not permit torture. Add to this the biggest reason, returning the bodies to their loved ones, and Hunt didn't have much choice but to plea bargain.

Besides, under current law and the concurrent sentence system, he couldn't see how he could add one day to Brown's Portage County sentence. Even with life on second-degree murder, which was the best that could be hoped for, Brown still would be eligible for parole in ten years. Better to impress upon state corrections officials the inappropriateness of his parole by getting him to confess to the murders, by whatever means. As a self-confessed multiple murderer, he would, in all probability, serve the maximum time allowable under his current thirty- to fifty-year sentence. In any event Brown still would be subject to judicial review of his mental status whenever he was released from prison. Hunt could insure that by advising the Parole Board to inform the Helvetia County prosecuting attorney prior to his release, should he ever be released, so that mental commitment could be initiated then. Yes, a lot could be done to insure that Brown would spend most of the rest of his unnatural life behind bars without going to trial again—maybe more than if he did. For, if they tried him for second-degree murder and he was convicted, Brown would come before the Parole Board in a little over thirteen years with only the two Portage County convictions, neither involving a death and both arising from a single criminal transaction, and that would be all the Parole Board could legally look at. They would almost have to grant him parole if he accepted mental treatment and had been on good behavior.

Hunt laid down Knutson's latest proposal, dated yesterday, July 1. Still, it was a hard decision. Of course, the citizens of Helvetia County had elected him to fill a position that often required the making of hard decisions. Sometimes those decisions required him to make a choice between rigidly adhering to policies that he believed in and making humane exceptions. Maybe he should leave it at that. If the families of the victims agreed to let him make a deal with Brown to recover their loved ones' bodies, he'd go ahead and do it.

If he could. If Brown would. Yes, there was still this one little flaw in their dealing—getting Bill to confess. A little something he had shown no inclination whatsoever to do so far. Bill was still stonewalling behind Elsinore's. The whole thing hinged on somebody breaking into Bill and getting the truth. He couldn't bargain without Bill's plea.

His best hope now was Sakarov. Hunt's finger stubbed the intercom switch. "Kristanna, get me Feo Sakarov up at Elsinore Prison."

Kristanna did. "Hi, Feo, how's it going with Brown?"

"I'm working on him, Michael," the supercharged voice came back. "We're barely into treatment."

"Look, my hat's getting mighty tight these days. I need something to go on. At least some assurance that you can crack him if he knows something. Knutson and his shrinks claim it's possible he's suppressing so deep he may never be able to remember just what and where. After all, they've been working on him off and on for months. The Forensic Center couldn't get anything out of him—"

"So what makes me think I can?"

"Yes, that's about it."

The voice crackled, higher-tensioned than the wires. "I got him pegged, Mike. The answer is yes on both counts. He knows something, and I can get it out of him. It's just a matter of time. But it must be done right—"

This time Hunt cut off Sakarov, his voice just as charged. "I have very little time. The trials are barely two months away."

"Good. My boys invariably remember a whole lot better the closer they get to trial. Particularly if you sweeten the pot a little more."

"Feo, this guy's killed at least four people!"

"At least, Mike, at least," Sakarov agreed amiably. "OK, I hear you. I'll move him into daily sessions, start hitting on him harder."

39

Bill finally met his match in Elsinore Prison. If Martin had been born to prosecute him and Knutson groomed to defend him, Fyodor (Feo) Sakarov had trained himself to crack him. Once a fugitive from organized justice himself—wrongly accused as a teenage rapist, he had been hunted down and jailed until the real culprit was caught—he had set out early on to learn everything about his nemesis he could lay his mind on and then infiltrate the system and knock it off its wobbly knees. As great good luck would have it, some years later, when he became superintendent of the Reception and Guidance Center for the Wisconsin Department of Corrections, he was finally able to turn the table on the sheriff who had wrongly done him in way back then. Fyodor Sakarov, the son of Slovakian immigrants, was not one to forget easily or give up often, then or now.

That's not to say he always succeeded. He just rarely failed. Climbing the criminal justice ladder two rungs at a time, he had assumed the superintendentship by age thirty, the youngest in the state's history, and was recognized now, at age thirty-two, as one of the foremost authorities in the United States on the murdering mind. As superintendent, he had general overall responsibility for the center's functioning and management, as well as disposition of all newly received male felons throughout the Wisconsin Department of Corrections. The Reception and Guidance Center is a 500-bed, close-security institution just outside the walls of Elsinore Prison, designated by the Wisconsin Corrections Commission as the state's primary clinical and diagnostic facility. It includes facilities for those individuals requiring in-house hospitalization in the Clinical Services Unit, a 123-bed, close-security institution. Sakarov's position also involved responsibility for the Psychological Services Unit, into which Bill Ray Brown was quickly routed.

As former administrator of all psychological services for the entire Wisconsin correctional system and past chief psychologist of the Clinical Services Unit itself, whose responsibilities included the evaluation and treatment of psychosexual offenders, particularly those who had committed bizarre offenses, Sakarov was uniquely trained to deal with the likes of Bill Brown. In fact, most of his education and on-the-job clinical training had dealt with the dangerous and/or mentally ill offenders, both from an evaluative and a treatment point of view. Not so incidentally, his research pointed out that, contrary to popular belief, inmate informal group leadership structure is similar to that found in industrial and civilian society. He was able to apply this thinking as superintendent of the center, aiding and abetting inmates into informal leadership positions, allowing to an extent what many civilians feared most, the inmates' takeover of the asylum. For example, when a freshly plucked "chicken" like Bill Brown came in, in order to keep him alive and healthy long enough to evaluate and treat him, he might call into his office the inmate leaders of the Black Panthers and the Hell's Angels or some such dominant group and negotiate some kind of a deal to place him under their mutual protection. This was done for a mutual price, of course, but one Sakarov was well willing to pay to keep his simmering center from blowing as high as some of the other penal institutions around the country. But, regardless of how he conducted it, his sex-offender program was considered by many to be one of the best in the country, if not the best. Somewhat modestly characterized by Sakarov as at least the "largest and most experienced," it employed about twenty mental health workers, including two psychiatrists.

Sakarov, at heart more clinician than administrator, put the toughest nuts in his own stocking, particularly when the nut was as intriguing and was purported to have a shell as thick as Brown's. Not that he had a head to grind for anybody but the patient, but, as he told Hunt, if in the course of Bill's evaluation and treatment anything came out amongst the filings that indicated Brown was really the killer, he'd be the second one to know. Other than that, he planned to treat Brown as just one of many, for, of course, to Sakarov, that's all he was. The day Bill Ray Brown walked meekly through Elsinore Prison's Reception and Guidance Center's double-barred doors, May 31, 1979, Feo Sakarov had some thirty-odd bona fide multiple murderers scattered about through his center and Elsinore Prison proper, which, with 6,000 blighted souls behind its great gray walls, was the largest walled prison in the world. No, there was no shortage of product for Sakarov. Bill Ray Brown was just another long prison number walking through his swinging door, with his thirty to fifty for rape and assault to commit murder nowhere near as infamous as, say, Jimmy Lee Jones, another All-American boy presently in residence who had terrorized the Iola area between July of 1969 and August of 1971, killing and mutilating seven females between the ages of thirteen and twenty-three in the process.

No, there was nothing about Bill Ray Brown that was going to make him drop whatever he was doing and rush to the nearest typewriter and hack out a quickie blood-and-guts book, an all too common practice of late that Sakarov loathed, particularly when done by or in conjunction with a mental health "expert" exploiting a patient in a sensationalistic manner. Nor did Brown appear to be such an extraordinary diagnostic specimen as early reports and his forwarded file would like him to believe. Sakarov soon found that Billy, as he came to affectionately call him, fit very neatly into his Symbiotic-Offender category, a psychosexual murderer so common to Sakarov he invented a label for them. Neither paranoid schizophrenic nor multiple personality, they nevertheless represented the classic case of good and evil residing in the same body, neither really recognizing that the other exists. The erupting volcano of contemporary society, Sakarov believed. With the breakdown of the traditional family unit and the rapidly diminishing role of the male as head of the household and disciplinarian, rape and psychosexual murder were moving from the ghetto to suburbia. Unless Sakarov missed his guess, the women's liberation movement would also unknowingly contribute a great many more such victims cum murderers in the very near future.

Yes, the longer he looked into and listened to Billy, the more he came to categorize him as a classic example of the "Boy Next Door" phenomenon, as Sakarov vernacularly named them. Now, after his conversation with Hunt, he once more dug out the data he had compiled delineating everything from their ancestry to their birth, through childhood and adolescence, to killing and capture and treatment, and ranged it across his desktop alongside Billy's file. He wanted to make absolutely sure he did have him "pegged" before tightening the screws on him, setting him up for the big bust.

He glanced through an essay he had recently written summarizing his findings: Superficially, the Boy Next Door appears to be just that, another average or above average boy next door, until, along about his nineteenth year or sophomore year in college, he begins to murder females of relatively the same age, continuing to do so at ever-increasing interludes until he is either caught or allows himself to be through commission of a catch-crime. His inception, conception, and progression are virtually formulaic. It almost always takes a three-generational mix of all the right ingredients to successfully produce a Boy Next Door. The paternal grandfather is invariably passive within the family. The grandmother is narcissistic, masculine, often takes over functions of the husband in family, pushes religion, is very strict. Their son, in turn, the father of the Boy Next Door, is generally a weak, tyrannical man who relinquishes family to wife and grandmother but is usually industrious outside of the home, looks good to the outside world. He invariably marries a woman who had a very stern father and now finds it hard to adjust to the female role and becomes a narcissistic mother. She is very close to the male child, who becomes the Boy Next Door, invariably a firstborn and only son, identifies with him at the expense of the daughters that follow, usually two or more, to the extent that this male child ultimately receives the signal that he is better than his sisters. As time goes on, the mother becomes aggressive-hostile toward all males except her son, yet she is envious of his sexuality, comforts herself by excessively stroking her male offspring . . .

Sakarov nodded his head here, needed to read no more of this part. Yes, he told himself, "Pour that good old-fashioned American mix together and stir well and approximately one out of every four hundred thousand males will grow up to be a psycho-sexual murderer." That is, if he's Caucasian—fortunately, his formula didn't seem to hold true with non-Caucasians.

He read on: Obviously, the die is not cast at birth alone. If he is to achieve his deadly destiny, the Boy Next Door must be stirred improperly too. The mother, and/or grandmother, continues to smother love in all ways upon him, fosters narcissistic feelings within him as well, arousing his latent incestuality. He assumes a passive role, for he has to do nothing to elicit his mother's extreme affection. He clearly realizes her as his sublime source of affection as opposed to his father, and hostility toward the father starts and quickly begins to solidify.

It is at this stage of the male child's personality development that many of his later traits become ingrained. He starts to unnaturally love his mother, becomes passive-compliant to get love, is the proverbially perfect kid, and is often told so by his mother and grandmother. He takes on the prudish moral standards of his mother, becomes industrious like his father. But his sexual attitude to himself is one of abstinence. He excessively masturbates, experiences great guilt, has emission dreams. At around age fourteen he begins to overtly experiment sexually with one or more of his sisters. This, the mother enjoys, the father ignores, and the grandmother covers. He fights incestual feelings toward his mother, but as he and they grow it becomes harder and harder to suppress this powerful longing. He has become very narcissistic by now and expects female love as a passive right. But a minor crisis may develop about this time. His sisters may begin to cut him off, start looking for less demanding boyfriends outside the home.

The Boy Next Door will usually go underground for a while then, seek external support outside the home. He becomes religious, is extremely nonaggressive, even bashful, retarded, in a social sense. He simply can't risk societal awareness of this terrible anxiety he doesn't understand.

"How does one say to his buddies, I want to screw Ma?" Sakarov muttered aloud.

His anxiety soon starts to surface. He wants relief from his incest feelings. He starts to expose himself; this stems from his narcissistic need for passive affection. He is asking those who view him for reassurance that he's still lovable, still has a penis. He is becoming compulsive, wants to cut the mother cord while being smothered with mother love at the same time. He wants to please females while he is insulting them. He is becoming torn, conflicted, compulsive, racked by guilt and shame. This begins the good/bad death struggle over his dying perfect self.

By this time the Boy Next Door needs even more external support and structure so he may move from traditional religion to fundamental or occult groups, almost anything, as long as it has high, even fanatical moral standards. He becomes even more subservient to mother and church, surrounds himself with people who firmly reinforce his good-boy image. But it doesn't work, he is starting to become angry, an emotion he denies as rigidly as his incestual longings. Yet he looks even better to the outside world. They only see the choirboy, youth minister, stellar athlete, honors student, model son. He starts seeking a solution in the Bible, starts to rationalize evil as the devil. This allows him a ready explanation for his wicked inner feelings and satanic thoughts.

Now comes the big crisis. His favorite sexual sister takes up seriously with an outside boyfriend, may threaten to, or does, cut the Boy Next Door off completely. The grandmother fears her granddaughter may become pregnant either by this outside danger or by her hitherto "perfect" grandson, signals him to do something about their familial pail of sexual worms. The mother is also becoming increasingly concerned about the twisted nature of things. Whatever vicarious sexual satisfaction she still receives has become outweighed by such societal fears as the grandmother's and indications that her husband, the father, may be showing signs of waking up and belatedly demanding something be done about cleaning up their mutual mess. If, at this critical juncture, the mother directly or indirectly reproaches her son seriously for the first time in their oedipal lives or threatens to withhold her unalloyed love from him, he may compulsively strike out at whomever he perceives to be the cause of his downfall, such as the erring sexual sister.

Sakarov just glanced through the next few pages, tried to concentrate only on what pertained to Billy: When and if he dates, it must be an equally religious girl, or the Boy Next Door will strive to create or cast her as such. They will have a strict sex code, and Mom will have to approve of the girl. If they should happen to have some kind of sex, usually abortive, there is much guilt. His anxiety level grows higher and higher. Physical symptoms begin appearing. He becomes restless, fearful, apprehensive, has headaches probably for the first time in his life, feels warm and tight all over, perspires unduly, becomes sporadically diarrhetic. Vague feelings of some sort of impending doom hover near, no matter how closely he tries to walk with his ramrod-straight God—

"Yeah, the religion shit is starting to fall apart. Now I got to make him see it for what it is."

The world is only black and white to him now, good and evil. The anxiety attacks grow. The first indications of later fugue states arrive, he may walk around aimlessly in a dreamlike state. Impossible fantasies begin, cannot be requited. He sees himself as Christ when he's not the devil. Prays for relief from this hideous duality, but it does not come, from either source. He may try to create himself into a pseudo-God like Jim Jones. He descends deeper and deeper into religion, joins occult groups, begins to interpret the Bible literally, and projects himself into these literal interpretations.

As Billy had when he wrote Linda his miracle letter about having jumped off a cliff and been caught by God, noted Sakarov on the running checklist he had placed on his desk between his essay and Billy's file.

He went back to reading: He is seventeen, eighteen, nineteen, now. The manifestations of his anxieties become more flagrant, his exhibitionism grows, his incestual yearnings are almost unbearable. His hands become evil, in masturbation as well as sex. He starts to feel his penis is magic. He may still expose it for this minimal relief but may discontinue, for he's now starting to fear having it devoured by females. Herein are the roots of the cannibalism that may show up later when the Boy Next Door eats comparable parts of his female victims, sucks their blood, desecrates them anally. The mutilation of their bodies in any way starts here.

Now comes a rapidly escalating period. He crosses over onto a very dangerous plateau. He starts to project, transfer, put his self in place of the female in his fantasies or actual voyeuristic prowlings . . . that woman can be his mother.

The cord is being drawn tighter and tighter around his shrinking penis; his fragile manhood cracks. His anger toward women and fear of them swell proportionately. He may become virtually impotent for he cannot risk what little he has left to their devouring mouths. He may start to burn down buildings for relief. It is safer than killing women. He wants to destroy, devour women in his own turn, but is still too

fraid so may temporarily turn to arson for his anger outlet—
r to his car. His car will take on a special significance. It can
:ap forward with great thrust while his penis cannot. Many
peak of their hands as evil, taking over the car, becoming
lued to the wheel.

Yet the Boy Next Door may still be able to hold back his
vil hands for a limited period by repressing them in intellec-
ual outlets, though their real thrust will invariably scream out
hrough their endeavors: bizarre paintings, writings addressing
heir dilemma subtextually; they may make dolls with curious
ncoded markings and dress.

Sakarov smiled within himself, laid aside his essay to pick
p the doll. Certainly it's Billy's doll, dummies! He even left
ou a clue, as he usually did, put the same glowing almost
hosphorescent cross on the pupils as he had in the Christ's
yes in his painting.

Picking up his large round magnifying glass, Sakarov hov-
red close over both the doll and the painting, wondered why
thers of his ilk paid so little attention to what a man did and
o much to what he said. The doll was Billy dressed up like
is mother. So he could hide himself away under the cottage
vhere it was found and hug it close and peaceably love the
oth of them at once, while begging for relief from his rapidly
scalating compulsions.

Sakarov held the painting out at arm's length. Looked to
im like Billy was all three of the figures in the painting. The
ery human devil, clad only in the briefest of flesh-toned bi-
:inis, muscles bulging, clenched fists having just snapped the
hains that bound those evil hands, huge archangel wings
oised for flight, eyes bugging wildly, hair literally standing
n end. It was Billy snapped, in a psychotic seizure, ready to
:ill. The radiant haloed Lord, fully dressed, wreathed in
:indly cloud, was Billy right after he had killed. Killed the
levil in him, crucified himself into Christ, walking on air,
ooking back down at the cowering, naked mortal left behind.
)nly the upper torso of the mortal man showed above ground;
is sexual self was buried. He was the Billy between the
gony and the ecstasy. The everyday self he has left to live in,
ry to pass off as "normal" to the world.

Sakarov picked up the magnifying glass and swept over the
ainting again. Of course, it could be Billy's version of the
3rown Trinity too, father, son, and holy ghost, all in lower

case—or, just what he claims it to be, a nice little religious painting.

Sakarov didn't bet a lot of money against his initial analysis. He slid the doll and painting off to one side. As bizarre paintings go, it wasn't that bad, one of the best his little group of Van Goghs had ever done. Wasn't likely any of his artists would cut off their own ears though, maybe their whole head, but—

Sakarov stopped himself; he had this habit of getting a little bizarre himself whenever he got to feeling sorry for his boys, and it was too early to start getting sentimental about Billy. He went back to comparing Billy and his file against his charts and outlines, reading his essay.

Often about this time, nineteen or so, the Boy Next Door will even make an external attempt to close with the enemy within him—becoming involved in mental health, studying police methods, working for the police—both for the feeling of power that comes with the territory and to try to find out more about himself, see if he can't come across a case that addresses his problem. This fact spoke directly to the belief Sakarov held that often the Boy Next Door knows that he is sick and might ultimately do something criminal, a sticky situation if he or anyone else were to present his theories before a jury for or against a not-guilty-by-reason-of-insanity defense. But did these facts, if indeed they were facts, make him any less mentally ill or less likely to ultimately act out his compulsions as he was virtually programmed to do? As far as Sakarov was concerned, in Billy's case the defense shrinks were probably right in their contention that he was mentally ill and not criminally responsible. The only thing was, they had tried to put the right guy in the wrong diagnosis.

Sure, Billy goes schizophrenic when he kills, then integrates, but they never really told how he got there and back. That's what really confuses a jury. Any juror with any kind of a brain can understand if the mental health expert is knowledgeable enough to take him by the hand and lead him to his intellectual and emotional destination. Just telling what a psychosexual murderer does and hanging labels on him for doing so doesn't mean diddly shit if you don't yourself know the real why and can tell others. To a great extent, he felt the defense shrinks had misinterpreted their own information, particularly the sodium amytal interview wherein time and time again Billy was giving them clue after clue and as much as coming right out and telling them everything they wanted to know had they but the wherewithal and the real background knowledge of the Billys of our world. Billy, from day one kept telling the cops and later his shrinks and anyone who cared to listen that he had "dropped off" Linda Lou Craig— this was a code phrase, one of the clues he kept dropping. Sure, he had dropped Linda off, after he had killed her. Sakarov would bet a dollar to a day-old doughnut and throw in the sodium amytal transcript he was rereading that Linda would be found someday propped up in exactly the same position that Billy kept telling them he last saw her sitting— "kind of on one hip, sort of, not really sitting but kind of leaning . . . in the snow." Sure, she was in the snow, but not on her front porch! She was probably kind of propped up under or against a tree somewhere. "She took her coat off and kind of wrapped it around herself, sort of tucked it under her . . . seat." Exchange the she for he and you got it. He already had her stripped nude, had "dropped off" the body, was somewhere else laying out the clothes to make it look like she was still alive for all his own sick reasons.

Sakarov reached up and took off his horn-rimmed glasses, looked at them, ran his hand up over his aching eyes into his thinning hair. Held his glasses out and looked at them . . . it was Billy's grandmother that wore horn-rimmed glasses, not his mother.

Putting his glasses back on, Sakarov resumed reading the sodium amytal transcripts. Here were other examples of Cantwell and Wendel missing clues, as far as he was concerned. After Billy had used his cunning and personal knowledge of the demons within him to explain away the Mathews catch-crime—instead of giving the real reason, which would show him to be even sicker and more compulsive—the two doctors had tried to get him to admit killing Linda and were side-tracked with all the garbage Billy fed them about his good and bad selves. Finally they gave up, when Billy appeared to be just babbling about "the night we finished I dropped her off a little after 2:00, but I felt like when I got home, going right back over there and talking to Linda and try to straighten this up and I thought, 'no.'" Then they waltzed around a little more until Billy leaped right in and repeated his litany about leaving her sitting in the snow and gunning out of her yard and driving home: "Then Mom was up and I raced around, I ran, I was trying to burn off some of this energy I had. I ran around, I went in, talked to Mom, told Mom I'd be seeing her, you know, in a few days, couple or a few days. We studied the Bible that day. We always tried to do that at least once a week and then go on . . . we do extracurricular activities too. So I talked to Mom and that." Then the two doctors had told Billy to rest and ended the interview.

Good a time as any to stop the tape, Sakarov had to agree. Billy had just told them he'd killed Linda, "dropped off" the body, had had a psychotic seizure and was still trying to integrate when he got home, saw his mother was waiting up for him. He didn't dare go in, so he ran around in the night trying to physically burn it away, finally risked going in and was confronted by his mother, who did or did not recognize the symptoms. After all, she'd seen them before, after Billy had attacked Elizabeth.

Sakarov nodded. Almost anything could have happened that New Year's Eve after Billy got home. Nothing whatsoever would surprise him.

Sakarov pushed conjecture aside, returning to his essay. The Boy Next Door was closing with his enemy, studying the police, maybe even working with them. Billy switched his major from primary education to Abnormal Psychology his sophomore year, right on schedule, started participating in religion, became a Youth Minister, etcetera, etcetera.

Cruelty toward animals may begin. The Boy Next Door is practicing the infliction of pain and death. It is now only a very short jump to unrelated females, but this is usually still part of his practice period for he usually does not harm them yet. He just starts to attack them, maybe rushes at them on a subway platform but stops short of pushing them off. It is enough now to feel his hands on the female and see the great fear in her eyes. For that is one of the things he truly wants to see, the great fear in the eyes, whether animal or female, fear and later pain, suffering. Torture begins here.

But still, with females at least, the Boy Next Door can only fantasize the pleasure after the aborted attack. He lapses into a dreamlike state, runs the episode over and over through his mind like a slow-motion movie, watches the principles perform, sees that it is his physical being doing the attacking but still doesn't think it is him. He is also practicing disassociating his good self from the bad act, so that when the real thing comes along he is ready to deal with it properly.

"A man can sure screw up a polygraph that way," Sakarov muttered aloud, flicking through Billy's and casting them aside.

His compulsion is still building, building, picking up an internal head of steam. He starts becoming fetishistic, coprophiliac, obsessed with his own human waste and that of others, obsessed with the human waste process as a sexual outlet symbol. He may start secretly placing upon his own body various articles of female clothing and either defecating while wearing them or upon them. Many of his actions become more bizarre, his impulses harder to deny, more difficult to suppress.

Now, when he slips into his dream state, rage is the dominant feature. He is ready to kill, programmed, prepared, practiced, made for murder. It may be a girlfriend demanding sexual satisfaction or a random female—or so it appears, but he knows who he is murdering. The woman he picks often matches the fantasy girl he has been practicing on all along. There is nothing to it; it is over before he has fully realized it. Death is usually the victim's only destiny, defense. The Boy Next Door is the deadliest of killers for he attacks from need. He attacks with no warning, and little or no communication, invariably stabbing his prey twenty-three to twenty-six times. It is the knife wound that gives him the sex experience, particularly the turning of the blade inside the wound and feeling the blood gush out over his hand as he withdraws, the exact number of stab wounds dependent upon how many withdrawals it requires for him to climax, reach orgasm.

Parts of the victim may be missing. He may cut off evil hands. There is almost always a ritualistic-compulsive cutting and carving on the body after death. He may carve eyes in the forehead, slice off breasts, gouge out anus and vagina. He is here to humiliate his lifelong love-hate tormentor, so he violates this surrogate body to do so.

Then he leaves it, "drops it off," so to speak. The invariably nude or partially disrobed body may take on a mystical, even supernatural, import to him. Her clothing may also be laid out some distance away as if the person were still in them. If this is the case, it usually complements the murderer's own dualistic nature—the body is evil, the clothing good. Depending on need, he invariably returns to either or both sites, unless something scares him off. Either of these actions indicates the culmination of his coprophilia and fetishism qualities, the compulsive use of some object or part of the body as a stimulus in the course of attaining sexual gratification. He may take a part of the body or an item of clothing with him.

The cache Hunt expected to find in Billy's bedroom—he's got one somewhere, I'll bet, Sakarov wagered himself. He may have forgotten where it is, for sometimes the Boy Next Door will repress that also, particularly when he thinks he's getting better and moving back into normal sexual relationships, as Billy may have tried to do with Sarah Fortunato. Of course, it hadn't worked out. Sarah had told Sakarov that her life with Billy was "sexually frustrating." Yes, I'll bet it was, Sakarov thought now—and scary.

She was now beginning to remember little things she had tried to overlook before: Billy playing his *Tommie* records over and over behind a locked door, her children's youth minister fascinated by a movie and song lyrics about sticking pins in people and other forms of physical and mental and emotional torture. She went to a drive-in with him one night to see two trashy S and M movies and listened to him laugh "weirdly" during a scene of a campy werewolf fondling the heroine's breasts. Billy had explained away his preference for midnight movies and drive-ins by saying they were cheaper.

She had walked in on him one night while he was undergoing what he himself had explained to her as an "out of body experience." He saw himself lying down on the bed, but at the same time he was floating up near the ceiling, watching himself lying down on the bed. The next night Danielle Forshey turned up missing. Before he had committed the Mathews assault, he had suggested to Sarah they run away. She had refused, told him that he couldn't run away from his problems. When Sakarov had asked her if she knew what his problems were, she had answered, "No, I didn't want to know." In December or January after the Mathews arrest, Billy had written to Sarah, in a code he had worked up for their communication, "Damn it, Satan, take me!" Fred had told her that when he first met Leona he had been attracted to her because "she had a glow around her head." Billy had told her he loved his grandma deeply—she was "very orderly"— and preferred his grandparents' home to his parents' home.

When Sakarov asked Sarah who Billy's hero was, she answered, "Jesus. He was perfection. Bill felt closer to Christ than to man."

Yes, Sarah had a lot to tell, if one knew how to listen. Had told him a lot more than maybe she even realized, particularly about what went on behind the Browns' closed doors. She was the best window so far into Billy's head. Now all Sakarov had to do was crawl through the casing.

A sudden thought occurred to him. Maybe the cops had looked in the wrong bedroom for Billy's cache. Maybe it was closer to Sarah's.

Sakarov shrugged, then realized why he had. Enough of it fit. He was almost ready to confront Billy with his murders. Yes, he told himself, noting the possessive pronoun, I am now sure that he committed them. Now all I must do is confront him with my knowledge.

Sakarov returned to the essay, firmly vowing never to digress again until he got to the end.

The Boy Next Door will not only take a part of the body or an article of clothing with him but usually also leaves a calling card for the police. This bespeaks his rising masochism, the need to be punished, his desire to be punished, which, of course, in the extreme, can result in suicide. Yet at the same time he wants to taunt the police, and his father, whom he equates with the police as being ignorant and weak, so his calling card clues are usually so cunning that it would take a person as superior as he feels himself to be to decipher them, and he can gloat when they do not.

The Boy Next Door usually doesn't remember his initial attack, as opposed to the sadomasochistic murderer who does, and kills for that reason—that is how he gets his kicks. It was here where the Forensic Center went astray, Sakarov felt, compounded their foolishly simplistic antisocial personality diagnosis. The Boy Next Door gains some measure of relief from his terrible tension through the attack and now feels relatively good and does not remember, for the simply complex reason that, if he does remember, he can no longer feel good. So he does what he had been practicing so assiduously to do most of his life; he intellectually compartmentalizes the attack in his evil bank and accepts only the good. Again, the base motivation of his attack, as opposed to the true sadomasochist, is not to be cruel but to relieve his awful tension.

He is not, in the clinical sense, mentally ill like the sado-masochistic offender he is often confused with, who is not treatable, as far as Sakarov was concerned. Nor is he like the psychopathic offender, for whom the only treatment is to make the cost of offense so high it might deter him; fear of death might make some psychopaths think twice. But the Boy Next Door responds readily to treatment. If he will allow himself to really face himself and see and accept what he has done, he can be essentially cured in eighteen months to two years of intense psychotherapy.

The dynamics of his attack, his thinking while he is doing it, is circumscribed by the incestuous relationship he's always wanted with his mother and cannot have. The fear, anger, frustration comes out in the attack. The surrogate dead female is safe, passive. He has overcome the resistance of his mother by killing her. Yet, because it is not actually her, she is still chaste unto him and he unto her.

But this female body is not, and he will do what he will unto her. He may make love to it. He likes this defenseless corpse; it does not threaten to devour his penis by making feverish claims for its own sexual gratification. He can have his passive love again. In fact, its coldness is one of its most prized and sought assets.

He may eat it. Suck the blood and lick the wounds. To him, this cannibalism is only natural. Now he gets revenge from the devouring female by devouring parts of her, symbolically or otherwise. The coprophilia that has been building throughout is now vented by humiliating the anus. He glories in the stench and waste. His castration fears are solved by desecration of the female genitals. He may, as already noted, cut off and up offending parts of the female such as the evil hands. He may return again and again to the scene to partake of the passive coldness of the winter body, revel in the stench of the summer decomposition.

Do not bother to think of this man at this time as you would another, for he himself does not, Sakarov noted. He evaluates his values differently. His only connection with civilization at this time is its beginning. He is a foraging human, driven by one of the oldest and most compelling compulsions yet known to man. He is out of control. To argue in courts before juries about this man's level of insanity and criminal culpability is to indulge in an act almost as bizarre as his.

The spring is completely coiled. Time goes on, he goes on, trying desperately to maintain his high-wire balancing act of good and evil. It becomes harder and harder to suppress his bizarre actions, incestuous feelings, another murder. His tension level is even higher than before the first murder, the compulsion greater, the physical pain more acute. He can actually feel hot knives cutting away inside his chest, needles probing into his skull. He must kill again to feel good. But it only helps for a little while. Now, with each succeeding attack it becomes more difficult to satisfactorily suppress the evil aspect of the killing and his actions with the body, and his unwanted knowledge comes creeping closer and closer to cognizance. This freer floating fear adds even another dimension to his already unbearable tension, so there is nothing to be done but to kill and kill and kill, closer and closer and closer together, kill and kill and kill—

He is totally out of control now, and knows it. By another bizarre twist, the more out of control his actions become, the more he is aware of them. To stretch the point to its ultimate, he is starting to get better. This is his first step toward real recovery from the possession of his sickness. He is starting to accept some form of ownership of his guilt, starting to really see himself as sick. He is running amok, knows he cannot continue this way.

So he commits a catch-crime, sets himself up to be caught committing a lesser crime. He makes sure that he is caught by doing it in broad daylight, on a busy street, and invariably displays himself and his license number . . . Yes, Billy's had been almost letter perfect, a classic catch-crime. It was one that he could easily handle; it was within his realm of experience. Billy would never stoop to stealing or anything like that, even for a catch-crime. That would be against his external religion, but he could surely handle the assault and phony rape of Dawn Mathews and the aborted stabbing and throttling of both her and her little brother, for he would have to remain in control enough to know when to stop, to keep this one in the catch-crime category. "Confessing" to it in the dream letter and throughout the sodium amytal interview was easy enough. All he had to do was dip back into some of his real murders and fugue states and psychotic interludes and whatever else necessary to paint a very convincing portrait to the perspiring shrinks taping and retaping his every breathless word. For he wanted to make damned sure he remained caught on his catch-crime, so he would not have to be brought naked before the big ones waiting in the wings.

Sakarov caught himself, read the conclusion of his essay.

. . . makes sure he gets what he is after. To be safely out of his mother's house, away from her and temptation. He is being punished but not too much, and without having been stripped of his emperor's clothes and presented to the world totally naked. Without having to divulge what else he is hiding, for the symbiotic offender has silent partners. To tell his whole story in the courts of the world, you have to drag in the whole family for three generations, whether you want to or not. That is, if you want to tell the whole story, and get down to the real sickness and parcel the guilt out where it belongs.

For the real conspiracy covers every day of the Boy Next Door's sad, sick life. The conspiracy of silence about his condition within the family. Had they any sense of care whatever for their fellow citizens, they would march him forward to the nearest doctor the first day they saw the first sign of his sickness, for there are many. But, as they don't really care about their fellow citizen, in the final analysis, they don't really care about their sick son either. They sacrifice him to maintain their petty prides and prejudices, cover their own sins within the family, disguise their contribution to his victimization. And as ignorance is no defense in the eyes of the law, it can no longer be in the eyes of society either. We must start looking beyond the murderer, the obvious, to assess guilt. If need be, and it need be, if we are to seriously come to grips with this burgeoning phenomenon, the whole kit and kaboodle must be dragged forward into the public dock and let the chips fall where they may.

The Boy Next Door subconsciously knows he is also a victim. It is one of the wellsprings of his great anger. He is torn by conflicting desires, religion, loyalty, love, hate, the old compulsions. He wants relief, justification for being, gains some measure of revenge on his family by committing his catch-crime, just by getting caught and paraded publicly. For, not only does this help satisfy his masochistic wish to be punished, it punishes his family publicly as well, particularly his mother, whom he wanted to pull down with him in this way too. If he couldn't have her solely to himself, then he's going to fix it so his father won't have her either, by letting the world know she has failed to raise properly his only son. But then, the Boy Next Door doesn't believe his father deserves her in the first place, for he has been taught by his grandmother and mother that his father is unworthy to start with. And so it goes and goes and goes, on and on and on, around and around and around—

And so do I, Sakarov noted wryly. But he had finished reading his essay, brought Billy's accounts up to date, had traced him through to where he sat today, the second of July, waiting for Sakarov in his treatment room, stonewalled somewhere behind God and the devil. No, Sakarov corrected himself, glancing at Billy's treatment charts, I guess by now the devil belongs to the occult. He has placed himself and his destiny completely in the hands of Jesus.

40

Hunt's hand reached out and flipped on his intercom. "Kristanna, send in Knutson." He had just finished reading the latest proposal, dated today, July 6, and hand-carried over by Knutson.

"Hi, Mike," Ken said, as he came in, shook hands, and drew up his usual chair. They'd been seeing an awful lot of each other lately.

"'Lo, Ken." Hunt's aristocratic lips creased in his cynical little smile, as he commented on that fact. "I'm starting to wonder whose office this is, yours or mine."

"I don't want it, you can have it, it's too fat for me," Ken drawled, parodying the song. A little humor might help; Hunt looked like he hadn't been sleeping too well lately.

Hunt merely sniffed, got right to it. "Let's go over this once more. I guess I can live with this one, or I shall I say, have to. But there's a few things we have to clarify."

"Like what? Nothing of essence, I hope. I've conferred at length with Bill and his family. I don't see how we can do any better, offer more."

Hunt shrugged, the bad taste already starting to fill his mouth. To think that it would all come down to Bill and Fred Brown dictating the terms! Damn them, business as usual. "Ken," he answered, trying to keep his feelings out of his words. "Specifically paragraphs one, two, and three are acceptable without change. One, and correct me if I'm wrong— I'm reading from your proposal—'that if Bill Ray Brown indicates that he was involved in a wrongful homicide of Beverly Lukken and is able to lead your investigators to identifiable body parts, you will amend the pending indictment by adding a Count 11 charging manslaughter and allow Bill Ray Brown to enter a plea of guilty but mentally ill to the added Count 11.'"

Ken nodded.

"Two, 'that if Bill Ray Brown indicates that he is involved in a wrongful homicide of Linda Lou Craig and is able to lead your investigators to identifiable body parts, you will amend the pending indictment by adding a Count 11 charging manslaughter and allow Bill Ray Brown to enter a plea of guilty.'"

Ken nodded again.

"Three, 'Bill Ray Brown will provide an adequate factual basis for the acceptance of both pleas.'"

Ken nodded again.

"I would agree to paragraph four," Hunt continued, "if it is amended to read as follows: 'If in addition to indicating his involvement in the disappearance of Beverly Lukken and Linda Lou Craig, Bill Ray Brown should indicate his involvement in the disappearance of Cindy Fall and/or the killing of Danielle Forshey, you will agree not to prosecute him in that/those case(s).'"

Ken frowned, his gaunt gray face wrinkling with concern. "I dunno about that, Mike, that goes quite a ways away from my original, what I was able to get Bill and his family to agree to—"

"Ken, I can't give him carte blanche on any other unsolved criminal case like you're asking. Who knows, he might have killed eight, ten others. I can't speak for those six status-open bodies up in Oconto County. The two over in Iola—"

"We're not asking you to address those cases—"

"No, not those, but there may be others right here in Helvetia County. Your paragraph four reads '. . . should indicate his involvement in *any other* unsolved criminal case.' I will agree only to Fall and Forshey, the ones we feel we have evidence to link him with, not any of the other cases that we still have pending right here in Helvetia County but have nothing so far to connect to Brown. We've got status-open cases that go back to 1972 that could as easily have been done by him as the others—"

"Mike, you're getting carried away. He was only a junior in high school—"

"Seventeen years old, turned eighteen December 27, 1973.

Attacked his little sister, hit her over the head with a jewelry box when he was nineteen. We get kids hauled in here who start killing when they're twelve years old."

Ken nodded, but not about paragraph four. "I'm going to have to go back to them about this . . ."

Hunt nodded too, sighed. "I know you do, Ken. Now, as to the rest of it, I'm only going to agree to two days at Crisis Center instead of the four you ask for. If at any time during his stay at Crisis, you or Brown should request transportation to any other part of the state of Wisconsin for the express purpose of locating a crime scene, we will provide same with our police personnel. The way you've got it written up now, he could call up the cops to taxi him to McDonald's for a hamburger."

Ken had to grin. "Maybe that's what he's got in mind."

Hunt was not in the mood for humor and never lifted his eyes from his counterproposal. "Yeah, Wendel and your other shrinks can ride along to 'ensure the availability of professional care throughout the trip.' I'll go along with allowing four hours to elapse before releasing any public information on any body parts he might lead us to, give Brown the time to personally visit with his immediate family regarding this development. I can't go along with twelve the way you've got it written. It's too broad. Again, I can't agree that any information obtained as a result of his examination at Crisis and any evidence obtained through the use of that information not be introduced as evidence at *any* trial, just in the four we are dealing with now or any other similar prosecution against Bill Brown. And I would add to those four that we can use such information or evidence gained to establish the fact of the victims' deaths."

"I'll have to, ah, check that one out too."

Hunt merely grunted. "Finally, I'm proposing an additional paragraph." He picked up his counterproposal, read, "It is understood that during Bill Ray Brown's stay at Crisis Center members of his family will not have contact with him until such time as he has disclosed his involvement, if any, in the aforementioned cases and produces identifiable body parts of the victims."

Ken just sat staring at Hunt for a while, his eyes narrowing. "He ain't gonna like that, Mike," he finally said.

"You know something, Ken," Hunt answered, leaning his

aristocratic face as far across his big, gleaming, official desk toward Ken as he could, resting his upper body weight on his hands, "I don't give a shit. This isn't a health spa I'm running here. I don't mind getting my nose tweaked, but he's not going to push it around all over my face. If he thinks he's just going down there for a four-day vacation, you just tell him he can just sit right there where he is."

"I'll tell him, Mike," Ken said, retrieving Hunt's counter-proposal off the desk and turning to go.

"You do that, Ken."

"Be seeing you."

"Yes, I'm sure we will." Hunt waited until Ken got out through his door, allowed enough time for him to clear his outer office, then buzzed his secretary. "Kristanna, get Elsinore Prison on the line, Feo Sakarov." He tapped his fingers on his gleaming desktop, let his eyes run back over the three single-spaced pages as he waited, listened as Sakarov brought him up to date, told Sakarov in turn about the new development, Bill returning to Crisis Center the sixteenth of this month, heard out Sakarov's succinct comments on that. "Feo, I know your first duty is to your patient, but crack him if you can. I don't like the smell of this whole thing down at Crisis either, but not for the same reason you don't. We may have to pay too much to get it, before and after. I want the confessions to at least Craig and Lukken on official territory, so we can control the situation before, during, and after. Promise him anything within reason you have to, but get at least those two confessions before the sixteenth."

41

It was six days later, the twelfth of July, one o'clock in the afternoon. Sakarov and Billy were locked inside the maximum security treatment room. Jake Janowitz was watching through a one-way mirror, listening on the bug. Sakarov was working Billy along slowly, carefully, just as he did every day. "Billy," Sakarov said suddenly, interrupting himself, "what about these murders? We've got to get into them sometime."

"All . . . what murders?"

Sakarov punched him lightly on the shoulder and grinned. "Cut the shit, you know which murders, the ones they got you indicted on in Helvetia County."

"Well, that's different. There's a big difference in indictments and actual murders. Badger's just trying to drop them all on me now—"

"Cut that shit, too. Forget about Badger. You've used him for your whipping devil long enough. I'm talking facts now. What about this plea-bargain stuff you got going with your lawyer and Hunt?"

"What about it, Feo?" Billy asked, but not quite looking at Sakarov.

Sakarov reached out and took Billy's chin between thumb and forefinger, turned his face to look in his eyes directly, kept his hand there. "Billy, you know you can't bullshit me, so why do you keep trying?"

Billy grinned sheepishly. "Just habit, I guess, Feo."

"Well, find a new one." Sakarov grinned back, squeezing Billy's chin playfully before he dropped his hand away. "Hey, I'm no dummy, man, you know that. I keep on top of things.

They keep shoving me the paper on you, whether I want to see it or not. I know exactly where you're at in your plea bargain."

Billy seemed a little surprised at that. "You do . . . ?"

"Certainly. This confession you're about to make is a very important part of both your— Look at me!" Sakarov suddenly commanded in no uncertain terms. "Dammit, boy, when I'm saying something important you look at me, you hear!"

"Yes, sir."

"Now you listen up, and you listen close, 'cause I'm only going to explain it once. Now I don't even have to do that, because you already know what I'm talking about, but I'll give you the benefit of the doubt in case you've overlooked a few little things." Sakarov winked when he said the last, talking easy again now. Billy smiled sheepishly, glad to be back in good graces again, careful to pay close attention and look Sakarov in the eye as much as he could. "Now I know you murdered those two women, and you know you murdered them. You just haven't owned up to it publicly yet. You also know that they're going to bring you to trial on those two indictments damn soon and try to hang you on murder one, and if they do you'll get life. And I do mean life. 'Parole' will just be a word that means something to other guys if they hang you on murder one and the big Life. Particularly when they start dragging in some of them other murders you squeezed off too, Billy, which you know damn well they will, if they get you on those first two—"

"They couldn't prove premeditation, Feo, not after all this time."

"Who told you that, Billy?"

"Ken. He says they have to be able to prove premeditation for murder one."

"Don't make that mistake, Billy. No, don't be foolish, don't you ever make that mistake. If the system wants you bad enough, baby, and they do, they can find a way to prove most anything. Once they get their hooks in you, which they have already with your thirty to fifty on Portage County, they'll find a way to keep you in here too. They only parole the guys they want to. And if you don't cooperate, they won't want to. So now Hunt and your lawyer Knutson are working out the details of your plea bargain, and if we play our cards right, we'll be able to use those murders to help you rather than hurt you.

But it's got to be done fast and right. You're going to have to trust me like you've never trusted another person in your whole life, including your family."

"I trust you, Feo, you know that."

"Yes, but how much do you trust me? You haven't told me you murdered those women yet."

"You never . . . you never really asked me before."

"I'm asking you now."

"Well, I . . . I still don't really know myself. If I did or not."

"Yes, you do. You just can't allow yourself to admit it. You're not man enough yet to accept ownership of that kind of guilt."

"I don't see . . . where it has anything to do with . . . manliness."

"Don't you? Don't you really, Billy? I mean in the larger sense, of a whole human being, being big enough to accept the ownership of your own guilt?"

"Well . . . I guess I do, in that sense."

"That's the only sense there is, in the end. And we'll work that out too, if you give us a chance. But first we got to get these murders out of your way. You've got to speak right up and say it out loud so you can hear it yourself. Really let yourself believe it yourself. For, right now, even though I know you know you did it, you just can't find it within yourself to admit it to yourself and your family and Sarah and Ken Knutson, all the people you think depended on you so much not to have done them. You think you let them down, don't you, Billy?" Sakarov asked, putting his arm around Billy's shoulders and hugging him a little.

"Yeah," Billy admitted, letting his head sag sideways to rest a little on Feo's strong comforting arm.

"Don't you see, Billy," Sakarov said softly, so low Jake Janowitz had to strain to hear, "it's not your fault. It wasn't you that said you had to be perfect, it was them. They raised you up to make you think that way. You know in your heart that you can't be perfect anymore, never were, so why do you let it keep grinding away at you so? Let some of it come out. Start by really owning up to what you did to those women, and then, when you can hold that guilt up to the light and look at it properly, then we can get in you, to all the other things you feel guilty about, get them out of your way too. See, you're not God, Jesus, the devil. You're just plain old man like all the rest of us. But you got saddled up with one of those four hundred thousand to one shots. You kind of got selected and programmed to kill women. . . .Billy, listen to me.

"In that way you are as much a victim as the women you killed. You were unconsciously selected and groomed to kill, you in turn unconsciously went out and selected those to kill. Now you got to accept ownership of these facts, so we can work back through those killings and your other actions to find out why you did them, turned out the way you did. How you happened to be 'selected.' What went down in your life to make you that four hundred thousand to one shot, a psycho-sexual murderer."

Feo tightened his grip around Billy's neck, was practically whispering by now. "Billy, wouldn't you like to get rid of that? Find out who you really are, beneath that? You're only twenty-five, surely you can make more out of yourself in the next sixty or seventy years you got left than that, no matter where you spend them. But you got to start somewhere, and that somewhere is here and now. Right here in my arms. Tell me you killed those two women. Just whisper it in my ear."

"Which ones . . . ?" Billy whispered.

"Linda. And the Lukken woman."

"No, Feo, not Linda. I loved her, honest I did—"

"The Lukken lady. Tell me about her then?"

Billy started to try to twist away, but Feo just clamped down tighter. "No, Feo, I . . . how . . . ?"

"How?"

"How . . . how do you tell something like that, even if you did, knew . . . ?"

"You just open your mouth and say it, Billy. You just say, 'Feo, I killed the Lukken lady.'"

"No, that wouldn't . . . work. No, even if I did do it, just saying it like that wouldn't mean anything to me. Do you understand that, Feo?"

"Sure, Billy, sure I understand. You want to really feel it when you tell me, don't you, Billy? Then you'll know for sure, right?"

"Yeah. I got to know for sure."

"Sure, you do, Billy," Sakarov agreed soothingly, both arms around Billy's neck by now, kind of rocking him back and forth as they stood standing facing each other. "Billy, if I show you how to tell me, the right way, so you get what you need out of it too, will you promise to tell me? Where the bodies are too?"

"I . . . I'd have to talk to Ken first. Ken and my dad, see if it is OK."

"Sure, talk to anybody you want to, tell them anything you want. But promise me first, Billy, promise me first, no matter what they say, you'll tell me what *you have* to tell me to make that terrible pain you got inside go away."

"Will I still get to go to Crisis Counseling?" a barely discernible babyish voice asked. Jake Janowitz wasn't sure at first it was Brown's, but it sure wasn't Sakarov, so it had to be.

"Crisis?" Sakarov asked, thrown off stride momentarily too.

"Yes. Ken promised me that I'd get to go to Crisis Counseling for four days, all the McDonald's munchies I can eat, if I confess down there."

Janowitz laughed out loud, Sakarov almost did. "Ken got anything against you telling me up here?"

"No, I don't think so, Feo," Billy answered, speaking more in his twenty-five-year-old voice now, "so long as I get to go down there too."

"Tell you what, Billy," Sakarov said. "What if I fixed it so you can have your munchies and eat them too. You tell me here and still get to go to Crisis Counseling for your four days. Deal?"

"Deal," Billy agreed impishly.

"Promise? Crisscross your heart?"

Billy did, adding for good measure, "Hope to die."

Sakarov got on the phone to Hunt, told him that Brown "in all probability" was now able to discuss the murders of Linda Lou Craig and Beverly Lukken and the location of their bodies. That he expected to have that information by the end of the day, but that Brown wanted first to confer with his attorney. Hunt hastily convened a meeting in his office with the head of his appellate division, Pete Wright, and his chief assistant prosecutor, Jim Barry. After quickly going over their position on prosecution and appeal vis-à-vis plea bargain, they resolved to continue with the plea bargain and called in Badger for his view of the matter. Badger was quickly briefed and grudgingly agreed to go along with them to Elsinore

Prison, both legally and physically. Captain Henry Hague and the Wisconsin State Police were contacted too, and also agreed they should take manslaughter if they could get the bodies.

Ken was closeted in his office this Thursday afternoon assembling case law and arguments for Bill's defense against the murder indictments when, contrary to his instructions to her that he would take no calls, his secretary interrupted his thought processes to tell him, "The prison is calling—line four."

Disgruntled, he picked up the receiver only to find no one was on the other end, at least, no one that was talking. After holding the phone to his ear for a goodly while and hearing nothing but the wind whistling down the line, he replaced the receiver. He sat looking at it some more, pondering the possibilities. It could only be Bill. Unless something was happening. Or had happened.

Dialing Hunt's office to see if anything was developing, Ken was put through immediately to Mike.

"Ken, Bill's breaking," Mike said, in lieu of amenities. "I'm surprised you haven't been contacted."

"Apparently, somebody tried to, or thought better of it."

"Well, you'd better get there. We're en route now."

He must have been. Though Ken pounded his rusted-out Olds eighty-five miles per hour and ran every red light on the way to Elsinore Prison, Hunt and his party were already there waiting for him in front of the main gate. Ken was slightly surprised to see Badger there too, but merely said, "Hi." Badger nodded. Nobody was talking much, and Hunt just said, "Bill's waiting for you."

After the group had displayed proper identification, prison security officers escorted them through the double-door entrance into the prison proper. While the others went up to meet with Sakarov, Ken went to find Bill. He finally spotted him through the glass window of the visiting cubicle he was waiting in. Seated alone, Bill caught sight of Ken at about the same time and casually waved at him through the glass, didn't appear to have a worry in the world. "Hi, Ken, how you doing?" he inquired pleasantly through the phone hookup.

"Fine," Ken answered automatically. "How's it going with you?"

"Fine—"

"Bill, what's going on? What the hell's going on!"

Bill appeared somewhat startled by his friend's rapid transition, but dryly responded, "I don't know. What are you doing here? We were supposed to meet on Saturday."

Ken just stared at Bill through the glass. He looked the same as usual. "Bill, what's this about you having some kind of . . . breakdown?"

"Breakdown? What breakdown?"

"Telling."

"Telling . . . what?"

"You know, telling. About the . . . murders."

"What murders?" Bill's face crinkled with boyish wonderment. He couldn't have been more mystified.

"Bill," Ken began, with some annoyance. "Dammit, we've been talking around them for weeks. All the while I been trying to set up this plea bargain for you. You know, like you and me and Fred have been talking about. I've been telling Hunt you're planning on going down to Crisis Counseling next week and telling Wendel what you have to do to fulfill our end of the deal . . ." Ken trailed off, seeing by the bland unconcern in Bill's eyes that he was getting nowhere. "You sure you're . . . all right? Not on the verge of this 'breakdown'?"

"Ken . . ." Bill spread the hand wide that wasn't holding the phone. "Look at me. I haven't felt better in weeks, not since this whole thing got started."

"You're sure?"

"Positively. Look, I categorically deny any 'breakdown,' or the prospect of same. You know I'd tell you if anything was up. You're my friend." A fleeting shadow flitted across Bill's face; maybe it was just the guards walking by. "Tell you what, Ken, why don't we go talk to Dr. Sakarov. He'll tell you, he'll know what to say. But I tell you, I'm OK. Absolutely OK."

While Bill repeatedly assured Ken that he was now and would continue to be "OK," they were escorted to Dr. Sakarov's office, where they were invited to remain in the reception room while Sakarov finished his "update" with Mike Hunt and the members of his staff plus Badger. Reading nothing from their solemn faces as this group filed out, Ken and Bill were ushered in to sit down in their still warm chairs. Sakarov too appeared very relaxed, affable. Ken soon came to the realization that he was the only shaken person in the room as he listened to the doctor casually explain that Bill, utilizing the "movie" technique he, Sakarov, had perfected, "might very likely be in a position to express any involvement, if any, in the pending Helvetia County homicide investigations."

Ken just sat staring at the blade-thin, angular doctor. He kind of reminded Ken of Joseph Wiseman back when he was playing revolutionaries, such as the one in *Zapata*. He had that same kind of barely suppressed zeal, fervor, honed steel inside and out, bridled power crouching in the blocks, just enough of the madman in him to get the job done. Yes, he believed every word he was saying. And so did Ken. "Could you tell me a little more about this 'movie' technique of yours, Doctor?"

"Certainly." Sakarov did, directing his explanation as much to Bill as Ken. Sakarov spoke rapidly as though he had no time to waste on frivolous speech and frivolous people who don't understand. "I think," he concluded for all of them when he had finished his concise explanation, "that Billy and I, if we both do our jobs right, have a good likelihood for success . . . don't you, Billy?"

Billy ducked his head, but not before he had given a short affirmative nod. Ken was watching Bill closely, had been, as best he could since they came in to Sakarov's office. It seemed to him that Bill acted quite differently in the doctor's presence, some of the poised, whipcord steel flowed from doctor to patient, man to man.

"I should like to have some time to think about this, Doctor. I request an hour's delay. I want to be sure in my mind, and Bill's, that this whole thing is legally proper."

Sakarov nodded. "You should. That's your job. But I also have mine. To do what is morally and psychologically proper. And it is my studied opinion that the best thing for our friend Bill is to proceed on this as quickly as possible."

Ken nodded, to show that he heard. "I should like to confer with Bill directly, and privately."

Sakarov nodded, smiled, got up to leave. "Be my guest."

Ken waited until they were alone, then suddenly asked, "Bill, did you try to call my office an hour or so ago?"

"Try . . . ?"

"Start? Did you place a call to me then . . . maybe . . . think better of it?"

Bill shook his head; he appeared sincere. "No. What makes you think that?"

"Just wondering." Had Bill decided to go ahead with it, without even telling him or his folks? "Forget that—Bill, is this what you really want?"

Bill ducked his head, but he got the nod in first.

"I thought we were all set to send you down to Crisis Counseling next week."

Bill looked up, a devilish glint in his eyes. "Maybe I'll have to go down there too."

"How so?"

"Feo, Dr. Sakarov, thinks I may have to go both places to get this whole thing all wrapped up, done right."

Ken stared back at Bill. Finally he slowly nodded his head, even though he still didn't know quite why. "I see."

Bill reached out his hand toward Ken in an appealing gesture. "Ken, will you make sure that I get to go? For all four days? Between you and Feo, will you work it out with Hunt in my plea bargain that I get to go for all four days? I'd sure like to get something for myself out of all this. You don't know what it's like to be locked away in a place like this forever."

"It won't be forever, Bill."

"It might be, Ken. So make sure I get the four days first, Ken. With all the munchies I want."

Ken nodded. It was all so sad he couldn't trust himself to speak directly. "Tell me something, Bill. Why didn't you just wait and go down to Crisis Counseling next week like we were planning? I've almost got it all worked out with Mike."

"Feo . . . I . . . don't think it's for the best. For me. In my own best interests. For my treatment. My future . . . whatever that might be. All that video equipment they got down there. Tape machines, they tape every word I say, film every move I make. Ken, seems like they got something else in mind besides just me and solving all this. Sometimes I get the feeling that they're more interested in what they need to get out of it themselves. Now, Feo, Doctor Sakarov, he's different. I can feel it. He cares. About me and all we have to do together, if ever I am to amount to anything, become a real man. Just like you care, Ken, I've known that all along. Care, in the right way. Not like my folks, they care for all the wrong reasons. They got to keep their rotten apple in the barrel with them, the cover nailed down tight, so that nobody can peer down in and see where my rot came from . . ."

Ken nodded, not knowing what else to say. This was all very interesting, he would love to listen to more some other time, but right now there were a few things a good deal more pressing. Their hour was passing quickly. "Bill, this is all very interesting, I'm sure it's important too, but—"

"Yes," Bill interrupted, smiling slyly, "I'm sure it's all very important."

"No, I didn't mean that sarcastically. I'm sure it is. And I'd be glad to listen to anything you might have to tell me about how you and maybe all this got started—"

"Maybe I'll write you a letter someday," Bill interposed, "put it all down on paper and just send it to you."

"Good idea," Ken agreed quickly, not knowing if Bill was pulling his leg or not, anxious to get back to things legal. "Bill, we've got to go over a few things we still got dangling on your plea bargain before we close with Mike. Call your folks. Acquaint them with this new development, and see what they got to say. But first, I want to ask you one last time. Do you really want to go through with this 'movie' thing of Sakarov's?"

Bill didn't hesitate. "Yes. I'm willing . . . to try it."

Bill's parents didn't hesitate unduly either. After deliberating for a few minutes on the telephone, as much to find out what was going on and what this movie technique was all about, they agreed to go along with Bill's decision and said they would leave for Elsinore Prison immediately.

Ken then met with Hunt and his group in Sakarov's conference room, to work out the final deal. Sakarov addressed them all briefly, told them that the confession would come more quickly if Billy went into the session knowing where he stood. He said he felt that Billy was now ready to talk to him about the Craig and Lukken murders but wasn't very sure about the other two, Forshey and Fall, that Billy might need more "motivation" before he would be able to deal with them. Ken agreed with Sakarov, urging that he not try for too much too soon, but Badger and the prosecutorial unit insisted that Sakarov try for all four if at all possible. So Badger was dispatched to brief Sakarov and Janowitz on all four of the

suspected murders. The four remaining legal experts then got
down to hard plea-bargaining, came to an agreement on the
manslaughter pleas, contacted Captain Henry Hague of the
Helvetia County Sheriff's Department and the Wisconsin
State Police and obtained their final agreement also; Badger
had already agreed. Knutson held out for Bill's scheduled
four-day trip to Crisis Counseling the following week,
whether or not he confessed to all four murders here in Elsinore. After all, it had been billed as a "competency evaluation"
in the first place. Hunt disagreed on the semantics and the day
allotment, but grudgingly agreed that he would go along if
Brown didn't confess to Forshey and Fall this day and would
to Wendel under the stipulations laid out in his counterpropo-
sals of the eleventh, yesterday. After some haggling, they also
reached agreement on the other dangling issues, all minor relative to reducing murder in any degree to manslaughter.

"Well, that should do it, I guess," Ken commented, pushing away from the table, anxious to get back to Bill and tell
him the good news.

"Not quite," Hunt injected, steel-eyed. "There are a few
more fairly interested parties that we haven't contacted for
their approval."

"Yeah, who's that?" Ken asked, trying to think who they
might be, who they could have possibly forgotten or overlooked.

"The victims' families. Particularly the two we have indictments on, Craig and Lukken." Hunt stabbed one hand out
at the plea-bargain littered table. "None of this goes unless
Vern and Irene agree to it."

Ken sat stunned staring at Hunt, normally a very sensible,
pragmatic man. He had never heard of such a thing. Surely he
could understand Hunt's feelings on the subject. He sympathized with the victims' families too, but this had no legal
logic. They couldn't take a chance on all their efforts being
jeopardized or outright killed by the emotional reaction of
some family member.

"Mike," he began slowly, "I know where you're coming
from. I feel for the families too—"

"Do you, Ken?" Mike asked wearily. "Do you really? Or
have you been a defense attorney too long?"

That pissed Ken, really pissed him, but he tried not to
show it. "Mike, you have no right to say that. For that matter,

I might say you're only doing this for political reasons, but I wouldn't."

Hunt smiled, but not his thin little aristocratic smile this time, more like the one he grew up with back in Big Falls. "You just did. And who knows, maybe it's partly true. Maybe I've been on the other side of the fence too long. Maybe I've become just a prosecutor. But today . . . today . . ." Mike pushed back his chair, came slowly to his feet, gathered the scattered papers up in his hands. "Today I'm going out to visit with Vern and Irene. Before I sign these." He turned and looked full into Ken's eyes. Ken held his probing gaze. "Why don't you ride along with me, Ken. Get out of this joint for a couple of hours. The fresh air might do us both good."

It was after four by this time. After five by the time they turned up Elmwood, rolled into the cul-de-sac around which ranged the houses Vern built, the one he lived in alone, 1600. Vern was just getting out of his pickup truck, mud from the construction site still caked his boots, stained his tan khaki pants up to his knees. He looked much older than he had just eleven months ago, almost to the day, since Beverly disappeared.

"Vern, remember me?" Hunt asked.

Vern's hands were filmed over with dried fill, so he quickly wiped them along the side of his pant leg and took Hunt's hand. "Yeah, Mr. Hunt."

"Mike Hunt," Mike corrected, then indicated Ken, who by now had come around the front of the Helvetia County car and stood watching. "Shake hands with Ken Knutson."

Vern hesitated but shook his hand anyway. Ken noted he had a nice firm handshake. Suddenly Vern's head gave a little jerk, his eyes narrowed. "You've found Bev!" he blurted, still holding Knutson's hand.

It was Knutson who had to answer. The man was still holding his hand. "No, sir. I'm afraid, not quite yet. But we think we might."

The eyes flared wide, then slowly shrunk, ice cold. He dropped Ken's hand and abruptly turned to Mike. "What's that mean?"

"We just came from Elsinore Prison. The doctors up there think Bill Brown is about to confess to some murders. Including Bev."

The big man just stood staring into Mike's eyes, frozen stock-still. The only movement Ken could see were the tears moving into his eyes. Finally Vern nodded curtly, just once.

"In order to get him to tell, Ken and I here had to get together and work out a . . ." Mike wanted another word, but he couldn't honestly find one, not to this man. ". . . deal."

This even stopped the tear from dropping. "Deal?" the big man growled, the hurt incredulity in his voice awful to hear. "What kind of a deal . . . could you make . . . about Bev?"

"Plea bargain," Mike said forthrightly. "Vern, it's the only way we could see to . . . get her back for you. But that's why we're here. We're leaving it up to you."

"To me? To me? What do I have to do with . . . getting Bev back . . . if she's dead?"

The guttural spiraling scream ripped from the big man's mouth, slapped Ken across the face harder than one of those big hands ever could. Both he and Mike moved in fast and grasped Vern's bared forearms, gripped him tight as he stood there shaking for control. Finally they felt the tremors under their fingers slowly subside. "Vern, I'm sorry," Ken heard himself say. "I'm damned sorry too. Please believe me."

"Vern," Mike was saying at the same time, "Vern, we're trapped with Brown. If he doesn't confess, and we don't get the—Bev and the others back, we haven't got much to go to trial with. If we just bring him to trial without his confession and the bodies, he will probably just keep on repressing it and carry it all to his grave. Maybe we lose at the trial. Then we got nothing, we lose everything, but most of all we lose this chance to get our loved ones back. And let you know . . . for sure."

Vern just stood there looking over both their heads. Neither Ken nor Mike could see just where he was looking or at what, could tell more by the feel of his swelling arms. Suddenly, they went limp; the great strength seemed to drain out of him.

"Do anything you want. Whatever works best for you. The rest of the families. Me 'n' Bev . . . hell, this ain't got nothin' to do with us anymore. That's the real dead part. Our love . . ." The big man, bent over double, went stumbling that way up his front walk and through his front door, shielding that love from their eyes.

Mrs. Craig had never been able to overcome her grievous

loss nor quite understand why others should counsel her to try to do so. She wanted revenge, and who is to say she didn't deserve it. But not just revenge, she wanted something more to come from the tragedy, so that her daughter would not have died in vain. At the very least, she wanted a heightened public awareness of such killings, what effect they have on the survivors. To think that her beloved Linda's young life could just be snuffed out and nothing of consequence rise from her ashes was almost more than her proud mother's heart could endure. She still lay awake nights grieving, grappling with elusive plans as to what she might do if the true story was ever brought to light. She had known from the beginning in her heart of hearts that Bill had somehow killed Linda; that fact had long since been buried in her rage of rage. But just to punish him and his family was not the ultimate anymore. There just had to be more than this hatred and her memories of Linda to console her. Maybe she could start some kind of movement in memory of Linda, acquaint other mothers and fathers of teenage girls with what they ought to watch for in their daughters' boyfriends. If they started to see some of the aberrant behavior that she knew now she had seen in Bill Brown and hoodwinked herself into overlooking for not good enough reasons, they would then know enough to intelligently acquaint their daughters with their misgivings, at least warn them of what to watch for. Certainly, that made some sense. Most young girls know so little about the male psyche that almost any behavior might be considered the norm. Of course, she would tell them to watch their daughters too, in case they showed indication of being unduly attracted to boys displaying such symptoms. She had been reading more and more of late about this phenomenon of victimology, where some victims almost seemed to have a pathological need to seek out their killer—

She threw the book down, went to answer the doorbell. Was astonished to see Prosecutor Hunt standing there, even more so when her reeling mind realized that the other man was Bill Brown's attorney, Knutson—the same man who had stood between Bill and justice all the while!

Her staunch Southern breeding saved her. "Won't you come in," she asked, turning to Prosecutor Hunt.

"If we're not disturbing you," Mike inquired solicitously,

"there is something important we'd like to discuss with you. I take it you've met Mr. Knutson?"

"Yes . . . we've met."

"If my presence offends you, I could wait in the car," Ken offered delicately, substantially repeating what he had suggested to Mike as they pulled up outside. He had known this was a lousy idea all along, but after his heartrending but strangely satisfying visit with Vern Lukken, he had let Mike talk him into trying this one too.

Again breeding conquered emotion. "Nothing or no one connected with the Browns could offend me any more than they already have." She guided both men to her parlor, invited them to sit down. She leaned over and picked up the book she had so hastily thrown down just as the doorbell rang—*The Murdering Mind* by Dr. David Abrahamson—unobtrusively slid it under her chair as she sat herself, settled back, and folded her hands in signal for the men to begin. She sat stiff-backed on the edge of her chair, her face set grimly, her smoky, blue-gray eyes glinting. Hunt had the feeling she kind of knew what was coming.

"Mrs. Craig, we have reason to believe that Bill Brown is about to confess and tell us where he placed . . . your daughter."

Her folded hands gave a little jump, but that was all she showed externally. "You mean . . . her remains . . . don't you?"

"Yes. The mental health doctors at the prison feel Bill is about to enter what they call a psychotic interlude and tell everything."

Mrs. Craig's lips curled disdainfully. "Yes, I would expect he would."

"How . . . what do you mean?" Hunt asked.

"It fits Bill. The trial is only a month or so away. He always seems to remember things when it behooves him to do so. Serves his own best interests. Lieutenant Badger warned me that something like this might very likely happen."

"Like what?" Hunt asked, though he was sure of her answer.

"Plea bargain. You're here to plea-bargain with me over Linda's body, aren't you?" she asked, turning her head slightly to direct this last question at Knutson as much as Hunt.

Ken felt his body stiffen even more than it was. He had never thought of it just that way before. She was still looking at him for the answer, and Mike wasn't helping out any, so he gave it a try. "Mrs. Craig, ma'am, I'm afraid, legally, the plea-bargaining has already been accomplished. We are here to seek your permission to go ahead."

The taut, tough lady stared right back at him like no opposing witness ever had before. "How can that be? It is not for the murderer to say what should be done about Linda's body. It is for me. Neither you nor Mr. Hunt nor Bill Brown has the right to buy or sell what little remains of her. That . . . privilege . . . is all that her father and I and Pat have left."

Ken could find no answer within him, so he passed the cup to Mike. "You're right, Mrs. Craig," he heard Mike say. "You're absolutely right. That is why we are here. And I want you to know, for what little it's worth, that I've never felt sorrier about a situation than this. But, still, I have to urge you to allow us to go ahead with our distasteful decision. It may well be the only way we have left to find out for sure just exactly what happened—"

"I know what happened, Mr. Hunt," Mrs. Craig interposed. "I've known all along that Bill Brown was responsible."

"I know you have, Mrs. Craig. But . . . this may be our only chance to get her remains back."

Now she stared two smoking holes in Hunt. Ken gave him credit for holding his ground and not looking away as he had done. "Yes, Mr. Hunt. Certainly, I want Linda back . . . but not at any price." Now those awful eyes swiveled back to stab Ken again. "No, Mr. Knutson, you can trot right back and inform your evil little client that the deal is off. The Craigs don't do business with the Browns." Her lips shook, but she got the words out. "Give Bill my hate. Tell him that I'd rather see him roast in hell where he belongs than help buy his freedom back with Linda's body."

"Mrs. Craig," Mike pointed out, "we're not trying to help him in any way, but rather you, and us. I'll be totally candid with you. As things stand now, I don't believe we can win both cases and have only about a forty percent chance of winning one."

"Which . . . one?"

"Lukken. We actually have better evidence in that case than with Linda. And even if we got a conviction at circuit court level, we might lose on appeal. Mrs. Craig, I don't have to delineate the legal difficulties we have with these cases. You've been involved on a day-to-day basis more than I have. You worked closely with your attorney, Mr. Clark, working up a great deal of the precedential information we used in our indictments."

"But Jack Clark thinks that we stand a good chance even without the bodies, the courts are starting to look at corpus delicti differently—"

"Irene, we went over this in my office when you and Jack brought his research and conclusions in. I told you both then that, though I agreed in substance with your position and finally did present to the grand jury and got indictments, our evidentiary position was skinny; it hasn't changed, it's still skinny, incredibly skinny. Now you know I've got all the respect in the world for both you and Jack, but—" Hunt suddenly turned to Ken. "Ken, level with me and Mrs. Craig. Do you think you could beat us in court with what we got right now?"

"Yes. I think your Flowers hypnosis evidence is police contaminated, most all your evidence in the Lukken case tainted in one form or another. This one . . ." Ken shrugged. "You have nothing physical. Under current corpus delicti law and precedent, you have a circumstantial case, at best. If you won, you would very likely lose on appeal."

Mrs. Craig merely glared at Ken this time. He could feel her steel resolve begin to weaken.

"Mrs. Craig," Mike pursued, "Mrs. Craig, I'm sorry to have to say it just this way, but you must remember yours is not the only victim family involved. We just came from Vern Lukken, explained the whole thing to him, he told us to go ahead. We've got the Forsheys and Falls down the line. They all want their loved ones back too. You see, this thing has kind of grown bigger than any one of us—"

"What's he want?"

"Manslaughter."

She looked first to Hunt, then at Ken, then back to Hunt. Finally shook her head slowly, just let the single word drop wearily from her lips. "Manslaughter . . . ?"

"He must plead guilty to both Linda and Mrs. Lukken. Show us where they are. If he tells us about Danielle Forshey and Cindy Fall within five days, he would be immune to them. I don't see how we can . . . get more."

"More . . . ?" she asked pathetically. "More? Mr. Hunt, I get nothing. The victims and their loved ones always get nothing. How can we get more of nothing?"

Neither man had an answer to that. They just stood waiting for her to give them her final answer. Finally she nodded grudgingly, but she nodded, whispered, "Go now. Pray for the dead souls."

It was supper time by the time they got back to Elsinore Prison. Ken immediately went to Sakarov and requested him to go ahead and "try it." Sakarov advised Ken that he would feed Bill first, then initiate his procedure, which could very likely require three to four hours to complete successfully. By the time Ken finished these last-minute preparations for Bill with Sakarov, they found that Hunt, Wright, Barry, and Badger had already left for Ox's Steakhouse some several miles away. Sakarov suggested that Ken would do well to join them, which he did. The steaks were good, but the social conversation a bit stilted, to say the least.

Returning to the prison at 10:00 P.M., Ken found Fred and Leona huddled alone in the cavernous control room of the prison. Almost afraid to speak, the three merely exchanged greetings and settled down to wait on one side of the room. Hunt and his group arranged themselves along the far wall; Ken couldn't help but think that he was a bit outgunned at the moment.

Badger pinched his mind now and again to make sure he was finally here, just sitting waiting, while some doctor shrink was supposed to get his little Billy-boy to confess through his own home movie what he, Floyd Badger, hadn't been able to get in three years. This shrink had impressed Badger though; there was no tricky-dicky bullshit about him. He was one of Badger's own. So he waited as expectantly as the rest.

No one said anything. Not one word was passed between the two camps, hardly any between associates, and then only in a whisper. The only sounds were soles shuffling back and forth across the tiled floor as they took turns pacing like expectant fathers. Mothers too—occasionally Leona would pull herself heavily to her feet and join the milling men as they aimlessly walked the hours away. To think that her motherhood had come to this, waiting in the eerie bowels of Elsinore Prison for her only son to confess to murder. Murders—more

than one, they said—but she still didn't believe any of it! Nor
did the father. Neither could really accept ownership of that
kind of guilt, even if they heard it from their son's own lips.
Never really would, they vowed silently, separately.

Time ticked away. Now and then a muffled sound would
filter down through the concrete and steel to remind those in
the waiting room where they were. Then those walking aimlessly or staring nowhere would suddenly stop and look fur-
tively about, to see if the others had heard too. But they in
turn would give no sign. It was almost as if they all felt guilty
for these seemingly faraway sounds, the pointless scream in
the night, the choked sob, the long-drawn-out anguished wail.

But, open momentary reflection, all seemed to silently
agree that the sounds didn't really sound real. They were just
something they imagined, so all went back to walking aimlessly and staring nowhere for certain. Maybe they were just
echos, some thought; the great overgrown structure settling in
the night. The mewling of ghosts, others imagined, for they
sounded too ghostly to be the real thing. Whatever, it had
nothing to do with them. They were all just here because of
Bill Ray Brown, only for a part of this one night. The ghostly
cries and sighs and screaming whispers had nothing to do with
them; they were only the by-products of this haunted house.

They were in a ten and a half by ten and a half "office"
cell. Upstairs, in the old wing of the prison, what was once a
prisoner's cell had been converted into an interrogation room,
a confession chamber. The knowing prisoners called it "the
wing-out room." The steel walls are painted a pale green.
There is only one heavy steel door with a four-by-four-inch
steel mesh window about two-thirds of the way up. Jake Janowitz is crouched outside below this window. Sakarov is seated
in one of the two steel straight-backed armless chairs, his back
against the inside of the door. Billy is seated in the other chair,
facing Sakarov, a short arm's length away. The only other
piece of furniture in the otherwise barren room is a plain steel
prison desk at Billy's right elbow, upon which lies a yellow
lined legal pad and a yellow pencil. Some pages have been
torn off the legal pad, but nothing shows on the topmost page.
Sakarov sneaks a look at his wristwatch. It is already nearing
eleven, and nothing of real consequence has happened so far.
Though they've gone over the facts as they know them, have

made a pass or two at going to the movies, they haven't dug deep enough as yet to warrant gaining admission, paying for the ticket.

Billy just wasn't ready to watch his private murder mystery. He kept trying to change the subject, talk about his dog, Dunce, the history of Elsinore Prison, how far away they were from another living soul this time of night in this old part of the prison, anything but what he was here for. Sakarov went along for a while, biding his time, looking for an opening, some trapdoor through which to push Billy into the main feature.

"Isn't this nice, Billy? You and me just sitting here, having this nice talk. Bet you and your father do things like this all the time, don't you?"

"Well, no, not really. 'Course, we can't now anymore—"

"I mean, before. Back when you were a little kid?"

"Well, maybe not so much as we could have."

"He's still very fond of you though, you know. Still proud of you, no matter what. Told me on the phone the other day that 'He's still a better man than I am.'"

Billy ducked his head, smiled a quick little smile. Sakarov could see he was genuinely pleased, touched. "Aww, he didn't really say that, did he?"

"Sure did." Sakarov ducked in a little closer toward Billy, so he could see his eyes better. "Billy, what was life like at the Brown house when you were little—say, before you were eight?"

"Ah, well, not so good, really. Seemed like, we didn't get along so good. Everything was always in a jumble, seemed like. Everybody hollering at each other over every little thing. Seemed like, when I look back on it now, I was getting punished for something every time I turned around—by Dad, I mean, Mom never really got after me all that much."

"What specifically would he punish you for?"

"Well, I remember this whole bedwetting thing. Seemed like I just couldn't stop wetting the bed—but I guess that was earlier. I think he finally cured me of that—by making me sleep on the cold linoleum—when I was about five. About the time I killed the bird."

"You think there's any connection, Billy?" Sakarov asked softly.

Billy looked up at Sakarov, some kind of startled fear

fleeting through his eyes. Maybe kind of like the bird's, Sakarov thought.

"Connection?"

"Yes, connection, Billy. Between your dad 'curing' you of wetting the bed and your killing the bird?"

Billy looked away. "I . . . I don't know . . . how. How there could be."

Sakarov leaned forward, arching his head in an effort to better see into Billy's eyes; their faces were only inches apart now.

"Oh, maybe you were so angry with your father about this and/or other things, you just took it out on the bird? After all, you couldn't get even with your father, take your anger out on him, he was too big, too powerful—how'd you kill the bird, Billy?"

Billy's head jerked a little. His hands, resting on his thighs, involuntarily twitched, his fingers began to curl into fists. "I . . . choked it, I guess."

"Choked? You got your big hands around its little throat?"

"No. No, I guess not. It was . . . just such a little fluffy thing. Just a baby."

"So, you more like got your hands around this little fluffy bird's whole body?"

"Yeah, I guess. More like I . . . crushed . . . crushed it, I guess."

"Crushed it between your fists?" Billy's hands were tight fists by now.

"Yes, I suppose so—"

"Yes!" Sakarov said sharply. "Look at me."

"Yes." Billy answered dully, but looking at Sakarov.

"Billy, now you've told me before about all the turmoil in your family when you were little, after your dad came home from the service and your folks finally got a home of their own, when you were about five—the same age you crushed the bird, incidentally—"

"Maybe it was a little later when I killed the bird. Suddenly, seems now like I was . . . maybe closer to eight."

"I don't think it matters exactly when it died, do you, Billy?"

"No . . . I guess not. It's been dead . . . a long time."

"Yes. Yes, it has. And it does seem, if I hear you correctly, like about the worst time your family had were those first three years after you and your folks and baby sister moved out of your grandparents' home—"

Billy was already nodding. "Yes, that's when Dad got religion, when I was eight. Things got a lot better after that."

Sakarov reached out and cupped Billy's chin in his palm, asked the question directly into his eyes. "Billy, I think all these things are somehow connected, don't you?"

"Like so?"

"Like, obviously there were some fairly drastic things going on in your home—maybe even more drastic than you've told me or can even tell me. Maybe you've just pushed them down so far that you can't quite get a fishhook into them—"

"Like what?"

"How should I know? I wasn't there. But if you have this sense of constant strife and turmoil, loud arguments and possibly even physical violence—you've already told me of your being physically abused for every little thing—"

"I said punished, not abused."

"They're not much different, Billy. Then, suddenly, your father, your entire family, gets religion. And things change, hopefully, for the better—"

"Oh, yes, it was much better then."

"What do you suppose was the final straw, Billy? Why, suddenly, did your father 'get' religion?"

Sakarov's hand still cupped Billy's jaw so he couldn't move his face away but his eyes could and did. He knows something, Sakarov concluded.

"Feo, gosh, you ask me some tough questions. I was only a little boy—why don't you ask them?"

"Maybe I will, someday. But right now I'm talking to you. Don't forget what we're up here for. We got to get into that sooner or later. More sooner. This ain't just some little circle jerk we're up here for. You got Hunt and half the law in Wisconsin waiting down there for you. This might just about be your last chance, Billy Ray, if we don't come through with our half of the loaf, they might even find some way to turn Badger loose on you—"

"Badger's still down there . . . !"

"You better believe it. He ain't about to leave until he gets a piece of your ass, one way or the other—"

"There . . . there is this one thing, Feo. I keep having this . . . dream . . ."

"Yes?" Billy was looking away from him again, but Sakarov made no move to re-engage his eyes, let his hand drop away from Billy's face. "Billy, this isn't just another one of your little ploys? To keep us from getting to the real thing."

"There . . . well, I don't know if it's really something or not. I mean, it's not even real. But it won't go away. Call it what you want, a bad dream . . . nightmare. I don't even know how it got in my head—certainly nothing like that ever happened in my home."

"Billy, just tell it—I'll decide whether it means anything or not."

"I'm little. Really little. There's a little girl, almost the same age as I am. Both virtually babies, I mean it's weird, Feo, sometimes in the nightmare I'm a baby, then I'm as big as I am now—I wake up in my cell all slippery with sweat, want to scream my head off."

"Let's hear it, Billy."

"Well, I'm looking through something. An opening. It's kind of jagged oval. If it were real it might be a keyhole. But it's not sharp and distinct like a metal keyhole would be, it's more soft . . . fuzzy . . . anyway . . . I see . . . I see this woman spreadeagle a little girl on the bed. She is about three. The man stands over her with a huge fountain pen in his hand. Aiming it at the naked little girl like a sword."

"Then what, Billy?" Sakarov prompted softly.

"The woman is talking to the little girl. The little girl looks terrified but at the same time fascinated. The woman is telling the girl child how wonderful it will be. How special. That she had it this way herself when she was a little girl and though it hurt it was very special too and now she wants to share it with her."

"Keep going."

"Now an infant boy baby appears on the bed beside the girl child. He is naked too. All are naked. As the woman speaks soothingly to the girl child, she reaches sideways and fondles the little boy's genitals, stroking, stroking, all the while she talks . . . bids the growing boy watch closely . . . the boy child has an erection under the woman's stroking hand."

"Tell it all, Billy," Sakarov murmured.

"The man suddenly leaps forward and forces the fountain

pen into the screaming girl child. Blood spurts out of her onto the boy's face but the man does not stop, even slacken his vicious thrusts. Each time he withdraws the pen, more blood spurts from the little girl onto the growing boy's face, he licks his lips. The woman, her eyes glittering, continues to hold the girl child securely with one hand while she strokes the young man to climax with her other hand.

"I have a little fluffy bird in my hands. While I have watched what I have seen through the soft fuzzy keyhole I have crushed the bird to death."

Sakarov nodded, crouching in even closer as he did so, his hands out, hovering over Billy's knees, eyes reading Billy's face: Billy sat hunched forward, his eyes almost closed, begging sleep from this waking nightmare.

A long, slow sigh seemed to rise up from somewhere deep in the prison below. Billy seemed to hear it, too, for he cocked his head more to one side and closed his eyes completely. It was so quiet now, Sakarov could hear the ghosts beating their wings against the bars.

Show time.

"Billy, how come you fucked your little sister?" he asked quietly.

"Wwhaa . . . What . . . ?"

"You heard me. How come! Didn't you realize how you were hurting her, maybe messed her up for life too?"

"Whaaa . . . Feo . . . ! I never . . ."

But his body was starting to rigidify, his pupils dilate, his hands grip the seat of his chair down alongside his hips. Billy's legs stiffened, his feet trying to push his chair away. Sakarov could hear the rollers squeak in the eerie breath-holding silence. Sakarov's hands claw-snapped onto Billy's knees, jerking him forward so they now sat pinned knee to knee, eyeball to eyeball. "You lying bastard. You've been banging your sister since she was barely able to crawl. Did she scream when you nailed her the first time? Did she bleed? But you liked that too, didn't you, Billy? Her pain? For you really wanted to hurt her, didn't you, Billy? It was the pain you caused her that you liked even better than screwing her, wasn't it, Billy?"

"No, Feo. No! Noooo! Noooo, nothing, none, none, no, I love her—" He was trying to get up off the chair, stand up, get away from his awful tormentor. Push past him, get out the door some way. But Sakarov just squeezed down tighter, his own adrenaline pumping now, his fingertips probing into nerve and muscle to render Billy immobile, short-circuit the power of his legs. It was fast becoming the ultimate struggle, but Billy hadn't tried to come at him with his hands yet.

"Sure you loved her, you hypocritical little prick. Almost as much as you hate her. That's why you tortured her half her life, because you loved her so much—"

"I never torture— No! Never torture her—"

"What did you do, then! What do you call it! Sucking your little sister who don't know no better into your dirty rotten life—that's torture! That's mental torture! That's emotional torture, you sick sad-assed narcissistic little shit! You just think because it's you that's doing it that it's alright! That little baby girl loves it! Shit, yes, you ripped her diapers off, didn't you?"

"No, never, no—"

"Look at me, you worthless piece of shit! Look at me!" Sakarov screamed. "You're not dealing with some little baby sister in diapers here, sisterfucker. I'll tear your kneecaps out and stick 'em up your ass."

They were locked staring into each other's eyes now, their faces not four inches apart, both crouched up off their chairs as far as they could go and still retain contact with their chairs and each other, Sakarov's fingers still digging into Billy's knees. "No, Feo, noooo, not baby, not baby—"

"But when she got bigger? About nine or ten, you started screwing her then, didn't you!"

"No—"

"Yes! Yes, you spineless creep. You think you can lie to me. To me! I can see right through you. I know everything that goes on in that creepy sicko head of yours. I can read you like a book. I'm stronger than you, in all ways. Don't think you can turn that shit sickness you got inside of you on me and get away from me. Let it come, see if I give a shit! I can handle you any damn night of the week and twice on Sunday. You don't scare me, you prick, I'm looking right square in your eyes right now, and I see a sisterfucker who ain't got enough guts to own up to it, but I see a sisterfucker. One who's finally maybe got enough man guts left in him to nod his head and own up to how he ripped into his little sister all these years because he didn't have the guts to face the fact that who he really wanted to get into was his mother."

Now came a short, hot breath-holding silence. Billy's eyes had flared progressively wider as Sakarov slashed at him with his "evil" words, now some kind of devil began crawling around under the choirboy demeanor, twisting good into gargoyle.

The body under his hands gave a fast hard jolt, like a massive dose of electricity had suddenly been injected directly into his veins. Then Billy settled back into his chair a little, his face fell away from Sakarov's a few inches.

It was starting to come. The psychotic seizure. This was the spooky time, the calm before the storm. They had entered into the eye of the hurricane together, but only one knew where they were. The homicidal rage was here, Sakarov could smell it, feel it on his own crawling skin, taste it in his dried out mouth. Now he would have to try to manipulate him, back him off a hair. He needs to kill now, Sakarov thought, staring into the dilating pupils, virtually the only sign of life in a seemingly dead body. This nice, young kid would kill anybody he could right now.

"Billy, we're going to hell and back. We're going to descend into the low place, visit your devil, but we're coming back. I'm God now, you're in my hands. I've got my hands on you, and I'm going to keep them there, never to let you go. I'm going to lead you down down into hell to visit with your devil. You're going to see your devil—"

"Don't . . . don't . . . leave. Don't . . . leave . . . leave me . . . You won't leave me . . . there."

"No, Billy, I won't leave you there. I won't ever leave you. Look over my shoulder. There. Look over my shoulder at the wall. There in the corner is a movie screen. That whole corner of the wall is a movie screen. You're going to see on that movie screen what you want to tell me. You're going to see now what you want to tell me. You're going to see now what you want to tell me."

Billy is starting to shake now; his whole body is shaking. His eyes continue to dilate. He is breathing very deeply and loudly, beginning to hyperventilate—

The movie is starting. He goes rigid. He is entering a catatonic state. His eyes are fixed on a spot over Sakarov's shoulder and off slightly to the right. Sakarov remains frozen in position also, the steel grip he retains on the other man's knees his life insurance and Billy's bridge to reality. For while in his catatonic state seeing his movie Billy has lost all contact with present reality and with all his senses except tactile. This has to be what Dante had in mind, Sakarov hears a small voice deep down inside his own self whisper.

The movie has ended. Sakarov knows that because Billy blinks, breaking the cold dead stare. Billy suddenly breaks out in a cold clammy sweat, signaling to Sakarov some form of realization, some degree of guilt ownership.

"Can you talk, Billy?"

The continuing cold dead stare answers him.

"Can you lift your arm?"

The arm twitches, then moves slightly.

"Good. Here, lift your right arm up here . . ." Sakarov helps him, lifts his arm up upon the desk, still gripping his knee with the other hand, places the pencil in his fingers. "Draw on the pad what you saw in the movie." Billy's only response was the cold dead stare. "Billy, if you can't quite do it yet, let the evil hand draw what you saw in the movie."

The hand with the pencil jerked once, a moment or two passed, then started to draw. At first Sakarov couldn't make out what Billy was drawing, but when he did, he sucked in a quick, fast breath himself. It was the same symbol he had speculated over in Billy's "Man in the Middle" painting. The curious symbol that had intrigued him enough to do some research and find out that it was an old pre-Biblical symbol for the Church in the days before organized Christianity, a triangle with a cross inside. Now Billy was drawing an antichrist pitchfork, just below the archaic church symbol. Then a line from it that extended down to the bottom of the paper, made a right angle to the far right edge of the sheet, then straight up, nearly to the top of the page; Billy marked the end of the line with an X. He dropped the pencil and slowly turned his head and stared at Sakarov.

Sakarov let loose of his knees and grabbed him by the shoulders, pulled Billy up close, stared deep into the dead eyes. "Can you understand what your evil hands have drawn?"

The eyes blinked; the head jerked affirmatively.

"Did the evil hands kill the girl Linda in the church?"

The cold dead staring eyes blinked again, slowly signaled no.

"Church parking lot?" Sakarov guessed. "The evil hands killed her in the parking lot."

This time the head nodded affirmatively.

"The evil hands stabbed her with the devil's pitchfork—a knife?"

The eyes blinked but the head shook no. Billy's hands suddenly jerked again, his fingers formed semicircular claws.

"They choked her?"

Again the head nodded yes.

"Why the line from the pitchfork then?"

Nothing in the cold dead eyes this time.

"It's a map, isn't it, Billy?" The eyes blinked, head nodded. "You sure the evil hands didn't kill her where the pitchfork is? Instead of at the church? They were on the way to the church, but they didn't quite get there. The evil hands killed her where the pitchfork is? Then the evil hands drove the car along the lines on the paper; those are streets aren't they, Billy?" The head nodded. "If you follow them, they take you to where the evil hands really dropped off the girl Linda's body, right?"

The cold dead eyes blinked, the head nodded, the lips tried to move, say something. "Dr, dro, drop, drop, dropped off."

Sakarov nodded. "I know they did, Billy. Good boy, Billy, for telling me where the evil hands dropped off the body. See, I told you I wouldn't leave you. I'll stick with you to hell and back, just like I promised. I'd never leave you there, you're too good a boy. Billy do you suppose you could follow those lines again if I got in the car with you, show me where the evil hands dropped off the body?"

The eyes blinked, the head nodded. But something else was starting to show in the eyes again. Life. Life was coming back. They were warming, warning Sakarov that Billy was starting to regain present awareness.

"Billy, I want you to see another movie now. The evil hands have done more things you want to tell me about tonight. Quite a few more things you want me to know. We have to get that devil with his evil hands out here in God's clean light once and for all. So you and me, Billy, we've got to do God's work for him here on earth. We've got to go back down into hell and see what he's up to this time. What those evil hands have done to that Beverly Lukken woman. I'm right here with you, Billy, I'm holding on tight to your knees again.

There ain't no way in this world he's gonna pull you out from
under me. Pull you down away from me. I'm too powerful for
that weak devil man. You and I, we'll get him together. So
you just look over my shoulder again. See on the movie
screen what those evil hands did to that Beverly Lukken
woman just walking along the street one morning, that warm
summer morning. Those evil hands were glued to the steering
wheel . . ."

Billy had sunk back into the catatonic state while Sakarov
was whispering urgently into his ear. He was seeing in his
mind movie what he had to see. Sakarov knew it. He could
always tell when they were seeing their movie. He didn't
always know exactly how, but he had developed a seventh
sense over the years while perfecting his technique and by this
time just knew when they were at the movies. Some had even
been able to tell him what it was like afterward. They invariably said it was like watching someone who looked very much
like themselves committing the crime in slow motion. It was
themselves, but then again it wasn't . . . yet.

This movie came to Billy much more quickly than the first.
It ended sooner, taking only about a minute. This time he
suddenly nodded his head to let Sakarov know that it was
finished.

But Sakarov didn't question him about this movie immediately thereafter. He merely asked Billy to see another. And
another. And another and another. "Just let me know when
you've seen them all," he commanded Billy, responding much
like an automaton by now. "All of the movies, as many
movies as you need."

They came quickly now, the next two requiring only about
a minute total. With each succeeding movie Billy's body
seemed to relax somewhat, even while remaining catatonic.
Sakarov believed that, as the memories came back, frightful
as they were, the patient began to relax internally, was somehow aware of his memory coming back and that this was the
beginning of his ultimate wholeness. Frightening as that might
be to face, it was better than the awful anxiety and tension of
only half-knowing who he really was and what he had done.

Billy suddenly turned his head directly toward Sakarov,
dropped his eyes from the movie screen, and nodded abruptly.
Sakarov could tell he was almost all the way back now; Billy's
eyes looked into his rather than through him.

"Can you find them for me now, Billy?" he asked him simply, dropping the intermediary evil hands device and asking Billy directly.

"Yes," Billy answered simply, directly, unthinkingly, owning-up, assuming the responsibility for the murders.

The two men just sat there that way for some time, still connected physically through Sakarov's hands squeezing Billy's knees, linked emotionally through their eyes. "You won't leave me now either, will you, Feo?" the one asked finally.

"No," the other answered, "I won't ever leave you, Billy. We've been to hell and back together. That will never leave either one of us."

They just continued to sit that way for another half minute or so. Billy appeared completely relaxed, his breathing and appearance back to normal, eyes no longer dilated, looking at Sakarov instead of through him. Then slowly, slowly, the eyes seemed to somehow roll over in their sockets, look in instead of out. The belated guilt was coming to him. For the first time in his entire life he was really owning up to himself. Accepting ownership of his awful guilt like any other relatively normal human being. "My God . . . it's true . . ." he whispered sad and low. "That was me. It is me. I did . . . kill them."

"That's right, Billy. You killed them."

"Linda . . . ! My God, Linda . . ." A gut-ripping sob wrenched out his ovaled mouth. "I really loved Linda. I was going to marry her. How could I have killed her too?"

There was no answer. Billy let loose a long low steadily rising keen and pitched forward, past Sakarov's knees. He made a grab for the downward hurtling body, but it tore from his hands. It was dead weight, and he had nothing much left right now either. Slamming into the steel floor face first, not even attempting to get his hands in front of his face to break the fall. Billy pulled his knees up into the head first fetal position and teetered there on face and knees, held up by umbilical guilt. Sounds of such desperate despair issued from his mouth to beggar description, higher keening wails riding up and over guttural, gut-kicked grunts, chokes, slobbers. He gave currency to the cliché—he was crying his heart out.

And they say he has no conscience, Sakarov thought, as he invariably did when observing this part of this kind of murderer's life.

He bent over and reached down and picked his fellow man up again. It wasn't easy, the rigor mortis of unbearable guilt was already setting in. Billy was trying to crawl back in and start all over again. Sakarov had to literally force him out of his dangling fetal position, physically bend his upper torso backwards and wrestle him back up onto the steel prison issue chair, where he finally sat, still crouched forward over his shriveled manhood, his arms hanging to either side of the chair, tears coursing steadily down his floor-begrimed face, the series of sounds still emanating from his loosely hung mouth.

Sakarov wearily began trying to put Humpty-Dumpty's defense back together again, to see if he could really bring him back from hell. "Billy, you did good. You've finally done the right thing. Now the families can get their loved ones back. Linda can be properly buried now. Their souls are at rest. They can all get a Christian burial. God will forgive you in the end. The Lord Almighty. The resurrection of the dead. You were sick. You didn't know what you were doing. But you know now, and we can start getting you well. You can become the whole human being you always wanted to be. I won't leave you. I'll help you all the way. There's still a place in this world for such as you, we just have to get you well and find it for you. Where you'll never have to kill again. You won't need to kill again. The compulsion will be gone. The tension is leaving you already. Billy, believe me, you're not dead yet. You still have a lot to live for, and we're going to find it . . . together . . ."

Sakarov talked on and on. Whatever came to mind. He was so weary by now he hardly knew what he was saying, had to trust his instincts, rely on rote, for he had given the speech many times before. But slowly, it took the better part of an hour, he finally got Billy to stop crying, engage in halting conversation. Billy asked for a drink of water, but found he couldn't walk when he tried to get up and go for one. So Sakarov gathered him in his arms and carried him out the door and down the hall to the drinking fountain. Billy didn't appear to recognize Jake Janowitz when he opened the door for them, or wonder what he was doing here. When Sakarov got him back inside the room, Janowitz coming back in with them now too, he perked up some, wanted to talk some more, keep

Sakarov from leaving him. But Sakarov told him, "No, you need to rest, we'll talk again some more tomorrow."

Billy seemed to accept this so Sakarov left him with Jake and started down to the control area where he had told Knutson and Hunt and the rest to wait. The session, like many others Sakarov had experienced, left him with a peculiar high —not pleasant, but predictably effective. The sheer force of the words he spat out like ripping bullets was, to a man contained and controlled within his own language sensibility, what he knew to be his job. With punks off the Chicago streets, it could be wasted sound and fury. But against the goody-goody facades of such as Billy, it was harsh medicine—a forensic emetic. And Sakarov remembered how often before it had worked. But at the moment, the only self-congratulation he gave to himself was to concede that he knew his business.

As he walked in he noticed a couple that could only be Billy's parents seated near Knutson on the defense side of the large room, so he altered course and veered in their direction. They started coming to their feet as he approached, the man half helping the woman to her feet. They sort of leaned against each other as he drew near. Hardly realizing he was doing it, Sakarov nodded his head yes, more to the man than the woman. But it was she who took a half-step toward him and kind of reached out a hand at him, so he directed his full attention toward her.

"What are you saying?" she hissed.

"He's guilty, ma'am," Sakarov said quietly, looking her straight in the eye. "Your son murdered those women."

She let out a vicious screech, ripping the deadly quiet of the sleeping prison, clawed at Sakarov's face with one quick reptilian motion but missed. "You . . . ! You're the murderer! You're the only other one that knows! You murdered them and planted the seed in Bill and made him tell for you! Murderer!"

Sakarov didn't state the obvious, merely turned on his heel and walked over to the dumbstruck Knutson. "Come with me," he said tersely, executing a military about-face. Knutson followed, Badger and Hunt and his men remained across the room, staring at Leona.

Ken had to hurry to keep up with the briskly stepping Sakarov. Followed the ramrod-straight back through the double steel door entrance into the inmate quarters, along a darkened corridor. All was now quiet, the only sound, the scuffling of their soles over the footworn slick concrete. For some strange reason the word blissful entered Ken's thinking, it almost seemed blissful now here in the darkened quiet prison. Or maybe it was just him. After all these months and years of toil and torment, it was now finally almost over. Except for Bill.

He surged forward and caught up with Sakarov. Caught his arm just as he was turning to mount a flight of steel stairs. "Doctor, what happened?"

Sakarov paused, swiped at his face as though to brush away the deeply etched fatigue, his hollowed eyes blinked owlishly behind his old-fashioned thin-framed glasses. "Prepare yourself, Ken, Bill will not be a pretty sight to see. Follow me, he's on the fourth floor."

Sakarov turned and proceeded up the stairs, got to the first landing before Ken caught him again. "Okay, I'll get prepared. But, how did Bill do—what happened—"

"Shush, not so loud. Okay, let's stop here." Sakarov turned toward Ken. "He did them all. But he only confessed to Linda and Beverly. Looks like he'll have to go down to Crisis Counseling next week to confess to the other two."

Sakarov's left eye either suddenly developed a quick tic or he winked. He turned and started up the steps again. Ken followed, mulling over the no-nonsense doctor's cryptic statement and conjunctive wink as they ascended the remaining three flights to the top floor, walked a shadowy corridor to its end, stopped before a steel door with a small square steel-grated window about chest high. "Go on in," Sakarov indicated, with a flick of his hand.

Ken opened the door and entered the dimly lit office. Stepping a few uncertain steps, looking about, he quickly saw Dr. Sakarov's psychology associate, the man he had been introduced to earlier in the day as Jake Janowitz, sitting on one of the two chairs. Looking about again for Bill, about to inquire as to his whereabouts, he heard a foreign sound, an unearthly groaning sobbing sound coming from the corner behind the desk. Ken turned slowly, almost afraid to, took a few faltering steps toward the eerie sound. There was Bill lying on the barren steel floor in an obvious fetal position, weeping like a motherless puppy. An intense sadness smote Ken, wiping

away any false feeling of momentary relief or whatever subconscious human reaction he might have felt in the inmate
corridors below. All he could think now was, there but for the
grace of God go I.

Unable to move yet himself, Ken felt as much as saw Dr.
Sakarov brush by him to crouch over Bill and verbally console
him and physically embrace him like a father an injured son.
Why didn't I do that? Ken had to ask himself. What is there
not in me that causes me to just stand here and watch another
do for me? Is not this broken murderer my longtime friend
too? Who am I just to stand by and watch a stranger do for me
and mine?

These and other questions swarmed through Ken's mind as
he stood frozenly watching Sakarov administer to his friend,
heard clearly what he was saying. "Billy, it's okay now. It's all
over now, Billy. Your friend Ken is here now, he'll help me
take care of you now. So why don't you try to get up, go over
there and sit down in that chair. Ken wants to talk to you now.
Your friend Ken wants to help you too, it's okay now."

Yet Ken still couldn't move those first few steps forward.
What is it? he raged internally. What is it? Why can't I just
spring forward and prostrate myself before the love I feel for
this fellow human being? Must I intellectualize everything
first? Filter it so many times through my head, there is nothing
left when it reaches my heart? Yet I feel for him, too. I want
to move forward and express my love as Sakarov is doing. It
is just that I do not have it left in me to move those first few
steps forward—

Sakarov was looking up at him, beckoning with his eyes.
"Ken, why don't you help Billy up?"

"Yes . . . yes, why don't I . . . ?"

So he did. He moved forward those last few steps and
stooped himself down and placed his hands under Billy's
shaking sobbing shoulders. He lifted him up and cradled him
in his arms and hugged him against his own fatherly chest. He
carried him to the chair, saying soothing words to him as he
did so, seated him on one of the straight-backed, armless
chairs. Billy slumped forward, his arms hanging to either side,
tears still streaming down his cheeks, but the shaking sobbing
had subsided to just a lifeless jerk now and again. Staring at
the steel floor, the fingers of one hand twitching as though to

feel for Ken's, Billy proffered in a whisper, "I'm sorry..: I loved Linda...I really did...! I...I...I hope...and pray that God...God Almighty and Linda can...can for... forgive me."

42

They all gathered again in the early predawn hours of the next morning to look for the bodies. Hunt and Badger, Wright and Barry, Sakarov and Janowitz, Ken and Bill. His parents did not join them for this final grisly chapter. But Jensen did, so did Lieutenant Orin Leigh of the Wisconsin State Police. They were both in the second car with Badger and Wright as the three-car caravan pulled away from Elsinore Prison at 7:00 A.M. In the last car with Hunt, Captain Henry Hague represented the Helvetia County Sheriff's Department. The first car, driven by Barry, contained Sakarov, Janowitz, Ken, and Bill. Needless to say, this lead car was shadowed closely by cars two and three as they proceeded south on state highway 22, a pleasant tree-lined country road that curved around and over gently rolling hills until it flowed into I-97.

It was a warm, humid July morn, Friday the thirteenth, Badger noted ironically. Two years, six months, and thirteen days since Linda Lou disappeared, and here he was just riding casually along toward Big Falls to finally find her body. He could even watch the back of Bill Brown's head in the car ahead of him, mentally keep the gunsights of his mind trained upon it. Now this. Yesterday, last night, and now this again, all because of what went on in that little pinhead, framed so nicely in the rear window of the car ahead, pressed cozily between Sakarov's and Knutson's. Badger instinctively adjusted the knurled knob that controlled the crosshairs of his mind to compensate for the other two heads in the frame, kept turning it down tighter and tighter till he was absolutely certain that he could touch one off from here without doing either

of the others any harm, other than splattering them with a little
Brown blood. It's soft heads and hearts like theirs that keep
the Browns of our world alive and well, he groused, for people like me to grow old and weary and cast aside trying to
catch and put behind bars. Maybe the world would be better off if he could really just touch one off. Wait until he
had showed them where the bodies were first, of course, then
just walk up to him and put it to the back of his head as cold-
bloodedly as he had done it to them. For this fine bright
warm, July morn, coming so shortly as it had after what he
had heard and seen yesterday and last night, he was in no
mood to be jerked around anymore.

The whole charade had sickened him.

High-powered doctors and lawyers and prosecution chiefs
scurrying back and forth city to prison, prison to city, city to
prison, meetings, plea bargains, more meetings, more plea
bargains, the whole thing planned and plotted and finally carried out, all orchestrated to the minute the little psalm singer
finally sang. He called the tune! The sneaky little psalm singer
had called the tune, right up to the chickenshit-crying cre-
scendo. He still was. Just riding down the road in the big
comfortable official car ahead like any one of them instead of
being dragged by his balls behind like he deserved. Conde-
scending, now that it was safe, to remember and confess and
guide us to the bodies. How in Christ's name could he now up
and show them just where the bodies are after over two and a
half years if he wasn't aware of everything that was going on
that night with Linda and that day with Beverly? If he was
crazy mad out of his gourd like the doctors claim and couldn't
even remember killing them in the first place? But now, just
before he was slated to go to trial, he could remember not only
the murders but just exactly where he dropped the bodies!

"Nah! Hellsfire, boys, I just can't buy all of it."

Wright laughed. "What's eating you now, Floyd?"

"I just can't buy all of this mental horseshit. Sure, maybe
I'll go along with him being a warpo-weirdo, though I have to
admit I didn't think so at first, for the longest time, but damn
them, how much do they really know when they're killing? If
buried within them is all this other knowledge of what they
did wrong and how and where they did it and where they hid
the bodies, some awareness of right and wrong, good and
evil, all the horseshit he was harping about on his good days,

why wouldn't some of that good rub off on him as well as the evil? In the big ways? But it didn't. Far as I can see, he was only affected in the big ways by evil—assault, raping, murder. Good in a big way would be to come forward and tell somebody he knew he was sick. But he didn't, and I gotta believe he knew he was sick from way back when, so I also gotta believe one more big thing. He liked his evil self a whole lot more than his good self. He gloried in his evil. Loved it so much he couldn't risk giving it up. Didn't until he himself knew it was out of control and we were closing in on him with the big M-one.

"I'd have got the lucky son of the devil sooner or later, and after Bev Lukken I think he knew it would be sooner. You know what, boys, I think he came back in my cow pasture and did her as much to tweak my nose as the other reasons the doctors were telling me over a beer late last night. That he wanted me to catch him but was afraid to let me. So he went out to Portage County and did the Mathews thing before I had a chance to close in on him." Badger stopped long enough to sneer. "Tells the doctors this morning that he only knocked Bev down with his car, she dies from the impact. Hmmmhmm, you believe that, you also believe he's the Cookie Monster. Yeah, he's good and evil all right, good and evil! And don't you ever let anybody forget it."

None of the other law enforcement officials in the car chose to comment on Badger's fiery outburst, but none of them ever forgot it either.

Upon arriving in the Big Falls area, Bill directed Barry to Keller Lake Road, north of the city of Little Falls. Bill, while subdued, had been speaking freely and coherently on the trip down from the prison, but now he grew silent and only spoke to give directions or comment upon them. "I've only traveled this road once," he observed when they got to Keller Lake Road, "so I'm not completely sure which direction to take." He finally chose north. Barry drove north for some miles. Bill would anticipate landmarks he felt should appear, and, indeed, those landmarks would appear as they continued north. A tension could be felt building in the car as they drove on. Bill correctly called landmark after landmark, Sakarov nodding assurances occasionally but saying nothing, Ken watching Bill out of the corner of his eye. Janowitz was quiet too, the only conversation, if it could be called that, between Bill and his driver, Barry.

Badger, in the car directly behind, could feel his guts start to roll when they hit Ghent Township. His old hunting grounds and Hatch Lake were not far ahead. Damn him, I knew it, he told himself despairingly. Linda is up here somewhere near her clothes.

Just as the caravan approached Boelter Road in Ghent Township, Bill directed Barry to turn east on a two-track road that led into the Viking Park area. After proceeding approximately three-tenths of a mile along this dirt road, which had Viking Park on the right and a series of single-family dwellings on the left, another two-track road was observed. "That might be it," Bill pointed out. Barry stopped the car. Bill debated with himself, then decided it was the road, so Barry turned in onto this dirt trail, the first entrance into Viking Park. "Stop here anyplace," Bill said. Barry parked, the other two cars stopped either side. Everybody got out, encircled Bill.

Yet Bill was still unsure this was the precise location. The landscape was rather flat, only an occasional clump of trees here and there, most standing individually. Bill swiveled his head from side to side but didn't move forward. He appeared pale but spoke and acted characteristically. "When I dropped her off, I walked down then up. Then left the path to the left on a flat area."

He stepped forward, the circle parted to let him through. Badger reached inside his jacket and unsnapped the catch on his shoulder holster. Bill led them down the car path another fifty yards or so, stopped, motioned with his left hand to the left. "She should be in there." "There" was a rougher, more densely wooded area, bisected by a series of shallow ravines. In long gone days meandering toes of melted glacier water had walked gently through here, but their prints had been many times smoothed by daily strollings of wind and rain and successive generations of living and dying plants and animals. And now all that remained was an undulating plain pocked by trees and shrubs and underbrush. Ken reached out and touched Hunt's bare arm. "Stick close to me, Mike," he whispered. "I just know I'm going to find her."

The eleven men fanned out within sight of each other. Bill was in the middle, supported from either side by Sakarov and

Janowitz. Badger never took his eyes off Bill. He and Hague walked to the left, Leigh and Jensen off to the right. Hunt and Ken were the double tight ends of this polyglot pickup team. Wright and Barry flanked out to the right. From above it would look like they were running in slow motion an old-fashioned wedge against the opposing trees and brush. It was 9:50 A.M. by Badger's watch, getting hotter and more humid by the moment.

They searched for sixty minutes without success. Badger never had any real faith that she would be found here. His thinking now became consensus. In the wintertime, when the leaves were off the trees and brush, the entire area they were searching would be visible from the houses across the road from the entrance to the park. Sun flashes off their parked cars could be seen even now as they gathered near where Bill still maintained she should be. Badger assessed the situation with his colleagues, then crossed over to where the rest of the group panted under another shady tree. He was pleased to note that his little Billy-boy's hair was all mussed up, bits of leaf and twig highlighting his coiffure of the day, sweat trails dirtying his soft baby-cheek-ass of a face. "You know something, Bill, I think this is just some more of your usual bullshit. You're tweaking our nose again. You just wanted a little break from prison—"

"I think he's doing the best he can, Lieutenant," Sakarov quickly interposed, "considering the time that has elapsed—"

"Doctor," Badger interrupted, "I have all the respect in the world for you. As a matter of fact, I can't remember when I last met a man I have more respect for, particularly one of your profession. But I'd like to believe I deserve a little respect too, for I've spent an even longer time with these guys, looking at them from just the other side of the fence."

"You have my respect, Lieutenant." Sakarov watched Billy out of the corner of his eyes as he said it. He was hanging his head sheepishly. Yes, Sakarov thought, maybe he does need a little taste of Badger now.

"Thank you, I need it," Badger answered. Those who didn't know wondered why he had answered just that way, but Badger didn't bother to explain. The eleven were by now huddled around Badger, and, to some extent, Bill, who seemed to have somehow got himself trapped inside the huddle with Badger. "Now Mike Hunt here is in charge of prosecuting; Leigh and Hague have got the other two. I got Linda and Bev. Until we find them, they're mine. And when the rest of you people are ready to quit letting Bill jerk you around here, and he is ready to come tell *me* where the bodies really are, we'll go find them. In the meantime, I'll be sitting over there in my nice, air-conditioned car. Yeah, you guys with the nice suits go search for a while, spend a little time on your hands and knees and really search for a change. It might do you all some good!"

Badger turned and stomped away. Got halfway across the small clearing, whirled back to see that all the rest of the police officers were following him. "That's right, let the doctors and lawyers and prosecution chiefs guard him. And if he chokes two, three of them and gets away, let them go after him too—find out what a cop's life is really like!"

Badger damn near ran the rest of the way to his car, jumped in, and slammed the door behind him. He was puffing some and soaked with sweat, but he felt better than he had for months. He had gotten it off his chest. Besides, what did he give a shit for anyway. They were going to take his Detective Bureau away from him. The letter was lying there on the kitchen table when he came stumbling in from Elsinore Prison in the middle of last night. Officially, he wasn't even supposed to be out here today. The letter said his position was terminated immediately upon registered receipt. He was to report to Uniform Division and suit back up again; at least, they'd let him keep his rank.

No, he breathed into his tightly fisted hands, them babies don't know who they're dealing with. After all the work I've put in, the sweat and strain and half-nuts agony trying to piece this all together, if they think now they can take this case away from me before I see it through to the bitter end, they just don't know who they're dealing with. They just ain't never met a country boy from Sand Lake before!

It only took Bill and the remaining white collar searchers thirty minutes to give in to Badger's wild logic, the heat, and the realization that Linda's body actually wasn't here, roughly in that order. Straggling back to the three cars, one containing four well-chilled detectives, it was frostily but thawingly agreed that from now on Bill would ride in Badger's car, up front alongside him, with his three security blankets, Sakarov, Knutson, and Janowitz, in the back seat.

Backing out onto Boelter Road, the caravan again proceeded in an easterly direction along the two-track road for another one-tenth of a mile, until the second dirt path entrance to Viking Park hove into view. "That's it," Bill said immediately. They were approaching the top of a small hill when Bill spotted this second entrance. The surrounding area looked to Badger very much as Bill had been promising.

Badger turned in, followed the dirt car path approximately fifty yards south. "Stop," the puppeteer ordered.

They did. Again three cars were emptied, the puppets assumed their positions around Bill. It was even hotter now, extraordinarily humid, nearly noon. Whether it was just the heat and humidity or even plain old-fashioned hunger, there was much more of an edge to the proceedings and participants now. Voices were muffled, the talk was terse and directly to the point. "Show us where, Bill," Badger commanded.

Bill pointed down the trail and off in a southerly direction into the encroaching wood, aspen and oak and an occasional slim birch angled for sustenance up through the larger hardwoods. A barely discernible path fell away from his hand into the wood. Shorter-growing grass showed where deer and other animals wended their way. A deer runway was always the easiest walking in the middle of winter too.

Badger nodded. They set forth, Bill leading the way, Badger close behind, the rest strung out single file behind. The deer trail led down, then up a hill to a level area, a small clearing in the wood totally devoid of shrub or sapling or underbrush of any kind. They herd here, Badger thought. This is some big buck's territory. This is where he does his work.

Bill stopped here too, his followers in turn. They had come just about seventy-five yards from where they left the cars. The wicked July sun beat down on them here in the open of the buck clearing. Badger could hear the heavy smokers and sedentary types breathing hard behind him. A carrion crow cawed in a huge white pine off to the left. A raven answered. Then all fell silent.

"She's over there," Bill whispered, pointing to the east. "I dropped her off over there somewhere. Sat her down against a tree."

Despite the heat, an eerie chill pervaded Sakarov's body, ended up in his brain. So far the map Billy had drawn for him last night when he couldn't yet speak was deadly accurate. As William James once said, the muscles remember, the brain doesn't.

Ken felt as though he must faint. He stood transfixed, staring across the little clearing to the bank of trees Bill had indicated. He could literally see the whirling dervish heat thermals dancing, twisting with twirling satyrs, horned Lucifers cavorting on the green with naked, bloodied maidens. He brought one hand up and pressed it over his eyes, clammy skin met clammy skin, his knees almost buckled. My God, he told himself, this can't be real. Even after last night, I still can't quite believe this. Maybe I've become a true son of the Browns.

His feverish thoughts were mercifully cut short by the actions of those about him. They all started walking across the clearing toward those trees to the east, automatically fanning out abreast as they had done before. Ken instinctively took his place alongside Mike on the far right wing of the wedge. He just stumbled along almost uncomprehendingly. As they reentered the wood, the terrain pitched steeply downward into a deeper, thicker copse. Ken slipped in some leaves, slid to his knees, and came to rest against her skull . . .

"Iiiiiiiiii!" he screamed, though he didn't know he had. He still knelt where his slide had ended, finally touching her skull. He tried to kick it away from him, to get away from her again, but as he wildly propelled himself sideways from the skull, he also broke through the clump of juniper bushes which had heretofore shielded the base of a large oak tree. There sat the rest of her skeleton, remarkably intact, more leaning than sitting, one hip kind of—

"Iiiiiiii! Iiiiiiii! Iiiiiiii!" he screamed over and over until Mike came smashing through the underbrush and grabbed hold of him.

"I found her, Mike," he said when he could talk so Mike could understand. "Now I know . . . now I know . . . for sure."

Yes, now Ken finally did know for sure. Not only that Bill had killed Linda and the others but that Linda had once really lived.

Another big man was at his side now. It was Badger, Ken realized now, just as he realized he was sobbing unabashedly in the presence of others for the first time in his life. Badger on one side, Mike on the other, lifting him gently to his feet, helping him to walk away from the truly dispossessed.

As Ken sobbed in the arms of his former adversaries, Bill cried in another part of the woods. Immediately upon hearing Ken's scream, seeming to recognize the voice and knowing what it must mean, Bill burst out crying and had to be held upright by Sakarov and Janowitz. Barry, who went to their aid while the rest of the party attended Knutson, noted that Bill was visibly shaken and somewhat emotional but not overwhelmed. As Knutson appeared to be; Hunt was afraid at first that stumbling over the body might be triggering a nervous breakdown. Though distraught men and women were no strangers to Badger and Hague and the other veteran law enforcement officials, they too were concerned over Knutson and told him so. Ken was genuinely touched by the gentleness of these rough-hewn men, the humane way they treated him, and soon was nearly his old self again. He had learned his second big lesson of the day.

Posting Hague and Wright to guard what remained of Linda, the remaining nine men returned to their cars. Badger stood beside his car, looked back down the car path to the entrance into the park from Boelter Road, saw how the path had gotten progressively narrower the farther they had driven into the park, squeezed to either side by clumps of tough wiry hazelnut bushes. "This is where you got your car scratched up New Year's Eve, isn't it, Bill?"

Bill stopped sniffling long enough to nod and say, "I guess so."

He knows so, Badger thought. "Let's go find Bev."

The three-car caravan traveled north on US-49. Bill told Badger to watch for a white building. It would be the primary landmark for locating Bev. They had traveled north for approximately seventeen miles when Bill sighted the white building, Ole P's Cheese Factory. "There will be a dirt road leading to the left about a mile further," he said, and there was, Wagner Road. They drove west for about two-tenths of a mile until they came to a T in the road. Bill then directed Badger to turn left onto a two-track farm lane that ran between an alfalfa field and a cornfield. "Turn left again at the end of the cornfield," Bill directed surely. They now traveled east, following another farm path two-tenths of a mile. "You'll come to a tree-lined ditch," he predicted. They did, a hedgerow with a gravel covered culvert dissecting the two-track farm trail they were traveling. "Stop here," Bill ordered, when they were atop the culvert bridge. "I don't want to show you, but I dumped her down there, in the ravine." Bill was pointing out the car window at a spot not more than fifteen or twenty feet away.

Badger got out of the car, sucked in his gut, worked his way through the hedgerow and down into the drainage ditch. There lay a decomposed body at the bottom of the ditch, just exactly where Bill said she would be. The whole search took one minute. It was now 1:20 P.M.

Hunt stood looking down at the skeleton for a few moments, shook his head sadly, turned and walked off by himself into the cornfield. He had seen all he wanted to for one day. But he had got the job done. He had at least these two bodies, if you could call them that, back for their loved ones. These two skeletons would no longer haunt him . . . or would they? Had he done right, really done right by the families, society? The victims? Himself? His word? His conscience?

This time it was Ken who came looking for him. "You ready, Mike? They're waiting for you back there. Everybody's ready to go," he heard Ken's voice say softly behind him.

Yes, they would be waiting for him back there . . .

Mike turned, forced a smile, so did Ken. Ken reached out his right arm to the prosecutor. Mike took it. "Mike, I know it took guts . . . but you did right, believe me."

Mike nodded, inside his head. God, it was hot—110 in the shade and no shade. The corn leaves were starting to curl again, just like they were almost exactly a year ago in Helmer Wrolstad's cornfield when they found Danielle Forshey. Cindy Fall still to go. God knows how many others. The skies were darkening in the west, heat lightning danced through anvil heads, an ominous rumbling could be heard.

"I hope so, Ken. I sure hope the people understand what I've tried to do. They should. They really should . . ."

43

Bill went down to Crisis Counseling on the sixteenth and confessed to the murders of Danielle Forshey and Cindy Fall, as scheduled. The grim searchers went out once more, Bill led them unerringly to Cindy's last vale in a clump of bushy woods alongside a housing development. All that was left of Cindy was a long blond hank of hair attached to a fragment of skull and a few gnawed bones. Domesticated animals had finished their master's work.

While the rest of the party gathered up her pathetic remnants, Bill moved off to one side and picked a bouquet of wild flowers. Lilies of the Valley. Virginal white petals. Pale green stems. Blood red roots.